THE CREEPS

A HALLOWEEN NOVEL

JUSTIN ZEPPA

CHAPTER 1
The Girl In The Cape

THE KIDS WERE gloomy, that much was clear. Whether this was a simple sense of dread befitting the Monday it was or a depression of more cryptic depths was less clear, but neither mattered for long as the late morning of a guttering harvest was devoured by the noise of machinery engaged.

The tractor roared, belching a fountain of black smoke with a tremor that made its painfully thin driver bounce out of focus like a freshly struck tuning fork wearing overalls. Behind the rusting beast rattled a large flatbed trailer loaded with bundles of straw, and behind that stretched the sprawling acres of Ash Orchard. The apple trees, gnarled and gray like the hands of an old blacksmith, went on for ages in rows ending well beyond the crest of the horizon.

Elyse Korbin leaned back against the wall of the cider mill. She eyed the inky vapors as they rose into the sky and vanished against the backdrop of menacing clouds, which seemed to be moving so low that she felt certain she could reach up and grab a handful of the churning ceiling.

Gone were the soaring and majestic days of summer, days of lawn flamingoes and hot-air ballooning. Once, the world awoke to a benevolent sun, eager to begin its triumph across the sky, sinking beneath the horizon only when it was good and ready. Now, in its stead, lived an elusive sun, one content to hide among the clouds and move harried, like a dad ducking into a market just to buy some batteries. There was no more lingering or showing off an impressive display of heat or blinding light, no more heliocentricity to give way to—no, the sun had given all it could and more for those four months, and like even the best of friends will do, had gone its own way to pursue glory elsewhere.

In had come atmosphere and cold, a shallow vault of slate billows prowling sinister and slow, breathing wind, spitting rain, and forcing the days to shorten so much that you might miss them if you blinked. The decline of summer into something terminal was eulogized in ways as striking as the seasonal transition itself; sleeves were reluctantly rolled down, and caps relocated from closets to wall pegs. Wind-blasted faces sighed dramatically while gardening supplies were moved into storage to make room for rakes and toboggans. And so the fall had revealed itself, slipping from a disguise of yellowing leaves and static grasses into that of reaper of summer—the harbinger of a frozen world.

The class had arrived by bus only moments before the tractor's racket. While Elyse was not one to be excited about anything to do with school, she had to admit that a half-day Halloween field trip was far better than learning about the stodgy goings-on of centuries-dead New Englanders.

Pulling her black cape around her, Elyse watched as her classmates split off into pools of friends, each one an ecosystem of gossiping and shenanigans. Some boys began throwing rocks at each other to show off for the girls (who weren't really watching them anyway), while a few random couples canoodled and gazed dreamily into each other's eyes, seemingly oblivious to everything around them and relieved to be reunited after an entire bus ride apart.

Elyse shuddered, feeling quite alone, and turned to the parking lot where another bus was emptying onto the grassy clearing. She craned her neck, searching for a sign of her own friends, and sighed with relief at the sight of Will Castle and Colin Niemann stepping off, followed by their teacher, Mr. Burnett, who looked as though a pack of hyenas had mauled him. Mr. Burnett had moved to Bootville from downtown Metropotamia over the summer and was still an authority figure of an unknown quantity. As he picked a paper airplane out of his hair, Elyse thought she recognized one of Will's trademark aileron folds—apparently the class was still testing his limits.

"Good morning, sunshines," she said to the boys as they approached. Colin waved hello while Will raised a foam coffee cup in salutation.

"Is it?" he yawned, scratching the back of his head with his free hand.

"Well, it's 11:30, so yes, technically, it's still morning," Elyse said, falling into step beside them. "Things could be worse—you could be at school."

"Mmm…" Will nodded. "Field trip on a Monday—you've gotta love it."

"Since when do you drink coffee?" she asked, raising an eyebrow at the beverage.

"Since we started learning about Cotton Mather at 8 o'clock in the morning," he grumbled.

Elyse scoffed. "What kind of mother names her child 'Cotton'? You're just asking for a fussy baby when you do something like that."

"I heard that's why the Pilgrims wore so many buckles," Will said, sipping his drink. "Cotton Mather was always being pantsed and dragged around the track, so he just buckled everything."

Colin's eyes went wide in mystification. "Really?"

"Nah, I just made that up," Will said, waving him off.

He crumpled his cup and tossed it into an empty barrel beside the old mill just as Elyse's teacher, Ms. Blithe, emerged, clutching various receipts and brochures. She looked up from the papers and spotted her fellow chaperone.

"Oh good, John, you're finally here," she said, hustling past the students and over to Mr. Burnett.

Mr. Burnett threw a wave to his disinterested driver as the bus pulled away to park and turned to Ms. Blithe, who promptly shoved a mess of yellow carbon copies into his arms.

"Now, here are the receipts for the trip, and the copies of the receipts for the head office, and the receipts for the receipt of the copies," she said, referring to her own papers. "I've gotten us hayride tours of the orchard, an exploration of the apple press, a walk-by of the pumpkin patch, and a group photo outside the mill."

"Oh, well, that sounds really—wow. Is this the price for all this?" Mr. Burnett asked, his eyes bulging at an absurd figure on one of the pages.

Ms. Blithe sighed. "I know it seems a bit much, but they have us over a barrel here—the kids are already distracted, and I need to get out of the classroom before they give me a case of the wicked-twitches." She stuffed the copies into her shoulder bag and rewrapped the scarf around her neck. "Oh, I can't wait until the snow flies and they become sluggish and docile—they're so much easier to manage that way."

Elyse and Will shared a skeptical look as Ms. Blithe whistled to her charges. "Okay, ladies and gentlemen—eyes on me!" The students quieted down for the most part and turned in her direction. "We're doing hayrides by homeroom—my class first, and *no* monkey business, or I will see it, and you will feel my wrath, understood? Okay? Okay, now let's have some *fun!*"

THE CREAKING TRAILER was a rough assemblage of wooden planks so bleached and warped with age that they looked like reorganized whale bones. The tractor offered groans of protest as it heaved Ms. Blithe's class deeper and deeper into the orderly forest, the bales of hay emitting small puffs of straw with each bump in the lane. The trees looked exhausted in the autumn weather, their limbs sagging from the weight of ripened apples adorning them like clusters of jewels on a crown fit for Charlemagne.

While her classmates laughed and yelled and took pictures of each other, Elyse sat at the rear of the flatbed. She pulled her cape around her for warmth from the chilly gusts running down the gaps between the orchard rows. A look of abject misery smeared itself across her face as she observed her peers at close range. Her mom and dad were biologists who split their time between teaching at the nearby university and observing various forms of wildlife in the field. It was at times like these that Elyse most felt like she understood her parents' work. They must have felt the same way while crouching in some tree-blind for hours on end, eyeing the local fauna and asking themselves the crucial question: What *is* that jaguar thinking?

It was not that Elyse felt in any way *better* than her classmates; it was just that she didn't relate to them at all. Like an alien sent to Earth on a reconnaissance mission, she had thoroughly analyzed them from all angles to figure them out and find a way to be welcomed into their company. They, in turn, had judged her infrequently and reluctantly, and each time she was found wanting.

Perhaps this was because she was quiet and naturally introverted, or maybe it was because other adults in town largely viewed her parents as being a bit batty—*literally* batty. There was a long-standing rumor that they had spent so much time caving in Australia for a study on bats that they now preferred to live in dim light, which was why the Korbin house always had the drapes pulled shut. The fact that this was partially true did not bother Elyse so much as the fact that it was looked down upon by other, more boring adults, who invariably spoke of it around their own kids in an isn't-that-weird-and-wrong kind of way.

But then, it was always something; if it wasn't the batty parents, it was the closed drapes themselves, and if it wasn't the drapes, it was the extensive collection of bone and tissue samples occupying the rooms behind the drapes. Likewise, if it wasn't because Elyse couldn't be bothered with the latest fads in technology or fashion, it was because her name had a 'Y' in it. If it wasn't that, it was because she didn't know the slightest bit about making fun of someone for things they had no control over and if not *that,* it was because her brother was dead.

Regardless of the reason, she was viewed with disdain, transforming the world into a slumber party she was not invited to. She was ignored, treated as though she was invisible—a weirdo, a freak, a wisp of oddity that, for some reason, embarrassed everyone and, as such, did not cast the slightest glimpse of a shadow on almost anybody's radar.

Elyse focused on the gentle rocking of the trailer as it crawled its way along the grooved orchard path and briefly indulged herself in the fantastic notion of a life in which she wouldn't be forced into close quarters with people like her classmates. Any consolation this brought quickly dissipated as her gaze absentmindedly fell on two such specimens, Jonny Monger and Teddy Rummage. With a small sigh, she watched as they grabbed the passing tree limbs that stretched across the lane as though offering to shake hands and ripped off handfuls of leaves they then threw at each other. They laughed maniacally as the now-naked branches snapped violently back into the canopy overhead.

At least she had Will and Colin; they were weird like her, and as long as they had each other, she felt like the rest of the world couldn't get to them, couldn't make them feel bad about themselves. She shivered as the wind picked up and huddled deeper into her cape. It was Halloween, but nobody in her class had bothered to dress up— that was for kids, and they were now terribly self-serious young adults. Even for Elyse, her choice of apparel was probably the least strange thing about her—she'd worn her cape every day for a year.

ELYSE WANDERED THROUGH the trees at the far end of the orchard, filling a small paper bag with apples as the tractor-trailer rumbled down the lane with the final mass of students in tow. Will and Colin sat towards the back, covered with broken bits of straw.

"How was your hayride?" she asked as they hopped off the trailer, followed closely by a pack of snickering classmates who continued to dump entire handfuls of the old horse feed on them as they passed.

"Oh, about what I expected," Will sighed as Elyse brushed the debris from his shoulders. "Colin told Travis Sinclair that he reminded him of a dog he once knew, and that pretty much set the tone for the rest of the ride."

Colin ran his hand repeatedly through his short black hair, scrubbing out the long, dried grass until a nearby tree seized his attention.

"Oh. I've found the apples," he announced in his trademark monotone, scampering over to his discovery. He crouched beside some of the fallen fruit littering the ground and stared at them expectantly.

Elyse watched him, concerned. "They didn't hit him again, did they? He doesn't know any better."

"No, they didn't get a chance," said Will, plucking a stray stalk from beneath his collar and examining it before putting it into the corner of his mouth. "Mr. Burnett started yelling before they could get a swing in."

Behind them, Mr. Burnett fell off the trailer with a groan, looking as though he'd been rolling around in a barn, his jacket askew and sprouting golden flakes. Ms. Blithe spotted him from beneath an apple tree and ran to him with a gasp.

"Oh, John, just look at you!" she cried, straightening his coat.

Slightly flustered, Mr. Burnett tugged at his sweater. "Oh, don't worry, Doris. I guess this is all part of that, uh, country charm I was looking for when I moved here." He spat out some bits of hay with a splutter. "I sort of feel like a scarecrow."

"Oh, they're just a bunch of animals, John—*animals!*" she cried over her shoulder to no one in particular.

Elyse snorted and turned to Will. "Is this how your class is?"

"Pretty much. There's a lot of sighing and headshaking."

Ms. Blithe turned to the students milling about. "Okay, people, please join us over here!" she said with raised arms, ushering the kids towards her as though directing jets down a runway. "Come on, come on!"

With surly grumbles, the kids began slowly making their way to the teachers.

"I suppose we'd better," Elyse said, dismayed at the sudden clustering of classmates. They joined the wandering stream of kids and were taken to the end of the path. Beyond this lay the desolation of the fens. The fens were locally infamous—a rolling wasteland of mire surrounded by stony crags in a great caldera of foul mosses that spat fog across Bootville on a nightly basis.

Ms. Blithe and Mr. Burnett made a wild and momentary stab at counting the heads amassing around them. They noted the same students two, maybe even five times before jotting vague and differing estimates on their respective clipboards and then abandoning the enterprise altogether.

"Well, everyone, I hope you're all having a lovely time today at Ash Orchard..." Ms. Blithe began while Mr. Burnett stood by, picking straw out of his hair.

"Um... there isn't really anything to do here," Jonny Monger called out, inspiring some other kids to nod in agreement. Ms. Blithe bit her lower lip and shot him a warning glance, for while Jonny was known throughout the teachers' lounge as a loudmouth, they feared him for sometimes making sense. "It's just a bunch of apples," he added for good measure.

"Jonathan, this is an apple orchard, not a peanut gallery," Ms. Blithe said. "Perhaps the rest of us can unplug our heads from the television for a moment and enjoy the splendor of nature and the history of our town—isn't that right, Mr. Burnett?"

"Hm? Yes, of course," Mr. Burnett replied as though waking from a dream. "Please, let's respect the splendor and the, uh… the history, okay?" He cast a blanket look of warning over them. Jonny Monger rolled his eyes.

"Now then, let's take a few moments to learn about where you're from: Bootville!" Ms. Blithe clapped her hands together with a modicum of excitement as the classes groaned.

She cleared her throat and began reading from her notes. "As I'm sure you're all aware, the first people of Bootville settled here in 1703, where they began a thriving boot-based economy that unfortunately collapsed following the War of Independence. Bootville was occupied for a short time, during which British troops set fire to the Asten Woods, presumably to prevent them from supplying General Washington and the Continental Army with their famous boots…"

Elyse began to let her interest wander as Ms. Blithe carried on. The Asten Woods inferno was one of those local tales that parents told their children from the age their ears had holes in them, usually during arduous family outings dedicated to leaf-peeping. Everyone in Bootville had heard about the raging fire so often that whatever horrific impact the burning of an entire forest and town may have had was now lost. It was like living within sight of Mt. Rushmore and keeping the blinds closed because, at a certain point, it stops being a monument and starts being just a bunch of giant heads watching you take a bath.

Elyse's eyes meandered over the field trip members in search of something better on which to focus. She noticed Colin absentmindedly turning an apple over and over again in his hands, counting the varying imperfections in its shape under his breath while watching the crows swoop in slow laps overhead like sky sharks in search of an aerial chumming.

Poor Colin. When he was younger, he'd been diagnosed as falling somewhere within the vast spectrum of autism, though the doctors could not say exactly where. He was high-functioning, sure, but there were definitely some vacancies at his emotional motel. As Colin once said, "My neurons are broken." He was frequently made fun of for being a weirdo, but Elyse and Will had long ago accepted that his brain was simply diffcrent and that differently-brained people can often be surprising.

Elyse turned her sights to Will, standing on her other side, watching Ms. Blithe weave her dull county history with an equally dull gaze. His eyes reflected a thorough numbing of the cerebellum. He was so *not* paying attention, but at least this would make for some good material to sink their teeth into at some point—Will was the one person who understood her cynicism, but he was usually able to flip it into something funny. She made a face at him as he turned to her. Will shrugged and mimed taking notes with his eyes closed as Ms. Blithe droned on.

"…and so, Bootville has carried on to this day, diverse and thriving." Ms. Blithe finished, looking pleased with her extended summation of local commerce. She looked over to Mr. Burnett, who had been examining a small hole in his sleeve, and quickly snapped to, clapping politely.

"Well done, Ms. Blithe, very nice, very, uh, informative—right everyone?" he said as a few students reluctantly joined him.

It was amidst this smattering of applause that a hacking cough rang out with the sound of extreme esophageal trauma. Everyone jumped at the abrupt rattling of lungs and turned to the dilapidated tractor for its source. They found it glaring back at them in the form of an equally ramshackle man in overalls, wielding an unmistakably well-kept knife.

CHAPTER 2
The Curse Of Bootville

THE OLD TRACTOR driver leaned against the engine, digging out black dirt from beneath his fingernails with a buck knife. He glared at Ms. Blithe from under the frayed brim of his oily hat and burst into an abrasive chuckle. Ms. Blithe shot Mr. Burnett a nervous glance and received an equally perplexed face in return. She turned back to the codger and began speaking to him as though he had recently escaped from the zoo.

"Um… Mr. Leo, did you have something to add to our history?" she asked.

"It's just 'Leo,' ma'am," the old man said before hocking up a mouth of spittle and shooting it into the tall grass. "And yeah, I'd say there's quite a bit to add to that pack o' lies you've just told there, ma'am," he said, stabbing the air with his blade.

Mr. Burnett leaned towards Ms. Blithe, mumbling under his breath, "I think we've found ourselves a primary source, Doris."

Ms. Blithe frowned. "Um, Mr. Leo—"

"Just 'Leo,' ma'am."

"Yes… *Leo*—have I left something out of the town history? This is all taken directly from the Chamber of Commerce tourism bulletin," she said, waving her notes at him.

The students waited in dead silence as the old man cracked the knuckles in his veiny hands. He straightened and laughed his disgusting laugh once more.

"Ha! The Chamber of Commerce… Aye, you could say they left out a thing or two, ma'am. This ain't no normal town, you know. 'Safe.' 'Thriving.' Them are just words folk use to make a place seem better than it actually may be." He turned to the classes with a wild look of contempt. "For if you kids knew the truth, I'd wager a bushel of corncobs that none of you'd ever sleep a wink again."

The students muttered to each other as Leo began pacing before them. Even Colin seemed captivated.

"I thought the fossil museum was next month's field trip," Will whispered in Elyse's ear. She turned to stifle a laugh and elbowed him in the ribs.

"And how could you!?" Leo shouted, silencing his audience with such force that even the crows seemed to fly in a hush. "How could anyone sleep, grown-up and youngster alike? How could you lay in the dark and truly rest when the shadows are full of mistakes from the past? Mistakes with *memory*. How could you ever close your eyes while resting over the dirt of a place such as this? A place carrying on its shoulders a wickedness that will not be erased—a *curse!"*

A gust of wind shot through the trees, causing scattered apples to fall from their branches with dull thuds. One by one, the prowling crows landed on the tractor behind Leo. One of the students quickly took a photo.

Elyse sighed. "Really? We're still talking about curses, huh?" she muttered.

Mr. Burnett began looking through the receipts Ms. Blithe had given him earlier. "Uh, Doris, is this part of the tour?"

Leo threw his hands up in the air, demanding silence once more. "Your Miss Book-reader there," he said, jabbing the knife in Ms. Blithe's direction, "she may have the skeleton of the tale, but the *flesh*… ah, yes, the flesh…" He smiled as though remembering a treasured birthday gift. "The flesh has long been lost to those pages in the county courthouse, I can tell you that much." He chuckled to himself.

"I guess you had to be there?" Will murmured.

"The flesh?" Ms. Blithe said, her voice strangled and birdlike.

"The flesh!" Leo snarled. "The flesh of old Spicy Jack—the commander of fire! The very same man who set flame to Old Man

Asten's woods! The flesh that destroyed this town, sucked the life from it and left it on the side of the fens for *dead!* Where is that flesh now—*where* is that flesh?"

"Okay, I think someone forgot to put Granddad down for his nap today," Will whispered to Elyse.

"His family must be hiding his meds from him," she whispered back.

The old man's lip curled as he surveyed his audience. "My family still tells the tale of that dreadful night, though it were forbidden by the town council to ever speak of it, such was their fear." Leo prowled the ground before them, warming to his story. "Old Spicy Jack, that brazen fool colonel—he didn't think there'd be resistance from the people of Bootville, and he sure didn't expect their vengeance for destroying their trees in the name of the crown. But vengeance came 'round when it were called, two spurs to the sides and the fury of a murdered forest upon its back."

Leo reached up to a nearby branch and snapped the end off with a turn of his wrist before letting it drop to the ground like a failed parachutist.

"And who can rest without knowing what became of old Spicy Jack? He, who vanished into the fog like a ship, scuttled at sea, rattling on the brink of death, with only a hollowed-out pumpkin to light his way. I speak the truth when I tell you his body was never found and that, to this day, his fate remains unknown."

Everyone stood in wide-eyed silence as Leo turned and gazed over the empty wastes of the fens, his eyes darting across the mire as though he half-expected the haunted soldier to emerge from beneath the loam.

"Where did he go?" Colin blurted out, breaking the tense silence.

"Shhh," Will said, giving Colin a poke.

"It's just a story, Colin," said Elyse, her voice gentle.

Leo turned to them, his eyes alive like fresh embers, and raised an eyebrow. "A story, eh? Maybe it is, maybe it is..." he mused. "As for Spicy Jack, well, I ask again—*where* is that flesh? For as much as the old colonel were cursed, so too were this very town cursed. Cursed with the threat of his imminent return to *punish* this place he hated so much.

"And when that happens… where will *you* be?"

Leo spat on the ground, and the crows on the tractor launched themselves back into the skies in a burst of black feathers. This sudden flurry seemed to break the old man's hypnosis over his audience.

Mr. Burnett blinked, cleared his throat, and muttered to Ms. Blithe, "Okay—I think we've had enough history from the frightening man-crone for one day, how about you?"

Ms. Blithe let loose a tiny yelp and straightened her glasses. "Yes, of course." She turned to the withered man. "Leo, maybe it's time we returned to the mill?"

Leo looked at them without attempting to conceal his disgust and spat one more grunt. "Yep. I reckon you'd like that."

"Okay, people, back to the tractor!" Ms. Blithe called out before turning to Mr. Burnett, her clipboard at the ready. "For the love of Pete, do not let any of them out of your sight—the last thing the district needs is parents wondering why their kids have become blood sacrifices for the haunted apple-people."

Elyse turned to Will, her eyebrow raised, and he shrugged before moving towards the trailer. With a shake of her head, she bent down and poured her apples from the paper bag onto the ground, releasing them back into the wild.

THE REST OF the afternoon was spent touring the various sites of historical importance, which Ms. Blithe and the silently nodding Mr. Burnett revealed with all the excitement of hack illusionists completing a magic trick. Elyse watched with pity as each lackluster story and thing was revealed to a less-than-enthusiastic audience.

Behold! The banks of the Whirry River—the same river that has run through this land every single day of your life! Voila! The cider mill! It dates back to the town's earliest days, when it used to be— abracadabra!—a *sawmill!* Ladies and gentlemen, please contain your excitement as we pass by the pumpkin patch and discover that it used to be—alakazam!—the site of Asten Manor, burnt to its foundations in the very same inferno you've heard about since preschool!

It had all been mildly interesting but certainly nothing extraordinary. The only one truly captivated by anything was Colin, whose eyes traced the complicated gearing of the hydro-powered cider press and who was equally fascinated by the lever used to drop the apples down their chute. "Up," he said as the lever was raised, "and down," he finished as the lever was dropped and mashed fruit slid down to the cider vat beneath the mammoth pressing stone. Over and over again until, at last, Elyse led him away.

All in all, despite the students whispering amongst themselves in the bemused tones of those who have recently been scolded by the elderly, it had been a relatively average field trip on an average autumn day at an average apple orchard. It was only when Elyse, Will, and Colin—by all accounts three perfectly average, angst-ridden 14-year-olds—lagged behind their tour group and stood staring into the tangled vines of the pumpkin patch that the air of something decidedly *not* average began revealing itself.

They had been avoiding it all day. The natural defense mechanisms of their minds had been blocking out all thoughts of what they'd been plotting over the past month. Only now, in the cloud-filtered light of October's dying day and with their school busses rumbling in the nearby parking lot, did they acknowledge that this would be their last moment together as they were and had been for so long. It was their last moment before they tried to do the impossible and change everything.

Will ran his hand through his hair and exhaled heavily. "So…" he began, unsure of how to finish. "Tonight's the night, huh?"

Elyse's dark eyes scanned the pumpkins without really seeing them. Her cape billowed behind her in the light breeze. "Yes, it is," she said, her voice thick.

"At the cemetery?" Colin asked, looking up at her with his strange, blank eyes. She nodded.

"And we're sure about that?" Will asked.

"It makes about as much sense as anything else," Elyse said. "And it's out of the way, so we won't be interrupted."

Will nodded. "And what time?"

"Dusk. Before the trick-or-treating starts."

Will turned to her, his face uncomfortably serious. "Listen, 'Lyse… I know this is sort of a dumb question, but… are you *really* ready to do this?"

"Yes, I am," she said without hesitation.

Will nodded in resignation and turned back to the overgrown ruins of Asten Manor as her words hung in the air, daring anyone to doubt them. "Okay, so let me ask you this: Are we absolutely crazy?"

Elyse sighed, her thoughts a million light-years away. "Yes. Yes, we are."

CHAPTER 3
The Family Korbin

LISTENING TO A teacher lecture is tedious at the best of times, but had anyone been bothered to pay attention to Ms. Blithe's less-than-thrilling town history, the unusual events of that same evening may have been offered some sense of historical context rather than seeming like the hot mess they ended up being. To see Bootville in its current form was to see glimpses of what it used to be, and to see what it used to be, was to see what it could have been.

At its birth, the town was built in the heart of the Asten Woods, named for the town founder and mayor, and as pure an example of old-growth majesty as one could hope to find in the New World. The trunks were as broad as smokehouses, shooting skyward in endless deltas that spawned rustling clouds of incomparable green.

The townsfolk, being equal parts industrious and destructive (as people are wont to be), immediately chopped several down and discovered the wood to be extraordinarily durable and flexible. They put it to good use for themselves, slicing the timber into thin slats to be attached as soles for their boots. In a world of handmade leather footwear with no sense of sizing and clunky heels subject to the perils of dry rot, the newfound comfort and sturdiness were seen as quite a boon, and the town soon gained a reputation for its boot craftsmanship. The town was named Bootville, the surrounding trees were called boot trees, and Mayor Asten's boot business boomed as much as a small-town Colonial business could, with boots flowing like wine throughout the area. It may not have garnered them the continental attention of the immaculate shirt collars produced by their neighbors and perpetual rivals in nearby Collartown, but it was enough to keep the small, rustic population in bacon and bonnets.

By all accounts, Bootville should have grown and thrived as much as it wanted, bound only by the limits of the fens, that vast expanse of mire and waste simmering on the outskirts of town. It was so poetically dismal that it seemed to exist solely as a contrast created to enhance the grandeur of the magnificent boot trees. Or, perhaps, it was a punishment lying in wait, a reminder that the world would never allow any one place to be so gifted without being equally blighted.

The roots of the boot trees had long locked themselves into the soil, but following the Asten Woods inferno, the fens had begun the process of slowly taking back the land. As the surviving townsfolk struggled over the following centuries to rebuild and replant, the fog rolled in thicker, and the fens stretched their wastes ever closer, one inch at a time. It was as though they were anticipating some far-distant millennia when the boring second-growth trees, less colossal than their predecessors by more the half, would be replaced by heather and peat. The erasure would then be complete, and Bootville would be no more.

And so, if this was what it was like to see Bootville, then to *hear* Bootville was to journey into the old downtown neighborhood of Bootville Proper, turn right onto Thorn Street, give a friendly wave to the mailman, and enter the great room of the old brick house the Korbin family called home.

MOTES OF DUST sprang to attention as horsehair hit catgut, sending them into the air, where they constellated briefly before being swiped into oblivion by the slashing of a violin bow. An orchestra thundered through the dimly lit space, its rich tones rattling the old stereo speakers before reverberating across the room, bouncing from bookcase-lined corners to hardwood floors and carrying over the massive glass panel of a wall-sized aquarium.

Elyse's eyes never left her hands as her fingers danced nimbly along with the music on the neck of her violin, digging into the strings so hard that they would soon be numb, while her left hand scrambled the bow at a furious pace. She blew a stray lock of black hair out of her eyes, almost missing a note as the orchestra rumbled on, winding its way into a point of tension before stopping without resolution.

Elyse took this brief moment to flex her fingers with a wince while still cradling the violin's neck between her thumb and forefinger. Leaving the end of the instrument to rest on her shoulder, she stretched her neck to the side, her thoughts wandering ahead to the disaster she knew was in store. With a deep breath, she tried to control her nerves as the orchestra began to pulse softly, the ambient hiss of a needle in a groove whispering in the foreground.

And now, for my favorite part, she thought, grimacing.

Hitting her cue on time, Elyse began the violin's gentle lead, a part of simple beauty, spinning into the air as though woven by musical spiders and as fragile as newly blown glass.

She furrowed her brow and tried wringing as much emotion as possible from the strings while keeping in mind the seemingly endless instructions on mechanics and technique impressed upon her by Maestro Brunhilda Glutenberg, the long-dead author of Elyse's tattered violin practice manual. She'd always imagined the Maestro to have been a barrel-shaped woman who spoke with a thick Germanic accent. In this voice, the buzzwords filed through her head like a mantra of musical discipline: *'Tempo, volume, posture, voicing, inflection...'*

The music gradually gained speed, and her lithe frame began to bend with the movements, a sapling in the orchestral tempest.

'Tempo, posture, voicing, position...'

An image of the dour Maestro Glutenberg repeating these mechanics began to take up more and more mental real estate—so much so that she didn't even notice the moment in the song she usually dreaded attempting.

'Posture, position, tempo, timbre, volume...'

Her vision of the Maestro began jabbing the air with a baton and scowling beneath a tightly wrapped bun of graying hair. Elyse snapped back to her violin, horrified by the realization that she was now twelve notes into her part, a complicated run up the neck she had always found terribly confusing. The orchestra continued to swell as she pushed her fingers as hard as she could, her body teetering onto one foot as the song continued to accelerate until—

Screee-ee-eech!

Her wrong note rang out against the rush of the music like the whining of a cat being ignored. Sweat began to bead at her temples as she scowled her way through her mistake, desperately trying to hold on to where she was. The next batch of notes were the right ones at the wrong time, slightly behind the unstoppable concerto, and then—

Screee-ee-eech!

This one sounded like slightly deflated tires squealing on a paved road surrounded by baby coyotes suffering from low self-esteem and hunger pangs.

Before she knew it, every note that followed was wrong, and with their wrongness came volume, and with volume came confusion as her string of bum notes drowned out the rest of the orchestra with their steaming tea kettle of dissonance. Her fingers fumbled while the thought of Maestro Glutenberg's guttural (or so she imagined) shouts fought for attention in her brain.

'Ach, the tempo! The volume! The posture!' she imagined the Maestro crying out, her baton shooting lightning bolts of furious disappointment. Overwhelmed by the passage, Elyse's bow squealed its way against the strings at an awkward angle while her hand gave up entirely in one final sour note.

"Damn," she grumbled, disgusted with herself. "Like lemons sucking on limes."

She held her instrument at arm's length as though it was some kind of intruder and growled at the infernal contraption she both loved and despised so much. In the background, the orchestra played merrily on.

Laying her instrument down on the bench of her brother's old baby grand piano, she turned to her parents' ancient Hi-Fi record player, which sat on a side table like a museum piece of artfully constructed tubes and dials from a bygone era. She lifted the needle from the record, causing the concerto to scrape to an awkward halt, and snapped the stereo off with a twist of the silver dial, the dim green light of the front console display fading into nothingness without complaint.

Feeling like an embarrassment to musicians everywhere, she carefully packed her violin into its case and grabbed her bag. She looked up to see the fish fluttering through the reefs of the wall aquarium, annoyed by her recent sonic assault. The tank was her father's pride and joy, big enough to take up an entire adjoining room and suitable for the most prestigious marine-life research centers. She enjoyed living with the fish—they made the house feel less vacant than it was. As she headed towards the front door, she paused to tap on the glass and watched the rush of briny bubbles as the fish, sharks, and seahorses scattered before her.

Stepping onto the porch and into the drowsy light of late afternoon, she paused, her hand on the doorknob, instinctually feeling as though she should let someone know she was going out before remembering that there was no one home. Her parents had been gone all summer, studying wildlife in the islands of Polynesia. They were supposed to have been home by now but had been waylaid by a series of pounding typhoons.

"It's that damned Coriolis effect," her mother had said the week before over a static-riddled satellite phone link-up.

"Um, yeah, I hear that's a real problem," Elyse said, at a loss for any other words regarding the tropical consequences of inertial circles.

"You know your father—he just *had* to see the Samoan flying foxes."

"Yeah, that's Dad, all right."

All of this was to be expected. Since their son's accident, the doctors Korbin had become increasingly paranoid about their mortality and were forever calculating the risk of everything they did. It was astounding that they had even made it to the islands in the first place. Despite feeling like a parent to her parents, Elyse couldn't really blame them; it had been a strange year for everyone, and everyone was dealing with it—or not dealing with it—in their own way.

THE PREVIOUS NOVEMBER had fallen upon them like schooner-sail canvas blasted by an Atlantic squall. The rain had refused to give way to even a moment of polite dryness, and everything in the world had seemed damp that day at the funeral parlor. The images still ran through Elyse's mind like a soggy living room slideshow depicting the world's most depressing vacation.

Will's suit coat had always been ill-fitting and uncomfortable, and the unfortunate weather had made it somehow more so, its soaked heaviness weighing him down and slowing his movements as though he was wading through a shallow pool. Colin's hair, usually an untidy mop of bristly black, suddenly found itself neatly slicked down and parted to the side with a hair oil that smelled of grandfathers and barbershop quartets. The rest of the cloudburst belonged to Elyse's tears, which filled innumerable sleeves and tissues as she mourned the loss of her big brother. Rain may fall as fresh water, but some would argue that the November of that year was a bit saltier than most, for it seemed that she would not—or rather, *could* not—stop crying.

Patrick Korbin had only been a year older than his sister, and while he was still over a year shy of being able to drive a car, he was already perceived as being apart from the other kids in town. Their mother would say that he was an 'old soul,' the kind who would undoubtedly be able to appreciate the cruel irony of comprehending the inherent uniqueness of someone or something only *after* it had gone away forever.

This feeling haunted Elyse the most. While she understood that it was, in fact, forever, she had never considered the idea that a death would actually kill a part of herself as well and would do so using that most torturous of murder weapons: guilt.

For it was not until after Patrick had shuffled off that she began to consciously acknowledge how good he had always been to her. Brothers and sisters have been at odds with each other since the days of saber-toothed tiger attacks, but always with the tacit acknowledgment that it is with love that these squabbles occur. A broken toy here, a bitten toe there—conflict enough to keep each other in line—siblings will forever offer each other's lives some small misery, with the understanding that no matter what happens in life, you're stuck with one another. That is until you're not, and this was the stumbling block for poor, heartbroken Elyse. Stuck together in life, you may be, but what about in death?

Her time of mourning began with this knocking about in her head on an endless loop, worrying her to no end. Only now that he was gone could she see what he meant to her. Only *now* was their family bond brought into focus, and she realized, to her great horror, that he had always protected her and shielded her from the small cruelties of life that his Big Brother-ness had been able to handle.

When Jonny Monger and Teddy Rummage had ambushed her with snowballs from behind Teddy's garage, it had been Patrick who had chased them down Lime Street and into the bare mantle of one of the towering oaks. And it had been Patrick who had waited patiently beneath that oak, throwing the occasional snowball up at the pair and finally grabbing Teddy's boot off his right foot and throwing it onto the roof of a nearby porch.

When Elyse's first baby tooth had fallen out, and she was convinced that her head was falling apart, it was Patrick who explained that she would get a new one and a bit of pocket money as well.

"I'll tell you what we should do, Sis," he said as she sniffled her worries away. "We should figure out a way to get some really good fake teeth and pass 'em off as our own, you know? We'll be *swimming* in loot!"

And when their parents caught them trying to pry a molar from the lower jaw of a giraffe skull they often used for lectures at the university, it had been Patrick who had taken the blame, claiming he had simply asked Elyse to hold the pliers while he attempted a better grip on the ossicones.

Like all people, Patrick was many things, but what separated him from the rest of Bootville was his infinite quality of *quality.* In the beginning, no one suspected him of being anything more than the good-natured, troublemaking child he appeared to be. It was not until the curious five-year-old climbed onto the bench of the old baby grand, a family heirloom that had been relegated to the role of 'heavy-thing-that-holds-the-rug-down,' that the scope of his potential was realized.

After several minutes of noodling, he discovered a tune that he expanded on over the next few hours. The day after that, he added his left hand. At the age of ten, he incited a minor sensation at the Asten Elementary School talent show, bringing the house down by playing a flawless rendition of Beethoven's 129th Opus, the Rondo in G. The front page of the next day's local paper, *The Bootville Boilerplate*, still hung proudly on the refrigerator door, featuring a photo of young Patrick sticking his tongue out and giving a thumbs-up beneath a headline reading "LOST PENNY FOUND—SHINES BRIGHTER THAN EVER."

Inevitably, his abilities and intuition isolated him from his peers—such acclaim never goes unpunished—but he didn't care. If the other kids didn't need him, he certainly didn't need them, so he breezed his way through life, strange and loudmouthed, never caring much for school or sport, never caring much for anything other than the music. It didn't matter what kind; he loved it all and so wiled away his days seated at the baby grand and hunched over the Hi-Fi, crawling inside the epic chord progressions and key changes of music's long history.

It was this love of the euphonic that had pushed him to find newer, better ways to scratch his musical itch, and it was through this search that he had ensnared his little sister. Elyse had been reluctant when he had first foisted the violin into her tiny hands and not without a few good reasons.

First, this was their father's old violin from back in his 'bohemian college days' as he liked to chuckle, his eyes glazing over as he lost himself in memories of halcyon times gone by—perhaps that interesting goatee-and-beret combination they'd seen him wearing in old photographs, or maybe even the scooter he'd rented with their mother when they'd stormed the arcades of sleepy European cities and long-dead civilizations. No sooner had Elyse and Patrick pulled the miraculous wooden sculpture from its case and plucked one poorly tuned string than Mr. Korbin poked his head into the great room, eyebrows raised.

"Say, kiddos, did I hear—ah! *Der Sturm!*" he said, his face lighting up.

"Gesundheit," Patrick replied.

"No, no, Pat—*Der Sturm;* that's its name!" he said, taking hold of the violin for a closer look. "It's German for *'The Storm'*—pretty wild, huh?"

"You *named* your violin?" Elyse asked.

"Nah," he said, blowing a layer of dust from the arched top, "that's just what your granddad told me it was called. It's been in the family for ages." After a moment's further consideration, he handed it back to Elyse, who held it gingerly, suddenly very aware of being entrusted with a family heirloom. "Well, hopefully, you'll have more luck with the thing than I ever did."

"Is that why I've never heard you play?" asked Patrick with a knowing grin.

"Well, you know, I sort of found it to be a little bit *square* in my heyday. And, um… maybe a bit beyond my skill level. I kept it around mostly to impress girls, but at some point, I decided to tuck it away in my dorm room closet in exchange for some bongos—I always was more *rhythmically* inclined, you see," he said, snapping his fingers wildly.

Patrick bit his lip, desperately trying to hold back a laughing fit. "Wow."

"Skiddly-diddly-bop-lop-a-*doo!"* Mr. Korbin sang to no one in particular, shuffling in a jerky motion that only vaguely resembled dancing. His progeny exchanged looks of abject horror.

"Dad, what are you *doing?"* snorted Patrick.

Mr. Korbin continued snapping, his head bobbing up and down to the mysterious and somewhat disturbing rhythm in his head. "Why, that's called 'scat,' son!"

Elyse stifled a laugh as Patrick's eyes narrowed. "You know you're setting me up, right?"

"Ska-dooby-dooby-dooby-ba-*doo!"* Mr. Korbin wailed. "See? Just like the Velvet Fog."

"Sounds more like the Velvet Smog…" Patrick murmured.

"Don't let him kid you, my loves—he couldn't play anything worth a darn," their mother said as she passed through the room, watching as her husband shimmied over to his record collection and began flipping through the vinyl. "He did look adorable in his blazer and turtleneck, I must admit," she sighed, her face misting with nostalgia.

"Honey, is Gene Krupa still alive? The next time he swings into town with the big band, we are *there!*"

This was the first reason.

The second was that the very makeup of the thing was immediately confounding. As soon as Elyse's 10-year-old hands reluctantly wrapped themselves around the neck of the violin, she realized that there would be no way on this planet she would be able to get a sound out of it. The strings were thick and taut, defeating the soft skin of her fingertips when she tried to hold them down.

"Ah, don't be such a baby, baby Sis!" Patrick had razzed when she grimaced at the red welts forming along the whorls of her fingerprints. "What are you—some kind of 10-year-old?"

It was an infuriating process that was not helped by the prodigy with the big mouth—and what did *he* know about it? Sure, developing muscle memory for odd chord shapes and runs up and down the piano's ivory keys was difficult. Elyse knew this first-hand (her attempts at the instrument had led to a sound her brother had described as "plunky and unfortunate"), but that pain was nothing compared to this gouging and cramping.

"And people do this for a living?" she asked him, rotating the numbness from her wrist.

"Oh sure," he replied. "Of course, those people are making actual *music*, not imitations of bellyaching pets, but the principle is essentially the same."

It was true—her first drag of the bow across the strings had been nothing less than a piercing shriek of the muses. Elyse had been disheartened, but Patrick refused to let her give up.

"Come on now, Sis, who am I supposed to duet with?" he'd tease, sitting at the keyboard and thumping out his own atonal dirge. "We could play exclusively for tone-deaf cats in some of the finest alleys in the world! They'll fill the tops of fences and the lids of trash bins night after night to hear us play our greatest hits! La-lala-*laaa*…"

Elyse couldn't help but laugh at the noise and soon joined in with her own squeals, the violin nearly peeling the wallpaper as they howled along. Moments later, their mother burst in, clutching a specimen jar containing a horseshoe crab, a panicked look on her face.

"Goodness, my loves!" she said, breathing a sigh of relief at the sight of them swaying back and forth to the cacophony of their design. "You had me worried there—I thought one of you was dying!"

Elyse and Patrick rolled on the floor with laughter, and in no time, Elyse realized she'd completely changed her mind on the subject. And so it was during those cold winter months, deep into the cruelest of seasons, when there were no more vacation days from school and no more holidays to look forward to, she practiced and tried to follow her brother's example of living through music.

While other girls her age were joining up with the neighborhood troop of Firelight Femmes in search of tent-pitching skills and merit badges, she stayed in and listened to the scratchy vinyl recordings of airs and quartets her parents had collected over the years. And when her classmates fell recklessly in and out of love with whichever teen idol was ruling television at the moment, Elyse daydreamed about the love letters Beethoven might have written to her and wondered if Chopin had a girlfriend.

Across abysmal snowbanks, through icebox temperatures and winds of chilly teeth, she made her way to the Bootville Public Library. There she borrowed the Glutenberg How-To book for beginning violinists, entitled *Violin Tendencies,* which, according to the back cover advertisement, was followed by a second volume of exercises for improvisational technique, *Random Acts of Violins.*

"Huh. Never even seen this one before," the bored librarian said, glancing at the cover through the lenses of her cat-eye glasses. She keyed its number into the database with such an absence of enthusiasm that Elyse felt safe in assuming she could keep the book as long as she needed.

From the Maestro's pages, she learned her scales, mauling the different progressions of notes day in and day out. Her family took to walking around the house with earmuffs on to preserve their sanity.

"Did you want pork chops tonight!?" Mr. Korbin would shout to his wife, who would respond in turn with an I-can't-hear-you shrug

and point to her earmuffs while the strained gargling of the violin seeped through every room in the house.

"It's nice to have music in the house, isn't it!?" she said as her husband nodded with a scrunched-up expression, as though squinting would bring her voice into sharper focus.

"Yes, exactly! Pork chops it is!"

Meanwhile, Patrick tried his best to be patient and frequently noted that any other brother would either try to stop this racket or at least consider viable housing alternatives. At the time, he was not yet twelve, so sub-letting was out of the question, leaving him ear-sore and exhausted.

Finally, one day in the late winter, he decided enough was enough. Elyse had been at work sawing up the neck of the antique instrument (which she now fully considered to be 'hers'), repeatedly working on the same five notes, ending high in a position where the sounds reached frequencies only appropriate for dogs. Patrick lay sprawled across the sofa at the far end of the great room, earmuffs on and flipping through the latest *Danger League* magazine, which featured an extensive cover article on some new excavations in Egypt.

'When Dr. Bastet Madu looks over—' he read to himself before being interrupted by Elyse's bow sliding into the wrong note again. He tried his hardest not to look at her, but the sound had succeeded at finally gnawing its way through the fabric of his left muffler. He shuddered and started to read again.

'When Dr. Bastet Madu looks over the recently uncovered ruins at Site 15—'

Screee-ee-eech!

Patrick winced as the noise again made its way through the left-side padding. Clearly, the sound had made itself a solid passageway and was looking to make it into a full-on burrow if he wasn't careful. He hazarded a glance over at Elyse, who was mouthing some unpleasant words Patrick thought looked familiar. He returned to his article.

'When Dr. Bastet Madu looks over the recently uncovered ruins at Site 15, he sees the history of—'

Screee-ee-eech!

Dr. Madu must have said something about Site 15, though Patrick never found out exactly what it was. He sat up and tossed his earmuffs aside as Elyse cursed loudly.

"Hey, Sis, you're really torturing that cat today."

"Argh, I know!" she said, throwing her bow across the room where it ricocheted against the aquarium's thick glass, frightening a school of pilotfish. She dragged her hand over her face. "I'm sorry, it's just that these scales are *ruining* me."

Patrick got up and headed to the baby grand in the corner. "You know, little Sister," he said, taking his seat behind the keyboard, "there is such a thing as over-practicing." He plunked some notes at random.

"Yeah, but if I don't know the notes, how am I ever going to play them well?" she asked, glaring at the violin in her hand.

"Ah-*ha!*" Patrick said, striking a mysterious-sounding minor chord, "I think the question you should be asking is: if you don't *play* with the notes, how will you ever really *know* them well?"

With a cracking of his knuckles, he began playing the familiar opening notes to *Für Elise*, the one Beethoven bagatelle anyone could recognize. "This is a little ditty I wrote for you, Sis," he said over the music. With a roll of her eyes, Elyse watched him for a moment as he played with an ease and assuredness reminiscent of putting on a tatty-but-loved sweater.

"Come on, lay it on me, cat!" Patrick shouted at her, morphing the song into a bluesy improvisation.

Elyse thought for a moment, nodding her head to the beat. Crossing the room, she picked up the discarded bow and began playing a melody that slowly floated to join the hammer-struck strings, wrong notes be damned. As their improvisation stretched out over that afternoon and across a hundred afternoons beyond that, Elyse began to wrap her brain around the idea of really *feeling* music.

Of course, that was then. The violin was discarded after Patrick's death, and it would be months before she would take it up again. She tended to avoid the great room, and when she did pass through it, there were times when she was convinced she had seen his spectral form behind the keyboard, banging out some silent tune. But this was madness, and she knew it. Dead was dead, and like so many notes struck on an instrument, so to did people hover on Earth for but a moment before quivering and fading into nothing but a memory.

CHAPTER 4
The Widow's Watch

ALL HAIL THE Widow's Watch, rubble be thy name! The grey stone tavern crouched at the crossroads on the eastern outskirts of Bootville, its weather-beaten walls as stoic and unyielding as Marcus Aurelius himself. She was a meditation in mortar posted as sentry to keep the gloom of the fens at bay while the town carried on carrying on.

The lamppost was lit, just as it had been for the past 250 years, casting a faint glow in the late afternoon light upon the intersection of Flareback Road and Nightjar Street. Beneath the random peaks of eaves and gables scattered amongst innumerable chimneys, the tavern's carved wooden sign creaked over the unassuming entrance on its iron rungs. A study in perseverance, the thick, quarried walls had seen the entire history of Bootville play out from founding to fire and everything after, a silent witness to this particular social experiment and the lone constant in an otherwise inconstant world. It was also known for serving a fair-to-middling shepherd's pie on Fridays.

To be at the Watch was to be at a place where time had no meaning, and the smoky, pitted stones were so thick with memories that one almost had to swat them from the air just to read the menu. Likewise, to work at the Watch was an equally exhausting study in the past being the present and the future looking much the same. It was this conundrum of timelessness that Will Castle was grappling with, deep within the recesses of the great immoveable object as he waited for his dishwashing shift to end.

What, in reality, was a few hours of jockeying tableware from the dining room to the industrial-sized kitchen sink had taken on the scale of a Homeric epic in the brain of young Will. He scowled as the rattling of pots and pans bounced around the walls and off the tiled floor, the irritating soundtrack of an honest day's work. Dropping his final bin of food-encrusted plates beside the sudsy water and wiping his hands on his apron, he tried to ignore the dull ache in his lower back, instead focusing on the existential pains of labor. Every second he was trapped in that steamy kitchen was like the further aggravation of a deep knife wound to his heart. He could feel his life leaving him, sucked away into the ether of gainless employment. Could the world not see he had things to do, places to be? He was young! He was restless! He had *angst! Why* was there no clock in this stupid kitchen, and *where on earth* was his boss to relieve him!?

As though she could hear the whooping sirens signaling his psychological meltdown, Will's boss, in the form of his mother, pushed through the swinging kitchen door.

"You're still here?" Mrs. Castle asked, an eyebrow raised.

"Yeah, look, Ma, can I go now?" Will replied, about to launch into a carefully constructed, perfectly reasonable story he'd been rehearsing in his head for the better part of three hours. "Colin has this really important project, and he needs me—"

"You can go, Will," she said, her bulky frame conspicuously blocking the door. "Your shift was over twenty minutes ago."

Will looked at her in disgust. "Ma! Why didn't you tell me that before? I've got plans tonight, you know." He shook his head as he untied the damp apron. "This is exactly why we need a clock back here—I've been telling you and Dad this for years now. If I don't know what time it is, there's no way of knowing when I can leave, and I'll just keep working and working like some kind of sucker."

Mrs. Castle rolled her eyes. "Well, that's true, I suppose—whatever have we been thinking?"

"I don't appreciate the tone, Ma," Will said, pointing an accusatory finger at her as he made for the door. Mrs. Castle took a step to her right, further obstructing his escape.

"Ma…" Will sighed.

"I know it's Halloween, but it's also a school night," she began.

"I know…"

"I want you back by ten o'clock, got it?"

"But, Ma—"

"Ten, Will. Not a second later." She meant business.

"Yeah, Ma, okay," he sighed, already formulating a plan to come home and sneak back out again if he needed to—the Watch was a difficult place to keep track of someone.

As she stood aside, he brushed by her like a storm of surliness. Never deterred, she followed him to the dining room, which was at its usual 1/3 capacity of shady characters eating equally shady food. None of them paid mother and son any mind.

"Did you do your homework?" she called after him as they crossed the hearth of the vast, five-foot-tall fireplace.

"Yes," he lied.

"Are you lying to me?" she pressed.

"No," he lied again.

"Is Elyse Korbin going to be with you?"

The query halted him in his tracks just as he was about to mount the stairs. He turned back but refused his mother the right to decent eye contact. "Um… yeah, I suppose." He felt his face turning red and briefly considered throwing himself into the fire out of sheer embarrassment.

Mrs. Castle's typically hardened expression softened as she eyed her son with the relentless precision only a parent can have. She sighed and crossed her arms. "You know, part of me thinks you should stay home tonight. After what happened last year." Will was about to protest when she raised her finger, silencing him. *"But… I recognize that seems unfair—I can't help it, I'm your mother. I just need to know you're going to be safe."*

"I'll be safe, Ma, I swear."

"I'm serious, William," she said, leaning towards him. "No trouble."

"Right. No trouble," he said before turning and bounding up the stairs.

"And if anything happens to that girl, you're working doubles until you're 40!" she called after him.

Will shook his head as her words followed him up the stairwell, past the second-floor rental rooms, and up to their third-floor apartment.

He entered his small, low-ceilinged bedroom and grabbed a beat-up baseball glove from his desk, absentmindedly slamming his fist into the leather webbing. He'd quit playing the year before, his interest suddenly shifting from a frustrating game of failure to an equally frustrating world of failing to get girls' attention. But it still felt good to hit something on occasion—especially when his parents started nosing into his business.

Sure, he thought as he tossed the glove aside and began changing out of his work clothes, Elyse may have always suffered the suspicion and derision of being the spawn of two oddball scientists, but the truth remained that they *were* merely oddballs. *His* mother was a regular menace to society.

"Remember, dears," he'd often overheard Mrs. Korbin tell Elyse and Patrick, "it's not about what *they* think about you. It's about what *you* think about you."

The 'they' in question were the stunningly lackluster people of Bootville, largely considered one of the most painfully buttoned-down towns in a state brimming with teeth-grindingly pleasant counties. It was these people who could at least begrudgingly respect the doctors Korbin for being doctors, even if they weren't the proper, tongue-depressing kind. And it was these same people who could just as easily disrespect the family Castle while reveling in the fact that they were being served by them.

The Widow's Watch had been in Will's family since the great land grab of the mid-19th century; the previous proprietors had gone West to seek their fortune, which would hopefully not include changing sheets mussed by strangers or washing the same tankards over and over again. With their departure, the Castles had seen their own long-sought fortune and grabbed it.

As it turned out, their fortune was so small that some people in town privately joked that it should be referred to as a misfortune. Still, it was enough to keep the Watch open for business, even as the idea of Bootville Proper had morphed and migrated its way down the road following the Asten Woods inferno, leaving the stone-and-timber tavern by its lonesome.

It was here that Will bussed tables, and it was here that Will was raised—in that order. It was not that his parents were unloving, but running the day-to-day goings-on of a relic such as the Watch was indeed a full-time job. Business and service were run by Mrs. Castle and executed with an iron fist. She surveyed the rooms, set the menu, balanced the books, and ensured her small cooking staff was paid on time. A gentle person at heart, she was nevertheless feared by her employees as a woman not to be trifled with. If Mrs. Castle said to use more sea salt, more was used, and if she said the tables needed a thorough wiping, wiped to a polish they would be, for she was an engine of proprietary means and a combustible one at that.

Conversely, Will's father seemed content to stay in the shadows and maintain the nuts and bolts of the building. He was fond of disappearing into the basement to fix leaky plumbing or sand the legs of the dining room tables down to an unrockable evenness. Dating as far back as the town's records could go, the Watch was a veritable buffet of oddjob-fixits in the waiting. When the kitchen was slow, he'd often bring Will along on his various excursions into the odd angles of expanding and contracting wood-paneled rooms, closets, and hallways, teaching him common-sense techniques to deal with any future problem that may arise.

"Yep, they don't make 'em like this anymore, sonny-boy," Mr. Castle once enthused as he scraped up a dollop of concrete with his trowel.

With a skeptical eye, Will surveyed the stone cellar, now leaking in the southwest corner, as he continued to stir the bucket of sealant. "That's a good thing, right, Pop?"

His father smoothed the concrete along the cracked grooves of the rounded foundation stones and snorted. "Will, you wait until you see some of these newer houses being built—drawn up in perfect right angles in an office by some pencil-pusher who will never see the real thing. And built with the strength of wet cardboard! Dozens of 'em! All exactly the same in make, and all prone to the same bruisings of time. Light?"

Will stopped stirring and trained a flashlight on the spot his father was patching.

"Now our girl here," Mr. Castle continued, patting the wall with a tenderness usually reserved for his wife, "she's built to last."

And she had; it was true that the Watch had survived the town catastrophe only because it had been built early and with stone. The construction process had apparently been so grueling and heavy that, upon its completion, it was decided to do the rest of the town in timber. Now the Watch was almost all that was left of that era, the victim of claptrap whisperings, forever questioning whether it was still needed in this modern age of hotels, motels, and obnoxiously stylized bed-and-breakfasts. Many thought it more worthy of being condemned than preserved as a landmark, but the Castles were nothing if not resolute and continued to pour their efforts into the twisted crag.

HAD HIS PARENTS not had their hands full with the Widow's Watch, perhaps they would've been able to put a finger on what was wrong with their boy. As the situation was, they only knew Will had gone from being a bit of a cutup to one of the most saturnine creatures they'd ever encountered. At times, he seemed like even more of a stranger than the people who breezed in and out of the rental rooms.

It was his smart mouth that had introduced him to Patrick in the first place. Friendships between people of different grades were hard to come by—first and second-year students have forever feared the knuckles of the upper classes, while older kids have always dreaded an association with young losers. After all, there were reputations to look after. However, none of this so-called class warfare meant very much within the cool cinderblock walls of detention, where Patrick and Will had first crossed paths.

Will entered the victim of one tardy slip too many and handed his write-up to Mr. Vespa, who took it without looking up from his paperback mystery and waved in the general direction of the classroom.

"Just take a seat anywhere and keep a desk between you and everyone else," Mr. Vespa mumbled, turning the page and leaning back in his chair.

Will sighed and shuffled to the back corner of the room, where Patrick was sitting, one sneakered foot on his desk, folding a quiz sheet into a paper football. He rolled his head lazily in Will's direction as he collapsed into a desk—one aisle over—and let his backpack drop to the orange-carpeted floor. Will looked over to him and gave a half-sneer.

"Man, I'm so *bored,*" Patrick said, folding the end of the football into itself.

Will glanced up at Mr. Vespa, who was busy mouthing the words he was reading.

"Don't worry about him," Patrick said, waving him off. "He's used to me. I'm in here all the time."

"Oh yeah, why's that?" Will asked, somewhat surprised. It was not every day that one was treated like a peer by an eighth grader.

"Oh, well, today it was because I was being, uh, which was it now? Oh yeah—an 'insufferable nuisance.'"

"And what's that supposed to mean?"

"Well, see, I play this game with the teacher—no matter what she asks, I give her the exact opposite answer she's looking for, and then when she corrects me, I act like that's what I was saying the whole time."

"Uh-huh."

"It drives her crazy, man—everything's totally wrong, but I agree with her, and by the time the class is over, even she doesn't know the answers."

"And this works?"

"No, of course it doesn't."

"But you're in detention."

"Yeah, because it works like a damn charm—this is what I'm telling you!"

"Okay, I get it," Will said. "You're right—that is really annoying."

"No, it's not. It's hilarious!"

"No, it's annoying—trust me."

"Yeah, that's what I said, it's *super*-annoying—don't you listen?"

Will nodded. "Yep. Got it."

"And it just goes back and forth like that."

"Uh-huh," said Will. "Super-annoying."

"Mm-hmm," Patrick said, teeing up the football on his knee and flicking it towards nothing in particular. It landed thirteen feet away and bounced briefly before coming to rest under an empty desk.

"Nice," said Will.

"You know, my teacher once called me a 'Wisenheimer,'" said Patrick.

"What does that even *mean?*" Will asked, shaking his head.

"I don't know, man. I think it's Dutch or something," Patrick said, grinning like a loon.

And that had been it—class clowns as they were, the two were pleased to have found each other, for two knuckleheads are clearly better than one, and the world was now outnumbered. They were the best of friends until the end, and it was through Will that Patrick met Colin (who was odd enough to remain unfazed by their relentless tomfoolery), and it was through Patrick that Will met Elyse.

Ah, the lovely Elyse. Will had fallen for her—so deeply, in fact, he felt he might now exist permanently below sea level; he found himself short of breath around her, and his insides felt like they were being pressured by several pounds per square inch more than ever before. It was an exciting sensation, and it made him feel like an intrepid explorer, daring to risk the perils of a Challenger Deep-like depression in pursuit of a glimpse of her rare, bioluminescent self.

With this in mind, he emerged from the apartment and scurried down the stairs to avoid his mother's talons. He barely broke stride as he passed his father, working at the greeter podium by the front door. "Hey, Pop, I'm going out—see you later."

Mr. Castle looked up from his crossword with surprise as he took in his son's all-black apparel. "You're not wearing a costume?"

"Nah, I'm over it."

"Is that right? Hm." Mr. Castle scratched his chin. "I suppose you could always say you're dressed as a jewel thief—you know, if you needed to."

Will gave him a look. "That'd be a pretty weird need to have, Pop. I'm just hanging out with Elyse and Colin. I'll be back later."

He hurried out the front door and, with that, had successfully escaped. Outside the Watch, he paused, breathing deep the chilly wind and deciding then and there that it was best not to think about what he was about to take part in—it was too strange an idea to consider, even for Halloween.

Intrepid explorer indeed, he thought.

Stuffing his hands into his pockets, he began walking towards Bootville Proper for the second time that day, his thoughts safely anchored in the same place they had been the first time—the same place they always were.

Will had begun his morning like every other morning. For someone who was not particularly fond of school and endured each class with the same attitude adopted for visits to the dentist— annoyed but with a reluctant acknowledgment that it was inevitable—each dawn saw him practically leap out of bed with an enthusiasm usually reserved for the promise of free cake. As he went through his morning regiment of showering, dressing, and breakfasting, he would compile a mental list of conversational topics to have at the ready should he need them in the coming hours. Television, movies, stupid jokes, rumors about teachers or classmates—anything he felt comfortable speaking on for more than ten seconds—were all fair game and haphazardly cataloged and filed away by his lazy memory for the approaching moment he lived for: that first moment every morning when he saw the black hair and equally black cape of Elyse Korbin.

The statistics have never been accurately gathered, but there is a very good chance that were it not for girls, most teenage boys would never show up to school at all, and the nation would dissolve into a state of chaos as their idle hands went about the business of blowing things up just for the fun of it. Packs of teenage boys would roam the streets with shoulders bruised black and purple from punching each other, their knees torn to shreds from daring each other to skateboard down one flight of concrete steps or another while blindfolded. And the economy would melt down around them as they loitered in drug stores reading comic books, cursing at old ladies, and playing with yo-yos without ever buying anything. Thank goodness for girls.

For Will, every school day was an exercise in self-restraint. Elyse was his best friend's sister, and now that his best friend was dead, she had become the only thing he gave a damn about in the whole world, and he refused to lose her. As such, he tried his hardest to keep things as normal as possible. Unfortunately, this meant Will was always walking around the swimming pool of their relationship and dipping his foot in to test the waters rather than closing his eyes and cannonballing into the deep end. It was an excruciating drag, but he had come to find pleasure in the pain of it all—at least he was feeling *something.*

Each morning, he met her at her locker with a heavily calculated air of cool detachment and offered a nonchalant "Hey," even though he meant to say *'I love you.'* She would respond with the closeness they had developed over the past years—close, but not *too* close. He would then proceed down his list of casual conversation topics in search of something that would hopefully not reveal him to be the tongue-tied idiot he felt like, inwardly thrilled that she still wanted to speak with him.

At times he felt similar to a Cold War-era spy speaking in code. Almost everything he said to her during these moments together was simply a substitution for his inner monologue, which was usually on the verge of throwing up as it shouted *'Run away with me,' 'You are so beautiful my head is going to explode,'* and, again, *'I am so totally in love with you.'* He hadn't been drunk yet, but Will was pretty sure this was what it must feel like—he was out of control, intoxicated by his infatuation. And he was absolutely *loving* it.

The funny thing was, this curious form of double-speak he had meticulously crafted was now so entrenched in his day-to-day interactions with Elyse that he had almost convinced himself that everything was as simple as it appeared. They were close—closer than most friends. And even though he wanted nothing more than to sweep her off her feet and take her to… *someplace* (he hadn't figured out where yet), his love was forced to just sit there, a zoot-suit-wearing elephant in the room he had resigned himself to ignore, for the time being. All to keep things normal and steady. Steady for her.

It hadn't always been this way. Once, she was just a classmate who happened to be his best friend's little sister, which was as far as it went. This scenario lasted only as long as it took for him to end up at the Korbin house, where he was surprised by both her willingness to talk to them and Patrick's unblinking acceptance of it. Every other sibling of a friend he'd ever known had been seen as a warring enemy.

"You know, she's probably stranger than the rest of us put together," Patrick once mused as they watched her polish the inside of the wall-aquarium glass. Her head was submerged, upside-down with a snorkel in her mouth, unbothered by the nearby school of clownfish assembling into a clutch of deep-sea lookie-loos.

Everything was as it should have been, and nary a second thought was given to spending so much time with a girl until that summer had rolled around, humid in both atmosphere and sweaty palms. Like a cloud of cicadas, the hormones of a new mating season had swarmed Bootville thicker than ever, feasting on the already lean crops of common-sense grey matter in Will's head.

Patrick and Elyse had spent the better part of the early summer traveling the Indian sub-continent with their parents, who had been anxious to eyeball the mysterious Asian lions of Gujarat and marvel at the Bengali felids of Ranthambore. As was always the case, and in accordance with the summer holiday laws of accelerating perception, these early days of vacation from school were the longest and the laziest, and while these would have been considered virtues under normal circumstances, a mere week of being couch-bound and playing video games at Colin's house (Colin always won), had left him pining for his distant friends' company.

After an idle June the length of three decades, the Korbins returned from abroad just as July was born, loaded down with freshly stickered steamer trunks, neatly sealed and labeled specimen jars, and hook-handled knives smuggled from the Khyber Pass. Will and Colin had spent the previous two weeks in an extended one-on-one street hockey tourney, smacking an old mossy-green tennis ball around while dropping shoulders and cross-checking their surplus energy into the air. They were ecstatic about having something else to do and hurried to see their long-lost companions.

Patrick greeted them wearing a pith helmet and issued a snappy salute that Colin gamely returned.

"Really?" said Will.

"Why, I've just returned from the Raj, old boy!" Patrick said in a voice vaguely reminiscent of James Mason as he led them into the great room. "Don't you know we salute our greetings at the bungalows rather than say them aloud so as not to disturb the ungulates?"

"Uh-huh," Will said. "Boy, we sure missed this, didn't we."

"Yes," replied Colin.

"You're so cynical, Will, you know that?" said Patrick, slipping back into his own voice and shaking his head pityingly. "Isn't he cynical, Colin?"

"Yes," Colin replied, tapping the glass of a jar labeled 'King Cobra Venom.'

Patrick dragged a chair to a corner of the room and climbed onto it so that he was nearly eye-level with the tarnished metal grating of a circulation vent. He rapped his knuckles on the grillwork. "Elyyyyyse! Bill's here with his pet robot—come see how real he looks!"

Colin offered the shadow of a smile as Patrick stepped down from the chair.

"It's always gloom-and-doom with you," Patrick continued, turning back to Will and tossing his pith helmet onto a side table. "And can I be honest with you?"

"Do I have a choice?"

"I must say, it's sort of a culture shock, especially having recently come from such a colorful and joyous people."

"Were they?"

"Sure, sure," said Patrick, brushing him off. "I'm… 98% sure that they were. Not that I speak the language, of course, and actually, come to think of it, some of them *were* downright hostile…" he said, rubbing his chin.

"Uh-huh."

"Are you confusing him again, Will?" Elyse said as she descended the stairs.

Any capacity for thought Will had brought inside with him promptly evacuated his brain and went to wait on the porch as she entered the room, bringing with her the warmth and confidence of exotic travels. She was foxier than he had ever noticed before, and he found himself overwhelmed by her sudden… *womanliness* as she threw her arms around him in greeting.

"Hey, 'Lyse," he managed to put together as she squeezed him in a way that was suddenly far too platonic for his liking.

"Aw, I'm so glad you guys came over," she said, beaming as she hugged Colin as well. Deep within the recesses of Will's heart, the panthers of misplaced jealousy roared, unfamiliar and reckless.

That afternoon had been auspicious in the joy of reconciliation it brought and the fire of love it had sparked. Will spent the rest of the day mooning in a googly-eyed fit as he eagerly lapped up Elyse's stories of adventure and intrigue in India's jungles and dusty flats. He nodded and encouraged her with enthusiasm so unlike him that Patrick began to eye him as though he was speaking Russian.

"You feeling all right there, buddy?" he asked as they slipped away to raid the kitchen, leaving Elyse and Colin to pore over well-worn maps and guidebooks.

"Yeah—why?" Will said, still thinking about his friend's sister.

"You seem awfully interested in the goings-on of old Bombay," Patrick said as he rifled through the refrigerator. "What, are you, like, some sort of tambura-nut now?"

"A what?" Will said, attempting to maintain an air of indifference. "You know, it's just really, uh, interesting hearing about all the stuff you guys saw over there. I've barely been past Collartown."

"Right…" Patrick said, emerging with two root beers and handing one to Will. "Here, drink that—it'll put hair on your arms."

"Cheers," said Will, clinking bottles with Patrick and taking a pull while his friend examined him with a suspicious eye.

"Speaking of things worth seeing…" said Patrick, "…have you seen Binzie Park at all this summer?"

"I did," Will said, glad for the change of topic.

"*And?*" Patrick's eyes were greedy for information.

"She's back with Fletch."

"No!" Patrick howled, slamming a fist onto the counter.

"Man, I saw them holding hands and sharing a brie-and-sprouts sandwich at the Grasshopper Café. You totally blew it."

"No!"

"Yes."

"Sprouts!?"

"Yep, you went to India, and you blew it," Will said, relishing Patrick's agony. He'd been fixated on this particular girl for the entire second semester, and she'd only become single mere days before the Korbins had left the States.

"She didn't ask about me?" he begged.

"No man, she was too busy wiping pita crumbs off Fletch's face. Sorry, dude," Will added, not caring either way.

"Damn, I *hate* the Grasshopper!" Patrick said, shaking his fist like a foiled supervillain.

"Yeah, it's no good."

"This year, friend," Patrick said, a far-off look in his eyes. "This year, we get girls."

"Uh-huh."

"Well, you know—we *find* girls, and then we get them."

"Right."

"I wonder where you find cool girls…" Patrick ruminated.

"Yeah," Will said, looking back at Elyse through the kitchen door. A small bloom of moon jellyfish floated aimlessly in the aquarium at the far side of the room, framing her in a corona of amorphous, forced-perspective membrane. She was laughing at something Colin had said, her smile radiating an electromagnetic field that shook him at the knees. "I wonder."

UNFORTUNATELY, IT WAS not to be; the loss of Patrick had been hard on all of them, but especially his sister, and Will suddenly felt more than the primal lust and adoration he'd been indulging himself in. He still loved her deeply—Marianas Trench-style—but now found himself assuming the mantle of a protector.

He did his best to shield her from the intrusive eyes of their classmates, who would only sense her weakness and prey upon it. He attempted to distract her from the darker corners of the grief she now carried in her delicate frame. He refused to let her frequent those blind alleyways of the heart which invariably led to sorrowful dead ends. He tried to anyway. The dark hollows beneath her eyes said otherwise, and he knew that the late hours of every evening, when there was no one else to lean on, were spent frequenting these places.

As he approached the cemetery gates, he saw Elyse and Colin waiting for him as planned. This was it—he could no longer avoid thinking about it, and from the fidgety postures and uneasy expressions of his two friends, he knew that they were thinking the same thing. Elyse clutched her bag to her chest, and he knew the transformative object was waiting beneath the canvas.

As he joined them on the curb, he looked around the neighborhood one last time, delaying his inevitable passage into unknown madness. The autumn colors of Nightjar Street seemed singularly beautiful to him at that moment. Beautiful like her.

CHAPTER 5
The Macabrium

IN MOST EARTHBOUND and lesser-cosmic matters, there is a simple rule: for every question, there is an answer. If you've ever wanted to know why a candle melts when it's been lit, it is because the heat has changed the molecular makeup of the wax, turning it from a solid into a liquid before wicking its way up to be vaporized by the flame. If you've ever wondered why your seventh-grade science teacher gave you a lesser mark on your papier-mâché volcano, it is because you have offered nothing of any educational value aside from how to make a papier-mâché volcano. If you've ever pondered why your seventh-grade science teacher *always* seemed to give you a lesser mark, it is because you look like his middle school bully, and he's still working through some issues (though the resemblance really is uncanny).

We live in a world of actions and reactions, causes and effects, the dominoes of occurrence careening one thing into another into another into another until this chain of events finally leads right to your doorstep. Or Elyse Korbin's doorstep, as it was, in the form of a timeworn leather book, which lay unobtrusive on her weather-beaten porch, in her weather-beaten neighborhood, beneath a decidedly orange-and-purplish weather-beaten sky.

If Halloween is a series of mysterious characters knocking on strange doors, it began one month early for Elyse. She'd been in the kitchen at the back of the old brick house, washing out safari canteens, when there was a sharp rap at the front door. She found this curious at first since the Korbins rarely had visitors, especially in the evening. Wondering who it could be, she wiped the suds from her hands and left the kitchen's warmth, making her way to the front hall.

She opened the heavy front door to find nothing, and as nothing is rarely so polite as to knock, she then stuck her head out the door and looked up and down the street. The clouds of early October filtered out all but a few lasting remnants of what was probably a glorious sunset, and the changing leaves, still painted with large splashes of green, rustled in the slight breeze as though the entire neighborhood had the chills. Still, rustling aside, Elyse saw no cause for the phantom knocking—most people were inside watching early-evening game shows at this time anyway.

She was just about to return to her rinsing when she happened to look down and find the old tome, quiet as most books are and patiently waiting to be read. She glanced in all directions to be sure there was no one about who may have dropped it on accident and, satisfied that it belonged to no one in the immediate vicinity, picked it up for closer examination. The heft of it surprised her, having been raised in a world of cheap paperbacks and mass-market pulp so flimsy that even inclement humidity would make the ink bleed off the page and onto the fingers. Here was a volume bearing all the trademarks of handcrafting and generations of wear and care. A true labor of love, the likes of which were rarely found outside of private collections or museums.

With this in mind, she looked around again, suddenly feeling a pang of criminal guilt. Still failing to find an accuser, she ducked back into the house, closing the door behind her slowly, fully expecting to hear a voice shout something like *'Hey, that's my book, you book-thieving pillager!'* at the last moment. But with a sigh of finality, the door clicked shut, leaving her alone in the dimly lit foyer with the aged volume.

And so, to be more specific about the general rule we started with: for every question, there is an answer—*if* you know where to look. Elyse had been left with no clue as to who her mysterious book-leave-behinder might be, save the very book itself. She stared down at its hand-tooled cover, slick and shiny from the oils of countless hands,

and the one word embossed in black gothic script stared right back:
Macabrium.

What on earth did that mean? She hadn't the foggiest, but it didn't sound like a best-seller or anything remotely modern. She flipped the cover open to see what this peculiar codex was about—Murder? Intrigue? Totem pole symbology?—and was so surprised by the contents that she nearly let it slip from her fingers. She caught it with a gasp and felt momentarily dizzy at the idea found scrawled in a shaky hand on the first page.

Shaking her head, she slammed the book closed and leaned against the wall beside the front door, breathing heavily and suddenly hyperaware of the cavernous silence in the old house. She stared down at the strange word, sinister in its ambiguity, and knew she would need some help with this matter of new-old strangeness.

"'LYSE, YOU GOT any snacks?"

Elyse rolled her eyes as Will and Colin stepped through the door.

"I don't even get a 'hello?'" she asked as the boys took their jackets off.

"Oh, c'mon—we're growing youths!" Will said, pounding his chest with his fist and adopting a much deeper voice. "We require dietary supplements to grow into our ever-changing bodies, right, Colin?"

"Yes, snacks," Colin said with a nod as Will threw both of their jackets onto the floor beneath the coat rack.

Elyse gave him a cutting look. "I see. Well, I hope your ever-changing bodies—gross, by the way—like crackers because that's about all we have right now," she said, leading them down the hall and into the kitchen.

"What, no mammoth?" Will asked, sliding into a seat at the kitchen table.

"Round crackers or oval crackers?" Colin asked, seating himself beside Will as Elyse ducked into the pantry.

"Oval crackers, Colin," she called back.

"I mean, I'd at least expect your parents to have a specimen we could fry up or something, right?" Will continued. Elyse tossed the box of crackers at him with more force than necessary.

"Don't be disgusting," she said, heading out to the great room.

"Here we go," said Will, handing Colin a stack. "A sleeve for you and a sleeve for me," Colin took it eagerly and began crunching away. "You know, I feel like the round ones are a bit classier—more buttery and posh," Will mulled, holding a cracker up to the light as he chewed. "But the ovals are so much more affordable, which I suppose makes them more reliable, right?"

"The ovals taste better," Colin said, crumbs spraying from his mouth.

"A working cracker for the working man, right? The round ones are so bourgeois."

Will was interrupted by the thump of the *Macabrium* landing before them on the table. Both boys stopped mid-chew and stared at it before looking up at Elyse, who stood over the table, her arms crossed.

"What's this—homework?" Will asked as Colin examined the book, his head tilted to the side.

"You've never seen this before?" Elyse asked, examining his face closely.

Will frowned and leaned over to inspect the leather cover more closely. He shook his head. "*'Macabrium.'* I've never heard of that," he said, looking up at her with curiosity. "Is it, like, a classic or something?"

Elyse stared fixedly at the black lettering and shook her head once. "No, I don't think it is. I've never heard of it either."

"Well, I don't know what to tell you," Will said, picking the volume up and hefting it, "The last book I read on purpose had 'Calvin and Hobbes' in the title."

Colin nodded sagely in remembrance of that particular masterwork but did not take his eyes off the *Macabrium*.

"Open it," Elyse said, leaning on the table.

"Yeah?" said Will, suddenly suspicious. "I don't have to read it or anything, do I? Because I don't really—"

He stopped cold as the cover fell open to him, revealing its insides. The pages were connected and folded in on themselves, and as he turned them outward, the contents were revealed.

"What is *this?*" he said under his breath.

Spread across three page-sized panels on each side was a design unlike any he had ever seen before; like stalactites and stalagmites, wisps of black hand-inked flames reached towards the center of the yellowed pages like furious jaws caught closing on the blankness. The elegant contours of the design undulated across the length of the paper, frighteningly complex and alien and yet somehow organic in their arrangement.

The book was shorter than it looked when closed, but the pages were heavier than he was used to, thicker than normal paper. He felt the texture of a corner with his thumb and forefinger.

"Vellum," Elyse said, watching him as he looked up, confused. "It's treated animal skin," she said.

"Oh, right," he said, nodding as though he'd known this all along. "That's really… odd," he replied.

"It's really odd, and it's really old, but the quality is pretty brilliant," she said.

Colin was now out of his seat and hovering over Will's shoulder, his black eyes scanning the book over and over again, unblinking.

"What *is* this?" Will asked again, staring at Elyse.

"Turn to the front," she said in little more than a whisper. Will squinted at her suspiciously and, refolding the left-side panels, turned to the first page. He read it aloud.

"*'To Find the Dead.'*"

It felt as though the kitchen temperature had dropped twenty degrees. The hair on the back of Will's neck stood up like the quills of an aggravated porcupine, and he lost all sensation of place as his limbs went numb.

Colin put his handful of crackers on the table and let his arms hang at his sides as his eyes became even more unfocused and distant than usual. Elyse watched the boys closely as the idea took root in their minds.

Finally, Will looked up at her, his expression neutral. "What are you thinking about here, Elyse," he mumbled.

"I think you know what I'm thinking," she replied.

"I think I know what you're thinking," Colin offered.

Will shook his head and looked back at the eerie passage. "You're right. I know what you're thinking, but…" he trailed off as he turned the pages and became lost in the design.

"We could at least explore the idea—" Elyse began.

"We don't even know what this means, Elyse," Will said, flipping back to the words. "They're just words on a page. It could mean anything. It could be an inscription, a chapter title, some kind of… lousy poetry—hell, I don't know."

"You know it's not any of those things, Will," Elyse said. "Don't you feel it?"

"Feel *what?*" he asked.

"The feeling that this is a command or instruction or something— the feeling that this is something *more?*" She stared at him with pleading eyes.

Colin grabbed a cracker off the table and stuffed it into his mouth, his eyes darting back and forth between them.

"I don't know, 'Lyse," said Will. "I mean… what is this supposed to *mean?*" He flipped to the menacing black wisps and held them up to her. "I've never seen anything like this before. Not even remotely close."

Elyse sat down across from him and pulled the book to her. She ran her index finger lightly over the top line of the strange pattern. "But isn't that reason enough to at least try to find out more about it?" she said, her voice calmer. "And see if we can figure out what it has to do with… you know…"

"Yep, say it out loud," said Will. "Hear how crazy it sounds."

Elyse sighed. "…finding the dead?"

Will exhaled heavily and ran his hand through his hair, his eyes wide at the thought of this venture. He took a breath and let his hand fall on the table.

"Sure," he said, his voice clear and resigned. "Let's figure it out."

Elyse beamed at him and looked up at Colin, who nodded his assent.

"But don't think this means anything more than it is," Will said. "I know what you want. And as much as I want it too… dead is dead, right?"

"I know that. But you said it yourself, and this book proves it," Elyse said, her voice catching for a moment. "There are some things in this world we've never seen before."

"YOU KNOW, SO far, this bears all the hallmarks of a lousy novel," Will said as the trio made their way up the steps of the Bootville Public Library. "I mean, a mysterious old book possibly harboring some ancient secret to defeat death—are you sure none of us is enrolled at a prestigious Ivy League college or, like, a member of some secret society or something?"

Elyse rolled her eyes, pushed through the heavy double doors, and entered the high-ceilinged lobby beyond. "I thought you didn't like reading anything that didn't have pictures in it."

"Well, I guess I mean to say that this feels like a lousy miniseries event *based* on a lousy novel." Will shrugged. "Even I'm not immune to the occasional saucy thriller—at least they don't make me think."

"Sure, why start now."

"That really hurts, Elyse."

They entered the library's main floor and decided to split up to cover more ground. Colin shuffled off to canvass the computer database while Elyse and Will went to the musty card catalog, hoping to stumble upon some new way of looking at the *Macabrium*.

"You have your list?" she asked Will, who pulled a wadded-up paper from his pocket.

The day before, they'd made a list of possible places to look, including everything from ciphers and codes to pictograms and folk art. Will smoothed it out on top of the card catalog and sighed.

"These days, there's nothing the kids like better than doing independent research on the weekend," he said.

"Indulge me," Elyse said, patting him on the arm and shooing him off to the stacks before turning back to her drawers of cards. She looked up and caught the librarian with cat-eye glasses frowning at her. She pulled her cape around her defensively and scowled in response.

"Don't worry, I won't hurt your precious books…" she mumbled as her fingers flew through the cards, energized by the thought of making progress on her problem.

Three hours later, the last resources of this energy evaporated into nothingness as the three reconvened empty-handed around a table in a private study room.

"I calculated the administration password and was able to gain access to their operation files, but I didn't see anything helpful, Elyse," Colin said, rubbing his eyes, which looked more hollow than usual. "It turns out the non-public files of the library are perhaps not as exciting as we thought."

Elyse scowled and shuffled through the stack of papers on which she'd written haphazard notes to herself of possible trails to follow, everything from cave paintings to chemical compounds to botanical etchings, all of which now seemed more inadequate and random than ever.

"I've got nothing here," she said, shaking her head. "I'd be fooling myself to think otherwise."

Will slammed the cover of a massive art book shut. "Well, *I* learned that the Italian Masters were *really* into painting naked people," he said, pushing the volume away with a look of shock.

"Nothing?" said Elyse.

"Not really—I mean, don't get me wrong, if there's anything else I've learned today, it's that there's a lot of… *art* in the world—I mean, really, it's a surplus. We've got art to spare. But no, I didn't see anything like *that*," he said, pointing at the leather corner peeking out from Elyse's bag.

"What about languages, encryptions, things like that?" she pressed.

Will shrugged, his eyebrows raised in surrender. "Cuneiform, hieroglyphs, Mayan calendars—nothing like it. Codes are typically numbers or letters, and anything else is obvious on purpose. Like, hide your secrets in plain sight, you know?"

"What is a 'Macabrium?'" Colin asked.

Elyse shuffled through her notes. "As far as I can tell, it's just a variation of 'macabre,' which dates back to France in the Middle Ages."

"Right, the Middle Ages," Will said, nodding and scratching his chin. "So that narrows it down to what? The last five hundred years or so?"

"The technical definition of 'macabre' is something relating to grim death," Elyse said, ignoring him and staring at her notes intently, trying to scramble and unscramble the information in some new way she hadn't already tried. It was all an enigma to her. She looked up at the books around her, stacked like cairns marking a potter's field of dead knowledge. There were so many of these graves, so many options. And yet the question remained: which one must be dug up?

WHEN RESEARCH AT the library wasn't going well (often the case), they headed further into town to the local Dog Ear Booksellers, where they casually picked through the entire inventory without purchasing anything. This noncommittal browsing continued until the clerk asked them to leave, proclaiming that books were 'for buying, not for reading!' Disgruntled, they headed to Colin's house to take their investigation to a digital level.

Colin's father was a software designer with a makeshift computer laboratory in their garage. With great care, they scanned two facing pages of the design into the bulky super-processor and ran it through every network database to no avail; the plugged-in community had nothing to offer either.

"Does this thing do HAM radio?" Will asked, bored-stupid next to a large panel of blinking lights and switches he proceeded to click on and off at random. "Maybe we can raise some lonely trucker who found the Macabrium on tape in Omaha or something." He adopted a rich, narrative tone: "'To find the dead—squiggle, squiggle, squiggle. Squiggle.'"

Colin walked past, engrossed in a sheaf of binary code printouts he seemingly had no trouble reading, and mumbled, "Please, don't touch the buttons."

Will absorbed this before deliberately flipping one more switch. "Squiggle," he said, more to himself than anyone else.

Elyse sat despondently in a swivel chair by a bank of monitors, her expression distant and sullen. Taking note of her depression, Will tried to soften and be more agreeable.

"'Lyse," he said. She looked up at him with red-rimmed eyes. "We'll figure it out. We're going to figure it out, right?"

"It never gets any easier," she said, her voice weary.

"Maybe we should ask your parents?" he suggested.

"Maybe we should ask *your* parents," she shot back in frustration.

Will couldn't help but smile—he enjoyed her ferocious side, even when it was unleashed on him. "Well, we could, but... unless this is the symbolic representation of a two-star menu or an invoice for twelve barrels of cod, I don't think they'll be much help."

Elyse scowled, though not at the endless dead ends in the maze of research they had taken on—she had taken on—but at the fact that before Patrick's death, her parents would've been the first place she would have gone. It was frustrating to think that this potential was now somewhat wasted by their hidden grief and the overly careful way they now stepped through their lives, not unlike the survivors of a shipwreck that had occurred because of their own carelessness.

"If only we'd thought of icebergs!" they seemed to cry out with every insulating gesture and tentative decision they made. No, they were too busy waiting out the tropical cyclones for a low-risk departure day to be of any help. With her brother had gone the family she had always known, and there was nothing she could do about it.

"'Lyse?" Will said, eyeing her warily. "You going nuts?"

"I think we've hit a dead end," Elyse sighed.

"Yeah?" said Will, exchanging a glance with Colin. "What does that mean?"

"I hate to say it, but we may have to ask for help from an untapped resource. Something we've never listened to or taken seriously."

"Like a Magic 8-Ball?"

Elyse put her head into her hands with a sigh of despair. "No," she said, despondent. "Like a *teacher*."

CHAPTER 6
Ms. Blithe

IT ALWAYS FELT strange visiting a teacher after-hours at school. Without the pressures of keeping a classroom full of kids within the boundaries of civility, a teacher's ordinariness (possibly even *humanness*?) was something Elyse's brain could not properly register. The quality was an optical illusion in which you could never really determine which side of the cube was closer to you.

So it was with no small amount of apprehension combined with a morbid curiosity that Elyse re-entered Ms. Blithe's room after grabbing her things from her locker. The classroom seemed different, unfamiliar despite the hours and hours she spent there every day, tucked into the back corner where she could observe but remain unseen. A heavy feeling of ozone hovered beneath the fluorescent lights, the last vestiges of the day's recently departed dramas, and it made the room feel like it had just been struck by lightning.

Ms. Blithe sat at her desk, napping in a silence that took her completely out of context. Elyse was used to seeing her as a blur of high-frequency vibration, mired somewhere within a constant state of riot control and lesson-plan perseverance, and left to spin these plates while trying to either remind or convince herself of her enthusiasm for the job. Seeing her now, red pen in one hand, her head propped up at a precarious angle in the other, she seemed wildly inexplicable, like a Caravaggio hanging from a refrigerator with letter magnets or aliens washing dishes after eating a lovely pasta.

It's weird to see her like this, Elyse thought, watching Ms. Blithe slip further into the land of nod and wondering if she should slowly back out of the doorway and leave well enough alone. *I always thought they just powered down or something.*

The sound of a delicate snore suddenly filled the room, causing Elyse to grimace at the awkwardness of it all. "Ms. Blithe…" she whispered, looking back into the hall, wishing some loud noise would spare her this impending embarrassment. Where was a clumsy janitor when you needed one? No sound came. "Ms. Blithe?" she tried again, in full voice.

Her teacher woke with a snort and instinctively straightened her glasses. "Hm—yes, what, I agree?" she said, looking around, bleary-eyed.

Elyse gave her a wave as though that explained things.

"Elyse?" Ms. Blithe said, surprised at the sight of her. Elyse could understand—she had never been one for class participation, and the past year had seen her withdraw even more, as though she was trying to will herself beyond the school walls. Usually, she settled for complete immersion in her cape.

To her credit, Ms. Blithe never seemed to mind—Elyse's grades were always good, though her recent report cards had noted her extreme lack of enthusiasm. Certainly, she was not enthusiastic about the task at hand.

"Am I, um… interrupting anything?" she asked her teacher.

Ms. Blithe emitted an awkward laugh and began shuffling a mass of essays into no particular order, moving them from one side of the desk to the other. "No, no, of course not! I was just decoding some of the mysteries of the semi-colon, and I must have dozed off a bit."

"Aw…" Elyse said, suddenly feeling for her.

"Not that twenty-four teenage interpretations of *Beowulf* don't make for thrilling reading, but…" she trailed off before turning back to Elyse. "I'm sorry, dear—was there something I can help you with?"

"Well, sort of," Elyse replied, now completely at a loss for why she'd thought this was a good idea.

"I'm afraid I haven't gotten to yours yet if that's what you're wondering…" Ms. Blithe said, placing her hand on the stack of essays while carefully examining her student's face. "…though, you've never really cared about your grades before, so I can't imagine that's it, is it," she said as a fact rather than a question, seeming somewhat relieved that this unexpected visit was probably not class related.

"No, it's nothing about that," Elyse said with a shake of her head. "It's something else I've been working on. It seems kind of crazy, but I'm, um, stuck on something, and I don't know what to do about it." The glaring insanity of her quest was now obvious in her mind. She began searching her brain for any excuse to escape before her poor teacher had her committed.

Ms. Blithe seemed to register the weight of Elyse's uncertainty and raised a curious eyebrow. "Mm-*hmm*…" she said, nodding deep in thought. "A real conundrum, eh?"

"Yeah, sort of," Elyse said, flustered. "I should probably just go—"

"Would you care for some tea?" Ms. Blithe interrupted.

"Tea?" said Elyse, confused.

"Yep, I think so," Ms. Blithe said, standing up and stretching. "I think a tea is definitely in order."

IF SEEING A teacher after school was odd, sitting next to one at a cheap Formica table in the teacher's lounge was like unexpectedly waking up in a Nepalese monastery. Ms. Blithe took a small kettle off a well-worn hot plate next to a surprisingly dirty microwave and poured the hot water over bags of Earl Gray into two cheap foam cups. Elyse watched, nervously folding the corner of a discarded morning edition into a crenelated wave.

"You know, I wasn't expecting it, but I'm glad you found the time to talk with me," Ms. Blithe said as she dunked the bags a few times.

"You are?" Elyse said, surprised.

"Well, of course!" Ms. Blithe replied, setting the cups on the table and taking a seat across from Elyse. "I had your brother in my class, you know." Elyse did know and had the faintest recollection of her in the parade of black-clad mourners at Patrick's funeral.

"Two years, in fact," Ms. Blithe added. "Patrick and I got on quite well—he was a bit of a talker but obviously brilliant in his own way." Elyse stared down at the tea steaming in her cup, unsure what to say. "I had hoped to get to know you better, but you're a bit of a mystery, aren't you."

Elyse looked up at her teacher, suddenly very self-aware.

"I'm sorry about what happened," Ms. Blithe said, her voice gentle. "We were all devastated. It must be difficult for you to get used to."

Elyse's eyes fell back to her cup. "It doesn't get any easier."

Ms. Blithe gave her a sad smile and nodded. "Yes, I'm sure."

At that moment, the door squeaked open, and Mr. Burnett entered, pausing at the sight of Elyse. He smiled at her and quickly turned his attention to Ms. Blithe.

"Hey, Doris—um, Ms. Blithe," he said, his eyes darting back to Elyse.

"Why, Mr. Burnett—fancy meeting you here," Ms. Blithe said, smiling and sipping her drink.

He stood in silence for a moment, looking nervous. "I just wanted to let you know that the, uh… *meeting* we had planned—you know, the, ah, teacher-teacher conference I had asked you about…?"

"Mm-*hmm…*" she said, raising an eyebrow.

"…Yes, well… it's taken care of. The reservations, I mean." He looked to Elyse again. She squinted back at him. "For the conference. For work. Uh… is Halloween at the Grasshopper good for you?"

"That sounds lovely," Ms. Blithe said. "I can't wait to… dig through those files you were talking about."

Mr. Burnett gave a nervous laugh. "Right, right—the files." Another awkward silence followed as he stood there, fumbling with his tie. With a start, he walked to the counter and grabbed an old donut, holding it up for them to see as he headed back to the door. "Just wanted to grab one of these guys. I'll see you, Doris—uh, Ms. Blithe."

The door squealed shut behind him, and Elyse turned to Ms. Blithe with a knowing look.

"He seems nice," she said.

"Doesn't he?" Ms. Blithe replied, smiling. She cleared her throat. "Well, where were we? Tell me all about this problem of yours— you've *intrigued* me."

At that moment, Elyse felt an overwhelming urge to tell this relative stranger about everything: her unending sadness, her alienation from almost everyone, her pursuit of something that was, by all sensible accounts, a complete impossibility, leading her to question her sanity… Instead, she found herself scrambling to sound reasonable and scholarly.

"Right, the… thing," she said, hating herself for it as she ducked down to grab her bag and place it on her lap. "I found this old book and wondered if you'd ever seen it before."

Ms. Blithe sipped her tea, which fogged up the bottom of her glasses as Elyse began rifling through her bag. "A book!" she said with no small amount of surprise. "Goodness me, there's hope for the nation yet. I wasn't sure we were still teaching people how to read."

Elyse gave her a look.

"Oh, don't mind me," Ms. Blithe said quickly, shaking off her skepticism. "Sometimes it feels like the entire world's been permanently plugged into video games." Elyse nodded sympathetically.

"I was an assistant librarian in college, you know," Ms. Blithe continued, blowing on her tea. "I used to love skulking through the stacks, sorting through the returns, and finding books I'd never seen before—never even knew existed! Thousands and thousands of ideas to be shared with the world," she trailed off, misty-eyed. "Not the most active social life, but still…"

"Did you see any older books?" Elyse asked, pulling the tome from her bag and delicately unfolding the pillowcase she'd wrapped it in.

"Oh, sure," Ms. Blithe said with a wave of her hand.

"*Really* old?"

"Mmm—some of the oldest in existence! My school had an extensive collection of rarities. Of course, you rarely see the obscure ones floating around these days."

The book fell on the cheap table with the heavy finality of a tomb being sealed. Ms. Blithe's eyes went wide at the sight of it. Even under the faintly flickering fluorescents, the *Macabrium* exuded as much dignity as a book would ever be able to muster. Elyse observed her teacher's reaction.

"Well, well…" Ms. Blithe murmured under her breath. "What on earth do you have there?"

"I was hoping you could tell me," Elyse replied, shaking her head.

Ms. Blithe set her cup down and leaned over the volume without touching it. *"'Macabrium,'"* she read slowly, frowning as the word escaped her lips. She looked up at Elyse.

Elyse shrugged and shook her head. Ms. Blithe leaned down further, so her glasses were just above the tabletop. She pored over it with a studied eye, tilting her head to the side.

"Well, it certainly looks old, I must say," she said.

"It feels old," Elyse said. "Leather and vellum."

"You've researched it?" Ms. Blithe asked.

Elyse shrugged again. "As much as I could—I never found anything about it anywhere. It's really weird."

"A possible one-of-a-kind, eh?" Ms. Blithe said, squinting at the book. "What's it about?"

"Um…" Elyse paused, unsure what answer would make her seem the least crazy. "You know, I'm not sure. It's sort of… complicated."

Ms. Blithe reached a hand out to it and stopped short. "Do you mind?"

Elyse shook her head and watched as Ms. Blithe drew the book to her, running her fingers along the spine. She took in the embossed title, her brow furrowed, before opening to the book's center and turning over a panel.

She gasped at the sight of the wild black markings within, clawing their way to the center of the pages with a violent tenacity. They seemed to taunt Elyse from across the table.

"Oh, wow," Ms. Blithe said, letting out a hiss of breath, her eyes wide as she took in the design. She turned the other heavy pages to find more of the same, her fingers gently rubbing the corner of the vellum. She seemed hypnotized, drawn deeply into the black flames. "Extraordinary," she whispered.

"Do you recognize it?" Elyse asked, her eyes darting from the pages to her teacher's enraptured face. Ms. Blithe looked up with a start as though she'd forgotten Elyse was there.

"I've never seen anything like this before."

Elyse dropped back into her seat, suddenly filled with despair once more. "Damn," she said.

Ms. Blithe ignored her cursing and turned the final panels. "Where in the world did you get this?" she asked, her face the picture of bamboozlement.

"Um…" Elyse started, unsure how much background she should go into without appearing mental. "Well, it was, uh, delivered to our house a few days ago."

"In the mail?" asked Ms. Blithe.

"No, no, the, um… you know, the book-bringers?" Elyse groaned inwardly at the blatant ridiculousness of this.

"The book-bringers?"

"Yeah—no. Nobody was home, so they just left it on the porch, you know? I found it there."

Ms. Blithe frowned. "But who sent it to you?"

"Well, that's uh…" Elyse said, eyeing the door. This line of questioning could lead to no good—one mysterious domino would fall into another until her base motive would be revealed, and she would be seen as the pathetic loon she very much felt like.

"Elyse, are you okay?" Ms. Blithe asked, intuiting her anxiety.

"Yeah, sorry," Elyse said, shifting uncomfortably in her seat. "I just remembered, my, uh… fish need feeding."

"Oh," Ms. Blithe said, confused. "But what about the book?" She began refolding the pages.

"No, it's okay," Elyse said, gathering her things into her arms. "If you don't know what it means, it's probably nothing, right? I was just curious about it."

"Well, of course—it's incredibly unique. Don't you want to see if we can deduce anything about it? I can call my old library and then—"

"Nah, it's probably just some crazy doodling or something. I always do it on my quizzes—well, you've probably noticed…" Elyse babbled. She had already shouldered her bag and drawn her cape around her, fully prepared to make a grand escape, when she reached for the book and froze.

Ms. Blithe had reached the front page with its shaky handwritten inscription. Elyse's heart sank at the sight of it. She felt so transparent she was sure the fluorescents were beaming through her.

"*'To Find the Dead,'*" Ms. Blithe read with a note of apprehension. Elyse's breath was caught in her throat as Ms. Blithe looked up at her, clearly perplexed.

"I know, crazy, right?" Elyse said with a too-loud laugh, making for the book. "I'm sorry, but I'm really late, and the cephalopods hate waiting."

"Protecting a fragile ecosystem, eh?" Ms. Blithe said, reluctantly closing the *Macabrium* and handing it back to her. Her expression spoke of confusion melded with suspicion, but she played along with Elyse's ruse anyway.

"Yeah," Elyse said with another strange laugh. "Gotta respect the habitat, right?"

"Mmm…" Ms. Blithe said, nodding.

"Well, thanks for the help and the tea—I really appreciate it, and I'll, uh, see you in class?" She could not get through the doorframe quickly enough.

"Of course," Ms. Blithe said. "And we should talk about this again," she called out too late. Elyse had already vanished around the corner in a swoosh of black cape.

CHAPTER 7
Aria For Encyclopedia

TO ELYSE'S RELIEF, Ms. Blithe never mentioned the book or their sharing of tea again, and things in class remained normal. Elyse sat quietly in the back and watched as her teacher battled through the usual classroom din. At most, Elyse occasionally caught Ms. Blithe looking at her with that tenaciously curious expression before quickly averting her eyes.

Despite their failure to determine anything new from the *Macabrium* itself, Elyse couldn't help feeling a surge of hope; Ms. Blithe, for all of her apparent grown-up worldliness, hadn't recognized the book and couldn't make heads or tails of its contents. If this was indeed the case, even with Ms. Blithe's extensive background in bookishness, then surely the *Macabrium* was something new and undiscovered. With no record of it ever having existed, there could be no record of it being unable to live up to its implied promise.

Still, she could not help see-sawing back and forth between hope and despair as the days rolled by, and the heavy thinking she and the boys had invested in the matter continually led to nothing.

IN THE LATER days of October, it was decided—well, Elyse decided—that their only option was to research at a virtually atomic level. They gathered in the great room after school, where the shadows of reef sharks escaped the aquarium and swept across the walls in great, winding arcs.

Nearby, Will tapped at the glass of a specimen jar holding a massive lobster. "You think this would boil up well?" Colin shrugged in response and turned back to watch the cluster of seahorses bobbing behind a corner of the glass.

"Okay, boys," Elyse said from across the room. She ran her fingers over the spines of some formidable-looking books on a shelf. "We need to get back to basics."

She grabbed a volume and held it out to them.

"What's that then?" Will asked, hesitant. "It's not another mystery book, is it? Because, clearly, one is more than enough."

"It's the encyclopedia, Matlock," Elyse said, exasperated.

"Oh," he replied. "And?"

"We're going to read it," said Elyse, a mad glint in her eye.

Colin bit his lower lip while Will rubbed his left temple and sighed.

"Yeah? We are?" he said. "You're not trying to distract us so you can tunnel into a bank vault or something, are you?"

Elyse's laugh bordered on the manic. "No! I just feel like it's the best way to cover all of our bases. This way, we'll know for sure we haven't missed anything. Great idea, right?"

Elyse's great idea hung dejectedly in the air as Will and Colin exchanged desperate looks.

"Ah, yeah, well…" Will said, looking for words that would not offend.

She shot him a look of warning. *"Yes?"*

Will sighed. "It's just… really? The encyclopedia?"

Elyse frowned and took her book to the sofa. She opened it on the coffee table and flipped to the first entry.

"I mean, it's not even a long book. It's a *series* of long books," Will pleaded. "It'll take us forever."

"I've got time," she said, taking the *Macabrium* from her bag and placing it next to the book of 'A's. She gave him a pointed look. "I thought you did too."

It was a dirty trick, she had to admit it. And yet she did not relent, even as she saw the jaws of this trickery snap shut and the teeth of deceit puncture Will's heart like the skin of an overripe mango. He winced visibly, and she knew he was wavering, having just been cold-cocked by the one-two fists of Love and Pain.

Despite everything that had happened over the past year, she remained well aware of his pining for her. Not that she minded, of course—her feelings for him were complicated—but his transparency sometimes made things all the more painful. To put it as perplexingly as possible, he often tried too hard to seem like he was not trying and then went ahead and tried anyway.

Again, it was not that Elyse didn't appreciate his efforts; she did not know what sort of state she would be in if he hadn't been there for her during the darkest times. However, their tension mixed with their collective grieving, his friendship with her brother, their unresolved and guilt-laden secret flirtation a million years ago, and the need to include Colin so that he would not feel like the outcast tagalong he had been before falling in with them—argh! It was all too much. Too much to deal with properly right now, especially while decrypting the vagaries of an old book of squiggles.

You stupid, stupid boy, she thought, watching him wrestle with himself over the Encyclopedia Plan. *Please forgive me for all of this one day.*

"It's not that I don't believe you, 'Lyse, and of course, I have all the time in the world to do this with you, but..." He pointed to the shelves of encyclopedias. "This seems a little more intense than I'm used to, reading-wise. You know?"

It was a testament to how far beyond their limits they had been pushed during their research. Will was now trying to ward off her wiles rather than jumping headfirst into them, and Elyse knew it. And it made her mad.

"Maybe I could, uh, build you something to help?" Will said, looking over to Colin, who nodded encouragement to this line of thought. "Like an encyclopedia holder that props it up, so you don't have to hold it."

"Or a wall sconce for your violin," Colin threw in.

Will snapped his fingers in agreement. "We could get some brackets, and—oh, oh... wait a minute. I have a vision here—three words, say them with me now: 'Cedar Cape Rack.'"

"Nice," said Colin.

"You know what you *could* do, is stop complaining and grab a consonant," Elyse said, now incredibly annoyed. "Or at least stop complaining."

"Okay, yeah," said Will, startled by the frustration in her voice. "Sure, we can do that." He leaned back against the nearby piano and awkwardly put his hand down on the keyboard. It plinked out a handful of atonal notes as though its tail had been stepped on.

Will frowned and examined the keys. "Does this sound out of tune to you?" he asked Colin, who looked on, curious.

From behind her encyclopedia, Elyse frowned and twitched as the boys hit the same sour notes over and over again.

Plink-plink-plink. "Is that right?" *Plink.*

"Try this…" *Plink.*

"What about…" *Plink. Plink-plink.*

"Ahem." The boys turned to find Elyse glowering contemptuously at them, her arms crossed.

"Oh. Sorry." Will turned to Colin and whispered, "Let's get the tuning kit from the garage." Colin nodded, and together they slinked from the room.

Elyse gave a sarcastic wave. "Thank you…" she said, breathing deep and submerging herself into the letter 'A.'

THIS TIME, IT was only a matter of two hours before the cloud of despair returned with a vengeance. As Elyse slogged her way through the entry for ACROMEGALY, the words began to blur into meaningless symbols representing the cultural equivalent of nothing. It was like trying to read carpet—it led nowhere, and she felt foolish for attempting it in the first place.

The boys weren't helping. Will had his head buried deep in the belly of the baby grand with the tuning wrenches while Colin stood by the keys, zoning out. By some random and infuriating twist of fate, Colin's 'different' brain had perfect pitch, despite having no musical aspirations of his own nor any gift of coordination for playing an instrument. He stood by, humming whatever note they were tuning (now in the third octave) and plinking the key in question while Will tightened or loosened whichever part needed attention.

Between the monotonous humming and off-key plinking, not to mention the creeping doubts regarding the folly of her encyclopedic endeavor, Elyse's jaw was so thoroughly clenched that she could feel a muscle in her cheek twitching in time to the tapping of the keys.

"Mmmmmmm…"

Plink-plink-plink.

Twitch-twitch-twitch.

"Aaaargh!"

With a fury no one had anticipated, Elyse exploded from the sofa. She flipped the coffee table on its side with a small bounce and a thump, sending the open books scattering across the floor and into the piano legs. The impact caused the instrument to hum with the sound of every note vibrating simultaneously.

Colin was frozen, his hand in mid-air, finger pointed down at the offending key. Will lifted his head from the piano to see what the fuss was about. His hair was matted to the side with sweat, and his face was covered with smears of antique dirt.

"What was that!?" he called out to Elyse. She was breathing heavily, her brow knitted as tight as her fists were clenched. "Elyse? Hey man, what gives? Now we gotta redo all these—"

"This. Is. *Ridiculous,*" she said through angry breaths. "I'm sorry, I'm sorry I'm a monster, but this is ridiculous. A waste of time. What was I thinking!? This is just… *argh!"*

Will and Colin could only look on in shock at the rare chemical event of a solid teenage girl melting into a puddle of liquid rage.

"Uh, 'Lyse? You okay?" Will asked, exchanging panicked looks with Colin. But no answer came, for Elyse was too into her mutterings of defeat, a potent fuel for the pacing and arm-waving she'd begun across the room, punctuated with bursts of crazed laughter.

"I just *had* to get my hopes up, didn't I? Oh-*ho!* I had to *convince myself* there was some purpose to all of this—*ha!* I had to go and read between the lines and invent an idea of what this *stupid book* is. Ridiculous!"

Will immediately reverted into his classic role of enabler, aiding and abetting her as best he knew, hoping she'd one day take notice. It was a comfortable part for him to play.

"It's going to be all right—" he began in the same soothing tones one would use when attempting to grab a cobra behind the head. He was then quickly taught the valuable lesson that soothing tones do more to soothe the one speaking in them than the upset animal being spoken to. Elyse wheeled on him and exploded.

"It is *not* going to be all right, Will! I've been following my gut instinct this entire time, and all I've learned is that my instincts *stink.*"

Will wiped some sweat off his brow. "Well, what did you expect?"

"I thought it meant something *more.* I thought it was leading us to a solution! But it's ridiculous! A ludicrous idea to think that stupid chunk of leather is—" Her voice caught in her throat as she stopped and followed the line of sight her finger made as it pointed to the *Macabrium.* Colin was bent over the book, his eyes transfixed. Elyse tilted her head to the side, dizzy at the sight of him.

Meanwhile, Will was still engaged in their conversation of outbursts. "To think it's *what?*" he asked, staring at her now-frozen form.

Elyse ignored him and stepped towards Colin, who had yet to move from his crouch. Will craned his neck around the propped-up piano lid to get a better view.

"Colin?" Elyse said, her tone calm once more. He didn't reply. She walked over and knelt beside him. "What is it?"

He didn't look up at her; his eyes darted back and forth between two items on the floor. "Oh," he said. "I've figured it out."

Elyse frowned at this, confused. Will put his wrench down and hopped off his crate, wiping his hands on his pants as he made his way around the instrument.

"Figured *what* out?" Elyse asked under her breath, as though speaking too loudly might scare away Colin's epiphany.

The *Macabrium* had careened off the leg of the piano, knocking down pages of sheet music, which had fallen slowly, like so many dead leaves off a tree, and landed next to the open tome.

"Do you see it?" Colin whispered as they all huddled over the mess on the floor.

Elyse looked back and forth from page to page and felt her stomach drop as if she was in an ascending elevator. "Is it… Oh, that's *mad…* " she said as the solution began to present itself to her in full.

Will could only squint and scratch his head, unsure of what the other two were marveling at. He eyed them warily as they lingered in their trances. "No offense, you guys," he said, his voice calm, "but what the hell are you talking about?"

In a flurry of cape, Elyse straightened and spun herself to the table she had just knocked over. She righted it with a thump as Will followed her, baffled. He watched as Elyse pulled a workbook of blank paper and a pen from her bag. Colin put the open *Macabrium* on the table alongside a page of sheet music.

"They are the same," he said blankly to Will, who still looked lost.

"Are they?" he said. "Because one looks like a bunch of painfully familiar squiggles, and the other looks like page five of, let's see here… *Elvira Madigan,* whoever she is."

"Will, don't be a hooligan," said Elyse. "Colin, you're a genius."

Will raised an eyebrow. "He is?"

"I am?" Colin asked.

"Of course!" said Elyse, excited by what had just been revealed to her. She began drawing a quick sketch of markings like the ones in the *Macabrium.* "See, we were looking at these as if they were something in and of themselves, but the marks represent something. But not words." She grabbed a page of music and began pointing to the notes.

"See, the music is just a detailed chart of what note to play where, when, and how. The staff tells you which one, and the notes are ordered left to right, just like how some of us read words. Then they're accented with the flags and double-bars and so on, right?"

"'Lyse, you know I don't 'get' music," Will said, massaging his temples.

"Right, right, right…" Elyse said, searching for a better explanation. "It's like a map, see? It tells you where you are, where you've been, where you're going, and what you did when you were there."

She paused, waiting for Will to process this. He frowned, still only half with her.

"Okay, so?" he said, shaking his head.

"This," she said, picking up her sketch, "is the same kind of map."

She slapped it back on the table and began drawing the familiar parallel lines of a music staff across the tongues of black flame.

"See how these marks end at points in intervals?" she asked, pointing to the new graph, which now looked astonishingly regular in its spacing within the staff. "This could be a song."

Will looked at her, momentarily at a loss for words. He didn't believe her, and she could tell, but she was far too excited by this idea to let his skepticism sway her.

"I don't know, Elyse," said Will. "I think the encyclopedia thing may have fried your brain."

"No, no!" she said, humming with energy. "This could be right! I told you it looked familiar, didn't I?"

"Did you? Okay…"

"And you know Colin doesn't see things the way we do, right?"

"Yeah…"

"He saw the pattern! Or the idea of a pattern—a different dimension of pattern." She turned to Colin again. "You're a genius, Colin."

"Okay," he responded, yawning.

Will stared at them as if they had just announced plans to rehearse a trapeze act. After a moment, he sighed and ran his hand through his hair again.

"Prove it," he said.

"Yes!" Elyse said, giving him a playful shove.

Ten minutes and several false starts later, Elyse and Colin had replicated a series of *Macabrium* markings and transcribed them onto a blank composition page. It had been painstaking work, and as Elyse watched Will's doubtful expression upon seeing the handful of notes, she couldn't help wondering if her intuition had been mistaken.

"That's it, huh?" Will asked as politely as possible.

"This is just a couple of seconds worth of notes," Elyse said, her voice betraying her apprehension. "We'll just play them and see if it sounds like anything, okay?"

"And if it doesn't?" said Will.

"I'll drop it, I swear."

"Really?"

"Probably not, but for right now, let's pretend I will."

"I figured," said Will with a roll of his eyes. "Play on."

Elyse walked to the piano, placed the sheet on the stand, then moved to a storage closet in the foyer, cracking her knuckles. Will crossed his arms, his face neutral, and glanced down at Colin, who was now looking over the *Macabrium* with new eyes.

"Okay," Elyse said, returning with her once-discarded violin. She exhaled deeply and stared between the music and the instrument in hand. She quickly tuned the strings and tightened her bow. "Wow. It's been a while. This is probably going to sound like a lot of sucking."

"You're talking to a couple of musical cavemen here—you'll sound great," Will reassured her.

Slowly, Elyse's pale fingers began the tune. The notes floated from the violin's body, bleeding into each other in the strange alchemy of melody. As she played, Elyse could feel the familiar sensation of the floor falling out from beneath her, a feeling that always accompanied her favorite songs. It was an overwhelming current of such power that the vibration felt like it could easily melt her down like an overworked electrical station. And then, as soon as it had begun, the song abruptly stopped as she reached the end of her hastily scribbled notes.

The silence of her house raced to fill the void left by the notes, leaving them with only the sound of the fish tank filter humming and their hearts racing.

"Well?" she said, turning to them and brushing a loose strand of hair away from her face.

"Aesthetically pleasing," Colin said, nodding.

"Thanks, Colin," Elyse said, smiling softly. She looked at Will, who stood motionless. His face was ashen, and his eyes were glued to a spot across the room.

"Hey," Elyse said, frowning at him. "Not bad, right? I mean, it kind of sounded like *something,* didn't it? Hello?" She waved her hand in front of his face, but his gaze remained locked elsewhere.

Slowly, his jaw dropped. "Um…" he mumbled. "Play that again."

"What?" Elyse said, surprised. "What's wrong with you? You don't have to humor me, you know."

"No, no," he said, shaking his head but still not looking directly at her. "I swear I'm not. Just… play it again."

Elyse looked at him as though he was ill, then turned to Colin, who shrugged.

"Okay…" she said, turning back to the workbook. Again, she began playing the notes, and again, she felt the floor drop out from beneath her. The song came more easily to her this time, the repetition bringing an assuredness to her playing that had been absent the first time.

"Elyse," Will murmured behind her. "Look up at the bookcase."

She frowned at the interruption but looked up anyway. She gasped; hovering in front of the bookcase stacked with encyclopedias, some five feet off the ground, was a wave of… Elyse wasn't sure what to call it, but *distortion.* It was the blurry feeling of tremendous, mirage-inducing heat—the kind that caused weary travelers to imagine oases in the desert or would hang, rippling like old glass, above firepits in the summer.

She had stopped playing, her finger holding down the last note. It carried through the room, a clarion creature creeping its way up the walls, reverberating along the aquarium glass, and running laps around the ceiling. There, it spiraled into nothingness and took the watery atmospheric disturbance with it as it died.

The trio stared across the room in shocked silence for a moment before Elyse turned to face the boys.

"What the hell was that?" she said, her voice shaking with excitement.

"Um…" Will said, his gaze riveted to where the waves had been.

"Cool," said Colin, rubbing the side of his nose.

"Will!" Elyse snapped her fingers in his face, causing him to finally tear his eyes away from the mystery spot. "Hello!? Hey! What *was* that?"

"Um…" he repeated.

"That was *crazy!*" she cried, starting to pace again.

"Crazy," Colin said, nodding.

They darted back to the coffee table and began the work of decrypting more of the bizarre markings. When she had written down a new handful of notes, Elyse would place herself in the same spot she'd been standing the first time and then play the results. It was a laborious process, but every experimental performance gave her a better understanding of the melody, and she began to rediscover that elusive state of mind Patrick had always harped on about—the *feeling* of the music.

Each pass she made through the song brought better results. The morphing of atmosphere became more pronounced, slowly expanding as she experimented with her mechanics, finally cashing in on the exercises from Maestro Glutenberg's manual. Playing her violin again felt like the strange mixture of relief and uncertainty felt upon seeing an old friend for the first time in ages. Her fingers protested as she slowly began to knock the rust from them, positioning and stressing them in exhausting ways she'd not attempted in nearly a year. Within an hour, her fingertips were scarlet with string-sized welts, and she had to stop.

As the final trace of rippling began to swirl itself away, she looked over to see Will and Colin staring at her as though she'd just beamed down from another planet. Even some of the fish had gathered by the glass to watch.

"Well?" she said, her face aglow with an energy she'd not felt since—well, *ever.*

Will shifted in his seat and cleared his throat. "Um…"

"Um-*what?*" she pressed.

"Um, at this point, I have to ask… what the hell is going on here?"

"Will, you stupid handyman, don't you see?" she said, barely able to control her excitement. "This is *it!* This is what we've been looking for!"

"Which is…?"

"How to find the dead! It has to be! Come on, admit it—you've never seen anything like this before."

"Well, of course not—this is totally demented."

"Totally!" she cried out, giving him a push.

"Totally," said Colin.

"Okay, as long as we're fine with that, I guess," Will said. "Then let's just be crazy."

AND SO THEY were. The trio approached it the best way they knew, playing it by ear. In the following days, Elyse practiced while Will and Colin tried their hardest to help her further decode the convoluted panels. Note by note, she struggled, adapting the top and bottom rows of black-flame scrawl into clefs and forcing the wisps into one concrete melody. She then transposed it over and over again in search of a key that would empower her violin to ensnare the song in its entirety.

With each step they took towards completion, the warping of the room became more distinct, and it was decided that the finished performance would only be appropriate at the cemetery—the scene of Patrick's dying breath. They would do it on Halloween—the first anniversary of the tragedy. They would take whatever risk needed to be taken if it meant finding him again, as the inscription promised. They would be crazy, follow the trail of nonsense, and hope the results would lead them to that elusive place where things were sound once more.

CHAPTER 8
Necropolitan Renaissance

THE FRINGE OF Bootville Proper was alight with candle-flame orange, courtesy of a sun dipping slowly beneath the tree line in the west and gilding the entire town in liquid fire. As the shadows grew long, Elyse, Will, and Colin converged amidst the banks of dead and dying leaves along Nightjar Street. From beneath the worn blacktop peeked a layer of vibrant maroon cobblestones, as though the past was trying to break through to the present.

Elyse and Will eyed each other but did not speak. Colin's eyes darted between them, awaiting some sort of cue. The wind gusted loudly for a moment. It carried the sound of a rusty creaking from somewhere along the line of wrought iron fencing surrounding the tombs and weaving between the quitting foliage. The trio inadvertently found themselves staring at a scarred and twisted tree that erupted just outside the gate and reached inside toward the graves. It offered little response.

Will cleared his throat. "Should we, ah, do anything before we begin?"

Elyse pulled her eyes from the branches and gave him a look. "What do you mean? Like, *say* something?"

Will looked mildly embarrassed. "Oh, well, you know… it just seems like quite a moment, right?"

Colin looked wide-eyed at him as Elyse wrapped her cape around herself.

"But we're trying to bring him back, not send him away," she said, her eyes slipping back to the scarred tree for the briefest moment. "It's like an anti-wake, right? If anything, we should say something *after* it happens—if anything does, that is."

Will nodded sharply and thrust his hands into his pockets. "Right, right. Well, let's get started, yeah?"

Elyse knelt and placed her violin case on the ground, carefully opening it while Colin unpacked her shoulder bag. He handed the spidery frame of a music stand to Will, who began assembling it with shaky hands. The wind blew a powerful cannon gale down the lane once more as Elyse removed the instrument, vibrating the strings into a moan of open tuning. She placed a hand over one of the f-holes and felt the reverberation in the wood pass as quickly as it had begun.

Colin removed Elyse's workbook from her bag and flipped through its used pages until he found her most recent notations. He placed it on the stand, turning it to face the cemetery. Elyse turned the end of her bow until it was taut and checked the instrument's tuning. The notes sounded in the encroaching twilight, ringing with a richness heard only amid an autumnal evening. She looked over to the boys with a last moment of hesitation.

They stared back at her with uncertainty, then moved well off to the side of the curb as though steering clear of a blast radius she was about to incite.

"You can do it, Elyse," Colin said in his near-monotone.

"Yeah, Korbin—play us some of that old-timey fiddlin'," said Will.

Elyse smiled at them but said nothing as she turned to the pages before her, her stomach alive with the fluttering moths of stage fright.

Stage fright indeed, she thought. *If this works, it'll be stage-terrifying.*

She set the violin under her chin and focused on the music before her. The notes began eking their way out of the instrument, the tune familiar to her from the hours she'd spent practicing. She'd never played the song as a whole—she'd felt it only appropriate to wait until the critical moment, as though doing otherwise might drain this astounding reservoir of discovery. She held her breath for a moment as she reached a transition point between two parts of fractured rehearsal but bridged them easily. Her phrasing of the baleful tune carried out into the crisp air, sedating the wind and serenading the nearby graves.

As she slowly traced her way through the labyrinth of notes in search of the eventual ending point, Elyse could feel the liveliness of the outside fall away into a muted still-life, and the lane took on a surreal quality of being paused. She dipped slowly to the pages of music, focusing as the ending phrases came upon her like an unstoppable river. Her fingers danced from note to note with the ease of a song once learned, forgotten, and remembered again.

As the final note sang its last into the hypnotic void, the slate sky spiraled quickly open ten feet above their heads with a sonic boom. The thunderous noise pulled the rest of the muted sounds of the lane into a pulse of vacuum, blowing their hair back and nearly knocking them to the ground with its power. They stared up in terror and awe as the vortex opened into what appeared to be a stormy, lightning-plagued night sky some fifteen feet across. It began to warp itself into a third dimension, like an inverted tornado funnel. This conical shape of night reached down like the barrel of a howitzer, twitching as though electrified and pushing the air against the three.

As they peered into the strange tempest above, a figure came hurtling down towards them with tremendous speed. Their eyes widened as the body accelerated to the mouth of the funnel. Despite being spellbound by this meteoric descent, Elyse, Will, and Colin were forced to turn away as the body crossed the threshold of the maw in a flash of blinding light that haloed out in all directions. The figure emerged screaming from the murky cyclone and hit the ground with a grunt.

The new arrival sat up with a groan and rubbed his arm, which had taken the brunt of the impact. Elyse felt her jaw drop as she noted the scorched jumpsuit he was dressed in—black, with a life-sized skeleton frame stitched on the front—and felt the dizzying sensation of the past creeping up behind her in an attempt to relive itself.

"Patrick!" she gasped, her eyes wide with disbelief at the figure, whose body mass seemed strangely vaporous.

"Hey, Sis! What goes on?" the brotherly specter said in a hauntingly familiar voice.

Elyse couldn't believe it—this could not be happening. She was delusional. She was suffering from visions brought on by food-borne illness. She had finally lost her marbles. Her dark eyes probed this probable hallucination in search of a giveaway that this was all some self-inflicted hoax. But despite her best efforts to prove the contrary, a further examination found it all to be true—the young man could be no one else but Patrick. Elyse knew her brother better than anyone, his shaggy hair, the inherent mischief in his relaxed posture. It was Patrick, all right, though incomplete and vaguely translucent, like a reflection seen beneath fluorescent lights through a dingy bathroom mirror. A hollow, dead look.

"Will, lad!" the ghostly Patrick said, moseying over to him. "Man, you look just *awful!* I mean, seriously, it looks like you haven't slept in a month—wow! What, are you out, hitting the casinos all night or something? Something? Hm? Should I be worried?"

"No—" Will started.

"Yes? Yes, I should be worried?"

"No, it's just—"

"I know, I know, it's just that you've been out all night, rousing the rabble, getting up to your shenanigans and your tomfoolery, wrestling the one-armed bandits from dusk to bloody dawn, am I right? Save it for your support groups, Will—let's get *real* here!"

"No, I was—" Will began as Patrick zoomed over to Colin, who looked up at him with his indifferent, alien eyes.

"Colin, you crazy son-of-a-gun!" Patrick shouted, a wild grin on his face. "Say, you look different—older or something. I can't place my finger on it... Hm. Do you guys see it?"

"Hello, Patrick," Colin replied with unblinking observance. "You're looking very see-through today."

"See-through, you say?" Patrick said, scratching his head. "Well, okay then..." He turned to Will and Elyse. "Have we figured out if he gets pills or anything? 'See-through?' I'm not sure how to take that, you know?"

"It's true," Colin said, looking up at the ever-dimming sky. "You're see-through."

"Well, I *am* known for wearing my heart on my sleeve, it's true," Patrick said, cocking his head to the side and staring at him.

Meanwhile, Elyse was slowly emerging from her state of momentary catatonia. "Patrick..." she started, watching as her brother pondered Colin. The ghostly images of dead leaves blowing down the street behind him could be faintly seen through his torso.

"Hmm..." he mumbled, his eyes slowly moving away from Colin. "Something's amiss here..."

"Patrick..." Elyse tried again, looking nervously over at Will, who was clearly still feeling the initial shock of this momentous appearance.

"Do you guys get the feeling that there's something *weird* going on?" Patrick asked as he began meandering around the area and examining the nearby trees lining the cemetery fence. They watched as he darted to a lamppost, looked behind it as though he might catch someone hiding there, and then made his way to a large mailbox along the curb. He rubbed his chin contemplatively as he grabbed the hatch handle and peered inside.

"It's just the strangest feeling," he said. "It's like there's something here that's, I don't know... out of place or something, you know?"

"Patrick!" Elyse finally shouted.

"Yes, my adorable, *shrieking* little sister?" He let the mail hatch swing shut and turned to her, eyebrows raised.

Elyse cursed herself for being so inarticulate—how was she supposed to deal with this? Her eyes brimmed with tears as she glanced over at Will. Patrick stared at her in a way she found chilling in its familiarity; it was the look of an oddball big brother, one she used to know well and took comfort in. She now found it overwhelming.

"Elyse..." Patrick said, the playfulness slowly draining from his face as he moved towards them.

From the corner of her eye, Elyse saw Will tense up and turn slightly in her direction. His hand was raised a few inches as though to shield her. The shift in body language was nearly imperceptible, but it was enough to bring Patrick to a halt.

"Elyse, please?" Patrick said. He stepped towards them again, slower this time, his hands raised. "You guys are being super-weird right now—what is the *deal?* You're all looking at me like I've got antlers or something." He quickly reached up and patted his head, then breathed a sigh of relief.

Elyse sniffled and exhaled deeply.

"Patrick… look at your hands," she said, pointing to them. Patrick looked down, only to discover that he could see his shoes through them. Frowning, he grabbed his right wrist and held it up to get a better look at it, tilting back and positioning it in front of the limbs of the large, overhanging tree.

"What the…" he started, peering at his palm as though it was some unknown marsupial species. He held his other hand behind it to test its translucence, waving it back and forth as his brow became increasingly furrowed. Elyse, Will, and Colin exchanged glances. Patrick dropped both hands and stared up at the sprawling branches of the tree.

"Wait a minute," Patrick said, the slightest air of panic creeping into his voice as he turned back to them. "What is this?"

"Patrick, don't you remember?" Elyse asked, her voice trembling.

"Remember *what?"* he asked. "What are you talking about, Elyse?"

"Pat, something happened to you," said Elyse. "Last year."

"Last year?" Patrick frowned.

"That's right," she responded, her heart hammering violently against her ribs. "Exactly one year ago tonight."

"Halloween," Will added. His face was drained of all color, causing him to look startlingly like his recently returned best friend.

"Do you remember?" Elyse asked, her voice gentle as she eased her brother into this revelation.

Patrick looked away, his eyes unfocused as he tried to recall what had happened. "Halloween…" he said, more to himself than to the others. Patrick shook his head and turned back to them. "I can't remember," he said, holding his hand up to his face again. "What about Halloween?"

"Well, it was… there was, uh…" Elyse looked over to Will for help, panic in her eyes.

"There was an accident," Will said.

"An accident?" said Patrick.

"It was accidental," Colin said.

"Well, what does that mean, 'an accident?'" Patrick asked. He looked at the surrounding neighborhood with newly suspicious eyes.

"Oh, Patrick, I'm so sorry!" Elyse sobbed, a tear running down her cheek. "It was an accident, I swear! We were just messing around, you know? We were messing around right here at the cemetery, and you were hit by lightning—"

"What!?" Patrick cried out, horrified.

"It's true! It was storming like crazy, and you were struck by lightning and fell, and then… and then you died." Elyse's words hung in the air like obtrusive party balloons as everyone absorbed this bold-faced statement of truth.

Patrick's eyes were as wide as dinner plates. "I-I'm dead?" he said, perplexed by the idea.

"Patrick, we haven't seen you in a year!" Elyse said. "A *year!* Do you realize how weird this is?"

"Do I ever," he said, astonished. "And I thought Mom and Dad were the crazies—whoa! Mom and Dad! Are they all right? Are *you* all right!?" Patrick was now in a panic as he ran over to belatedly console his sister.

Elyse gave him a sad smile. "They're not the same, Patrick— none of us are."

Will and Colin nodded in agreement. Patrick exhaled and leaned back, smacking his forehead with the palm of his hand.

"Dead! I can't believe it!" he said, as though insulted. "But I don't even remember it! You'd think I would now that I'm the undead. Or, whatever this is," he said, waving his vaporous hand in front of his face. "I mean, I don't know the rules to this or anything, but shouldn't I be ascending to some hyper-conscious plane or at least achieve some kind of general omniscience?"

"If not omnipotence…" Will mused.

"At *least*, right?" Patrick cried, throwing his hands up in exasperation. "I mean, I hate to be a griper and all, but this is not the cosmic experience I'd counted on…"

"Patrick—" Elyse started.

"I mean, it seems like a real drag so far," he continued, shaking his head.

"Patrick—" Elyse repeated.

"Look at this—look how hazy I am. I'm translucent over here—and you know, that's really only a half-step away from transparency, which means I'm *almost* invisible. And yet, I feel nothing." He said.

"Patrick—"

"When even *invisibility* is not enough to give you a charge, you know you could've done better, you know what I mean?" he said, looking down to Colin, who nodded. "I just want my mind blown, that's all I'm saying."

"Patrick!"

He turned to her, startled.

"What is it, Sis?"

Elyse wrapped her cape around her with a snap, sending up a whoosh of orange and red leaves.

"You have to follow me."

She turned from them and ran through the foreboding gates of the graveyard.

"Hey, where are you going?" Patrick hollered as they ran after her.

They snaked through the undulating burial grounds beneath a vault of autumn leaves and creaky limbs. After a moment, Elyse slowed until they were all standing before the massive slab of tombstone inscribed with Patrick's name. The four of them stared at it in silence for a moment before Patrick drifted towards it, his face a mask of ghastly disbelief. He reached out and absentmindedly traced the large 'K' of 'KORBIN' with his finger while placing the palm of his other hand on top of the flat stone.

"Everything is cold," he murmured while the others looked on. He turned to them with a sad smile. "I suppose you wouldn't go to all the trouble of setting this up just for the sake of a prank, right?"

"Patrick, we come here all the time," Elyse said, her voice trembling once more. "We've missed you so much—things have been just awful since you've been gone."

"Yeah, it hasn't been the same, brother," Will said.

"I only have two friends now," Colin stated.

Patrick's eyes went wide as a thought occurred to him. "Was there a funeral?"

Elyse nodded.

"Really!" Patrick said, amazed at the thought of it. "Man, I'd love to have seen that! Is that morbid of me? It feels morbid."

Will shrugged. "You yourself are kind of morbid."

"Am I?"

"Well… you're the walking dead…"

Patrick shook his head in disbelief. "This is crazy," he said, looking back at his grave. "It's a nice stone, I have to admit," he added, tenderly running his hand over it. "It's dignified, you know? Did Dad have his guy do it? He always said he had a headstone guy, but I never really knew what the hell he was talking about—"

From across the tree-lined burial yard came the sudden howl of a dog.

"It's the night watchman," Elyse hissed at them.

"It must be closing time," Will said, eying the fallen sun. "He's probably doing his clearing-out rounds."

"But it's *my* grave!" Patrick said in mock annoyance. "Doesn't that count for anything anymore?"

"We have to get you out of here before that stupid hound sniffs us out," Elyse said, taking her violin case from Colin and slinging it over her shoulder like a rifle.

"Do you think he'll notice something's off?" Patrick said, pressing his hand against the headstone, the engraved 'K' dimly showing through it.

"Let's go to the Watch," Will said, ignoring him.

Elyse nodded, and they crept from the graves, each keeping a nervous eye over the rambling cemetery lanes. Patrick followed suit, pausing briefly to race back to his headstone. There, he brushed away some dead leaves from its base before vanishing into the ever-encroaching blackness of Halloween night.

CHAPTER 9
Down In The Cellar

HAVING SUCCESSFULLY RETREATED out the rear gate of the cemetery and traveled the narrow path back to Flareback Road, the trio-turned-quartet arrived at the Widow's Watch. Sneaking around to the back of the inn, they huddled close to Will as his shaky hands fumbled with the lock on the angled cellar door, anxious to be hidden away before the prying eyes of Bootville caught sight of them.

Elyse felt like a bootlegger smuggling a brother-shaped barrel of bathtub gin into a speakeasy, shushing him any time he opened his mouth to make some wry comment, which was frequent. Always talkative in life, she had never considered that Patrick would be equally verbose in death. The padlock finally slid open in Will's numbed palm, and he hauled the plank door open with a groaning of the hinges, ushering them inside.

"Oh man, that was *awful*," Patrick said with an enormous exhale of breath as they made their way into the jet-black confines of the basement. "I don't remember ever being that quiet before. Can you, Sis?"

Elyse shook her head as she carefully placed her violin case on a rickety workbench along one of the stone walls. Colin joined her with her bag while Will turned on a string of emergency lights, illuminating the already depressing space into the homey feel of a wartime bunker.

"Try to keep it down—we don't need my Ma coming down here," Will said as he looked up to the ceiling where the shuffling of feet and the scrape of chairs and barstools could be heard at the bottom end of a roomful of muffled chatter.

"But I'm dead, right?" Patrick said, raising his hands in a ghoulish posture. "I'm supposed to be *haunting* things, bwa-ha-ha-*ha!*"

"Shhh!" Will hissed, throwing a loose can at him. Patrick dodged it easily and followed him to the stairs leading up to the kitchen. Will stood at the bottom step and could easily pick out his mother's voice as she ran the kitchen with dictatorial authority. Patrick slid up behind him.

"Do you think they can hear me?" he whispered to Will.

"I don't know—why wouldn't they? We can hear you just fine," Will replied.

"Yeah, but what if this is all just some elaborate delusion you've created for yourselves, huh? What if I'm not really here, and you guys are just playing some kind of pretending game?" Will gave him a look. "No, seriously," Patrick said. "Maybe you guys are having a psychedelic experience or something—hell, I don't know what you kids get up to these days."

From behind them came a crash. They turned to find Elyse leaning over the workbench, where she'd slammed the *Macabrium* down in a white-knuckle grip.

"That your diary, Sis?" asked Patrick as he and Will joined her.

"What're you thinking, 'Lyse?" Will asked as she unfolded the pages.

"I'm not even sure..." She stared at the incomprehensible scimitar curves swallowing the blankness of the page.

"'Dear Diary,'" Patrick said in his best girl voice. "'Today I raised my brother from the dead, and also, Will likes me, but I'm not sure if he like-likes me, or if he really *likes* me likes me.'"

Elyse looked back at him with a scowl as he peered over her shoulder and finally laid eyes on the *Macabrium* panels. He gave her a perplexed look.

"What is that?" he asked, the playfulness absent from his voice.

Elyse sighed, unsure of how to approach this subject. "Do you know where you came from?" she asked.

"Yeah, Dad had that talk with me—it was pretty uncomfortable. He drew these diagrams—"

"That's not what I meant, Pat."

"I haven't the foggiest," he said, shaking his head. "The last thing I remember was stepping out the door to go trick-or-treating, and *somebody* had a real attitude about it," he said, looking at Will, his eyebrow raised.

"Do you know how you got here?" she pressed.

Patrick pondered this for a moment before shaking his head again. "No, it was like being awoken from a deep sleep by a noise outside or something, and then falling and just… *here*, you know?"

Elyse frowned and looked back at the book, flipping to the front. "Patrick, I found this book, and it says here that it can bring back the dead," she said, pointing to the shaky inscription.

"Ha! That's ridiculous," he said. The other three stared at him pointedly. "Oh, well…" he said, looking down at his translucent self, "…I guess I see your point, but… but *what?* That still doesn't make any sense—like, *how?*"

With a sudden interest, he pushed between them and began examining the panels, his face scrunching at the sight of the alien markings.

"Colin figured it out—all of these figures can be sort of manipulated into music on a staff, see?" Elyse said, pulling her workbook from the bag and laying it next to the *Macabrium*. Patrick's eyes flicked from one book to the other several times before looking up at Colin.

"You figured this out, buddy?" he asked.

Colin nodded. "They make the music," he said, looking up at the beams of the dining room floor as footsteps sounded along the worn planks.

"You sly boots," Patrick said. "And you guys, uh, translated this whole thing?" he said, pointing to the passages Elyse had notated in her careful hand.

"Well, once Colin figured out that it kind of matched notes, I had to block it out and play it until I could find the proper phrasing and feel and all that—we've been working on it for a while," she said, looking down at her labor. "I didn't think it was going to work, though."

"That's pretty bonkers," Patrick said. He took up her notebook and began examining it as he wandered to the opposite side of the basement, his translucent eyes flashing as he traced his finger along the notes she'd written.

Elyse turned to Will. "I didn't know it was going to work," she said under her breath, her tone less than convincing.

"I know you didn't—hell, none of us knew," Will said.

"What are we going to *do* with him?" she whispered as Will exhaled heavily and flipped the *Macabrium* closed. "I mean, he's not really alive, is he? He's like a phantom or something."

Will shook his head, lost. "I have no idea. This is, like… pretty uncharted territory, you know? I mean, it's not actually him, is it. Or is it? It sounds like him, don't you think?"

"No, it's definitely him—or it's his personality anyway," said Elyse, shooting a glance at the specter of her brother. Patrick had begun picking through boxes of tavern debris in a remote corner of the cellar while Colin looked on, intrigued.

"Um… what's he doing?" asked Will.

Elyse shook her head and turned back to the *Macabrium*. "Will, this book works. Or at least it works like we wanted it to work, right?"

"Yeah, I'd say so."

"Right, and I think we'd better keep it under wraps until we can figure out what exactly we're dealing with here and how we're going to explain-–oh!" Elyse clapped a hand over her mouth.

"What is it?" asked Will, alarmed.

"My parents! *Our* parents," she said, pointing over to Patrick, who was now uncovering a large, tarp-draped object.

"Oh, yeah…" Will said.

"What am I supposed to tell them? They'll drop dead if they see him back like this."

"So what—we can just use the book, right?" He offered a half-grin.

"That's not funny, *William,*" she said, punching him hard on the shoulder.

"Ow, okay!"

"I'm sorry, but this isn't the time for screwing around," Elyse said, brushing a stray strand of black hair from her face. "I don't know if this was such a good idea."

In a moment of uncharacteristic boldness, Will placed his hand atop hers across the cover of the *Macabrium*. She looked up at him, startled.

"Don't worry," he said, suddenly flustered now that they were touching. Elyse felt his palm go clammy, and he quickly pulled it away to rearrange the other items on the workbench. "We're gonna figure it out, you know?" he said. Elyse tilted her head to the side a fraction of an inch, examining him. She watched as his face reddened, and he cleared his throat. "Wow, it's kind of hot down here, right?"

Meanwhile, Patrick cast aside a final case of old dishes, leaving only the enshrouded mass.

"Ah-*ha,*" Patrick proclaimed, whipping away the dusty tarp to reveal an antique clavichord. "There you are, my magnificent museum piece! Left here to rot in this cellar of the heathens—why, it's outrageous," he muttered, lovingly caressing the lid of the old instrument.

He quickly enlisted Colin to wipe the grime from the wooden body while he hummed the notes on Elyse's worksheets to himself. His ghostly hands shuffled the pages briefly, then placed them on the carved music stand above the keyboard.

The clavichord was a curiosity belonging to the Watch and had been taking up space since before the Castle family had begun resting their heads beneath the building's raised beams. Will's Dad figured it to be at least as old as the inn, if not older. He had once entertained the idea of fully restoring it to its original glory for display in the main dining room and had even gone so far as to string and tune the arcane contraption to see if it still worked. It played, but like so many things around the Watch, it was quickly put aside in favor of replacing that leaky roof tile or repairing the cast iron stove that had cracked and begun spilling molten embers across the kitchen floor to the consternation of Mrs. Castle. On days of ambitious daydreaming, Mr. Castle would still proclaim it to be the next thing on his ever-growing list of things to do.

As it was, Patrick was little concerned with the artistry and craftsmanship of the instrument but more with its ability to produce a proper noise. He plunked a key, and the string within was plucked, creating a nasal tone. He hit the key again a few times in rapid succession.

"Hm. You think?" he asked Colin with a shrug.

"G," Colin droned matter-of-factly as though that had been the implied question.

Patrick nodded. "I believe you're right."

With a flourish, he played the length of the keyboard from bottom to top in an assured run, then, after the slightest of pauses, began to play the song from Elyse's notes.

"I remember this one," Colin said, placing his hand on the body of the clavichord.

As the haunting melody was plucked and began to ooze into the rest of the basement, Elyse and Will discussed their plan of action at the workbench.

"We have to get him home until we figure out what to do," Elyse said, deep in thought.

"At least it's Halloween—kids will be everywhere the closer we get to town," Will said.

"Is that a good thing?" she asked him.

Will shrugged. "It'll be dark—maybe nobody will notice how, uh… see-through he is. We'll tell anyone who asks that he's wearing some new hologram costume or something, right?"

Elyse frowned, trying to concentrate as the music began to grow louder.

"I mean, he could stay here, but he'd have to stay in the cellar—there's no way my Ma would miss your dead brother coming up the stairs to book a room, you know? She's got eyes like a hawk. And a tiger. She's like a tiger-hawk."

"No, no, I want to get him home—maybe being there will help him remember or trigger some kind of reaction or something," she said, shaking her head. She paused suddenly, cocking her head to the side. "What is that?"

"What is what?" said Will.

"Patrick, *no!*" Elyse yelled, bursting past Will towards the clavichord, where Patrick played the final measure of the summoning song. Overhead, in the center of the space, a swath of ceiling had churned itself into a watery bending of light. He held the last note and turned to her.

"Yeah, Sis—you know, it's catchy, but I just don't think it's a Number One—"

He was interrupted by the flash and vacuum of sound that haloed throughout the dingy basement. Everyone ducked, throwing their arms up for protection. Their clothes blew outward, and the ceiling began to open like a camera's aperture, from which a massive, cloaked figure fell. In a billow of black fabric, the creature hit the packed dirt of the cellar floor with a heavy thud and a clatter. Will pulled Elyse out of the way, and Patrick yanked Colin under the clavichord. They looked up in awe at the opening, through which they could see a blazing firestorm. The edge of the passage began to melt and converge inward and, just as quickly as it appeared, twisted itself back into nothing but the underside of the dining room floorboards.

"Whoa. Did that happen last time?" Patrick whispered to Colin, who nodded. *"Whoa."*

Elyse gasped as the figure in the center of the basement floor began to twitch with a snort. Will turned to see the shape in motion and stepped in front of her. They watched as the thing, its back to them, rose to its knees and then to its feet with a groan, supporting its weight with a large staff of gnarled tree branch. Elyse's heart sank as the thing straightened to almost seven feet in height, the groan becoming the growl of some larger bear species. Her instincts kicked in and immediately reported to her brain that even with all of them working together, there would be very little chance they would be able to overcome this creature by force alone.

The figure raised its head, which had upon it a large, military-style crested hat, nearly scraping the low ceiling. It gathered its cloak and spun around to face its summoners with a ferocious roar. Even the considerably unexpected appearance of Patrick from beyond the grave was not enough to prepare her for the hideous death's-head glowering beneath the cockaded brim. The eye sockets were an empty black, and the jaw twisted into a violent rictus, translucent like her brother.

Elyse's instincts checked in once again to report that, upon further consideration, there was now *zero* chance of any of them surviving this monster. Her heart dropped even further into her guts, pausing only to wave at a passing scream headed in the opposite direction.

CHAPTER 10
Spicy Jack

UNDER NORMAL CIRCUMSTANCES, Will would've been more than a little disappointed with himself for his behavior in the face of everyone's ultimate demise—especially in front of Elyse, whom he had privately vowed to protect since Patrick had gone the way he had. However, looking back on the situation, he would find solace in the entire sequence of events being so unexpected and unusual (not to mention so frightening). He would eventually grow to accept that facing the possibility of his untimely end for the first of what would be many times had elicited little reaction other than screaming at the top of his lungs like an infant in need of changing.

He also found comfort in the fact that his scream met with Elyse's scream, which blended neatly with Colin's scream, all of which were drowned out by Patrick's. The large skeleton man seemed slightly taken aback by the noise and drew his cloak around himself in defense. He looked around the cellar, seemingly disoriented.

"What is this… *trickery?*" he boomed in a low, hoarse rumble, his lower jaw clacking against the rest of his skull as he spoke. The kids screamed again.

"It's a skull, *and* it talks!?" Will cried out, both horrified and annoyed.

"Here, take Colin. He's a great listener," Patrick said, nudging Colin in front of him with a forced smile.

Colin waved at the creature. "Hi."

The skeleton man brought forth his staff, from which hung a pumpkin suspended by an intricate weaving of vines, reminding Will of an eyeball dangling from its optic nerve. The creature slammed the staff into the dirt floor, causing the gourd to rock back and forth like a pendulum. A rudimentary face was carved into the orange shell, simple but expressive of its malice.

The towering figure turned to the pumpkin and exhaled a slow, shuddering breath. From within the shell, a flame quickened and rose with a *whoosh!* and the carved face became animated, its eyes narrowing and its jagged mouth spreading into a leer. The pumpkin chuckled. The kids screamed. The pumpkin screamed. The kids screamed some more.

"Silence!" the vaporous skeleton man bellowed, drawing a saber from within his cloak and pointing it at them. "In the name of his Royal Majesty, King George the Third, ruler of the British empire, you are hereby placed under arrest for insubordination and treason— a fate punishable by *death.*"

Patrick screamed again. "No, not that!" Colin gave him a curious look. "Well, you know, it's not like you get used to it," Patrick said, shrugging.

The pumpkin's carved eyes drew into slits as it glared at the quartet. "Go on then, Colonel—punish them! I'd *really* like to see them punished as much as possible—especially after what we've been through, eh, Sir? And don't forget wrongful imprisonment— why in the world are we in a *dungeon?"* The pumpkin eyed the stone foundation walls, appalled.

Elyse gasped. "You're Spicy Jack!"

The bone-man turned his skull to her with a grunt.

"Shh, don't bring his attention over here!" Will muttered from the corner of his mouth without taking his eyes off the hulking figure.

"But it's *him,"* she whispered, as though she'd spotted a minor celebrity. "It's Spicy Jack and his lantern, like the crazy old guy was saying at the orchard!"

"'Crazy old guy?'" Patrick said, scratching his head. "Was this one of those volunteer things where you sit with a senior and let them ramble for an hour?"

"Enough of this nonsense—*death to all!*" Jack roared, whipping the sword above his head in a fluid motion. His pumpkin laughed, its eyes bulging to reveal demonic flames.

"Elyse, duck!" Will shouted, grabbing her by the hand and pulling her behind the clavichord as the sword fell mere nanoseconds behind them. The blade landed heavily on the instrument's body, the painful sound of splitting wood filling the basement and instigating a hum of vibrating strings from within.

"Oh, Will, you're gonna be *so* grounded for that one!" Patrick said from beneath the clavichord. He reached out and quickly flicked the sword's blade twice as Jack struggled to dislodge it. "Yeah, buddy, that's real."

"Make for the door!" Will yelled, grabbing Elyse's workbook from above the keyboard as the sword came out of the wood with a violent snap, crashing into a stack of boxes and empty wine crates. Jack roared his thunderous animal cry again, swinging at them as they retreated to the far side of the cellar, the blade finding nothing but air and the bottom of Elyse's cape, which billowed behind her as she ran.

She cried out in surprise as she felt the cape tug momentarily against her and pulled Will behind some nearby barrels, a mere ten feet from the steps up to the kitchen.

"You all right?" Will asked her, gasping for breath.

"Yeah, just a close call," she said, examining the jagged tear with a shudder.

Across the cellar, Patrick and Colin were crouched by the steps leading to the angled door they'd initially passed through. Spicy Jack stomped toward them with thudding, deliberate footfalls, his riding boots kicking up divots in the dirt floor. In one hand, he held the staff from which his pumpkin lantern growled, irritated by the sudden elusiveness of its quarry. His other hand held the sword out at a right angle, dragging the tip of it along the stone walls, which bled clods of mortar.

"Will," Elyse said, her voice all business, "the book."

"What?"

"The *Macabrium*—it's still on the workbench."

Will looked to the bench and saw it was true. The book was where they'd left it, about the same distance away as it was from Jack.

"Forget it," he said. "We've got to get out of here."

"We need it, Will," she said. "If we're ever going to find out what's happening, we need that book."

Will sighed and brushed his hair out of his eyes. "What do you want to—"

She was off in a blur of black cape before he even knew what was happening, like a tiny superhero whose only power was pure boldness. Jack drew his sword back, grinning at the sight of her darting straight toward him.

"Steady, Sir, steady…" his pumpkin said, its hyena grin returning.

"What is she doing!?" Patrick yelled across to Will, who looked on, dumbfounded.

Elyse veered towards the workbench, reaching for the book. The sword flew into the table less than an inch from her arm as she got her hands around its leather binding. Jack pulled at the sword, and in an instant, it was out of the wood and pointed directly at Elyse's neck. She turned away, her eyes closed.

The pumpkin laughed, delighted as it swung from its vine, then went silent as its carved eyes focused their fiery insides on the *Macabrium,* still clutched in Elyse's hand. The pumpkin's face tilted to the side, its features becoming rounded and curious.

"Hey, look, Sir—isn't that—"

"*The book!*" Jack growled in realization. He slashed the sword back to strike her down.

"That's not yours to swipe, girl!" the pumpkin said, swinging towards Elyse. "Give it here, and we'll only kill you and your friends once!"

She took a quick breath and blew a puff of air into the pumpkin's face, extinguishing the fire within. Jack and the lantern were caught off-guard.

"Hey, that's my face you just—*whoa!"* the pumpkin cried out as Elyse swung her violin case off the workbench and into the exposed stomach region of the monstrous skeleton man.

Jack fell backward, dropping his staff and careening into a stack of boxes. The pumpkin hit the dirt floor with a small bounce and rolled in a tight arc.

"Ow!" it yelled out, its features grimacing. "Can't you see I'm a gourd!? I bruise easily!"

But Elyse wasn't listening. Violin case in hand and book under arm, she grabbed her bag and ran back to the others, who crouched, ready to make a break for it. Behind her, Jack was already throwing debris off himself with clenched, skeletal hands.

"Split up!" yelled Will to Colin and Patrick. "We'll go out through the kitchen, you leave through there," he said, pointing to the door behind them.

"We'll meet at Colin's—wait—" Patrick yelled back before turning to Colin, "—you guys still live in the same place, right?"

Colin nodded, "My Dad repainted the bathroom, but it's in the same place, yes."

"Crackerjack," Patrick said, turning back to Will and Elyse. "Yeah, meet you at Colin's!"

"Right—now go!" Will said as Jack threw the final crate against the wall with a crash and began to right himself.

"Patrick, be careful!" Elyse yelled to her brother, who was already halfway out the cellar door.

"Already dead, Sis!" he said, grinning and shooting her a thumbs-up. "Later, alligator."

"Elyse, come on!" Will said, holding the door to the kitchen open for her. She ducked inside and began making her way up the stone steps as Will followed suit, slamming the door behind them. He reached down and felt around for a chock of wood he knew should be there. His fingers finally grazed the doorstop and slammed it under the crack. He hammered his fist upon it for good measure.

They found themselves running up the stairs in pure blackness with both doors closed. For a moment, they could only hear their heavy breaths and the slap of their shoes as they climbed upwards. The effect was eerie and seemed too close to their ears.

Elyse and Will had almost reached the top landing when the silence was broken by a loud bang on the downstairs door. They froze, Will's hand on the doorknob, and listened. *Bang!* This time the thump was accompanied by the unmistakable sound of wood splintering.

"Go!" Elyse said, giving Will a push.

They emerged from the blackness of stony nothing into the steamy chaos of the inn's kitchen. Their eyes were blinded by the bare bulbs hanging from the rafters overhead, while their ears and noses were overwhelmed by the clatter of pots and pans and the sizzle of various foods strewn about on every available cooking appliance.

Will slammed the door shut and turned to bolster it with both hands, almost losing his balance as he slipped in a puddle of cooking brine. Elyse slung the strap of her violin case over her shoulder and stuffed the *Macabrium* into her bag, her hands shaking.

"Which way out?" she asked Will, breathless.

"We'll go out the side door where we take the trash out so my Ma won't—"

"Will!" a voice erupted from around the corner, causing them to jump.

"—see us. Well, scratch that, I guess," Will groaned as his mother made her way over to them, apron on and sleeves rolled up.

"Hi, Mrs. Castle!" Elyse said in the cheeriest voice she could muster.

"Hello, Elyse darling," Mrs. Castle said with a warm smile. "Are you all right, dear? You look a little winded."

Elyse choked out a nervous gasp of a laugh. "No, I'm just… excited about Halloween, you know! All the, uh, spooks and candy and, um, whatnot."

"I see…" Mrs. Castle said, frowning. She looked over to Will. "William, what are you doing to that door—closing it to death?"

"Ha! Good one, Ma!" Will said, starting to sweat.

"Come on now. You two know you're not supposed to be back here during dining hours," she said, grabbing the back of Will's shirt and herding them away from the cellar door.

"But, Ma—" he said, looking back at the unguarded door, panic in his eyes.

"We'll just go out the side there, Mrs. Castle, it's really—" Elyse began.

"Nonsense, dear—you go on out through the dining room and be safe tonight, okay?"

"Well, I guess so, if you—"

"That's right, you go on," Mrs. Castle said with a smile. She put her hand on Will's shoulder as he tried to follow Elyse out of the kitchen. "I need a moment with my charming son."

Will turned and gave her his most winning smile. "Ma, I should really go with her—it's getting pretty dark."

Mrs. Castle pulled him close and leaned into him with a scowl. Even though he was amidst a growth spurt, she was still a few inches taller than him.

"I thought you were all going out tonight," she said, raising a shrewd eyebrow.

"Yeah, we did—we *are*, I mean," Will stammered, his eyes darting back through the kitchen.

"And do I even want to ask what you two were doing together in the cellar?"

"You really wouldn't believe it," Will said with a nervous laugh.

"Oh, please," Mrs. Castle said with a knowing laugh. "I remember your father when he was your age."

"Look, Ma, we've gotta get going," Will said, trying to maneuver his way out of the kitchen doorway.

"I heard crashing," Mrs. Castle continued.

"Yeah, it was that thing that fell over—I'll clean it up tomorrow," Will said, continuing to inch his way out.

Sensing her son was possibly on the verge of a nervous breakdown, Mrs. Castle's suspicion vanished from her face for the briefest moment, replaced with motherly concern.

"Are you all right, Will? You look ill." She placed her palm on his forehead.

"Ma, I'm fine. We just really need to—"

And with that, Will was interrupted by the sound of an unexpected and almost polite knocking. He and Mrs. Castle both turned to the source, which seemed to be the cellar door.

MEANWHILE, ELYSE WAITED by the front entrance. Mr. Castle was chatting her ear off while he absentmindedly made some notes in the mostly empty reservation book. She gazed over the old dining floor, with its stone walls and unfinished timber beam ceiling. The massive fireplace broadcast a decent-sized fire's worth of flickering ambience across the craggy faces of the Widow's Watch's patrons. The dinner crowd could rarely be called an actual crowd, but tonight it seemed like all of the sullen regulars who even occasionally frequented the Watch had come in simultaneously.

Tapping her fingers impatiently on her violin case, she tried to distract herself by focusing on what Mr. Castle was saying.

"…and it turned out that I'd put the damned shingles on upside down!" he said, chuckling to himself, tears welling in his eyes. "Can you believe it?"

"You don't say," Elyse said, forcing a smile.

"Oh, but I tell you," he continued, sniffing and trying to catch his breath, "I've been working on this heap of rocks for so long that there's not much left that could surprise me about her."

He'd only just finished this sentence when the kitchen blew up.

THE EXPLOSION SENT everyone in the dining room ducking towards the floor, abandoning their stews but resolutely holding onto their spoons—one didn't regularly dine at the Watch and not expect the occasional disaster from the kitchen. This time, however, it was no disappointing tart or slab of unloved mystery meat that emerged from the smoke and debris of what had formerly been the kitchen door, but rather a seven-foot-tall skeleton man swinging a coughing pumpkin on a stick.

The Watch patrons squinted at the figure as though it could be something other than what it clearly was. Someone at table three waved the smoke out of his eyes, only to find Jack still there and still without flesh, while the newspaper reader at table nine peered into his stein and tried to count how many drinks he'd had that night.

"Will, are you all right!?" Elyse coughed across the room to where Will was helping his mother up from the floor.

"What in the world…?" Mr. Castle coughed as he raised himself from behind his door post.

Jack's eye sockets narrowed as he drew his cloak around him, a low growl emanating from within as the rest of the dining room looked at each other, murmuring for some explanation.

In a flash, Jack flung his sword out before him. "People of the colonies!"

Everyone looked around again, wondering if this creature was, in fact, addressing them.

"In the name of His Royal Highness, King George the Third, you are hereby placed under arrest and are ordered to—"

"No!" shouted Mrs. Castle, bringing down the handle of a mop onto Jack's wrist. Jack recoiled and dropped his sword with a clatter.

"Ouch, that hurt," he said, his usual grumble sounding rather pathetic.

"Honey, what are you doing!?" Mr. Castle cried out. Elyse stood by him, mouth agape.

"Now you listen here—we do not tolerate rowdies in this establishment!" Mrs. Castle said, pushing her face into Jack's skull, backing him up against the wall so that his hat slid down what would have been his forehead.

"But—" Jack started.

"I don't care if it's a holiday or just a Wednesday; we do not take kindly to troublemakers at the Widow's Watch. Do you understand me?"

"Madam, I—"

"Now, I don't know what you've done to my kitchen, but you can be sure that you'll be paying for it and that I'll be bringing down the full might of the *law* upon your head!"

"I *am* the law!" Jack declared.

"*You* are a grown-up dressed like a pirate!" Mrs. Castle shouted back, causing him to cringe away once more. "You are *nothing* to me. You are an immature clown and a useless, carousing waste of space! And you owe me a kitchen!"

"Enough!" Jack cried, drawing himself up to his full height and puffing out his ribcage. "How dare you speak to a commissioned officer of His Most Glorious Highness' army in such a way, you impudent troll! You shall all be hanged and left to rot on the gallows!"

"Right—that tears it," Mrs. Castle said, reaching through the kitchen doorway and grabbing a silver fire extinguisher from off the wall.

There was a sudden mass scraping of chair legs on floor planks as the uncouth diners of the Watch stood up, men and women alike, and began rolling up their sleeves in anticipation of an old-fashioned ruckus. Mr. Castle unplugged the handset from the phone and wielded it menacingly while adjusting his spectacles. Mrs. Castle aimed the extinguisher at Jack, a defiant sneer on her face as the two parties stared each other down. Will watched, breath bated, as Jack's pumpkin sized the situation up neatly.

"Um, Sir?"

"Yes, Lieutenant?"

"Run!"

Jack scrambled along the wall towards the kitchen, followed by the posse of disgruntled diners and Mrs. Castle, who ignited the extinguisher into a chalky-white plume.

Will ran in the opposite direction, weaving between the tables and kicked-over chairs, towards the front door where Elyse was waiting. They waved as they passed Mr. Castle, who remained at the front desk, calmly reattaching the phone to the cord and peering into the cloudy shambles that was once his kitchen.

"You get him, dear," he called after his wife. "I'll just mind the phones…"

Will and Elyse ran outside, pausing beneath the lone lamppost at the intersection of Flareback and Nightjar to catch their breath. The sound of melee could be heard over the patchy eaves of the stone inn, informing them that the chase had made its way out the kitchen exit. Someone's scream echoed down the streets and over the fens.

"That was crazy!" Will gasped, doubled over.

"Is your mother… going to be… okay?" Elyse choked out, leaning against the lamppost.

"Oh man, are you kidding? That guy better hope his femurs can take all the running he's gonna be doing—I haven't seen that expression since Patrick and I broke the antique fireplace bellows blowing up that inner tube!"

Elyse laughed and brushed a loose lock of hair out of her face. "Which inner tube?"

"The big blue one—we were gonna roll Colin down a hill in it, but we couldn't get the bellows to fit the mouthpiece, so Patrick cut up this funnel and—"

Will stopped and looked at Elyse, who gazed into the waning dusk hovering over the general direction of the cemetery.

"You all right?" he asked her, all joking sucked from his voice. Elyse looked up at him with watering eyes.

"Have we done the right thing?"

Will gulped but could think of nothing worthwhile to say. It seemed to him that this could easily be the first time these circumstances had ever transpired and that something of gravity *should* be said. But he found himself unable to live up to the challenge and left silence as a placeholder.

Another scream rang out from the direction of the mob, fainter this time, changing the subject for them.

"Come on, let's catch up," Elyse said, hoisting her violin case and avoiding eye contact as she headed down Nightjar Street.

CHAPTER 11
The Burden Of Conquest

SPICY JACK WAS having the devil's own time of it.

"Is this what I've been reduced to?" he asked his companion, Lieutenant Crain, former aide-de-camp and current pumpkin lantern. Having narrowly escaped the Widow's Watch, they'd found a safe harbor, cowering behind a large boxwood shrub.

Crain gave him a look with his carved features. "What *you've* been reduced to? *I* used to be a good-time lad with a body, and now I'm only fit for a pie—it's no kind of life, Sir."

Jack sighed and shook his head. Oh, the humility of it all.

Here he was, Jack Cavendish, a colonel in His Majesty's army, the greatest fighting force the world had ever seen, reduced to hiding behind some neglected shrubbery in this accursed town, having been abruptly ousted from that accursed tavern by those accursed colonists.

"What is it about this place, Crain?" he rasped through half-rotted vocal cords over the open beating of his heart, which throbbed visibly through the shredded remains of his once-regal officer-issue shirt and jacket. "Why do we seem doomed to be punished by this wasteland and these criminally uncivilized *peasants?*"

Through the trees of the nearby wooded walkway, they could hear the animal cries of the Widow's Watch patrons as they hunted for them in the dwindling twilight.

"Those people are relentless, Sir," said Crain as he rocked back and forth on his gnarled vine. "You'd have thought they'd never seen soldiers before, let alone ones who looked like us, eh, Colonel? Nothing but bits and pieces, that's all we are."

Jack wheezed a harsh growl and violently shook his staff, sending Crain into a nauseating corkscrew. He hated being reminded of their deformities, resulting from some power he had yet to fully grasp. Even worse, he hated how self-preservation often dictated cowardice as a means of survival. Him—hiding! He was Spicy Jack Cavendish, the scourge of a dozen or more American towns, feared by nobility and ne'er-do-wells alike, and commander of the most efficient killing regiment of foot soldiers the empire had to offer. And he was now reduced to wrapping his cloak around himself behind a hedge so the whites of his bones would not give away his position. Shameful. His only ally: a gourd. Ridiculous.

Oh, how far he'd fallen, oh, how foolish he felt. He did not need the tenacity of village half-wits empowered by sheer numbers and cheap drink to come crashing down like so many clubs upon his skull, for he knew that only clear thinking would be able to pull him out of this. The less distraction, the better. And until he felt secure within the trappings of power and respect he was used to, he would do whatever it took to maintain his dignity. For his dignity reflected the empire's dignity, and empires were forged by the mettle of men pushing their boundaries ever outward.

"I have had enough of losing the advantage to these… *American* serfs," he spat contemptuously, as though the very idea of the colonists was poison on his tongue, a tongue that now lolled about in a jaw of decomposed flesh.

"See, now that's the Spicy Jack I like to hear, Sir," Crain said, nodding with encouragement. "Petty and judgmental."

"It's time to take the reins of this decrepit village back into my hands and execute a justice befitting their betrayal of the Crown."

"Right!" Crain shouted, salivating stringy pumpkin innards at the idea before his features went benignly round and curious. "Wait, I'm sorry, Colonel—forgive my thickness, but what exactly does that mean again?"

Jack drove the bottom of the staff sharply into the ground, causing a fountain of flames to erupt from Crain's jaggedly carved mouth, incinerating the shrub before them. Crain coughed and gagged out smoke as the roaring current of fire ended as quickly as it had begun, leaving the bush to crackle and blaze, its late autumn dryness feeding its demise.

"Whoa, whoa, *whoa!*" Crain hacked as Jack swung around to stare into the tangerine-stained sky. "Sir, I know you like doing that—and it's a great little trick, I absolutely agree—but you've got to remember that every time you decide to burn your cares away, my *head* is set on fire."

Jack ignored this collective dry heaving of acrid smoke and complaints as his hollow eye sockets scowled into the half-sun. "Lieutenant Crain, there shall be no more running, no more hiding."

"Okay, great," Crain said through another bout of wet hacking. "Just, please… I mean, it's like that uncomfortable feeling you get when you go swimming and get water up your nose—except instead of water, it's *fire*, Sir." Crain continued coughing as Jack took a turn to the cobblestone street leading away from the Watch and into Bootville Proper.

"Rest easy, poor, foolish Crain," Jack hissed in his disgusting way. "Soon, we shall be rid of these shackles of misfortune that have ensnared us."

"Right, right, the shackles—of course, Sir," Crain said, unsure of where this rant was going. "We'll just… find the key and unlatch them and… and throw them away, right, Sir?"

"And remind these creatures of their place in the order of things. As food for the fire."

THE ACCELERATION OF Spicy Jack Cavendish through the ranks of His Majesty's army was not necessarily due to any great outpouring of respect or credibility lent by the highest commanding officers in the ranks. His was not a position of power warranted by social standing or inheritance, nor was he the sort to play politics or bribe his way into favor. No, his power had been taken up and wrapped around his shoulders in the classic model: through unending fear.

This particular brand of fear was compelling because a more cursory examination would have dismissed him as little more than a hard-living fool. To those who had never seen him on the field of battle or read his unapologetic reports of butchery and victory, butchery and victory—always in rapid succession—he was a good-time man-about-town and a character no party could do without. Yes, he may have enjoyed his drink a little more than was appropriate in public circles, and he may have talked too loudly and pounded his fists on the tabletops of dining rooms and taverns across the globe with a bit more force than would seem prudent. However, it was this very strength of spirit that enabled him to embody the nature of the empire. He lived on top of the world where the sun would never set upon him, and it would take the studied ear of another man who had also been tried by fire to catch the chilly edge beneath Spicy Jack's booming laughter. His hearty joy of living was, in fact, heartless.

This rush of ice water in his veins, combined with the demons he danced with in his drink, had blazed the way for his movement up the ranks. For if he could not be respected as a gentleman—or, in truth, *any* kind of man—he could be respected as a soldier who would happily bathe in the pools of violence spreading throughout the world. No matter which weapon of cruelty he exercised, his fellow officers had to admit that he always got the job done with a disturbing passion they could only acknowledge with wide-eyed wonder.

His appointment to the continental expedition led by the brothers Howe had been due to this unyielding commitment to life and death by the sword. Though he had hoped to liven up the campaign with his close friend, General Johnny Burgoyne, he had to admit he enjoyed the freedom General Howe had allowed him in his endeavors. Let old Gentleman Johnny drag his wardrobe and mistresses through the untamed wilds of the northern colonies; the good looting, the good plunder, the good foe torn asunder—all of these things were to be found in the more populated regions, and all were now his alone for the taking.

If it seemed to his superiors that Colonel Jack Cavendish was wholly invested in victory no matter the cost, it was because he was. It had been here in the American colonies, over twenty years prior, that he had experienced his first taste of battle. Seeking an escape from a position of urban servitude as a slummy city-cellar potato peeler, Jack had lied about his age to join the army. If this was what it took to draw the ladies' eyes and gain the respect of the uniformed and armed men he saw parading in the city squares, then so be it. He'd only been 18 when he was shipped off on the trans-Atlantic passage of legend as a member of General Braddock's army. The Crown had sent him to wrest back the lands so injuriously trod upon by the French and their Native allies, who'd had the gall to proclaim the territory their own.

Upon arriving in this new land, they were sent in pursuit of the fight with which he'd longed to try himself. His blood was his investment in the New World, along with the blood of so many of his compatriots on that fateful excursion north to Fort Duquesne.

His commitment to the fate of continental supremacy was stoked then. The harsh wilderness took its toll on their columns as they razed their way through a gauntlet of thick underbrush and endless colonnades of trees taller than he could have ever conceived. It was forged into its final, furious form when the Monongahela ran red, and he was drenched with the blood of both his brethren and his enemy. It had been a rout that not even General Braddock would survive, and it was the catalyst for the transformation of young Jack Cavendish into his current mindset.

The horrors of war so casually spoken of in song and verse, where its virtues were praised and immortalized, had been revealed to him as something more chilling than those writers and poets could ever articulate. It was so chilling that he was forced to respond with coldness in kind. The fires of his inner humanity were forever snuffed out, and his body was left numb.

Only the carousing could help to warm his belly, if not his heart, but despite the temporary relief offered him by wine, women, and song, they were no true salve for his wounds. And so, Spicy Jack became locked in the perpetual forward motion of cycling through violence and manic celebration without care for whom it might affect or how. He was Spicy Jack—scourge to all who would get in the way of his legacy, his efforts to secure the world for the empire, and secure himself from the vaporous ghosts of his own memories.

AS JACK AND Crain made their way down the empty side street into Bootville, Jack sulked his way down a different path in his mind as he tried to figure out where in the course of things he'd gone wrong.

Surely that blasted book the girl had was to blame in some practical sense, for something about it had been the means of their current physical monstrosities. However, it seemed that the true villains fighting against what he deeply felt was his deserved reign of terror were the people of the town itself.

It was bad enough that the entire confederation of colonies thought they had the right to excuse themselves from the empire. Did they not know what the cost had been to win their freedom from French oppression? England and France had collided like two swinging fists over this mass of untapped wilderness, and the price had been steep to emerge the victor. The colonies' bill had yet to be paid.

Aside from this larger offense, the town of Bootville seemed to represent the most extreme and offensive elements of the entire rebellion. They had made his invasion more difficult and disagreeable than he had ever anticipated but had also wielded some power that had destroyed his body and thrown him into retreat. It had been a lot to deal with.

It was at this moment in his ruminations that several things happened at once, forever shifting his way of thinking. As the oddly hollow clacks of his translucent boots and lantern staff sounded against the exposed cobblestones, a new noise entered the decayed sockets where Jack's ears once existed. An unnatural whining sound, not unlike the song of swamp insects, entered the twilight with a disturbing persistence. Within moments the dusk was destroyed by an explosion of light atop a black iron pillar Jack had failed to notice in the late autumn gloom.

"Aaaah!" Crain shouted, rotating on his vine to gaze up in terror at the pulsating orb of fluorescence. Jack turned away and shielded his eyes from the streetlamp, which was quickly joined by others igniting, one by one, illuminating the road ahead.

"Sir, *what is happening?*" Crain quivered in a whisper, his eye carvings round and fixed on the lamp. "Is this the… the *end-times?*"

Jack warily peeked over his forearm as though he half expected to be punched in the face. The streetlamp continued its relentless beaming, unfazed by Jack's rank, his talking pumpkin lantern, or the fact that he was essentially a mobile cadaver. Jack grunted after a moment and straightened himself, looking around in embarrassment.

"'Tis merely some form of torch, Crain," he said, frowning. "Some strange fire these people use to light their way, perhaps…"

After a moment of consideration, he turned them back down the road to take note of the line of streetlamps beyond, running interminably into the distant evening. "I actually find it to be rather pleasant," he grumbled.

Crain was not so easily convinced. His voice was weary as he looked around, waiting for the rest of the trap his pumpkin mind had envisioned to be sprung. "I don't like it, Sir," he said. "It's an unnatural occurrence—like an omen of bad tidings."

"Now, now, Crain," Jack chided. "We mustn't let ourselves be ruled by fear."

The words had barely escaped his mouth when they were suddenly assaulted from all sides. A motor-scooter rounded the bend with a guttural whine, cruising past them with such speed that Jack's cloak billowed out behind him as it passed. Jack and Crain screamed. Across the street, a bug zapper was ignited, inciting a lonely moth to immediately kamikaze its way into the light, crisping itself with a piercing shock. They screamed again. A low rumble of mechanics boomed as a garage door opener did its duty, causing them to scream again and whirl in the other direction. They promptly ran into a wall of electronic phone-ringing that blared through an open window. They turned again and were faced with a barking dog leaping at them from behind a fence. Somewhere, a toilet flushed.

They were now in absolute hysterics, their voices ragged but still reaching operatic heights. In another instant, the wind was knocked out of them as a car backed out of the now-open garage. It threw them into a wall of sidewalk hedges with ease before roaring into town with a friendly *honk-honk*.

Jack and Crain continued to gasp and pant little howls of terror in feeble falsettos from the bushes.

"Oh, my heart!" Jack cried, clutching his chest, through which the withered, fist-sized chunk of flesh could be seen rapidly pumping.

"Well, we've successfully made our way back into the shrubbery, Sir," spat Crain, rolling from side to side in a shallow arc on the dirty ground. "I don't know what just happened there, but I'm afraid we may be in a little over our heads, Sir—were we just run over by a bloody metal dragon!? We should turn back, right, Sir?"

With a groan, Jack propped his torso onto one boney elbow and delicately rubbed his head, now aching for many reasons. He reached into the thicket of hedgerow branches and pulled out his rumpled cockade hat, slapping it onto his exposed skull, twigs and all.

"No," he growled through gritted teeth as he planted Crain's staff into the ground and hoisted himself to his feet. "We must find that blasted book. Do you wish to remain a *pumpkin* for the rest of your days!?"

"I'm sorry, Sir," said Crain, "But were you not here just thirty seconds ago when a smoke-breathing, armor-plated carriage assaulted us quicker than anything either of us has ever seen before? Because I *distinctly* remember that, and—Sir?"

Jack was no longer listening. He had slowed at the sight of something passing by, deep within the shadows between the streetlight pools.

"Sir?" badgered Crain, looking around the street. "Sir, have I missed something? Please, fill me in. I was busy ranting."

Jack ignored him with a snort and took another few steps before stopping abruptly at the sight of more movement. It appeared to be a small, cloaked figure running in the opposite direction. Jack turned his skull to follow the shadowy figment over his shoulder.

Crain eyed Jack warily. "Really, Sir, if there's something amiss, I do wish you'd make me aware of it. You *are* my primary means of transport, and I feel like we need to establish an open system of communication and mutual respect if this is to be an effective—"

Crain gagged as Jack turned on him, swung a skeletal finger through his carved mouth, and hooked it through one triangular eye-hole. The lieutenant dangled there like a freshly caught fish on a line, his pumpkin features distorted and awkwardly sideways. Jack pulled his furious face close and stared at him, eye socket to eye socket.

"Will you *please* stop speaking for one moment, you insufferable, yammering *ninny?"* Jack said with quiet ferocity. Crain moved in a nod-like way.

"Nn-hnn, yesh, Cnhnnh," he said as best he could.

"Shh!" Jack hissed, straining to hear something carry in the evening breeze. After a moment, he unhooked himself from Crain's face and made to continue into town. Before a single foot could fall, he found himself frozen at the sight of a creature standing in the middle of the street. Crain yelped in surprise at its appearance.

Standing no taller than four feet and clutching a partially-filled burlap sack at its side, the thing was wearing a hooded cloak and matching mask with eye holes revealing only a shadowy void. The mask's grin stared up at them like an asylum escapee.

"Sir!" whispered Crain. "What *is* that?"

"I do not know," Jack replied, unable to tear his eyes from the eerily silent figure standing before them.

"Perhaps it is a Druid child?" Crain suggested. "Observe the shape of the mask and the elaborate stitching of the sandals—" Without warning, the masked creature padded off down the street without so much as a glance back at them. "—and there he goes. Well, that was intensely odd," finished Crain. "You know, I have to wonder if it's even worth conquering this town, Sir. It's been nothing but a strange sequence of—"

"Look," Jack interrupted, striding down the street, where a small flock of masked figures with bags walked. This slow trickle soon became a veritable flood as the colonel and his lieutenant rounded a turn in the road and stopped, overwhelmed by what they found.

"Oh my. Is this some sort of demon convention, Sir?" asked Crain as the volume of bird-like chatter rose from the mob of trick-or-treaters. A small, veiled reaper ran from amidst the throng, pausing long enough to give Jack a swift kick in the shin. With a grunt, Jack hopped and clutched his leg as the monster ran off with a squawk and a laugh.

"I do not understand this madness..." Jack grumbled in annoyance.

"Sir, why don't we just move on to somewhere else—Collartown perhaps, or—ooh! Metropotamia! We can have a right-proper drink-up there, eh?"

"Retreat is not an option, Lieutenant," Jack said, his head darting back and forth as he followed the trick-or-treaters' seemingly random motions.

"I know, Sir, I know all about your retreat issues, but take a look around, Colonel—this isn't exactly a population worth conquering single-handedly, is it? The bloody village seems to be run by deformed children. See? They are openly plundering each other's houses, and not only that, they seem to be having a marvelous time doing it!"

Jack had to admit to himself that this was true. Now that they seemed to be in the heart of the populace, he could see the extent of this lunacy. With a knock and a scream, they appeared to be gaining access to the most valuable treasures within each oddly lit home. It was an interesting technique, and Jack (who had been known to plunder with the best of them) wondered which oath or threat was being intoned in unison by these demons and why it was so successful in coercing such brightly colored riches so willingly from the adult townsfolk.

"They must possess some dark power or weapon of incredible destruction to hold such sway over these people," Jack ruminated as more loot was transferred from house to bag on the stoops of Bootville. "Look! They do not even offer struggle or resistance. Incredible."

"And smiling all the while," Crain mused, impressed. "Further proof that we may be out of our league here, Sir."

"Crain, your cowardice shames the empire," sneered Jack. "You used to so look forward to the mayhem of battle."

"Do not mistake me, Colonel—the mayhem is still my bread and butter, but please remember that this is the town that turned me into a vegetable. I'd just like to cut my losses before I'm done up into a dessert."

Jack began slowly walking once more, eyeing the strange decorations adorning the houses and fences with distrustful curiosity.

He paused briefly to take note of an effigy that looked suspiciously like himself hanging from a tree.

"With any luck, my orange friend, you will not have such fears for much longer. All we need is the book that impudent girl now possesses. I shall not rest until it is mine, and we can reverse this misfortune of decay."

"We've definitely looked better, Sir, but at this point, I raise the following questions: Who is the girl with the book? Where is she now? How do we find her? Why does *she* have the book and not the girl who *used to* have the book, *and* is that going to affect our getting back to normal?"

Jack had kneeled to examine a small grouping of carved pumpkins flickering in front of some dried corn stalks.

"Perhaps one of these would not speak so much…" he pondered, shooting a malicious look at Crain.

Crain gasped, deeply offended. "Sir, I was only asking because— Sir, behind you!" he cried as a wide shadow fell over them, cast by a figure whose hulking frame eclipsed the nearest streetlight.

In a flash, Jack was on his feet, sword drawn and ready to do battle with the mysterious intruder. Bootville may be the hell of his final undoing, but that didn't mean he would go without a fight.

CHAPTER 12
The Village Idiots

"PRETTY COOL, HUH?" the shadow asked with a chuckle.

The intruder in question was revealed to be a dumpy, middle-aged man wearing a windbreaker and chinos. "Yep, got myself one of those kits down at the market," he said, answering a question no one had asked. "Heck of a time getting the hang of the cutting technique, ha-ha. But it doesn't look like you need any help in that department, am I right, fella?"

The pear-shaped man took the blade of Jack's sword gingerly between two pudgy, feminine fingers. Jack grunted at the audacity while Crain stared at the little man, nonplussed.

"Todd Dempster's the name—I'm in sales," the man said proudly, as though being 'in sales' meant something more than just selling things to people. "Say…" Todd said, adjusting his glasses. "That's quite a costume you've got there—did you get that as a rental, or did you buy? You know, I think the most cost-effective route for most people is a rental—I mean, for a nice one like that— but it seems like most of them are put off by wearing something that's been *used* before, you know?"

Jack looked down at the tattered, scorched rags of his once-regal uniform, now colorless in its transparency, while Crain looked on in horror at the neighborhood man, who appeared to be having a one-sided conversation with himself.

"Not that I'm one to talk—me and the wife got a great deal a couple of years back on some really excellent vampire get-ups. We do a lot of those costume parties and things like that—my wife's in the Rotary Club—you know, strictly adults-only, what with the cocktails and all, but we have fun with it. Anyway, we found these costumes, these Dracula costumes—wait, was it Dracula, Tracy?" he shouted up the walk to a bored-looking woman sitting on the porch with a bowl of candy.

"What!?" she called back.

"The costumes we got at the convention center!"

"I don't know, I think they're just vampires, aren't they?"

"Right, right, just vampires," Todd said, turning back to Jack and Crain. "Anyway, we decided, what-the-hey—"

"Why would he keep thinking they're Draculas?" Tracy muttered.

"What's that, hon?" Todd said.

"They don't even look like Draculas. One of them has this shroud-thing—"

"Right, well, they look like they're for vampires—we do vampire make-up, the whole nine yards," he said over his shoulder to Jack.

"It's a dress!" Tracy said. "One of them is definitely a dress. I just don't know where you get Draculas from. He's said it like eight times tonight!" she hollered to Jack, who was rubbing his head, now aching from this sudden influx of passive-aggressive loud-talking.

"They're quite mad, you know," Crain said under his breath to Jack, who groaned in the affirmative.

"So we said, why not? It's an investment. Got 'em for a song!" Todd said, jingling some loose coins in his pockets. "But you know, funny thing—we don't dress up on Halloween. I know, I know, ha-ha: 'Why don't you dress up if you *bought* the Draculas?' We just figure, hey, it's for the kids, right?"

"It's for the kids!" Tracy called out.

Jack frowned, perplexed by the entire conversation. "What is this... *Halloween?*"

"Ha-ha, I know, right?" said Todd, giving him a playful sock in the arm. "Marketing—jeez. I mean, you want to help the economy, but all this *consumerism*—it's just so tasteless. You know, it's like I always say: 'You can buy the candy, but you can't buy the memories.'"

"He never says that," Tracy said.

Jack raised his sword, fully prepared to stab the man in the heart. Todd, however, stood his ground and rubbed his chin while staring at Jack's uniform.

"Say, that *is* a pretty neat get-up there," he said, taking Jack by surprise. "Wait, let me guess… hmm… oh, I know what—Civil War?"

Jack and Crain looked at each other, unsure of what he was talking about. Todd carried on, unfazed.

"Say!" he said, snapping his fingers. "Did you see that program on the PBS? Oh my goodness, I watched some of that—must have been three nights in a row! That was *unbelievable.*"

"He fell asleep every night," Tracy could be heard mumbling as she dropped candy into some trick-or-treaters' bags.

"Oh, the carnage—whew! Did you see it?" Todd asked, warming to the subject.

"Yes, I have seen much carnage," Jack intoned, the memories of blood-soaked battlefields flooding his rotten mind with a wash of unyielding despair.

"You've gotta see this thing, it is just *great,*" Todd continued, oblivious. Jack made to leave the conversation but was stopped by the snapping of Todd's fingers once more. "Oh!" he said. Jack sighed and turned back to him. "Are you one of those, uh, whaddya call 'em… honey, what are they called?"

"Draculas," his wife called back.

"No, no, the guys who dress up in the old uniforms and do the whole *thing… "* Todd said, squinting.

"I am going to kill you now," Jack said, visibly exhausted.

"Re-enactors!" Todd shouted with a smile, snapping his fingers yet again, a habit that now gave Crain a nervous tic with each *snap!* "Ha-ha, yeah, I was reading about you guys in the paper today— they're doing a re-enactment of the Battle of Collartown, is that right?"

"Collartown!" Crain hissed in Jack's ear.

Jack dropped his sword and grabbed Todd Dempster by the front of his windbreaker, lifting him a full foot off the ground and fogging his glasses with his breath.

"Collartown?" Jack rasped. "What news of Collartown? Tell me *everything."*

"Hey there, fella," Todd said, looking down at Jack's skeletal fingers. "No need to get upset now, right? I just thought with your outfit and everything—"

"What has happened at Collartown? What has become of the army!?" Jack pressed, his frustration mounting.

"What—today?" asked Todd, his puffy face slick with sweat.

"The *battle!*" Jack roared.

"Easy now, Colonel…" Crain murmured.

Jack dropped Todd and tightened his hand into a fist. The remaining tendons of his neck stood taut as he clenched his jaw in anger. "But he confounds me so!" Jack hissed back at his lieutenant. "Such a labyrinth of nonsense I have never before known—*argh!"* He kicked a nearby pumpkin into oblivion with his booted foot before picking up his sword and wheeling on Todd, who calmly polished his glasses on the tail of his shirt.

"Well," Todd said, somewhat smugly, returning the frames to his face, "I would have thought you'd know all about this, being a re-enactor and all, ha-ha. Actually, me and Tracy and the kids went down to the museum in Collartown last spring—was it spring, honey?"

"It was February. Remember, we had to go to your mother's for her birthday," Tracy replied, rocking in her chair.

"Oh, that's right—she's always right, ha-ha," said Todd. Jack growled and hefted his sword. "*Any*-who, we went down there, and they've got a really nice little museum—you'd never believe it because it's not on the main street, but it's there. Totally worth the price of admission, and we got a few bucks off because of the Rotary, you know. Anyway, they've got this whole map laid out showing where the Redcoats were routed, and it was just really something to see—"

"*Routed?"* Jack groaned.

"Oh dear," muttered Crain.

"But come to think of it, that was the Revolution, not the Civil War," Todd said, suddenly empowered by his memory. "Hope your uniform was a rental, ha-ha."

"Nooo!" Jack bellowed, stomping his staff down on the sidewalk. Crain belched a firestorm, igniting the dried cornstalks bunched around the nearby picket fence.

"Whoops, got a little blaze happening here, ha-ha," said Todd, moving to stomp the fire out with one sensible loafer. "Hey, it's not a big deal—you can call the credit card company for a receipt and just get a refund on the thing—I do it all the time! You know, last month, I ordered this sweater vest from the HinterLand Fringe catalog, and I *specifically* checked the color box for Tender Salmon. And what do they do? Of course: they send me Lilac Sunset instead— I mean, how hard is this, right?"

Jack had collapsed down onto one knee, his remaining face twisted into a mask of fury, his breathing heavy and hacking. Crain swung next to his ear.

"Sir, I know this information is not exactly what you wanted to hear right now, but this simpleton in the bad jacket does seem to be a font of knowledge about many things. Perhaps he can help us find the book we seek?"

"Oh, but I *loathe* him," Jack grumbled as he picked himself up.

"I know, I know, but he seems absolutely *obsessed* with the sound of his own voice, so let us exploit this for our own gains," Crain said as Todd scrutinized Jack with a curious eye.

"Hey guy, it's okay," Todd said, patting Jack on the arm. He quickly pulled his hand away with a grimace. "Wow! Chilly out here, eh? Did you have a relative in the war or something? You seem to be taking this pretty hard. Are you one of those Daughters of the American Revolution?"

Jack straightened and cleared his throat with authority. "Townsperson, I require certain information from you *immediately.*" Crain quietly coughed. "Please," Jack added.

"Sure, sure, anything I can do to help. You know, I did help put together a pamphlet of local goings-on for the Chamber of Commerce. Nancy—the assistant secretary at the courthouse, you know—well, she called me up, and—"

"Silence!" Jack roared, momentarily forgetting himself. Todd arched a curious eyebrow. "Um, forgive me, I meant to say, 'Please stop talking,'" Jack said, regaining his composure.

"He doesn't know how!" Tracy yelled from the porch.

"What can I do ya for, neighbor?" Todd asked, ignoring his wife and adjusting his glasses.

"We—um, *I*—am in search of a book. A very particular book, currently possessed by a young girl."

"Sure, uh-huh, okay." Todd crossed his arms in thought. "What kind of book is it? Like a coming-of-age story?"

"Alas, I am unsure of its contents. However, I believe it to be *musical* in nature," Jack croaked in his most civilized voice.

"Okay… do you know what it's called?" Todd inquired, rocking slowly on the balls of his feet.

"Again, I am unsure—hence my troubles," said Jack with a chuckle that could have frozen the ocean. Todd continued to nod.

"Okay, okay… do you know the name of the girl you saw with the book? Maybe my kids go to school with her."

Jack looked briefly at Crain, who subtly shook his pumpkin head.

"Um, no, I don't have a name, but she wears a cape," Jack said. Todd looked around at the costumed children milling around the street in force and shrugged.

"Of all the nights, right? Ha-ha," said Todd. "Tell you what you do—you take this road right into town, hang a right, and you'll see the Dog Ear bookstore. They might have it there, and if not, they can order it. Probably your best bet. It's where I get all my Clancys and my Grishams—you know, the real literature."

"A seller of books, you say? Hm…" Jack pondered.

"It does seem like our best chance, Colonel," Crain whispered. "We haven't much else to go on."

"Indeed," Jack replied, turning to Todd. "Townsperson, you have been preposterously annoying, and I should like to see you dead at dawn. But I am very busy, and you have, in your own foolish way, been of some help. I shall therefore leave your home and possessions intact, despite an overwhelming urge to burn them to the ground."

"Uh-huh, real good now, ha-ha," said Todd, beaming. "Say, you've got that old military thing down, don't you."

"Crawl on the ground like the worm that you are, and weep for the mercy I have shown you on this night!" Jack exploded, desperate to feed on someone's fear.

Todd chuckled. "Okay, you betcha, ha-ha. You enjoy the weeping mercy now—and drive safe tonight, okay?"

Furious, Jack wheeled around with a snap of his cloak and stalked down the sidewalk toward town.

"Don't party too hard, and don't do anything I wouldn't do, am I right?" Todd chuckled again with a wave before stuffing his hands into the pockets of his windbreaker.

"Don't believe a word of it," Tracy called out. "He's in bed by ten!"

"She's right—she's always right, ha-ha!"

CHAPTER 13
Persistence And Memory

HE WAS TRYING too hard. Of all the lunacy that had revealed itself since the sun had set, this one feeling was turning out to be the head case at the asylum who babbled the loudest. Elyse was stressed, and Will knew she was stressed, and she knew that he knew that she was stressed, and her knowing about him knowing was causing more stress as they wove their way through the gathering Halloween crowd.

Deep down, she knew he probably couldn't help it. When she thought it through (and why was he making her think it through *now* of all times?), she could deduce that the cause was the male's one-track mind, a concept so clichéd it had to be true. She momentarily wondered if her father had been as relentless with her mother but couldn't picture their comfortable coupling outside the warm, quirky family in which she'd been raised.

They did not touch or speak as they walked down the hedged sidewalks toward Colin's house. Yet, with every worried glance he threw her way out of the corner of his eye, she felt as though he was casting an enormous blanket of concern over her head, smothering her as she tried to organize her thoughts for the next step on this unusual night. She could feel the atmosphere around them rearranging itself as he focused his empathy on her like an industrial-grade laser beam, worrying about how *she* was doing and what he could do for *her* when he should have been focusing that energy on *their* situation and *their* collective well-being. It was exhausting.

He needed her—she understood that, and likewise, she needed him. These things taken together, they needed each other. This aspect could not be disputed, and she'd never bother to try, but when it was broken down to its components, the truth of the thing was that his need for her was founded on sturdy slabs of absolute certainty so leveled and true that he never thought twice about them. It was rather intense. Conversely, her need for him was kaleidoscopic and nebulous, forever changing and encompassing friendship, love, loss, sorrow, and the void. It was not as simple for her as it was for him, and only the passing of time and living of life would be able to correct this one way or another.

Naturally, life being the puckish journey it is, time seemed to be the one thing he couldn't give her. The resurrection of Patrick, the arrival of whatever that thing in the basement was, and their gut-wrenching brush with death seemed to have set off an alarm in his head and triggered an amplification of his anxiety regarding her. With the world turned upside-down, he kept *trying* with her as though to anchor himself to the one sure thing he knew so she would not be inverted with everything else.

Now, here he was, all twitchy and awkward with hyper-sensitivity, looking at her with such concern and protective ardor it was almost laughable. Almost, but not quite, for in her own weird way, she loved him too. The hows and whys of this love were not important right now. Right now, she needed to focus on what the hell they were going to do next.

"Hey," he said, burying his hands in his pockets in the least-casual way possible. "You doing okay?"

She nodded. "Yeah, I'm fine." Inwardly she sighed. Absolutely exhausting.

HE DIDN'T BELIEVE her. Sure, she was fine. Right. Over the past year, Will had learned to read her various emotional states—well, 'read' might not be the operable word in that he understood none of them, but he could at least recognize them like he might recognize German or French when written.

They were mutual substitutes of shared experiences who were close at hand to fill each other's vacuums left by Patrick—secondhand boots to retrace his footprints. His loss had been a turn neither of them had planned on taking, and their mourning had led them on a journey through places Will had never expected to find himself, while others were places he *had* expected to find himself, but under better, less grief-stricken circumstances. At times he felt like a wayward tourist being eaten alive; he'd always wanted to see the sky over Australia, just not on his back while being devoured feet-first by local crocodiles.

He'd always wanted to hold her for hours on end, to feel her against him, and he did—at her brother's wake, where she wept so hysterically she could barely stand. He'd longed to find out what she smelled like, and he did—on the hallway floor, leaning against the lockers when she rested her head on his shoulder and dozed between classes, having been unable to sleep the night before because her brain would not stop *thinking* long enough for her to rest. On a good day, he would find her hand in his, just as he'd always dreamt it should be, but only because she needed something tangible to hang on to.

They approached the corner of Nightjar and Lime Street and slowed in front of an old gingerbread house across the road, awestruck by the sight of it. Atop every flat surface, from porch to steps to walk, sat an army of jack o' lanterns, each with a different, carved face, aglow and taunting.

Elyse shivered. "And to think I used to *like* carving pumpkins."

A shudder ran through Will, and he turned his head to look behind them.

Elyse eyed him, frowning. "What is it?"

Will's eyes darted around the dimly lit street, passing over the growing parade of trick-or-treaters moving past tree trunks and black masses of shrubbery.

"Nothing," he said after a moment. "It just felt like we were being watched or something. It's nothing."

They turned back to face the pumpkins, which *were,* in fact, watching them, and quickly rounded the corner as though a prompt escape might erase those eyes of guttering fire from their memories.

Will sighed inwardly, promptly refocusing on the quiet girl in the cape beside him. Through all their time spent in distraught closeness, some part of her remained a mystery, a place he was not allowed access to. This element, above all else, was how he knew that none of his maladroit yearnings meant what he'd always hoped they would mean. He was the anchor, not the vessel, yet it had not always been this way. Once, he had been there, had set foot in that place.

Of course, this one small step for William-kind happened to fall right before his foot was torn off and eaten by fate's bloody crocodile.

WITH ONE HEAVILY taloned finger, Will rang the doorbell at the Korbin house. He shifted his weight from one foot to the other as he waited, silently cursing the uncomfortable dinosaur head from which his face emerged, sweaty and constricted despite the cool October air.

The anticipatory quiet of the pre-trick-or-treating dusk was interrupted by the heavy wooden door being thrown open, revealing Patrick, clad in a black jumpsuit with a full skeleton stitched on, tracing his scrawny frame.

"Ha-*ha!*" Patrick bellowed, pointing at the dinosaur costume.

"Aw, shut up about it, Pat—I didn't even want to do it this year," Will grumbled as his friend doubled over with laughter.

"Come on, that looks *amazing!*" Patrick said, wiping a tear from his eye.

"Oh, I look ridiculous!" Will said, scowling as he walked into the foyer. "And mind the tail."

"Sure, sure," Patrick snickered, pushing the tail out of the way and closing the door behind him.

The Korbin house was warm with the smells of pumpkin and cinnamon, briefly distracting Will as he tried to avoid suffocation in his outfit. The family had decorated the old homestead with dried multi-color corn and various squashes fit for a harvest feast. Fake cobwebs hung from every corner and dangled like Spanish moss from the chandelier overhead. It was pleasantly festive, and Will reluctantly began enjoying himself.

He turned to find Patrick eyeing the ridiculous stuffed raptor head he was wearing, his arms crossed, obviously stifling a laugh.

"You're lethal at eight months—and I do mean *lethal*," he said in a nasally British accent, mimicking the gamekeeper from *Jurassic Park*.

"Are you about through?" Will asked.

"Clever girl," Patrick added in the same voice.

"All right, I'm going home," said Will, making for the doorknob.

"Come on—that's the greatest movie of all time!" Patrick said, laughing hysterically once more.

"You're not thinking of leaving, are you, William?" Elyse called, swooping down the hallway from the kitchen, her vampire cape snapping behind her like a mainmast flag, her black hair pulled back to reveal a painted-on widow's peak.

"I'd love to, but my dumb claws are in the way," Will said, fumbling with the door. "Stupid evolution—why are you so *slow?*"

"Too bad," Elyse sighed, arching one dangerously attractive eyebrow. "My canines have finally grown in, and I was hoping to feast upon your jugular when you weren't looking." She bared her teeth to reveal a set of glistening plastic fangs. Will felt his face turn hot while Patrick rolled his eyes.

"You know, even the dinosaurs in the movie figure out doorknobs," Patrick said, shaking his head in pity.

"Come on," Elyse said, pulling Will by the tail. "There's carrion in the kitchen for you and Mom's pumpkin pie for us."

"No, let's get going—I want to hit the whole neighborhood this year," Patrick said as he unfurled a folded pillowcase.

Will eyed the skeleton jumpsuit skeptically. "No skull mask?" he asked, unrolling a black garbage bag with his awkward talons.

"No, no, I'm not a skeleton," said Patrick. "I'm John Entwistle, bass player extraordinaire."

"I don't know what that means."

"You know, from the Isle of Wight? 'Ba-dum-dum-dum-diddly-dum-dum-*doo,*'" he sang with a slight bobbing of his head as he grooved on a highly strapped air bass.

"Not getting it," Will said, shaking his head.

Before Patrick could explain, Colin drifted in from the rear of the house wearing a full astronaut suit, complete with a clear plastic dome helmet.

"Aw, there's our little space case," Patrick said, rushing over to knock on the dome with the side of his hand. "I always said he should be in a bubble."

Colin held up a fork with a chunk of pie impaled on it. "I can't get to my pie," he said blankly.

"Sorry, friend, but we've got to keep you sealed for freshness," Patrick said, taking the fork from him and stuffing the pie in his mouth.

"Don't be a jerk," Elyse said, pushing her brother aside and using the corner of her cape to polish the clear plastic. "Don't worry, Colin, we're just about to head out. You've got your bag?"

Colin nodded inside the helmet and held up a grey duffel bag. He froze at the sight of Will, fully velociraptored, and stared at him wide-eyed as Patrick and Elyse stepped outside. Will stared back, self-consciously guarded, as a momentary silence ensued.

"Life found a way?" Colin asked, awestruck.

Will sighed and followed him outside.

THEY REACHED THE outskirts of town three hours later, now weighed down with their bags of loot. Will was fatigued and glad to be almost done with the trick-or-treating, both for the evening and for good. Patrick had been relentless, and, true to his word, they had canvassed most of the Bootville Proper neighborhoods with military precision. Will appreciated his friend's enthusiasm but couldn't help feeling distracted by the presence of Elyse, whom he now looked at through love-goggles full-time.

For whatever reason, be it the festive occasion, the distractedness of Patrick, or simply being out late at night, Will couldn't help but feel like he was actually making some real progress. Elyse had walked progressively closer to him as they roamed the old sidewalks and had laughed a little bit more than usual when Will poked fun at her brother, who had been keeping up a steady stream of mostly one-sided conversation with Colin for their amusement. He also noticed that whenever he found the guts to look over at her properly, she was often looking back—and not only that but actually *seeing* him, her eyes spelunking new depths.

If only—*if only*—he wasn't wearing this idiotic dinosaur get-up. Will cursed Patrick to himself throughout the evening for having suggested it as the cumbersome burden of having a tail and a heat-locking quilted lining gnawed away and increasingly distracted him.

By this time, they'd reached his side of town, and as the Widow's Watch drew near and the neighborhood houses offering candy became fewer and farther between, Will couldn't help but feel relief. The night winds had picked up speed, lashing the branches of the great trees lining Nightjar Street and causing Elyse to shiver.

Emboldened by the holiday spirit and acting almost wholly on impulse for the first time in ages, Will put his arm around her. His insides immediately knotted up as they caught up with what he was doing, and he soon felt a blast of adrenaline as she moved in and let herself be held.

"Sorry about my claws," he mumbled, his ears ringing with the rushing of blood. Elyse laughed softly but neither looked at him nor said anything, as though doing so would break this newly formed bubble.

Unfortunately for them, Patrick upset the magic anyway, stopping suddenly and turning. Will's hand flew down to his side in the space of a nanosecond as he tried to look casual. He began examining his dinosaur feet for no reason while his jaw began chewing an imaginary piece of gum.

The next time I'm actually being casual, I have to remember to remember what it looks like, he thought. *Because this is not it.*

He was pleased to see Elyse from the corner of his eye, looking off into the distance at nothing in particular and fiddling with her cape as though she had just discovered it was there.

Despite this ugly bit of pantomime, Patrick seemed not to notice anything amiss and grandly raised his hands.

"Who wants to play…" he said, pausing for effect, "…*Ghost in the Graveyard*—bwa-ha-ha-ha-*ha!*" he boomed in a deep, vaguely foreign accent, clapping his hands together and rubbing them like a backlot mad scientist.

Will and Elyse looked up to see the forbidding iron gates of the cemetery before them, briefly lit into silhouette by a well-timed flash of lightning.

"Really?" Will asked, casting a skeptical eyebrow skyward as the ensuing thunder rumbled beneath them.

"Yes, *really*," Patrick said, mimicking him. "What, are you too cool for some good old-fashioned shenanigans now?"

"Um, kind of."

Patrick elbowed Colin, almost knocking him over in his heavy spacesuit. "Hey, Colin, check it out—Victor Mature over here's too serious for Ghost in the Graveyard, ha-ha-ha!"

"Ha," Colin said as Patrick slapped him on the back.

"Hey, Cicero—have you seen what you're wearing? It looks like a Muppet's trying to puke your face up!" Patrick said, delighted with himself.

Will rolled his eyes and whipped off his raptor gloves, tossing them into a gutter before pulling the dinosaur cowl off his head, leaving it to hang lifelessly down his back. His stomach dropped as Elyse covered her mouth to stifle a giggle.

"Sorry," she said, pointing. "Your hair."

Will ran a hand through his sweaty mop, his thoughts now on getting to the Watch as quickly as possible so he could change out of his absurd costume, run a comb through his hair, and piece together whichever shreds of dignity he had left.

"You don't even know how to play Ghost in the Graveyard, do you," he said to Patrick, impatient to move on.

"Oh, whatever—nobody does!" Patrick said, waving him off. "You just run around and hide behind the tombstones or something— who cares? It's our last Halloween!"

"Pat, you know they lock the gates at sundown," Elyse said, crossing her arms with the same look of impatience her mother wore in similar situations.

Patrick stared at them, appalled. "So, that's how it's gonna be, huh? My best friend and my own sister won't even indulge me a little harmless B and E, even though they're both minors *and* it's Halloween. Shameful."

Will had grown tired of this argument and decided to cut his losses. "Go on then. We'll just wait here and keep a lookout."

Anything to get a minute alone with your sister, he thought, feeling surprisingly little guilt in doing so.

"What about you, Buzz?" Patrick said, turning to Colin. Colin shrugged. "Yeah? Then let's light this candle, buddy." Patrick led the way to a large tree rooted just outside the fence, with plenty of canopy hanging over the other side.

"You know, I'm older than both of you," Patrick said over his shoulder to Will and Elyse, who looked on as he tossed his candy bag onto the ground and gave a few exploratory knocks on the trunk of the tree. "You guys should look up to me—I'm a role model."

Lightning pulsed again, brighter this time, followed by the ever-closer volcanic rumble of thunder. Elyse looked up warily at the starless, threatening sky.

"If I get wet out here waiting for you, I'm leaving," she called to her brother.

"Come on, Colin, let's leave the geezers to their Andy Griffith reruns. I hear *Mayberry RFD* is good tonight," he said, boosting himself with a grunt off Colin's space-pack and onto the lowest rung of branches.

Will turned to Elyse with a shrug. "I guess we're doing this now," he sighed, trying not to think about how suddenly unsupervised they were.

The powerful gusts snapped at Elyse's cape and made the loose strands of her black hair move with an unnatural, medusan quality. She reached up to her mouth and spat out her plastic fangs. "These have been killing me," she said, working her mouth back into normalcy as she tucked them into her pocket.

"Well, you know what Patrick says: 'You've got to *commit* to your ghoul!'" Will said, doing a spot-on impersonation.

"Yeah, well..." Elyse said, looking away and taking a tone that suggested she wasn't interested in talking about her brother anymore. She shivered as the storm churned more violently.

"You cold?" Will asked, hating himself immediately as she nodded and drew a shuddering breath.

Of course she's cold, moron—keep going.

"My Ma's got hot cider for when we get back to the Watch. And the fireplace…" He was losing it. Fortunately, lightning crashed directly overhead, and she jumped, almost knocking him over.

"Wow!" she said, laughing nervously.

"Yeah, that was close," Will said, putting his arm around her again. It was easier to do this time, and she did not pull away.

Thank you, nature, he thought.

They stood in silence for what felt like a decade before she slid her arm underneath his and they moved closer together.

"I've never been this close to a dinosaur before," she said.

Will laughed softly, his heart on the verge of exploding. "Yeah? We have a bad reputation, you know. What with the carnage and everything."

"Sure, sure," Elyse said, leaning her head on his shoulder as they stared into the empty cobblestone street.

"And we're pretty extinct these days, so we don't really get out that much," he said, turning his head to look at her directly.

"Mmm…" she said, nodding slowly with exaggerated fascination. "You really should, you know."

"Yeah?"

"Definitely."

"Would you come with me?"

In an instant, the squall was upon them. The sky flared with blue-white flashbulb pops as lightning struck once, twice, and then a third time behind them with a clap of thunder that charged through their bodies, breaking their embrace and leaving them temporarily deaf. The speed of it was almost too much to take in as a thick bolt illuminated the tree by the cemetery fence, now alive with electricity and an unparalleled natural fury.

Will could only just register the skeleton-clad form of Patrick frozen within the charge before the brightness made him shield his eyes. He refocused in time to see his friend's body plummet wildly from the high branches, his ringing ears barely picking up Patrick's scream before he hit the ground with a sickening finality and only silence remained.

CHAPTER 14
Back At The Lab

"Oh good, you're alive."

Patrick swiveled in his chair beside Colin to face Elyse and Will as they entered the side door to the Niemann garage. Will bolted the door behind them before lifting the adjacent window shade and peering into the gathering darkness while Elyse stashed her bag and violin case in the corner.

"Colin was just showing me demos for some new video games," Patrick continued, gesturing to the bank of monitors behind them. "It was pretty boring."

Will ducked beneath some low-hanging cables as he made his way over to them. "You fellas planning on cutting some meat later?" Befitting the protocol of a laboratory, Patrick and Colin had put on long, white coats.

"Will, don't be an idiot," Patrick sneered. "We're obviously doing the late shift at the maternity ward."

"Stat," Colin added as Patrick nodded his approval.

"Did you guys get away okay? You weren't followed?" Elyse asked, her voice tense.

Patrick shook his head. "No, we were as elusive as black panthers, weren't we, Colin?"

"We walked here."

"Exactly. What about you guys?"

Elyse shook her head. "I don't think so. It's hard to tell though—the streets are really filling up."

Patrick leaned back in his chair and put his hands behind his head. "Uh, so maybe I missed something while I was dead, but who was the talking cadaver-man with a flair for the dramatic back there?"

"That was crazy," said Will, his eyes wide.

"Crazy," Colin agreed with a nod.

"Will, that was *your* house," Patrick said, pointing at him. "Do you have something you want to tell us? Is this a Bates Motel thing with Mother in the fruit cellar? Do you think she's fruity?"

"What? No, you creep," Will said, simultaneously defensive and disgusted. "Stop trying to twist everything into some bizarre mummification fantasy—it's really weird when you do that."

"I do not!" Patrick said, aghast.

Elyse gave him a pointed look. "Remember when you had to do a family tree for school, and you couldn't find a picture of Grandma, so you used a photo of the Siberian Ice Maiden instead?"

"Or the time you were convinced that the Chamber of Commerce was just a front for a cult of sphagnum bog bodies," added Will.

"Or the time you told everyone to call you 'Imhotep.'"

"Oh yeah... wow, that *is* really weird," Patrick nodded with a frown. "By the way, Sis, I couldn't help but notice that Mom and Dad totally ignored the drawings I made for how I wanted my tomb to look."

"Sorry—the cemetery balked at the subterranean doors sealed with curses," Elyse said with a roll of her eyes.

"I *specifically* asked for antechambers!" Patrick hollered in outrage.

"Hey! Can we deal with the contractor disputes later, please?" Will asked, holding his hands up in truce. Elyse and Patrick shot each other warning looks as Will moved to peek out the window again. "So, what do you think, 'Lyse? Was that really that guy?"

"*What* guy?" asked Patrick.

"Spicy Jack," she replied.

"What, like the cheese?"

Elyse gave him a look. "No, you idiot, the legend of Bootville." Patrick shrugged and shook his head. She sighed. "You know, the story they always tell about the Redcoats burning the old town down and ruining everybody's good time—did you never pay attention in class?"

Patrick shook his head. "Seriously, like, never."

"It happened on Halloween! Come on, you're supposed to be 'Mr. Halloween,' right?"

"Oh, *that* town-burning. Yeah, okay. Got it," Patrick said, nodding.

"This guy had a talking pumpkin," Will noted.

"Oh, wait—I get it," Patrick said, smirking with dawning comprehension. "It's a lantern, right? 'Spicy Jack of the Lantern?' '*Jack O' Lantern?*' Is that where that comes from?"

Elyse shrugged. "Could be."

"Wow, so we're dealing with, like, an archetype, huh?" Patrick said, his translucent eyes going wide.

"A what?" asked Will.

"Like, the real deal, man. An original. Like Santa Claus," Patrick replied. "That's pretty wild."

"Yeah, but what does he *do?*" asked Will. "Is he friendly? Is he mean? Does he have powers? Can we make him go away? Does he have any known food allergies?"

Patrick nodded, considering all of these things. "Well, he did try to bisect my sister with a sword, so I think we can rule out 'friendly.'" He glanced at Elyse, who was now frowning and absentmindedly pulling her hair back over and over again. He leaned forward in his chair, squinting at her. "Hey, Sis."

"What?" Her voice was sharp with stress.

"You freaking out?"

She scoffed. "What? No, I'm in control."

Patrick arched an eyebrow. "Uh-huh. You're also wearing a cape, but I'll let that slide for right now. You know I know when you're lying, right?"

"Pat, I am *not* freaking out!"

Will's eyes widened as the sibling tension mingled in the air with the dry electrical discharge of overworked processing units. He turned away, glancing at Colin and making a circular motion with his index finger. Colin swiveled his chair away from the conversation and stared blankly at the black, data-crunching screens.

"Look, I'm sorry!" Elyse continued, throwing her hands up in the air. "This is all really weird, you know? You're *dead*, Patrick. You've been dead, and this was all my idea, and now this pumpkin guy is out there, and it's all really, really... *weird*."

"Yeah, but it's okay, right?" Patrick said, shrugging. "Look—I can sit on chairs and wear fun jackets. It's totally normal."

"Oh yeah, this is totally normal," she said, pointing at him. "Look at you—you're *see-through*. Mom's gonna kill me."

Will turned to Patrick, consumed by curiosity. "Are you, like, hungry or anything?"

"I could eat," Patrick shrugged.

"What about going to the bathroom?"

"Dude—really?"

"Hey, I don't know," said Will. "This is a new experience for me."

"You're telling me, buddy."

Elyse stared at them as though they were vest-wearing grinder monkeys in mid-jig. "You know, this *is* starting to feel normal— you're both really annoying me."

"Hey, Sis, don't worry!" said Patrick. "Things are totally looking up for us right now! Look, in the last couple of hours, we've gone from graveyard to basement to garage—if we play our cards right, we'll be in a broom closet by Wednesday!"

"Yeah," nodded Will. "And things definitely can't get any weirder than they already are, right?"

As if in response, a tapping came from the door. They froze, their eyes bulging from the sudden rush of adrenaline.

"Um... what was that?" Elyse asked, her voice low.

The tapping came again, this time louder. In a mad scramble, Will rushed to flip the overhead light off while Patrick and Colin dived to the floor, hiding behind their chairs as if they were nattily upholstered shields. Elyse shook her head at them pityingly. "Really?"

"What *is* that?" Will whispered to her as the tapping became more insistent. The sounds of muffled sobs filtered through the door.

"Is that crying?" Elyse asked.

The anguished weeping began to fill the darkened garage. In the soft, blue light of the computer monitors, Will and Elyse looked at each other, waiting for the other to act. Colin pulled his lab coat over his head as Patrick peered around the back of his chair.

"Let's do the sensible thing and ignore it," he whispered. "Um, anything good on TV these days?"

"We can't ignore it—what if somebody's hurt out there?" Elyse said as the phantom sniffling grew increasingly pathetic.

"Elyse, you know I abide by a very strict code: if you break something, hide it, and if you don't want to deal with something, ignore it!" Patrick shot back, ducking behind his chair again.

Elyse sighed, disgusted. She turned back to Will. "You should open it."

Will began to fidget. "Oh, um… I don't really make good first impressions…"

With a shake of her head and a snap of her cape, Elyse walked to the door, her hand slowing as it reached for the knob. The sobbing was steady now, mournful. With a final look over her shoulder to the others, she opened the door.

There, in the darkness, crouched a grotesque pile of bones, topped with a skull that gazed up at Elyse with its black eye sockets. "Hello?" it whispered.

Everyone, including the skeleton, screamed. Elyse ducked behind the open door for protection while Will retreated to where Patrick and Colin were shivering beneath the computer console. The skeleton flung its arms over its head. The bones were of the same off-colored translucency as Patrick's.

"Elyse, close the door!" Will said, his hand flailing behind him on the console in search of a weapon. His fingers latched onto a pencil, which he held in front of him like a switchblade.

Elyse peeked around the door to find the sitting skeleton shivering with fear. "Hello?" she said. The skeleton peeked through its crossed arm bones but did not reply. "Hey, are you okay? Are you hurt?" she asked.

"It's a talking skeleton, Elyse, of course it's hurt!" Patrick whispered around his chair.

"Please!" the skeleton wailed, startling them anew. It held one boney hand out to Elyse. "Please, help me!"

Elyse stared at the trembling hand, unsure of how to respond. Will shook his head and frantically motioned for her to close the door. She frowned at him and stepped from behind the door to get a better look at the pathetic creature, who was now openly weeping into his other hand.

"Hey, it's okay," she said in a soothing voice, unsure how to properly console a distraught cadaver. She reached her hand out to take the skeleton's and then drew it back in shock. The skeleton cried out and leaped at the sudden movement. "Shh, I'm sorry!" Elyse said, desperate to calm it. "Your hand's very cold—I wasn't ready for it."

She gathered the corner of her cape, held it out to grab the skeleton again, and gently led it into the garage as though coaxing a frightened animal to a handful of cereal. Once it had shuffled inside, she reached back to close the door and flip on the light. The boys yelped again as the shivering creature was illuminated beneath the overhead fluorescents.

"Is this a good idea?" Will asked her, unable to take his eyes off the thing.

"Don't you think if it wanted to hurt us, it would have done something already?"

"Yeah, but… you invited it in—you're not supposed to invite them in, right?" Will replied as Patrick and Colin peered out behind him.

Elyse gave him a look of disappointment. "That's for vampires, and also, that's made-up. Look how scared it is," she said, kneeling beside the skeleton once more. "Hey, little guy, what's wrong?"

The trembling skeleton turned its black sockets to her. "Spicy Jack! You have to hide me from Spicy Jack!"

Elyse felt her stomach drop. "Wait, what? You mean the… the skeleton guy with the pumpkin?" The skeleton nodded. "What is it? What do you know about Spicy Jack?"

"He aims to kill me, ma'am!" the skeleton sobbed. "He will kill us all! Please, help me!"

"Shh, it's okay—we'll try to help you," Elyse said, looking to the others for assistance. "Will you guys stop hiding like you've just seen a spider and come over here? It's really upset."

Slightly shamefaced, Patrick and Colin crawled from beneath the desk, straightening their lab coats. Patrick noted the pencil Will was still holding before him. "Nice weapon, Van Helsing—I think you really had him frightened."

"Shut up, Pat," Will muttered, tossing it aside as they gathered around Elyse and the skeleton.

"Do you have a name?" asked Elyse.

The skull bobbed up and down. "Isaac Morgan, ma'am. My beloved called me Ike."

"'Ike?'" Will repeated with a note of skepticism.

Patrick shrugged. "I like Ike."

"Okay… Ike," Elyse said, taking his hand in hers, this time without the cape. "How did you get here?"

Ike sniffed and shook his cranium. "I don't know, ma'am. We were in the dark place, and *he* was there. That *murderer!*" He began bawling once more.

"Wait a sec—did you follow us here?" Will asked. Ike nodded. "I knew it! I *knew* we were being followed, didn't I, 'Lyse? Didn't I say so earlier?" he said, looking at Elyse triumphantly.

"Yes, you're very intuitive," she replied, rolling her eyes.

"So… that means he must have come here with the other guy, right?" Will said, scowling as he tried to piece together the puzzle.

"We fell, sir," Ike sniffed. "We fell, and I hid myself. Please forgive me, sir, I had to—he'll have me *dead* if he finds me!"

"It's okay, Ike," Elyse consoled as he wept. "You're safe now."

Patrick looked at Will wide-eyed and nodded his head to the side. Will turned to join him in facing the opposite direction, exhaling deeply.

"You know, I didn't want to let him in because I thought he was gonna kill us, but this is almost worse," Patrick muttered to his friend.

Will nodded. "I know, it's kind of intense."

"Intense-nothing—he's having an emotional *meltdown* over there! I don't know if we're exactly qualified to run an invasive therapy session, you know?"

Will shrugged. "Well, he doesn't have a body, so he's probably got some self-esteem issues, right?"

Behind them, Elyse cleared her throat and beckoned for them to gather around as Ike's crying mellowed into a sniffle.

"Okay, Ike? Do you think you can talk now?" she asked. The skeleton gave a weak nod. "Okay, good. Now, this is very important—if you want us to help you, you have to start at the beginning, okay?"

"Yes, ma'am," Ike whispered.

"Oh boy, settle in…" Patrick muttered, grabbing the console chairs and placing them around their quivering guest.

Elyse shot her brother a dirty look and patted Ike's skeletal hand. "It's okay, Ike, just ignore him. Now… tell us what you remember."

CHAPTER 15
A Box Of Bones

WHEN I THINK about where I should begin my tale, I cannot help but think about where I know it must, one day, end.

The coffin was half-covered with loose dirt when I decided to catch my breath. Testing the ground around the grave with a few jabs of my shovel, I drove the blade into the surface and leaned my weight onto the handle. The soreness and futility of removing six feet of cold soil, only to replace it mere hours later, began to numb my arms and lower back.

I mopped a line of sweat from my brow with one ragged sleeve and surveyed the cemetery before me. It was a sad, rolling expanse tucked into the woods, usually deserted but now peppered with black-clad servants from the mayor's nearby manor house. Some of these mourners surrounded a weeping woman holding a small child, whom I took to be the dead man's widow and son. I watched as they were ushered gently down the lane while the others trailed behind the bereaved and murmured to one another with the solemn relief of a burial rite now finished. Or, rather, almost finished.

I gazed down at the coffin, its pale, freshly cut wood appearing grey as it reflected the remaining light of a bleak sky, seeming for all the world like a broken bone emerging from a blackened wound. I shuddered. This was a new one, this business of grave-digging.

As Bootville's resident slop boy, I was used to the dirty work others had neither the time nor stomach for. With rumors of massacres, rebellions, and an army of the king's fighting men sailing across the Atlantic to stomp out this fire in the colonies, there was plenty to distract the villagers from their day-to-day tasks. Having no skills or trade of my own, I took these rubbish jobs gladly. But burying the dead—this was an unexpected turn in the life of a mere slop boy.

Stretching the crick from my back with my fingers locked over my head, I turned and was surprised to find two figures from the funeral standing a short distance away. Their mourning garb was refined and of a quality befitting the mayor of Bootville and his daughter. I found myself entranced by the unnatural movements of their black cloaks as they were worked by a stiff breeze, exploding in all directions like a bottle of ink spilling across a page. The two mourners stared at me, the mayor with sad, tired eyes, his mouth fixed into a grim line, and his daughter's gaze unblinking and blue beneath her dangerously sharp eyebrows.

I gave them a quick nod and reached for my shovel. I found their presence unnerving, but then, I'd found the rest of the day to be unnerving as well.

The hour was early, and the sun had not yet risen when I'd been awoken by two sharp knocks on the door of the shack I shared with my father. I'd opened the door to find the mayor's valet standing there with a request on the great man's behalf for a day's worth of well-paid labor. Did I agree to this, yes or no?

Of course, I'd agreed; despite the vagary of the request, one did not turn down the mayor, no matter how inconvenient the hour or unusual the situation was. In this case, it was most unusual as the valet led me down a sequestered path through the forest and into the town's burial grounds. He'd then pointed to the overgrown vacancy I was to dig up, with instructions to have the plot prepared by late afternoon.

This arrangement was strange but no stranger than the circumstances leading to digging the grave in the first place. I'd heard them whispered about by everyone in town with morbid curiosity and laden with some admittedly wild and irresponsible speculation.

"Don't you find it odd that the mayor's butler should die so unexpectedly at his young age and with no signs of sickness?" the town's cooper had been heard to mutter as he leaned against a bundle of freshly cut barrel slats.

"Yeh, very odd—old Aberfoyle weren't really that old now, was he," the local blacksmith had been rumored to reply from beside his anvil while scratching his stubble with sooty hands.

"And don't it seem mad that old Asten should be arranging the burial in such a quiet manner? Aberfoyle was as much a town figure as the rest of us, wasn't he?"

"Mm-hm, spot on with that, sure enough. Most definitely mad."

"And did you hear that the mayor forbade everyone except the doctor from seeing the body?"

"Why, I think I did hear something 'bout that—and he had himself a wife and a young lad no less. Don't seem right that they shouldn't be allowed to weep over the corpse, do it?"

"Curious, innit, the way the matter is being dealt with—not quite a secret, but not very public-like either."

"You're bloody right, there—that is *most* curious."

Nobody could explain the odd behavior borne of Asten Manor, just as nobody could explain the coffin being firmly nailed shut before a viewing of the corpse. Likewise, nobody could explain the decision for the funeral to be limited to the house staff and to take place at dusk, which, considering the oppressive cloud cover, may as well have been at night. And nobody could explain the rumors trickling from the loose lips of the mayor's surviving servants after a few tankards of ale at the Widow's Watch. They whispered that the body in the box was not actually a body and claimed it to be a skeleton devoid of any trace of human exterior, as though it had been decomposing for a century.

I hefted my shovel as this unusual day drew to a close and was about to return to my labors when the mayor and his daughter, who looked to be about my age, made their way around the hole in the ground and paused beside me. I froze in the unexpectedly close presence of my betters, but the mayor did not speak. Instead, he placed a gentle hand on my shoulder and pressed a gold coin into my palm. The girl studied me with her stormy eyes.

Uncomfortable beneath their stares, I glanced down at my payment, which seemed to glow as it caught the dying, muted light.

I looked up to find the two walking away, arm in arm, winding through the tombstones jutting every which way like the stony fingertips of buried giants, clawing at the surface for a gasp of air.

Pocketing my fee, I noted that the nightly fog was rolling in from the fens and idly wondered if my dad had remembered to eat anything that day. With a sigh of resignation, I turned my attention back to the open grave. The newly cut headstone reading 'ABERFOYLE' had been laid in the tall grass nearby and was to be the last thing I would deal with that night. It all felt years away from being done.

I stabbed the shovel into the mound of black dirt and turned it into the hole, onto the grey box. A most unusual business, this. My back and shoulders burned as I repeated the motion over and over again. The task seemed endless, and I wondered if this was how things would be now—if I was doomed to spend the rest of my days here, alive amongst the dead.

CHAPTER 16
An Ike In America

ALLOW ME TO go back further.

I'd been raised on a farm in the West Country and had been to Bristol once and only once. From this old port, my father and I departed for our new lives as exiles in the American colonies.

My father was an industrious and clever man, though cleverness and smartness aren't really the same thing. While you might consider his scheme of stealing sheep from his neighbors, shaving them, and then selling them back to the neighbors as replacements for themselves to be clever, it was hardly smart. The ruse could only last so long before the other farmers in our county noticed that the only man not to suffer from being sheep-took was dear old Dad.

"Not to worry, lad," he said, flashing me a smile as the jailers shackled him and unceremoniously carted him down to the Cornhill Gaol at Shepton Mallet for trial and punishment. "You just mind the farm while I'm gone, and this business will sort itself out. Just be sure to—"

He was interrupted by a solid knock to the head from one of the guards, and I was left to imagine what his further instructions might have been. Since we specialized in sheep-flipping, 'minding the farm' meant literally doing just that—remembering that it existed—and so I spent the next few weeks sitting about and practicing tying knots, waiting for justice to be administered, knowing that he'd surely be hanged.

It was with some surprise that I was awoken one morning by the sound of hooves and the clatter of a cart. I hurried outside to find Dad being thrown to the ground from the prison wagon. He looked worse for wear but smiled through his rags and filth as though he'd just been crowned the Prince of Wales.

"Dad, what's happening—are you all right?" I asked, running to help him up while the jailers looked on, bored. "I'd thought you'd see the noose for sure!"

He laughed a ragged laugh and held up his hands, which were tied at the wrist.

"Aye, lad, you'd have thought, wouldn't you? But your old Dad still has the gift of a silver tongue, doesn't he."

"Why are you all tied up, then?" I asked, undoing his knots in mere seconds.

One of the guards coughed. "It needn't have been that way—he tried escaping on the way back here."

"Dad!" I said, appalled.

"Three times, actually," the other guard piped in.

My father shrugged and rubbed his wrists where the rope had left scarlet welts.

"It's not even that far away, Dad. Were you planning on abandoning me?"

"Let's not worry about that now, my boy," he said, putting his arm around me and walking me back to the house. "I need you to pack up what you can carry. We're leaving this shack for good."

It turned out that while Dad had managed to talk himself down from the hangman's gibbet, he still needed some punishment for his crimes and was exiled across the Atlantic.

He never talked much about the horrors he faced in prison, but forever after, he was a changed man, a half-man, as though he'd left his spirit behind in the wretched cells of Cornhill. He never thieved again, but he never really lived again either, keeping to himself and rarely leaving the cottage we managed to piece together once we'd arrived in Bootville. The only lesson he ever bothered to bestow upon me was one of obstinance.

"Whatever you do, son," he said one night as we tried to stay warm on a violent sea, "don't stick your neck out for anybody. Just keep your head down and mind your own. It's a cruel world, and they'll not thank you for it in the end."

HAVING NO HONEST money, we found a plot of land by the fens that no one wanted, and I found myself the provider for both of us. America was wild and exciting to me, and I discovered that, contrary to everything I'd been brought up with, honest work was satisfying work. I did odd jobs around the village—helping the elderly with heavy things, scrubbing the butcher's floors, lugging quarry stones for new foundations in the town square, gutting fish for the easily nauseated, and cleaning up after horses and the like.

The glorious thing about being in the New World was that no one knew anything about us, and we were genuinely able to start over. Mind you, the people of Bootville weren't exactly ecstatic to see us, but they weren't particularly thrilled about much of anything. At least they didn't look down on us as villains like they used to in the West Country. We lived hand-to-mouth, but still, we lived, and even Dad, growing frailer over time, managed to enjoy the idea of being an American and showed glimpses of his old, carefree self as he drifted around our useless acre of mire.

I'd been doing some steady jobs for Mayor Asten, who had the biggest house in the village and a spread of land that rivaled all of Somerset back home. He'd made a fortune logging his forest and employed half the village making those boots, which was good for everyone, including me. Though I was too young for the sawmill on the Whirry, I'd been hired to clean up his outbuildings for a few pence and tried my hardest to impress him.

He was a true gentleman and bore himself with the air of nobility, the likes of which I'd occasionally seen back in England, but mixed with a benevolent spirit of what I came to recognize as equality. Though he was the most moneyed man in the county, he treated the local shopkeepers and landed gentry with no more importance than he did the lowest of the lowly laborers like me.

He was as easy speaking about philosophy as he was about breeding horses and would engage for hours in discussions about the rights of man and the place of government. He was fluent in whatever other high ideas were running around Europe's salons and printing presses, but was gentleman enough not to trod upon anyone else's opinions on these matters. Be it in his parlor at Asten Manor or by the fire at the Widow's Watch, he was always good for a chat—a man of both ideas and integrity.

But for as much as I admired the great man, I am not ashamed to admit that I admired his daughter even more. How clearly I recall the day I first spoke to her.

I had been slopping the pigs in the warm morning of a late summer month and was covered in the filth of my toils. As one of the swine nudged my leg (for we had developed a fair friendship, as far as man and pig go), I noted that I could not recall a time when I had ever been more dirty. Disgusted with myself, I sloshed the last bucket of kitchen scraps into the trough and straightened, rubbing the mud-caked sweat off my brow with my forearm. As I looked up, I was taken by a vision of loveliness on the manor's porch.

She was fair, with a heart-shaped face and large, blue eyes that seemed to swallow the world rather than see it. It was the first I'd seen of her since that dreadful day of digging at the butler's funeral; those eyes had captured me then, and I had been hoping to cross paths with her ever since. Until that moment, the closest I had ever been able to come was listening outside the parlor window, where the sounds of her practicing music lessons could be heard floating from the manor's clavichord and out across the woods—a shop boy's serenade. I would tend the gardens beneath the sash and listen to her play for ages, wondering if I would ever be able to make her acquaintance.

I watched, entranced, as a servant brought around a saddled horse from the stables. She mounted it confidently and, with a flick of her heels and a whistle, incited it into a trot down the lane, slowing as she passed me.

I stared up at her dumbly, too drawn in by her beauty to look away, even though this was forgetting my place and betraying an unspoken rule of servitude. Her gaze examined me with the sharpness of a butchering knife preparing meat for the salt, yet she revealed little of what she might be thinking.

Entranced by her porcelain face, I smiled at her sleepily as though swimming in a dream. Unimpressed, she arched an eyebrow and addressed me in the authoritative way of the elite.

"What is your name, boy?" she demanded rather than asked, emphasizing 'boy' though she couldn't have been much older than me.

"Isaac?" I replied.

"Are you quite sure?" she asked.

"Um, I think so, ma'am," I said, now sweating even more than I had been.

"Fair enough," she said briskly. "Isaac?"

"Yes, ma'am?"

"Your pig looks hungry. I daresay you should let her eat before she ignores you forever, no?"

I looked down to find the pig staring up at me, looking as annoyed as a pig can look that I was blocking it from its trough, and jumped back with a startled "Oh!" Embarrassed by my idiocy, I looked up to find only a cloud of dust and the receding form of my newly discovered beloved galloping down the path toward the horizon.

I DID NOT find work at Asten Manor for another week, and during that time, my mind was occupied with questions concerning the lovely girl everyone in town called Moira—who she was, what she was like, *whom* she would like…

And yet, no sooner would I let my mind wander down these paths than I would remember who I was and where I had come from: lowly Isaac of little education, no prospects, and the son of an aging criminal. It would be a waste of my dreams to spend them on the magnificent Moira Asten, who was surely a slice cut from the upper crust of society. My imagination painted her into a portrait of some dull, aristocratic family resulting from a marriage arranged for mutual economic benefit. Her future husband would be weak-chinned and riddled with gout, her children spoiled and boring with heavily lidded eyes. No, she was too good for the likes of me, too fragile a beauty, too ephemeral to be real.

Imagine my surprise when she appeared at the shack I called home. I looked up from digging a post-hole to see her galloping down the road in a wild blur of stallion. My father had been wandering aimlessly behind me, lost in his thoughts, yet even he paused as Moira pulled up her horse outside the fence before me.

"Isaac," she said, patting her horse on its neck.

"Hello, ma'am," I said, once more conscious of how incredibly dirty I was. "Can I water your horse for you?"

"No, I think not," she said. "I've just come to tell you that my father would like you to clean the chimney if you wouldn't mind. I've already told him you wouldn't, so you'll have to say 'yes.'"

I was momentarily speechless with both joy and apprehension. "Of course, I don't mind, ma'am. Um…"

"Yes?" she pressed, locking her eyes onto mine.

"Well, it's just… I don't think I've ever cleaned a chimney before."

"I wouldn't worry," she replied breezily. "I don't think father ever has either. Who is this?" she asked, noting Dad watching our conversation closely and scratching his beard.

"Hm? Oh!" I said, looking back at him. "That's my dad. Dad, this is, um, Lady Asten," I sputtered as though introducing a courtier to King George himself.

Moira rolled her eyes. "'Moira,'" she corrected. "A pleasure to meet you, sir. I'm enjoying your lack of shoes," she said, noting that my father was indeed quite barefoot.

"Oh?" he said, taken aback by being treated decently by anyone. "Oh, well, thank you."

"So, we will see you soon for the sweeping," she said, looking back at me.

"As soon as I get a chance, ma'am," I said, distracted by the thought that our next meeting would yet again find me dirty and soot covered.

"And Isaac?" she added.

"Yes, ma'am?"

"The pig desperately misses you. Please say hello to her on the way in."

With that, she spat on the ground and rode off as quickly as she had arrived. I looked back at Dad, who met my gaze with wide eyes.

"Oh," he said, nodding slowly. "She is *spirited*."

CHAPTER 17
The Spirits Of '76

SUCH WERE THE circumstances leading to my being waist-deep in a chimney the next day. Using a broom from the barn, I jabbed awkwardly up the flue, inducing a small avalanche of soot to rain down upon me in a merciless, inky-black cloud. Hacking the remnants of fireside chats gone by from my lungs, I ducked beneath the mantle and stumbled onto the sheets of canvas I had spread around the hearth. Shaking my head with vigor, I managed to rid myself of enough soot to open my eyes. To my unending horror, my lovely Moira stood in the doorway, her arms crossed, watching my struggle with bemused curiosity.

I froze. "Oh, um… I don't know what I'm doing."

"Clearly," she replied with a sigh. "Well, it would appear that you have succeeded in moving the waste from the chimney and onto yourself, which is one way of cleaning the thing, I suppose."

"I'm sorry, ma'am, but I'm afraid if I clean anymore, the house will never be dirtier," I said, sheepishly motioning to the blackened canvas.

"Indeed," she said. "Very well, I suppose that's enough for the day. Come with me, and do not touch a thing—you are a filthy creature."

I followed rather willingly as she led me out of the house and across a field of long grass, on the other end of which sat the sawmill. The tall building hovered along the edge of the Whirry River, which turned the enormous waterwheel as it cut through the land. Moira stopped at the river's edge and turned to me as I trekked down the pale green embankment, leaving an expanding plume of black dust in my wake. I stopped beside her and looked down at the flowing current, steadily pushing the paddles of the wheel on an endless trip to the same place.

"That looks cold," I said, boldly stating the obvious on that late autumn afternoon.

"Oh, it is," she said with a slow nod of her head.

I watched as an orange leaf was carried downstream, ebbing and spinning on the clear surface. "Why are we—" I started before being suddenly interrupted by Moira, who nudged me in the back. Thrown off-balance, I tumbled down the remaining embankment, splashing head-first into the freezing water. I broke the surface, sputtering and gasping for breath, and floundered in a panic for several seconds before my feet hit the rocky riverbed. In a moment, I was standing, only to find myself barely waist-high in the river.

"Oh," I said, feeling more foolish than ever. I looked up to find Moira doubled over with laughter.

"And I was feeling so bored!" she laughed, wiping a tear from her eye. "Oh, you've just turned my day around."

Brushing my hair out of my eyes, I smiled at her outburst, the freezing water suddenly no match for the torch my heart had become.

"Should I just stay here, then?" I asked as she regained her composure.

"If you like," she replied with a devilish grin. "Though, you are almost clean again—one more dunk ought to do it, I should think. I don't feel like explaining to my father that his hired hand caught his death of cold because he decided to go swimming in October. You'd probably come off looking quite ridiculous."

"And we wouldn't want that now, would we," I said, looking down at my sopping self, murky fireplace refuse pouring off me. With my teeth now chattering, I held my nose and submerged myself once more. I broke the surface to the sound of Moira politely clapping before she offered me a hand out of the water. Slipping only twice on the overgrown slope, I emerged from the Whirry and eagerly followed her as she led me to the mill, away from the chilling autumn breeze.

Once inside the darkened building, with its creaking timbers and gentle burbling of passing waters, she lit a lantern and took me down to the cellar, where rows and rows of casks and barrels stood on a floor of straw and sawdust.

"What is this place?" I asked, shivering and hunched over to not knock my head on the low ceiling beams.

"This is the distillery. Father's been making his own spirits the last few years," she said, placing the lamp on the floor and arranging two empty, upended barrels in the corner. She patted one, indicating I should sit down.

"It doesn't taste good, but it does do the job of warming one up," she continued, dragging a heavy crate across the floor and sitting beside me. I watched in amazement as she flipped off the lid to the sound of clinking glass, revealing several bottles of deep amber liquor.

"Is this wise, ma'am?" I asked as she picked up a bottle and uncorked it with her teeth. I'd never had so much as one drink, let alone access to an entire bottle. I was suddenly anxious that I was about to make a fool of myself in front of this girl yet again.

"I don't care," she said, spitting out the cork. "Who's going to miss one bottle? My father *owns* the distillery. Now drink this before you catch your death of cold."

I eyed the bottle warily as she held it out to me, then looked around the cellar again to ensure we were alone.

"Is this a… a trap, ma'am?" I asked.

Moira sighed and pulled down an impressive slug from the bottle, making her eyes squint and her cheeks turn pink.

"There," she said, handing the bottle back. "No traps, see?"

Taking the drink from her, I examined the dark liquid before another chill ran through my body, and the dampness of my clothes became intolerable. Before I could think better of it, I took a drink. True to her word, it tasted awful, but it did burn like fire all the way down my throat and into my clenched stomach, where it somehow loosened all the knots of nervousness it found there.

"There's a lad," she said, slapping me gently on the face and grabbing back the bottle for another drink. "Better?"

I felt like I was going to vomit but nodded anyway, my head suddenly dizzy in a way I'd never known before. Moira laughed at me, and it was the sweetest sound I had ever heard.

I don't remember how much time passed, but the outside light seeping through the cracks of the floorboards overhead eventually faded into soft darkness. Our lantern seemed to cut more and more space out of the black, making our corner into a cave of flickering orange light.

Over half the bottle was now gone, and somehow we had ended up sitting on the floor and leaning precariously against the stone wall, which, at a certain point, had seemed a much more secure station than balancing on some barrels. Fascinated by the bottle, I held it close to my eyes and watched the remaining drink slosh around in a lazy circle. Beside me, Moira watched the liquor flow from one side of the bottle to the other, her head tilted drunkenly to the side, her enormously blue eyes as alert as ever.

"Splash," she whispered before breaking into her musical laugh. I looked over at her, surprised, and began laughing myself. It was the first word she'd said since we'd started drinking.

"Your father is going to be very, very... *very* upset about this," I slurred, nodding to myself.

"Ha!" she said, waving me off. "He won't have a clue, and even if he did, he's helpless before me. I'm the apple of his eye, don't you know."

"Is that so?" I replied.

"Mm-hmm," she said with an assured nod of her beautiful head. "I'm the apple of his eye and the potato of his ear—ha! Besides, I was just going to blame the chimneysweep anyway."

"Hey!" I cried. She laughed at my distress. "Oh, ma'am, don't joke like that—I get so nervous."

"It's *Moira!*" she exclaimed. "Not 'ma'am'—*Moira*. I'm not your schoolmistress, and I'm not sixty. Never again! You promise?" she said, pointing an accusing finger at me.

"Yes, ma'am, I promise."

She punched me a good one in the arm and took the bottle from me for another drink.

"And *you,*" she said, corking the bottle and rolling it on the floor, "I'm going to call you 'Ike.'"

"Ike?" I said. "Why is that?"

"Because 'Isaac' is *boring.* It's so stuffy, don't you think? It's just the least-interesting name I can think of."

"Oh, well… I'm sorry about that—I didn't realize you had such strong feelings about it."

"Would you rather I call you 'Ick'?" she teased.

"Oh, please, no—I'd never be able to live that down," I said, despairing at the thought.

"Well then, I've saved you, haven't I," she said, leaning into my face. I stared at her dumbly before she grabbed me by the collar with a yank. "Ike! Don't you see, I've *saved* you? I've saved you from being *boring!* Ha!" As she chuckled, pleased with herself, she dropped and laid the side of her head on my leg. "There's nothing worse than being boring," she murmured.

"I don't think I know what you mean, ma'am—Moira," I said, catching myself.

She turned her pale face up to me. "Don't you ever get bored? Don't you think this is all so *boring?*"

"What—this?" I asked, bleary and confused, pointing to us on the floor.

"No, you twit, not this!" she said. "*This* is *exciting!* I'm talking about the same town, the same people, the same… *routine.* It's just a toothless mountain lion gnawing on your leg, trying to pin you down and eat you up forever until you are nothing but bones in a pile."

"Hm… I don't know if I've ever seen mountain lions in these parts," I pondered.

She looked up at me again, her eyes great blue saucers. "Oh yes, the daughter of a rich man and a cleaner of pigs and feeder of chimneys—surely we are both living on the brink of extraordinary things." She laughed bitterly, and I soon found that I was stroking her hair.

"Actually, I just feed the pigs and clean the chimney," I said, enjoying the warmth of her closeness.

"Imagine feeding a chimney…" she said with a laugh. "Poor Ike. You know, there is adventure out there. I've read of it. Somewhere beyond Bootville, you can be your own person and not worry about what everyone says or thinks. There are stories to be told of bravery and heroism. Of great loves battling together against the storm of life rather than the fog. And you never have to be boring."

"And this?" I asked.

"*Exciting...*" she whispered, closing her eyes. They snapped open a moment later. "Did you know *I'm* having an adventure?" she asked, raising an eyebrow.

"Really?" I said, looking around at the dull wooden casks surrounding us. "And I thought this was just a basement."

"No, no, no," she said, waving me off and sitting up, much to my disappointment. She braced herself against the wall, suddenly motionless. "Oh… dizziness. No, not here—at home. Well, sort of at home—it's possibly the start of an adventure anyway."

"What sort of adventure?" I asked, both intrigued and immediately worried it might lead her away from me one day.

She leaned in close with excited eyes. "It's a *secret,*" she said in an exaggerated whisper.

"A secret?"

"A *secret* secret," she nodded. "Father says I'm never to speak of it."

"Oh," I replied, confused and disappointed.

"But not speaking of it is so *boring*, and I'm just *dying* to tell someone! And I like you, Ike. I want to trust you."

"You can trust me, I swear it. I'll not tell anyone."

She leaned in closer, her breath hot on my cheek. "Do you remember… the *funeral?"*

I was taken off-guard by such an odd question. "You mean… you mean the one where I dug the grave?"

She nodded.

"Well, of course I do. That was your butler, right?"

"Aberfoyle," she nodded, her voice soft. "Poor, poor Aberfoyle…"

I wasn't following her. "Yes, but… well, what about him?"

She looked at me with unblinking eyes that spoke of some unbearable weight upon her conscience. "Didn't you ever wonder why no one ever saw what was inside that box?"

The memories of those bizarre rumors flooded my head as she stared at me expectantly.

"Well, I—"

From outside, a loud clanging shattered the silence of the early evening, pulling us from the drunken cave of dreams we'd dug ourselves into. Moira sat up like a shot.

"That's the emergency bell," she said, panic in her eyes. "We must leave here before we're spotted." She leaped to her feet as though possessed by the very spirit of sobriety and pushed aside the crate of liquor before grabbing the lantern and my hand.

The cool air had begun to revive my blurred senses as we arrived out front of the manor to find the entire town assembled in the clearing. The aggressive ringing of the mounted emergency bell mixed with the unsettled murmuring of the crowd. Mayor Asten stood on the front steps, attempting to calm everyone.

"Father!" Moira cried as we approached the house.

"Moira! Where have you been? Inside the house right now, before they go mad!" he said, ushering her through the door. She cast a final apologetic glance at me before disappearing inside as her father shouted for the townsfolk's attention.

"Everyone, please! Try to maintain civility, I implore you!" he cried, his voice booming and vanishing into the nearby woods. As though scolded by an exhausted mother, the mob abashedly quieted itself. "I have just received word that the king's army is approaching Bootville."

The mob uttered a collective gasp and began muttering about 'that bloody King George' with anger and fear in their voices. The mayor held his hands out to calm them again.

"I understand your discontent, believe me," he continued, his voice quieter. "We've always known these horrible circumstances may one day befall us. It is true that the empire demands monies taken unjustly from the fruit of our labors."

The crowd murmured its collective agreement.

"And it is true that it is being taken without being offered the dignity of equal status as loyal subjects of the realm."

Again, the crowd agreed. A musket was fired into the air for good measure.

"And as mayor of this fine town—a town of its own values and sense of community within this colony of friends and family neighbors—I assure you that such actions will not stand!"

A roar as I had never known greeted this statement, a sound both primal and frightening, contained only by the assured presence of the great man on the steps. I watched, my stomach clenched like a fist clutching reins, as Mayor Asten raised his hands for silence.

"Now, I would beg of you, as mayor and friend to every Bootvillian: please return to your homes in peace on this night."

The mob groaned its disappointment at this, only to be hushed by its leader once more.

"I know that these circumstances greatly pain you," he said, "but this is not the night to exorcise those demons. The time will come for that, I have no doubt. Your energies would be wasted here and now, and you are better set to finding a *rational* solution to our problems."

The throng collectively gagged at the word 'rational' but was clearly defused in their passions.

"Go home to your families," Mayor Asten continued. "Go home and value what cannot be taxed or taken from you while you still can. Protect each other. Let us demonstrate solidarity in the face of the king's mighty arms and show these dogs of war that force alone may bend our branches… but it will not break them."

With that, the crowd watched as the great man entered his home and closed the door behind him, his face as placid as a lake at dawn.

CHAPTER 18
Color Change

THE SUN HAD not yet peeked above the horizon when I was awoken by the sounds of our future hell winding down the road.

It had started with the faint rattle of drums, which rang across the fens, bouncing from tor to tor, conquering the countryside before they had even set foot in the town proper. I alit from my bed and made for the window to see what on earth could be happening in this dismal and forgotten end of the village.

Through the wavy glass, I could only just make out the spiny creature that had slung itself over the crest of the wagon-worn path and had begun slithering in great ripples toward the town. At first, I thought I was still dreaming—surely this bristling dragon could only appear in the corners of my worst night terrors—but a wheeze and a snort distracted me, and I turned to find my old Dad looking out over my shoulder.

"Dad, what's that?" I said, my voice hardly a whisper.

"Mmmm," he replied with a slow nod, as though he'd been expecting this. "That'll be His Majesty's army, then."

The sound of clinking armor wares and the slapping of cheap boot soles pounded a rhythm of menace in the clear, windless morning. We ran outside in our nightclothes to watch as the epic collection of humanity passed. They flowed endlessly, their coats blending into one another so that it seemed the sky had been pricked and was bleeding through the valley beneath a cloud of flashing bayonets.

Dad and I watched from behind a jagged boulder as the might of the king's fighting force unfolded itself.

"Blimey, Dad—there are so many of them."

"Aye, lad—the fiercest fighting force in the world, that's what," he grumbled in reply, an aged hand absentmindedly rubbing his beard in time to the march.

"What are we going to do, Dad?"

My father turned to me, squinting into the rising sunlight. "We don't do anything, lad. We stay right here and pretend we're not even doing that."

"But the town, Dad!" I gasped, somewhat shocked by his plan. "They don't even know what's coming! Shouldn't we try to do something—warn them?"

The old man gave pause as he considered this. "You're right, boy," he said finally. "We should pack our kit and leave go of this place."

"What?" I cried out as he turned back to the house. "That wasn't what I was saying at all!"

"No, we must go," he said with a dismissive wave. "I've heard good things about Canada. Maybe we should go there and trade us some pelts or some such thing."

"But Dad—what about Moira?" I said, panicking at the thought of her in the clutches of the Redcoats. "They might do something to her! Doesn't that mean anything to you?"

My father grabbed me into his wiry grip and turned me around to face him dead-on, his expression more serious than I'd ever remembered.

"Now you listen here, boy," he said. "There's nothing you can do for them now, you understand? They'll be at the village green sooner than you could get there without being seen, and if they did see you sneaking about, they'd hang you. Or worse."

"But Dad—" I started. He shook me once, and I was startled to see true fear filling his eyes.

"You don't know what an armed fighting man is capable of, boy! They'll show you no mercy, do you hear me?"

I was shocked by his outburst—had never heard him so alarmed.

"War makes men into *animals*," he said, trying with all his might to make me understand. "And as animals… they will play with their food."

TRUE TO MY father's word, there was little hope of my reaching town before the army. The best I could do was make it to the square using a path through the back of the cemetery that only a local could have known about. Creeping my way parallel to Nightjar Street, I could round the butcher's stall and hide behind a barrel of animal blood and rainwater I knew all too well from my experiences scrubbing the killing floor.

The square was eerily silent, empty of the usual morning business that gave the village its life. Even the chimneys were quiet of smoke. The vendors and artisans had shut their doors and could be seen poking their heads through closed window hangings as the soldiers clattered their way to and through the crossroads, past the lamppost outside the Widow's Watch. They were led by a small pack of horse-mounted men wearing such elaborate uniforms that they could only be officers. Slowing their pace, they eyed the deserted street and shops with suspicion. From the group emerged a man who was nothing if not a commander, who led his horse slowly to the center of the green, where a flagpole bore the blue and gold colors of Bootville.

He was tall in the saddle and wrapped in a long, dark traveling cloak. His crested hat was cocked to the side over a lean face that bore no emotion, his eyes cold and dead as he surveyed the quiet shops around him, his hand resting lightly on the hilt of his saber. As he sat, taking in the silence with his chilling consideration, loud hoof-falls echoed from building to building as a small, rotund man with a nasty face approached from the opposite end of town. The tall officer sidestepped his mount to face this paunchy creature as he pulled up to a stop.

"Lieutenant Crain, your report," the tall man said in a deep voice that was clearly accustomed to speaking as authority itself.

"Sir, there is no sign of life to report as of yet," the lieutenant said. He turned in his saddle and quickly surveyed their surroundings as though to reaffirm his words. "The scouts have rounded the village and found no one about. Colonel, you don't suppose they've turned tail and run, do you?"

The colonel's dark chuckle threatened to shake the remaining leaves from the canopy above them as his face twisted ever so slightly into a serpentine smile.

"Come, listen with me, Crain," he intoned. "Do you hear what I do?"

The two men sat, unspeaking, as a breeze ran through the square, eliciting a creaking of the boot tree limbs.

The lieutenant looked up at his superior, confused. "I don't hear nothing, Sir."

"Precisely, Crain—what you do not hear is the sound of a hundred breaths being held as they watch their fates sorted before their very eyes. That is the sound of *fear*. No, Crain, they are here."

The lieutenant shifted in his saddle, clearly uncomfortable at the idea of being watched by those he could not see. "And your orders, Sir?"

"Have the force make camp on the outskirts. Fortifications for the officers' garrison shall go here, and we shall quarter at that hideous inn at the crossroads. But first..." he paused, turning his stallion in a small circle, casting his calculating eye upon the dead village, "...roust the locals."

Crain rode back to the clutch of officers gathered outside the Watch and relayed the orders. Within minutes the Redcoats were bleeding down the street, pounding on the locked doors, demanding an audience. The colonel and his lieutenant watched with an air of amusement.

"Careful, men," the colonel rumbled. "There may still be some fight in this old trough yet." Beside him, Crain laughed harshly as the townsfolk slowly emerged from their shops and homes, stone-faced and mute. When he was satisfied with the size of his crowd, the colonel spurred his horse into an apathetic walk before them.

"Denizens of His Majesty's imperial colonies, take heed. My name is Colonel Jack Cavendish, though you shall now address me as 'Sir.' As you are no doubt aware, a rebellion is attempting to take root on this continent, and as you are about to learn, I am here to dig it up before this sickness has time to spread.

"Now, I know you are all loyal to your king, and as such, I *know* you will embrace this occupation with open arms as you would the king himself." The menace soaking his voice left little room for argument. "In the weapon of war, the king is the fist that wields the sword, and we are the blade. Stand by and serve your soldiers—your countrymen—and you shall not find yourself in its path."

Here, the townspeople looked at each other but said nothing in response to this threat. Lieutenant Crain began laughing once more, eyeing them with a hungry leer.

"I am told by your neighbors," the tall colonel continued, "that you have a reputation for surly isolation and minding your own. I have no qualms with this, so long as you recognize my authority. Hear me now: *I* am in charge, and so long as the breath of rebellion does not warm your tongues, you shall be allowed to keep them. Now, what say you?"

Tension hung heavy as the colonel awaited Bootville's response. From my hiding spot, I could just make out the movement of his hand from the reins to his sword and could sense the eyes of the town following it as it rested there, palm-to-hilt. It seemed as though even the animals in the nearby woods had gone quiet.

Expecting the worst, I was astonished when a woman I recognized as the town baker took a step forward. Offering an iron glare to the colonel, she spat on the ground in front of him before silently walking back to her shop and closing the door behind her.

Soon, the entire town followed her lead, throwing icy stares and gobbing on the now-occupied soil of their homeland. As the shutting of heavy wooden doors rang out across the green like muffled musket fire, Colonel Cavendish chuckled his sinister chuckle once more. Lieutenant Crain stared at him in confusion at this unexpected response. "Sir?"

"Ah, Crain, but these Americans amuse me so," the colonel said with a nasty smile. He reined his horse onto its back legs before turning it toward the Widow's Watch. "Come along now—I could use a drink."

I watched, awestruck, as they made their way across the green while the remaining soldiers began setting about their duties. Amidst a final gale of laughter, I could hear the colonel's voice split the thick air as he barked out, *"Raise the Jack!"*

As THE COLORS of Bootville's standard were replaced with the red, white, and blue of the crosses of Saints George and Andrew, so too did the power of our village change hands, leaving me behind the stinking butcher barrel to figure out what could be done. To my simple eyes, the situation seemed hopeless beneath those lead skies, and my only solace came in the knowledge that my Moira was not around to be threatened. I watched in horrified fascination as morning became afternoon, and the town square became an occupied outpost. The Redcoats worked quickly and efficiently in constructing their camp, exercising the military industry that had let them take over half the world.

From across the green, the echoes of Colonel Cavendish and his underlings' laughter rang out from the narrow windows of the Widow's Watch as they waged war on the tavern's supply of ale. They did not reappear until the sun, buried somewhere behind the clouds above, began to descend in its typical autumnal haste.

Alerted by the slamming of doors and the preparation of horses, I peeked from behind my barrel and began panicking anew. The colonel and his lieutenant, along with a small pack of foot soldiers, began making their way across the square, where, to my unending dismay, they turned down the northbound lane leading through the proud forest of boot trees and, eventually, to Asten Manor.

My heart threatened to explode from my chest as I gathered myself. Something had to be done, and I would have to do it, though *what* exactly had to be done remained mysterious. Summoning my small reservoir of courage and calling upon the sneakiness I had inherited as the son of a criminal mind, I crept around the back of the town's buildings without being spotted by the many patrolling guards. I then quietly disappeared into the rampaging undergrowth of the towering woods.

I kept a respectful distance between myself and the colonel's party, and soon the grand house was in sight. As the Redcoats made their way up the path, I stumbled my way behind the tree line around the clearing before shielding myself behind the large timber mill, now eerily quiet. Ever so silently, I crawled my way around the side of the house and poked my head around the corner to watch the scene playing out at the front door.

Colonel Cavendish sat calmly upon his stallion as the sounds of his men rampaging through the house were thrown across the grassy clearing. He watched with a placid expression as Mayor Asten, that most civilized and dignified man, was thrown off the front steps in his shirt sleeves by two soldiers who then proceeded to stand him and hold him in place by the arms. The bayonets affixed to their muskets glowed like exaggerated candle flames as they reflected the soft orange of the setting sun.

The colonel leaned forward in his saddle as he addressed the great man, now humbled. Mayor Asten, his face bleeding and clothes dirty and rumpled, maintained the posture of a lord headed to Parliament and met the colonel's gaze with a look of stony resolve.

"*Ex*-Mayor Asten, I presume?" the colonel rumbled, sounding slightly bored. "Such a pleasure. My name is—"

"I know who *you* are, Colonel Cavendish," the mayor interrupted without a trace of fear in his voice, his face a mask of contempt. "The tales of your atrocious deeds and abuses of power have been ringing through the colonies since before you even set foot back on this continent."

"Ah yes, my… *reputation*," the colonel said with a smile that did not touch his eyes. "You know, it's a funny thing about those stories, Mr. ex-Mayor—no one has ever been found alive to verify them. Curious, is it not?"

"There is no amount of rain or flood that could wash away the blood you've shed. You're an animal amongst men and a disgrace to civilization. The king would kick the stool from beneath your feet on the gallows himself if he knew half the crimes you've committed in the name of the crown."

I closed my eyes, fearing the worst from the mayor's outburst, but to my surprise, Colonel Cavendish merely laughed. I could smell the stink of liquor on his breath from where I was crouched, several feet down the manor's façade.

"Ah, well-spoken, Mr. ex-Mayor," the colonel chuckled. "I do so love being lectured about the monarchy by a treasonous rebel leader—you've just made my night."

"Try as you might, your army will never find a foothold on this land," Mayor Asten said, his voice calm. "The fens will not bear the weight of oppression."

"Hm, perhaps not now," the colonel replied, "but what if they were filled with the carcasses of your famous boot trees? Wouldn't that be something?" He turned to consider the surrounding forest, chuckling.

"These trees are all we have," the mayor said, clearly shaken by the idea of their destruction. "They are our future."

Colonel Cavendish bent low in his saddle to meet the mayor's eyes dead-on. "And yet how quickly the future becomes the past."

A scream erupted inside the manor, and the colonel straightened as Crain emerged, pushing a struggling Moira along with him. I went mad at the sight of his hands on her, and my vision turned red as I leaped to my feet.

"Moira, no!" I cried, running towards them, fully prepared to rip the laughing lieutenant apart, piece by piece. My assault caught everyone off-guard, but Crain easily sidestepped my charge and cuffed me on the back of the head, sending me sprawling into the dirt. The pain was blinding and left me so dizzy that I could not find the proper direction in which to stand up.

"Ike!" Moira cried, struggling in the nasty lieutenant's clutches. "You leave him alone!" She stomped down on Crain's foot, but he remained her leering captor.

"Hey, look, Colonel!" Lieutenant Crain cackled, kicking a hail of stones in my face. "It's George Washington, come to save the day!"

The Redcoats laughed uproariously as I struggled to right myself.

"A noble effort, Young Master Washington," Colonel Cavendish said, offering a casual salute and a wicked smile, "but Boston this is not, I'm afraid."

He turned once more to the mayor. "As of now, you are under house arrest on suspicion of being a traitor. Bring the girl, Crain—perhaps her absence will remind the ex-mayor that he should be on his best behavior."

With that, he wheeled his mount and headed back towards town. Lieutenant Crain gave me a sharp kick to the midsection as he passed, laughing and dragging my poor Moira behind him.

"Ike!" she called back to me. "Ike, I'm so sorry!" And then she was gone, swallowed up by the depths of the woods.

Mayor Asten helped me to my feet. "Come along, my boy," he said, supporting my weight.

"Moira…" I mumbled as he walked me to the house.

"Step aside, you fools!" he barked at the remaining foot soldiers as he brushed past them and led me inside. "If you must be here, then at least stay out of the way!"

We entered his library, where he sat me in a chair and quickly shut the door behind us. Only when it was closed did he seem to exhale. He moved to a side table where a pitcher and cups sat and poured a drink of water with trembling hands before sitting in a chair beside me.

I gratefully took the cup from him and drank, hoping it might drown the ringing in my ears.

"There now," he said, his voice calm. "Feeling better?"

I nodded, but it only rattled my brains back into a frenzy.

"That was a very brave thing you did for my baby girl back there," he continued. "She's spoken very highly of you—it's Isaac, isn't it?"

I nodded again, wincing. "I'm so sorry, my lord," I said, my thoughts awash with despair. "I should have… I should have done something—"

"Fear not, lad," he said, placing a fatherly hand on my shoulder. He paused as though considering something, battling over a decision in his mind. "All is not yet lost. Things have gone bleak, it's true, but we can right the ship if we hurry."

"We can?" I asked, my thinking clouded with confusion.

"That's right, my boy," he said, looking me in the eye. "But I will need your help. You can stop all this madness and save your family, the town, and Moira. Now, will you help me?"

I was taken aback by his words; I was less than useless, a failure in everything, unable to even properly stand up in defense of my beloved. I had less value than the very dirt I had fallen into. What good would I be to this man?

He stared at me expectantly, and my father's words flashed in my mind: *Don't stick your neck out for anybody. Keep your head down and mind your own.*

They clung to my thoughts like an overgrown blanket of ivy, and just as I was about to carry out their mandate, their stifling vines were drawn away, and I was left with the memory of Moira's lovely face and the kindness she had shown me. I then realized that I needn't bow to our cynical family motto. I could be more if only I had the strength to choose such a path.

My throat was as rough as the raw timber down at the sawmill as I looked up at the great man.

"I will do whatever it takes."

CHAPTER 19
The Killing Floor

Night had swept in quickly upon fresh bat wings by the time I'd made my way back to the town square, where I was met with bonfires and drunken revelry. The officers' encampment howled with laughter and the random firing of muskets while the townspeople appeared to be safely locked inside their homes.

As I crept through the shadows and fog, I clutched the flat, rectangular package the mayor had placed in my care with shaky, almost reluctant hands.

"Deliver this to my daughter—she will know what must be done," the great man had said before wishing me luck and sending me out the window, so the guards would not see me.

Having arrived at the rear of the Widow's Watch, I looked down at the parcel, wrapped in a canvas sheet, and hefted it, wondering if it was worth risking my life for. I answered myself without hesitation: if it meant saving Moira's life, then, yes, I would gladly throw my own to the winds of fate. Resolved on this issue, I quietly opened the back door and entered the tavern.

The kitchen was disturbingly absent of its usual clanking and shouting, and I guessed that the proprietors must have locked themselves upstairs in their private chambers. Certainly, they were not the type of people who would serve this brutish army of occupation.

As I picked my way through the maze of iron stoves, ovens, and cured meats hanging from the ceiling, I could hear the faint sound of music and carousing from behind the door to the main dining room. I was nearly ill as I bumped into a freshly skinned pig, its viscera fully exposed, and I wondered if it had been one of the swine I had fed in better days.

Crouching low, I pressed my ear against the greasy wood of the door and heard the voices of my two new enemies, slurring their speech and bursting into fits of hysterical laughter. The music was some sort of formal waltz, at odds with the soldiers' barbaric conversation and reminiscent of music I had so often heard through the windows of the parlor at Asten Manor—my stall-mucking serenade.

I pushed the door open slightly and peered through the crack. After being surrounded by so much darkness, the grand stone fireplace was momentarily blinding. It cast dancing shadows on the old tables and chairs and illuminated a large pile of pumpkins, corn, and other fruits of the recent harvest. This yield would have been used for the yearly celebration of another farming season ended, but it now lay useless, stacked to the ceiling beams in a corner.

In front of this bounty sat the familiar profile of the lovely Moira, playing the tunes of civilized drawing rooms the world over on the Watch's beat-up clavichord and looking rather bored by it all. My breath caught in my throat as I watched her at the mercy of these animals. Their shadows taunted me, flickering and distorted along the wooden planks of the floor as they swam the seas of an ale-soaked evening. Their voices boomed as they reminisced about campaigns gone by and how they wished their mate—someone they called "Gentleman Johnny"—was with them. I judged them distracted enough with their clanking of tankards to make my way to Moira.

Gathering my wits, I slunk low along the tavern's stony wall, crawling on two knees and one hand with the other clutching the package. I paused in a large swath of darkness cast by the mountain of pumpkins in the face of the roaring fireplace and was about to scamper the few remaining feet to Moira when Lieutenant Crain slammed his mug down on the table and looked my way.

"Hey, *you*—stop right there!"

I froze, feeling as though I'd been caught nicking biscuits as the portly man stood, the sound of his chair scraping the floor like the moaning of a hungry banshee. Moira had stopped playing and warily looked over at the bleary-eyed lieutenant. With a wave of relief, I realized that he had been addressing her. I remained motionless in my uncomfortable-yet-hidden crouch.

"Enough with the funeral music, love—it's absolute *rubbish!*" Lieutenant Crain shouted as Jack sat beside him, running his thumb over the blade of his saber and looking amused by his underling. "Play us something a fighting man can dance to, eh? You bloody Americans wouldn't know a jig if it slapped you across the face!"

Moira sighed with exasperation and proceeded to bang out a simple martial tune more suited to fife and fiddle than a parlor clavichord.

"Crain, you are a masterfully loathsome brute," Colonel Cavendish commented over the tune, a wicked grin stitched across his face. "Remind me to recommend you for an ambassadorship when we return home."

"Aim to please, Sir," the lieutenant said, offering a crooked salute that knocked his hat from his head. They both collapsed into laughter and began singing along to the tune—something praising the king and his loyal regiment of foot, with a few words thrown in that even sailors would have found inappropriate. I felt drunk just looking at them.

Their party with themselves was quickly interrupted by the familiar clanging of the town bell. Colonel Cavendish turned in his chair and stared out the small window beside the front door, a peevish frown upon his face.

"Crain," he muttered to his lieutenant, who was too busy dancing to notice. "*Lieutenant Crain!*" he roared at the small man, who stopped in mid-jig, confused. "Do go and check what that racket's about—it's ruining my good time. Feel free to threaten them with the gallows if you must."

"Aye, Sir, will do!" Crain toadied, offering another awkward salute before stumbling out the door, screaming at anyone who might be in the area.

"It's my party, and they'll die if I want them to," the colonel mumbled before collapsing onto the maps and charts spread out on the table before him, his hand still clutching his tankard of ale. I watched as Moira took note of Colonel Cavendish's snoring and began playing a gentle lullaby, easing him deeper into the realm of nod. I knew then that this would be my only opportunity to act.

"Moira!" I whispered from my shadow. She turned with a start, her fist raised and wearing an expression that said she was not afraid to use it. I peered out from behind the package, which I'd thrown up in defense.

"Ike?" she said, hardly believing her own eyes. "Is that really you?"

Lowering the wrapped bundle, I leaned forward into the firelight and smiled nervously. "Hello, ma'am—er, Moira."

"What are you doing here?" she said, glancing over at the slumbering colonel. "If he sees you again, he'll kill you for sure."

I gazed up at her and shrugged. "At least it's not been boring, right?"

Her hand flew over her mouth to stifle a laugh. "It's good to see you," she said, beaming. "What is your plan?"

Keeping low, I shuffled over to her and passed over the package, which she accepted, tilting her head to the side in curiosity.

"Your father told me to give you that," I said, looking over at the colonel. "I don't know what it is, but he said you'd know what to do."

Her relief in seeing me faded, and the blood drained from her face as she made some realization about her father's mysterious package.

"Moira, what is it?" I asked, alarmed by this sudden change of temperament. As I spoke, the waters around our brief island of peace began to drain. I could now hear the shouts of Lieutenant Crain drawing near as he returned from the village green. Across the room, the colonel began to stir from his sleep.

Moira grabbed my arm, a panicked look in her eyes. "Ike, you've got to hide—and whatever you do, *keep your ears covered.*"

"But, what—"

The door to the Watch flew open, and I dived into the shadow beneath the clavichord just as Lieutenant Crain wove his way back into the dining room.

"Colonel, I've got some absolutely smashing news!" he bellowed, red-faced and panting.

The colonel sat bolt upright and dragged a hand down his face to sober himself. "Hm? What are you yammering about, Crain?"

"Sir, it's brilliant! The rebel army has been scouted out! They're moving under cover of darkness towards Collartown as we speak!" the lieutenant said, practically bursting with the news.

The tall colonel stood, his cloak rippling as he threw his hands upon the table, his mad eyes darting around the maps before him. "*Collartown...*" he grumbled to himself. "At last, we can force an engagement!"

"I knew you'd like it, Sir," Lieutenant Crain said with a sloppy grin. "I've already passed on orders to wake the men for mobilization."

Colonel Cavendish chuckled with sinister amusement, and as he did, I felt something brush against my arm. I looked down to find the canvas wrapping from the package in a rumpled pile on the floor. I'd no sooner picked it up when Moira began playing the instrument once more.

I feel safe in saying that it was the most off-putting tune I have ever heard. The notes began to fill the large room, floating over each other in such an odd way that it was uncomfortable to listen to them. I looked over to see the colonel and his lieutenant engrossed in plotting a course on their maps and was shocked to see the space between us moving. At first, I thought it must be from the heat emanating from the fireplace, but I soon realized the entire room was rippling and warping, precisely mirroring the way my stomach had begun to feel.

Colonel Cavendish paused as his finger traced a route on one of his more detailed charts. "Crain," he said, slightly cocking his head in concentration. "What is that?"

"Um… what is what, Sir?" Lieutenant Crain replied, suddenly looking ill as he mopped sweat from his pasty brow.

The colonel placed one spidery hand against his own temple, blinking rapidly. "That… that *music*." He began to pitch slightly as though the earth was avalanching itself away from beneath his boots. "What is that *dreadful music?*"

They looked over to their prisoner, who began playing with even more intensity, each plucking of string causing the air to move like swirling waters. Lieutenant Crain swooned and collapsed onto one arm on the table with a dull thud, and I suddenly remembered Moira's last words to me.

My entire body now aching, I clasped my hands over my ears and was racked with a burning sensation over my skin as I watched through blurring and bending vision as Colonel Cavendish stumbled, kicking his chair away behind him. He grabbed his saber and shouted across the room at Moira, *"Stop! Stop that sound at once!"*

But Moira did not stop; she only played louder and more aggressively. I could feel the vibration of the notes travel through the wood of the instrument to the planks below as the invisible scalding ran across me. The pain was relentless, and I collapsed onto my side as my body twisted unnaturally, my teeth grinding together. Unable to stop myself, I released a hand from my head and held it in front of my face as the dirge entered my ear again, its fractured, nightmarish melody crawling its way into my brains. I looked on in horror as the skin of my hand began to waste away before my very eyes, moving from something young and alive to something pale and thin, like weak paper. It began to grind itself into desiccation as though being attacked by an unseen mortar and pestle, the feeling sweeping across my body, tearing at me until I caught a glimpse of white beneath. The bones of my hand were revealed to me as they undressed themselves of my flesh, and I could only hope that I would soon be dead.

"No!" the colonel cried out across the room, lunging forward into the table, flipping it over, and scattering its contents onto the floor as his towering bulk collapsed out of sight behind it. The lieutenant was also scattered and thrown halfway across the room, where he landed in a writhing mess. His compact form had also begun changing as he threw his rapidly decaying arms over his head in a desperate crawl across the inn's floor, howling in a chilling, primal torment.

The music escalated in complexity as it fervently tore away at its audience. Through wave after wave of pain, I could feel my insides fall apart and watched, helpless, as the lieutenant scrabbled his way toward Moira, straining with the effort. I saw his head loll upon his shoulders in agony, and I swear I caught his eye as he clawed for his dagger, collapsing then rising, collapsing and rising, over and over again like tides lapping at the shore. Despite the crippling forces I knew to be at work upon his body, he was soon upon her, shaking and salivating through his exposed jaw, a death's-head with purpose.

In a final burst of energy, he forced himself onto his knees and lunged at my poor girl while she played us into our inevitable graves. The music stopped as he fell upon her, only to be replaced by her screaming. As I gasped my last breath, I could hear the scream cut off by a wet gagging sound and saw her legs stiffen while the lieutenant's skeletal form was thrown into the pile of brilliantly-orange pumpkins. I felt the vibration as Moira's lifeless body crashed onto the keyboard in a corpse-sized chord as sour and haphazard as this very night it seemed to echo. Her blood ran down her body and bled through the cracks of the instrument in a thick rain, pooling around me and spattering its way to the now-abandoned dagger lying mere feet away on the floor. I don't remember everything going black, but black it must have gone, for now I am here, lost and wishing more than ever that I was dead.

ELYSE PUT HER hand over her mouth as Ike collapsed into quiet sobbing once more. Will, Patrick, and Colin exchanged ashen looks as the weeping stretched throughout the otherwise silent room.

Gingerly placing her hand on the back of Ike's cold skull, Elyse tried her best to calm him. "Poor Ike," she whispered. "Poor, poor Ike."

"That is mental," Patrick said with a shake of his head.

"Yeah," Will nodded. "And those guys are running around out there right now."

"In our neighborhood," Patrick added.

Will turned to him. "You just had to go and play the song, didn't you."

"I'm sorry!" said Patrick. "You know how I like to show off if there's a keyboard around! It's what I *do!*"

"And look where it's gotten us," Will said with a pitying shake of his head.

"I didn't know some blood-lusting sociopath with a license to kill would be resurrected across two centuries, did I!? Give me a break—I've been dead for a year! It's a very groggy sensation."

"I hate to say it," said Will, "but there's probably a good chance you'll be dead again soon if those guys are willing to kill an unarmed girl." Ike howled in anguish.

"We're all dead," Colin intoned, scratching the side of his nose.

Will pointed to him and looked at Patrick. "Yep, see? The human calculator says he wants us dead."

"He wants the *book,*" Elyse said, rising. The boys watched as she crossed the garage to retrieve her bag. Pulling out the *Macabrium*, she held it out to Ike. "Is this the book you saw that night?"

Ike recoiled at the sight of it, his entire frame tremulous with fear as he threw his hands up in front of his face.

"You should take that as a 'yes,'" Patrick murmured.

Elyse absentmindedly ran her fingers over the smooth, worn leather of the cover, her brain whirring away behind black coffee eyes as she pondered. "It doesn't make any sense," she said with a shake of her head.

"Well, yeah…" said Will with a subtle nod in Patrick's direction.

"No, I mean, it actually doesn't make any sense—the *Macabrium* brings the dead *back,* right?"

"Um, yeah."

"So, why would it have *caused* death back in Ike's time?"

"I have no idea," said Patrick while Will shrugged.

"It's a nullifier," said Colin with a deliberate blink.

"Yeah." Elyse ruminated a moment more and then stood, stuffing the book back into the bag. "Okay, new plan: we need to know more about all of this, and I think I know where to go."

"And where's that?" asked Will.

Elyse ignored him. "You should take Ike back to our house, and we'll meet up there."

"Wait—why?" Will frowned as she handed him the bag and went to get her violin case.

"Because it's closer to town," she said, forcing the case into his hand.

"You're going into town? Isn't that sort of dangerous with the Spicy Jack guy looking for you?"

"Don't be a wreck, it's gonna be packed there—Halloween, remember?"

"Yeah, but I don't like the idea of you going off alone."

"I'll take Colin with me—you game, Colin?"

"Yes," he replied.

"See? We'll be okay. You know we can't take Ike with us."

Will sighed. "*Elyse*—"

"*William,*" she said, mimicking his exasperation while reaching up and grabbing a fistful of his hair. He winced in pain, completely at her mercy. Patrick stood beside Ike, his arms crossed, watching this exchange with great interest and uncharacteristic silence.

She leaned into Will, her voice low. "I'm a big girl, right?" He nodded, tilting his head to the side to alleviate the sharp pulling sensation. "Good, I'm glad we agree." She released his hair and gave him two gentle slaps on the cheek. "We'll meet up soon, I promise. Now promise me."

"Promise you what?"

"Promise me you'll take care of my brother."

CHAPTER 20
Wayfaring Hellions

WHILE IT MAY seem obvious, it does occasionally bear repeating that the human brain is an extraordinary thing. Resilient and adaptive during times of great stress, it is capable of convincing itself that the unusual is usual, the unnatural is natural, and the incomprehensible is easily comprehended. If the world as we know it is dictated by that which we perceive with the mind, then it makes sense that during these tumultuous turnings of the synaptic tides, a brain can break through previously unconsidered boundaries of acceptance and reaction. It is here that some semblance of normalcy is maintained, through which shall be found the grandeur of self-preservation.

It is as though the normal rules by which we are all governed are suspended indefinitely and without ceremony, pending a return to properly civilized conditions—a rain delay for sanity, if you will. The intricate tapestry of human history (sometimes exciting, mostly boring) is punctuated with these circumstantial shifts demanding a flexible brain, and to its credit, the brain's hunger for survival and perpetuation usually comes out on top.

Will Castle was surprised to discover himself breathing the cool, rarified air of this contradictory rule-bending, currently manifest in the shape of two skeletons—one quite real, the other a scorched costume—both in varying states of being undead.

"This is so weird," Will said, his mind neatly summing up the scene as best it could to continue functioning.

"You're telling me," Patrick muttered, casting a sideways glance at Ike. The new arrival's boney kneecaps clacked against one another as his few remaining muscles and tendons struggled to balance his precarious, off-white torso and skull in an upright position. "He's kind of creepy, isn't he?"

Will squinted at his translucent best friend, who had, until very recently, been a year in the grave and was currently calling the kettle black.

"You're pretty creepy yourself, you know," he said.

"Hey, you're the one hanging out with us, friend," Patrick said with a shrug.

In an evening thus far filled with incredible things, Will had found the ease of Patrick's return to be the most incredible turn of all. His friend's reappearance had almost completely erased the previous year's mourning, and while the recesses of his mind couldn't help grappling with the incompatibility of the situation (which existed as an almost imperceptible awkwardness, like a painting hanging slightly crooked from a museum wall), Will could not help but feel relieved that Patrick was back. It made things feel almost... *normal*. Like he'd only been away on vacation.

As the strange trio made their way from the Niemann garage laboratory, down the drive, and back to the crowded sidewalk, Will realized that the seemingly mundane task of going to the Korbin house and waiting for backup was easier said than done. Sure, Patrick was see-through, but at least he had flesh and eyeballs. Allowing for the inclination of adults to only see what they want to see, he could easily pass as an enthusiastic trick-or-treater with a talent for face painting. Ike, on the other hand, was truly a walking nightmare.

A skeleton hanging in the corner of an anatomy classroom seems normal, its relentlessly toothy grin lending it an almost rakish, devil-may-care quality, like a calcified Cary Grant at a cocktail party. A skeleton ambling shakily down a dark street, jumping in fear of anything that does not date back to the 18th century, seems exactly like what it is: an incomprehensible freak show.

Almost immediately upon their joining the flow of pedestrian traffic, a young witch looked up to see poor Ike in all of his unnaturally skeletal glory and began screaming the piercing scream known to beleaguered parents around the world. Some of those around them reacted similarly, while others merely gasped, and still others laughed good-naturedly at what must surely be a Halloween prank. Regardless of the form this attention took, it was still attention, and Will knew they would have to act.

Skittish as he was, Ike acted quicker and promptly ran down the street with his bizarre, loping stride, his gangly ulnas waving over his head as he screamed in fright as well. Will and Patrick stood frozen, mouths agape.

"Wow, look at him go," Patrick marveled as their boney compatriot was swallowed by a costumed mob, many of whom began weeping with unbridled terror. He crossed his arms and shook his head. "Memento Mori, crybabies."

"Um, this is not exactly what I had in mind," Will said, scratching his head.

"I suppose we should follow him?"

"I really can't see how it would lead to any good if we didn't. And believe me, I'm trying."

And so, following a thread of screams and laughter that wound its way around several blocks, the pair jogged their way through Ike's wake of terror, in which he'd left more than one child sobbing beside their bag of candy. After a solid seven minutes of this, the boys clomped to a stop and doubled over, gasping.

"Do you hear anything?" Will asked between breaths, adjusting the shoulder straps of Elyse's violin case and book bag.

Patrick shook his head. "Nah, nothing like it was—oh man, I've got a stitch like you wouldn't believe!" he said, clutching his side. "I feel like I'm being gored by a rhino."

"Can you really cramp up if you're dead?" Will asked, giving him an odd look.

"Dude, I'm a piano player, not Jesse Owens—the last time I ran on purpose, I was six, and that was only because Dad found out I was feeding nachos to the grouper," said Patrick.

"I don't know, I just figured you'd have some kind of mutant abilities or something if you're the walking dead."

"Man, as far as I can tell, I don't have *any* powers – no sixth sense, no laser eyes—nothing," Patrick replied with a shake of his head.

"Well, that sucks."

"I have to tell you, I'm feeling pretty ripped off."

Will looked around, trying to make out shapes in the surrounding darkness. Their chase had taken them to a small side street, along which sat backyards, trees, and a lone streetlamp.

"I suppose we better find this guy," Will sighed. "This is like having some kind of crummy new pet."

The boys began walking around, softly calling Ike's name into the shadows and bushes. Within moments, a rustle of branches drew their attention upwards, where he could be seen clutching onto a low branch.

"Hey, buddy—you doing all right up there?" called Will.

"I am so *hated!*" Ike replied, his voice hoarse and quivering. "They think me an abomination."

"Yeah, well… it doesn't look good, I'll give you that. But nobody called you abominable," said Will, grasping for anything remotely reassuring.

"Yeah, they were too busy screaming," Patrick added under his breath. Will gave him a look and sharply shook his head. From his branch, Ike sobbed.

"Hey, Ike, don't listen to him—he's just as nightmarish and hideous as you are," Will said. "You wanna stay up there for a minute and, uh… gather yourself?" Ike nodded, hunching lower on his branch. "Okay then, you do that. Me and Pat are gonna figure something out so you won't get screamed at, so just take it easy."

"Yeah, rest your weary bones," said Patrick as they turned from the tree to the street.

"This is not going well," Will said.

"You noticed that, huh?" Patrick replied.

"I can't imagine Jack is faring any better than this guy, right?" Will asked, pointing his thumb back to the tree.

"Well, you know, Jack was wearing pants, so I think maybe he is. And a hat—everybody looks better with a hat on."

"It was kind of jaunty, wasn't it."

"Wide-brimmed, sort of angled to the side—yeah, he'd do well in a job interview."

"First impressions are everything."

"Provided they're not rotting or end in murder."

Will considered things for a moment. "Well, I don't even have a jacket, and your clothes are see-through. *And* they have a skeleton on them, which does sort of defeat the purpose."

"True…" said Patrick, rubbing his chin in thought. He looked up suddenly. "Hey! We could get a branch…"

"Yeah?"

"…and we tie him to the branch with your shoelaces, so he looks like one of those puppets!"

Will frowned. "Like a marionette?"

"Yeah, I guess—everyone loves a good puppet."

"Do they?"

"Well, he'll look like a crazy Halloween prop, right?"

Will frowned. "No offense, but I don't really feel like puppeteering my way across town."

Patrick looked at him, annoyed. "Well, okay, joy-kill—he followed us from your place to Colin's, so let's have him stick to the shrubbery, how about that?"

"I'm not going to have him scrabbling through the thickets like a stupid ground squirrel, that's ridiculous," Will said, crossing his arms.

"Uh, did you not just hear his story? He was *always* creeping around! It sounds like he spent most of his life keeping to the bushes. And give me a break—you yourself just said he was a pet," said Patrick.

"He's a person!" Will said in his loudest whisper.

"Ah, he's a bone bag and a dead one at that," Patrick said, waving him off. "I say we have him go bustle in his hedgerow and get on with our lives! Or deaths, as it were."

"This is getting idiotic," Will said, kicking a rock down the sidewalk in frustration, "We've gotta get him some clothes."

"Okay, so we go to somebody's house and ask to borrow a sweater—how's that blow your hair back, Mr. Think Tank?"

Will sighed and considered this. "Okay, so, we'll go around the block and, uh… I'll pretend like I've lost my parents and I'm scared and alone and freezing. How about that?"

"Uh-huh," Patrick said, raising a skeptical eyebrow. "You're really bringing a tear to a glass eye over here. If Elyse were here, she'd play her violin for you."

"Let's just do this."

"I'm just saying, you're not exactly a Dickensian seven-year-old," Patrick said as they turned back to the tree.

"I don't even know what that means."

"And who leaves the house in October without at least a light jacket?"

After a long minute of coaxing and carefully worded reassurances, they gathered Ike from his tree and told him their loosely constructed plan. Ike nodded and didn't even object when Patrick told him to stick behind the shrubbery as they began their search for a front door that might somehow indicate a surplus of disposable jackets. As they walked, trying their best to ignore the rustling of bushes beside them, Will could not help but notice that, despite the emergency of their situation, this was the most fun he could remember having in a very long while.

"This is like old times, isn't it?" he said to Patrick, who turned to him with his trademark manic grin.

"Yeah, man, this is a real riot," he said. "I mean, it's weird to think I've been missing everything for a year. But then, it must be super weird for you too. It's kind of doing a real number on my brain right now."

"Yeah…" Will said, unsure of how to put his own thoughts into words. "It's just good to have you back, you know?"

"You don't think I'll have to go back to school, do you?" Patrick said, suddenly alarmed by the thought. "Oh man, that would suck."

Will shrugged. "You could probably do whatever you want, right? It's not like you have anything to lose—in a cosmic sense, anyway. I've heard some people pay good money to fake their own deaths to get out of stuff they don't want to do, so you've just kind of taken that to a new level."

"I could haunt houses," said Patrick, as if he was at a career-counseling office. "Damn, what are my parents gonna think?"

"Uh, well, they're probably going to freak out," Will said, quite sure of this. "When you died, things got really… awful. It's been awful, man." Will's stomach knotted itself into something Gordian as their conversation slipped awkwardly from the banter of best friendship into more troubling and emotional territory.

Patrick remained silent for a moment, clearly uncomfortable—getting serious had never been his strong suit.

"You've been, uh, keeping track of my sister," he said slowly, stating it as more fact than a question.

"Yeah, sure," answered Will in a tone carefully crafted to sound casual in response to something that could have been perceived as almost accusatory. "We both have—me and Colin, you know," he quickly added. "It's all we've got—well, it's all we had. Sticking together, I mean."

"Yeah…" Patrick replied in a voice of distant consideration. Silence reigned for eons.

"Hey!" Patrick cried, his eyes lighting up. "Let me ask you this: What is going on with Binzie Park? Does she talk about me? Did she come to my funeral? Did she cry? I bet she cried, right?"

Will smiled, glad for the distraction. "Sorry, buddy. She's still with Fletch."

"Are you bloody *kidding* me!?" Patrick said, clenching his fist in frustration. "But my death was so tragic! I was so *young*, Will! How did that not pay off in spades?"

"Yeah man, they're like *inseparable*. I haven't seen 'em apart in ages. Everyone refers to them as 'FletchandBinzie' now, like they've melded into one big body that just stands around and gropes itself all day," Will said, shivering at the thought.

"I can't believe it," Patrick groaned, shaking his head in disgust. "Her grief must have driven her into his arms for good. I'll bet she was overcome with loss and couldn't deal with it, right?"

"Uh… sure, whatever gets you through the night…"

"And that sneaky bastard was there to pick up the pieces. Unbelievable."

"Uh-huh."

"You think she could ever love a dead guy? I bet she'd totally dig it. I don't care how handsome that dude is, she's gotta go with the dead guy, right? I mean, come on—I'm *translucent* over here. That's got to count for something, right?"

"Um…"

"I'll bet she cries in private."

"Yeah."

"I'll bet she goes home, puts on a long, black veil, and cries herself to sleep."

"Sure."

"Totally."

Will stopped as they reached the corner of the block, beyond which stood a row of front porches attached to a series of small, boxy houses.

"Ike—you still there, guy?" Will whispered into the bushes.

"I am here, William," Ike called back, parting the dense branches with his disturbingly spidery finger bones and peering out at them with hollow sockets.

"Gah!" Patrick said, startled by this chilling visage. Will looked at him like he was a goon. "What? You think it's easy getting used to that?" he said, pointing at Ike, who sniffled in response.

"Get a grip, will you?" said Will, shaking his head and turning back to the houses. "Look, there's one right there with no porch light on. You guys wait here, and I'll—"

"Wait, I'm going with you," Patrick said, frowning at him.

"No, you stay with Ike. I'll get the jacket, then we'll go."

"Oh, give me a break, Castle—your Li'l Orphan Moron shtick is garbage, and you look about as innocent as a submarine captain. Let me do the talking and we'll leave Jolly Roger here."

"Whatever, let's just do this," Will said, resigning himself to the fact that you can't properly boss around a dead person.

As they strode up the walk to the nearby house, which was notably absent of Halloween decorations, the moment's immediacy hit Will like a steam shovel.

"This isn't going to work," he whispered to Patrick.

"Come on—this was your idea," Patrick said, pushing the doorbell without a care in the world.

"What if somebody recognizes you?" Will whispered, the idea suddenly popping into his head. "You're supposed to be dead!"

"Dude, there are hundreds of houses in this town," Patrick replied, looking down the street, his hands jammed into the pockets of his jumpsuit. "What are the odds this is someone we know? Nobody ever liked us anyway. Pretend I'm your cousin from Shanghai or something if it makes you feel better."

"Shanghai? Really?"

"Well, Tokyo then—what the hell do I care?"

With that, the door opened, and the odds in question inflated rapidly as they found themselves face-to-face with their classmate, Jonny Monger. In a wide-eyed flash, Patrick turned himself back to face the street, actively trying to look casual and leaving Will to deal with the situation at hand. Jonny stood there, lazily chewing some gum, a television blaring in the room behind him.

"Yeah?" he said, his voice bored. He looked back at the TV for a second before turning to give them a cursory glance. "John Entwistle, huh? Cool," he said, noting the skeletal back of Patrick's costume with an approving nod.

"Told you," Patrick muttered to Will.

"Look, we don't do the whole candy thing, and I've got this TV to watch and this gum to chew, so why don't you kids—" He stopped and squinted into the night, directly at Will. "Castle? Is that you?"

"Oh, uh, hey… Jonny," Will said, trying to sound as laid-back as possible despite all of his plans collapsing in on themselves like dying stars.

Jonny frowned at him. "You're not, like… trick-or-treating or something, are you?"

"What? Nah, no way, man," Will said, scrambling.

"Cuz that would be really lame."

"Ha! Yeah, for sure—good one. Kids are so… stupid?" Will did not like the way Jonny was looking at them. While he may have had a reputation as being something of a burnout, Jonny Monger did not miss many tricks.

"You sure?" Jonny asked, his inquisitive eyes noting Patrick's costume. "Who's that?"

"Oh, that's my cousin from Hong Kong," Will said, not believing the words coming out of his mouth.

"Shanghai," Patrick mumbled.

"Uh, Tokyo, I mean. My cousin from Tokyo," said Will, feeling suddenly lightheaded from the cloud of lies he was unleashing.

Jonny frowned. "How does that—"

"His parents—well, my aunt and uncle, I guess—they work over there in the, uh, offices?"

"Oh," said Jonny, crossing his arms and leaning against the doorframe. "Well, guten tag."

"Prego," Patrick said in a lousy attempt at disguising his voice and throwing a small wave.

"He's shy," Will said. "Culture shock."

"Uh-huh," said Jonny, jawing away at his gum. "So, why the bass player getup?"

"Oh, you know…" Will said, racking his brains. "It's his first Halloween, so he wanted to dress up…"

"Party," Patrick mumbled from the corner of his mouth.

"…and there's this party we're going to…"

"Girls," said Patrick.

"…with tons of girls, so… you know. That's what we're doing, pretty much," said Will, his eyes shooting daggers at his best friend, who continued pretending he was terribly interested in the front yard.

Jonny stopped chewing. "I didn't hear about any party."

Will sighed as he turned back to Jonny and prepared to dig himself deeper. "Uh, yeah, I know, it's—" He froze. There, just inside the doorway, hung a hooded sweatshirt. It was an arms-length away, yet it might as well have been on the moon with Jonny Monger standing there.

"Whose party?" Jonny asked, frowning at the now highly distracted Will. Patrick cleared his throat.

"What? Oh, you wouldn't know 'em," said Will.

"Like hell," said Jonny. "If there's a party with girls, I think I'd have heard about it. And what do you care—I thought you were going out with what's-her-face."

"Uh…" said Will, glancing over at Patrick, who had suddenly started listening attentively.

"You know, the weird one with the cape," Jonny continued. "Korbin, right?"

"No, it's not like that," Will said, hoping to defuse this risky topic.

"Yeah, right," Jonny sneered. "You guys are always creeping around together—everyone's seen it."

Will could sense Patrick tensing up beside him and desperately wished Jonny's mouth would stop making noise.

"I mean, don't get me wrong, I get it—she's kind of a fox, but she's sort of a freak, you know? A real gloom-and-doomer."

Will saw Patrick's head drop from the corner of his eye. "Jonny…" he started

"Hey, whatever winds your clock, man," Jonny rattled on, oblivious. "Girls are all crazy anyway—you just happened to get the head-case of all head-cases, I guess."

"Hey!" Patrick yelled, finally turning to face Jonny, his eyes alive with fury in their undead way. "That's my *sister* you're talking about!"

If he was waiting for a reaction of epic proportions to unfold (and knowing Patrick, Will suspected he was), he would be sadly disappointed. Jonny, a full head taller than Patrick on a bad day, was unmoved by this outburst—it was a combination of words that simply made no sense coming from this stranger in the skeleton jumpsuit.

Jonny looked at Will with a who's-this-guy expression before turning back to Patrick, who was now breathing heavily with rage. Will's eyes darted back and forth between them as he wondered who would be hitting whom first. He weighed the option of clocking Jonny a good one himself for slagging off Elyse.

Those three endless seconds of stand-off ended up being moot; Will saw it flash in Jonny's eyes, that mental burst of recognition and subsequent readjustment to the seemingly impossible. It arrested his ability to blink and caused his eyebrows to float skyward as though he had just noticed a torpedo headed directly at him. Patrick saw it too and curled his lip in a sneer.

"Boo," he said—a direct hit.

The color ran from Jonny's face faster than a turkey from November, and he stepped backward, stumbling as he hit the staircase. *"Korbin?"* he said, hardly believing what he was saying.

"In the see-through flesh," Patrick said, offering a lazy salute.

At that moment of newly revealed and freshly haunted chaos, Ike stuck his head through the doorframe and examined the foyer with a catlike curiosity. "Is there anything I can do to be of assistance, sir?"

he said, staring up at Patrick. Jonny yelped at the sight of him and collapsed into a shaking pile at the foot of the stairs.

"Hey, Ike," Patrick said cheerily, pleased to see him, if only for his scare value. "How'd you get up here?"

"I climbed up through the bushes beside the steps," Ike said, nervously chewing at the ends of his phalanges.

"Of course you did," Patrick replied, rolling his eyes.

Will kept a close eye on Jonny, who had covered his eyes and was whimpering. This situation was no good—even if they managed to leave quickly, there was no way Jonny would let them live if he remembered they'd seen him at his weakest.

"Um… hey, Jonny?" Will said, reaching across the doorway and plucking the hooded sweatshirt from its peg. "I'm gonna borrow this. Is that cool?" Jonny hooted something incomprehensible. "Okay, cool," Will said, turning back to Patrick and Ike. "All right, we've gotta get the hell out of here."

"Yeah, sure," Patrick said, looking over to Jonny once more. "Hey man, this was all just a dream, and, uh, it never happened, okay? And watch what you say about my sister, Monger, or I'll come back here and haunt you—*haunt you!*" he said in his best *Inner Sanctum* voice, his hands raised and fingers wiggling like a second-string Lon Chaney.

Will eyed him, looking bored. "Are you about through here?"

Patrick dropped his ghoul hands and cleared his throat. "Yeah, let's go."

CHAPTER 21
A Browse At The Bookery

HAD HE BEEN given the time to try hard enough, Spicy Jack could have very possibly seen his excursion into the exhausting strangeness of the modern world as the culminating act of derring-do and adventure in a long life of defying death and exploring uncharted territories. Again, this is how he *could* have been thinking had he been given the time, and therein laid the problem; certainly, he was used to reacclimating himself to situations in flux—that was the very essence of being a military man—but the aggressiveness of distraction in this particular neck of time and space was vexing in ways Jack never knew possible.

The sheer brightness and volume of all things coming from all directions made a person feel like he was losing his mind. It was in this state of tenuous grasping at some scrap of stability that Jack found himself as he stumbled through Bootville's bustling downtown district and finally arrived at Dog Ear Booksellers.

The sign was a carved wooden affair, painted with colors half a shade bolder than pastel and guaranteed not to offend or invigorate the mild-mannered locals and their bored purses or wallets. The effect was intended to remind one of a magical cottage from some pastoral fairytale land that never truly existed.

Jack and Crain cast skeptical looks at the picture window display, which featured various editions of Washington Irving propped up on a table covered with fake cobwebs and a carved pumpkin.

"They could stand to give the place a wipe-down, couldn't they," Crain said, eyeing a plastic spider perched on a web.

Jack leaned down to get a better look at the pumpkin on display. "Hells bells, is that supposed to be *you?*"

Crain shook his gourd. "No, I'm definitely taller than that."

"They haven't really captured your look very well, have they?" Jack mused, and indeed the display carving did seem more rounded and spooked than angular and aggressively chatty. "You look rather gormless here."

Jack straightened and slunk towards the door beneath the gingerbread sign, looking over his shoulder as though anticipating an assassination attempt or further conversation with a local. He paused to examine the decorative dried corn stalks flanking the entrance. "They seem to have had bad fortune with the crops this growing season," he murmured, rubbing a browned bit of husk between two boney fingers before entering the shop.

If the outside of the Dog Ear was a calculated portal of enchantment, promising entry to a scholarly netherworld, then the inside was a cold splash of consumer-driven reality. Adequately workmanlike piano-driven jazz-pop blared from overhead speakers, serenading the milling crowd of semi-holiday downtown foot traffic. A grown man dressed as a carrot stood at the magazine stand, flipping through the November issue of *Trendy Kinetics* magazine, while a small group dressed as hockey-masked serial killers sipped frothy lattes at a corner table just because they could. From deep within the recesses of the many rows of shelves, a baby cried with no sign of stopping.

"This town is bloody *barbaric,* Colonel," Crain hissed as Jack led them to an expansive checkout counter. "I mean, who has a baby out at this hour of the night? They *must* know that a baby needs a proper bedtime, do they not?"

"Inane musical noodlings and nocturnal infants—I'd almost rather be dead," Jack grumbled as they approached the young man behind the counter, who was busy ripping a scrap of excess register tape from the printer with authority.

"Cool costume," the young man said, peering up at Jack through his wire-framed glasses. He was college-aged with overly enthusiastic sideburns and stood painfully skinny in his oversized Dog Ear polo shirt. The laminate on his lanyard labeled him 'Phil,' while the headset in his ear labeled him another victim of the soul-crushing world of retail. Jack frowned and looked over his shoulder.

"He's talking about you, Sir," Crain mumbled in his ear.

Unsure of how to respond to this nonsense, Jack pressed on. "I'm in search of a book, and I was told your… *bookery* would be of some assistance. Are you the bookist?"

Phil squinted up at Jack through his wireframes as he scratched his unruly facial hair, utterly unsure of how to respond to this. "Um, yeah, I suppose I would be the… the bookist."

"Very well," Jack grunted with approval. "Now, do exactly as I say, and you shall live to see another dawn."

"Okay then," Phil said brightly, tapping a few keys on his register. "Do you have the title or author?"

Jack sighed. "No."

"If you've got the book's number, I can just punch it into the database here and see if I can order it," Phil said, pointing to his register screen. "Should be here in two to eight weeks, no problem."

"No, no, *no!*" Jack cried out through gritted teeth, slamming his fist on the counter and scattering a basket of tasseled bookmarks in the process. "I need it *now!*"

"Hey man, just chill out, it's cool—everything's cool," Phil said, putting his hands up in defense of his bookish mellowness. "Now, is this a particular book you're looking for, or do you want just, like, *any* book?"

"Oh, it is *very* particular," Jack chuckled, rubbing his skeletal hands together. "It is filled with strange markings."

"So… like an art book, maybe?"

"No, no—I believe it to be *musical* in nature."

"You're gonna have to clean it up, Tony," Phil said, his eyes darting to the side.

"I beg your pardon?" Jack said, his eye sockets narrowing.

"Sorry, it's just the walkie-talkies," Phil said, pointing to his headset. "We just had a Frankenstein monster throw up in the Classics department—ironic, huh? Too many circus peanuts, I guess. One sec…"

As Phil mumbled something into his microphone, Jack glanced at Crain. "Did you understand any of that?" Crain shook his gourd, his eye carvings wide with amazement.

"So, okay," Phil said, turning his attention back to them. "We're looking for some sheet music, maybe some tablature, right?" Jack stared at him, open-mouthed. Phil gamely continued. "You're probably gonna wanna check out the Performing Arts section in aisle five—we've got fake books, real fake books, fake fake books, tabs, classical crit., jazz crit., blues crit., country crit., rock crit., pop crit.—all kinds of stuff. Are you a musician? You know, I play in this band, The Didgeridonts—maybe you've heard of us? We're kind of a surf-rock meets northern soul by way of an Appalachian folk group thing. You should check us out sometime, you might—*then get a mop and a bucket and clean it up!*"

Jack and Crain were taken aback by this outburst. Snarling, Jack pounded his fist on the counter once more, inciting a shower of plastic gift cards to rain down on the well-worn Berber carpet. "How *dare* you make demands of me, you—"

Phil held up one shushing finger at him and adjusted his headset with his other hand. "No. Uh-huh… no. No, I'm with a customer right now. Uh-huh… no. Well, then have Keri help you, jeez…"

"He's talking to himself, Sir," Crain whispered to Jack. "We must be wary of his lunacy."

"What is this 'surf-rock' he speaks of?" Jack mumbled back.

"I don't know, Sir, but it stinks of sorcery and black magic. Perhaps he is a warlock who communes with spirits?" Crain hypothesized.

"Okay, guy—sorry about that," Phil said, turning back to them. "I'm the Assistant Manager On Duty, so I kinda have to run the show here, you know. It's sort of a big deal." He swelled with pride but was quickly deflated as Jack drew his sword and held it to his throat.

"I demand that you give me your enchanted surf-rock, wizard!" Jack threatened, his growl pulsating with authority.

Phil's eyebrows arced softly upwards like two fuzzy caterpillars beaming aboard a flying saucer. "Sure, man, no problem," he said, eyes flashing down to the blade at his neck. He reached into his pocket and pulled out a cassette tape, hand labeled 'The Didgeridonts

Demo.' Jack sheathed his sword and snatched the cheap tape from him, eyeing it greedily. He held it up to the light, tapped it, chewed on its corner.

"What is this contraption?" he wondered aloud.

"Yeah, we decided to use cassettes," Phil said, beaming with pride. "Pretty retro, huh? My buddy George has a four-track, so we just bounced all the tracks onto there—it sounds pretty sweet. Hey, are you doing a show tonight? Is that the deal? You don't think my band could maybe get a slot, do you? I mean, I'm scheduled here until 10, but after that—"

"*Silence!*" Jack shouted, tossing the tape over his shoulder in disgust. "Why is it that everyone in this hideous town speaks with no sign of stopping!?"

Unfazed, Phil continued. "Let me ask you this: would you like to sign up for our Dog Ear Booksellers 'Give A Dog A Treat' Program?"

"And still he keeps talking…" Jack sighed, rubbing his forehead in agony.

"Steady-on, Sir—perhaps he's simply touched in the head or some sort of town fool?" Crain consoled his superior as Phil the Bookist carried on with his sales patter.

"Basically, with a membership to the Treats Program, you'll be able to cash in on outstanding Dog Ear savings throughout the year. All I need from you is your personal info, and we can get you set up tonight to be rewarded for being a valued Dog Ear customer."

"Whatever you're talking about, the answer is *no*."

"Let me just assure you that all you need to do to take part in the Treats Program is to hang onto any receipt with the Treats Program printout at the bottom, which will then offer you 15% off any book with the purchase of any other book of equal or greater value on specially designated Tuesdays of the third week of every other month."

"15% of anything is hardly worth rolling out of bed for," Jack muttered, idly flipping through a nearby display of glossy entertainment magazines.

"Ha-ha, that's so true," Phil said, feeling confident about how his pitch was developing. "So, should I start the paperwork then?"

"No," Jack said, his eye sockets narrowing to slits.

"It'll just take a minute."

"No."

"All the Treats Program requires is your name, social security number, date of birth, place of birth, time of birth, home address, business address, home phone, business phone, hours of availability, and three to five friends and/or family who might also be interested in being treated to being a valued member of the Dog Ear Booksellers Treat Program. If you act now—"

"No!" Jack shouted, slamming his fist on the counter and sending a nearby display of chocolate-dipped Mark Twain peanut clusters into the air with the impact. "I do not want a treat—I have *never* wanted a treat! Again and again, I say '*no*' to you, and *still,* you keep talking! I've shown no interest in whatever wager you're offering, and yet you continue, unbidden, to offer it!"

"Hey, man, I know," Phil said with an empathetic nod. He motioned for Jack to lean closer and lowered his voice into a hushed, conspiratorial tone while covering the headset microphone with one hand. "Just between you and me, I think this whole system is totally *lame.* They have these scripts we have to memorize and repeat, like, *verbatim*, and then they subcontract these, like, spies who come in and 'mystery-shop' us to make sure we're actually saying this stuff to every customer, no matter how much they seem to hate it."

"Spies?" Jack repeated, apprehensively looking over his shoulder.

"Yeah, I know, right? And we have these quotas too…"

"Quotas?" Jack repeated, looking over his other shoulder, his anxiety now overwhelming.

"…and if we don't make our quotas, we don't get entered into the drawing for the $10 gift card, which I know doesn't *sound* like a lot of money, but I gotta commute to campus from my parents' house and gas ain't free, you dig what I'm saying? So, while I don't *think* you're a mystery shopper, I *am* required to keep reciting this Treats Program thing until you've refused it by *literally* saying 'no' five times, and you've only said it four times, so I guess what I'm trying to say is… would you like to take some literature about the Treats

Program home with you so you can sign up for it the next time you come in?"

Crain shouted as Jack threw aside his staff before reaching over the counter and grabbing Phil by the wrinkled poly-cotton collar of his polo shirt.

"You listen to me, you strange creature of whichever world this is, you miserable… *bookist* of the bookery: for the fifth time, *no.* I did not walk in here anticipating some devil's bargain involving treats or rewards—indeed, it makes no sense to proffer your wares for one price only to immediately negate them for a pathetic discount as soon as the transaction takes place!" Here, Jack clutched the headset microphone and spoke directly into it. "Why would they even approach you with a book if they did not have the money to purchase it at full price in the first place? Why wouldn't you gladly take their money and have done with it? Are the time and energy spent trying to swindle the consumer into some street urchin's game of bait-and-switch pick-pocketry worth the loss of clientele due to sheer annoyance? It *makes no—"*

Phil's eyes darted to the side, and he raised his index finger once more. "Yeah, Tony, what is it? Uh-huh… no. Uh-huh… no, absolutely not." He covered the microphone with his palm and turned back to Jack. "Could you excuse me for a moment? Someone's gotten themselves locked in the restrooms—taffy on the hinges or something. Only on Halloween, am I right?"

"You do realize that whenever you drop me like that, all I can do is roll around on the floor until you remember to pick me up, right?" Crain rattled at Jack in annoyance as they made their way to Phil's recommended aisle five.

Jack rubbed his aching forehead once more. "Perhaps if I had you burn the rest of my face off, I would no longer be forced into listening to the drivel the world seems preternaturally disposed to spewing my way."

"Wait, Colonel, stop a minute, Sir!" Crain gasped, his tone suddenly serious. Jack sighed and shook his head.

"No, Crain, I don't care if you *do* smell cinnamon, we're almost at the musical book section that idiot bookist spoke of."

"No, seriously, Colonel, you've got to turn it around right now—there's something you need to see." Crain sounded unusually panicked. "Dead ahead, Sir—second shelf from the top," said Crain as Jack frowned and grabbed the front-displayed hardcover from the Just Arrived section.

Jack tilted his rotten skull to the side as the figure on the cover registered in his memory. "What in blazes is that…" he trailed off as he scanned the gold-embossed lettering of the title. "*Champlain Uncorked: The Rise and Fall of Gentleman Johnny Burgoyne* by Chester J. Marley…"

"He looks ridiculous in that painting, doesn't he?" Crain remarked with a rueful shake of his gourd.

Jack was stunned and began paging through the book, reading certain passages aloud to himself and feeling more and more like he had slipped into some fresh, private hell.

Crain looked on as his colonel devoured the words. "Sir… I know this might seem like a ridiculous question right now, but… do you think we should go back and sign up for that Treats Program?"

CHAPTER 22
In Cold Pursuit

MR. BURNETT FELT confident that the evening was going well. He and Ms. Blithe had been seated at a cozy corner table at the Grasshopper Café, Bootville's premiere eating establishment, which ran an extraordinary gourmet soup-and-sandwich menu during the day and an even classier bistro dinner service by night. Pretentious, organic, and appropriately bohemian (though only just), the Grasshopper had established itself as the town's hottest date spot, a backdrop suitable for new lovers to project these same qualities like a magician's smokescreen in the hope of mystifying and enchanting the objects of their affection. A culinary sleight-of-personality.

"Fresh-ground pepper?" asked a waitress, clutching a mahogany grinding mill. The usual evening wait-staff uniform of a white dress shirt and black bowtie was accented with a crooked set of antennae and some lopsided plastic wings, a reluctant acknowledgment of the Grasshopper that, yes, despite all attempts at lending Bootville some dignity and class, Halloween did in fact exist, and let's not make too big a fuss out of it.

"Don't mind if you do," said Mr. Burnett, watching as the pepper fell to meet his fresh-caught salmon.

"I'll take a slug of that too, dearie," said Ms. Blithe from across the table, pointing to her strip steak with a knife. She gave her empty glass a wave. "And let's do another cabernet, hm?"

"Of course, madam," said the waitress, removing the empty bottle and leaving them to their conversation.

"Oh, John…" sighed the red-cheeked Ms. Blithe, digging into her steak with relish. "This is just what I needed—a night out to just *relax,* you know?"

"I'm glad you're enjoying yourself, Doris. It's not often I have the fortune of such charming company," replied Mr. Burnett with a smile as he tucked into his fish.

"Ha, you old smooth-talker—you're like Otis Redding or something."

"Oh, wow," Mr. Burnett chuckled nervously. "No pressure there, huh?"

"Oh, you flatter an old school marm," laughed Ms. Blithe, waving him off.

"You're nothing of the sort. I have to tell you, I really respect your tenacity. I wish I had half your passion for education," said Mr. Burnett, looking at her with genuine admiration.

Ms. Blithe shrugged and took the new wine from the waitress, pouring herself a glass that dangerously neared the rim. "Hardly. I do the best I can for them, but, you know, they can be so *resistant.*"

"Yes, they can be rather… spirited."

"They're monsters, John. Don't let their fresh faces and expensive dental work deceive you—they'd eat us alive if they could. We can only try to cram their brains with as much as we can with what time we have and let the criminal justice system work its magic after that," said Ms. Blithe, drinking deeply from her glass.

"Well, that's a relief to hear you say that," Mr. Burnett said. "I thought I was the only one who felt that way. I was actually worried I was going crazy, to be honest with you. Ha!"

They both laughed heartily at this and clinked glasses in a toast.

"You know, I used to think my life would be strictly purpose-driven," Ms. Blithe ruminated as she swirled her wine in the glass, gazing into the distance. "I was sure I'd be able to thrive in the trenches, molding young minds and adventuring with them across new philosophical landscapes in one great tumble towards some greater enlightenment. These days, I find myself living in the small moments. The quiet times."

"How do you mean?" Mr. Burnett asked, finding himself entranced by the way the candlelight flickered across her face.

"Oh, well, you know… times like this," she said, smiling. "A good meal, a lovely chat, a charming gentleman-caller…"

Mr. Burnett smiled self-consciously, feeling suddenly very hot. He eyed his wine glass suspiciously.

"Life is filled with such upheaval," she continued. "A life of distraction and ever-changing circumstances, tumultuous like the sea. I find it's the times *between* things always happening to be the ones that fill my memory. These are the times in which life is lived."

"Which does beg the question," Mr. Burnett said as they stared deeply into each other's eyes and leaned in ever so slightly, "what happens next?"

"Ms. Blithe!"

The electric silence of a quiet moment to remember was broken by the familiar shout of something happening. The two teachers snapped to attention and turned to find Elyse Korbin and Colin Niemann standing at their table, gasping for breath, looking both alarmed and, in Colin's case, curious at the tender scene unfolding before them.

"Elyse?" Ms. Blithe said, her teacher's intuition suddenly buzzing at Fret-Level 3.

"Colin," said Mr. Burnett, nodding at one of his odder students.

"Cufflinks," Colin replied, his eyes zeroing in on the one part of his teacher that was dressier than usual.

"Um, yes, yes they are," Mr. Burnett said, smiling at Ms. Blithe sheepishly and pulling the sleeves of his jacket down.

"We need to talk with you—like, right now," Elyse said between heavy breaths.

The sound of wait-staff whispers could be heard behind them as the maitre d' stormed his way through the dining room.

"Oh dear," Ms. Blithe said, taking note of the frown on his face and the murmuring of antennaed waiters and waitresses following in his wake. "I believe you've upset the doorman."

"Pardon the interruption, madam," the maitre d' said, pointing to Elyse and Colin, "but this is simply not done."

"They wouldn't let us in without a reservation," Elyse said to Ms. Blithe, shrugging, "so we ran for it."

"That is correct, madam," the maitre d' said, mopping his brow with a handkerchief, trying to maintain his composure through gritted teeth. "The Grasshopper does not allow admittance for dinner service without reservation; we have a three-star rating in the Bootville Chamber of Commerce's *Fen For Yourself* guide to local dining, and the according reputation to upkeep, and this is simply. Not. Done. Do these *creatures* belong to you?"

"Um… I suppose so, in a way. John, be a dear and get our coats, will you?" Ms. Blithe said, gently squeezing Mr. Burnett's arm. She turned back to the seething host. "My apologies for the interruption, garçon. We were just leaving."

"Sorry for doing what is simply not done," Colin chimed in blankly.

The maitre d' growled before being accosted by another diner, demanding that their breadbasket be refilled, while Ms. Blithe corralled the kids towards the front door. As they waited in the lobby for Mr. Burnett to return with the jackets, Ms. Blithe crossed her arms and stared at Elyse and Colin, her expression the perfect mixture of disbelief and annoyance.

"Well?" she exploded as quietly as possible.

"Sorry about ruining your dinner, Ms. Blithe," Elyse said, genuinely contrite. Colin nodded in agreement.

"Oh, whatever," Ms. Blithe said, waving the idea away. "It's not like *he's* going anywhere." She pointed across the lobby where Mr. Burnett was unsuccessfully attempting to stick his arm into the wrong sleeve of his trench coat while juggling Ms. Blithe's jacket as well.

Ms. Blithe sighed at the sight of him and then turned back to her students. "So, what's this big emergency—and where are your parents!?"

"Ms. Blithe, I know this sounds crazy, but… do you remember the book?" Elyse said, moving in closer.

JACK AND CRAIN exited the Dog Ear and staggered into the flow of costumed downtown foot traffic. The night's breeze drafted through the hollows of Jack's skull as he surveyed the bustling storefronts through the filter of fresh knowledge. His head was swimming with information gleaned from an hour of hopping from one heavy history book to another, retracing humanity's steps over the centuries in his absence. If the things he had read and the images he had viewed were even remotely true, then the world had become a far more confusing place than he ever could have anticipated.

The boney remains of his hand rubbed his forehead as he tried to apply all he had learned to their current situation. Poor Gentleman Johnny—he'd been told his expedition into the wilds of the north would be folly. Ah well, if that blithering idiot he'd spoken to earlier was correct, his own excursion to Collartown had been equally disastrous. It seemed there would be no winning here. Jack shook his head in an attempt to clear it and became aware that Crain had been yammering on for some time.

"…I mean, if you think about it, Colonel, it does make *some* sense, right? If we abide by the maxim that people are extraordinarily cheap and also a bit thick, then offering them *any* kind of deal will make them bound to come in and at least see what it's all about. And that means you've successfully drawn in potential customers, which is half the battle. It's a bloody genius system when you think about it, eh, Sir? Sir?"

Jack had long since stopped listening, his watchful eye sockets having fixed themselves on trouble coming their way. With all the reckless abandon that mob mentality would allow, a troop of Firelight Femmes swooped in on them from down the block, their faces painted like Serengeti animals, their crimson sashes blazing proudly in the glow of the streetlights. With his keen military eye, Jack homed in on their leader, a steely girl with enough merit badges to impress even the snootiest of palace courtiers. She whipped along on a scooter flashing with chrome and pink plastic, her handlebar tassels impressive and somehow menacing as she led her girls in the chanting of an old bonfire standard.

Crain's pumpkin jaw dropped at the sight of them. "Sir, it must be the local militia!"

Within seconds they were surrounded by the singing, skipping warriors, their crisp, blood-red berets bobbing up and down as they danced in a circle around the horrified undead. Each member reached up to slap Crain on the side of his gourd as they passed, taunting him with giggles of melodious belligerence.

"Ow! Sir—*ow!*—they have us outnumbered!" Crain cried as he was battered back and forth with each smacking palm.

"Stay calm, Lieutenant—they can sense your fear!" Jack snarled as his head darted back and forth, seeking some means of escape from this gang of thugs.

In a blurry whoosh of air, the troop leader appeared before them, skidding to a halt on her two wheels. Jack eyed the contraption suspiciously as she stared him down, whipping a flashlight from her belt and pointing its beam at the off-colored, translucent form of the colonel.

"You!" she said with authority.

Jack drew back a step, snapping his cloak over the lower half of his skull to shield himself from this strange lucency she wielded so assuredly. Her small legion of lion and cheetah-faced goons quieted into an unsettling tension, and Jack knew he was done for. He'd seen the American natives behave the same way during the old campaigns of the Monongahela, and the outcome never fell in favor of the surrounded. His skeletal body drew itself in as he awaited the leader's final command for his ultimate undoing. He was Rome before the Vandals, and he was about to be sacked.

She stared at him, unblinking, and uttered the final words: *"Send us to camp next year."*

The hyena-faced girl beside her held up a clipboard loaded with donation forms, and Jack grunted in bafflement.

"Crain..." he whispered out of the corner of his mouth. "Crain, what do I do here?"

Crain offered a nauseated moan in response, still spinning wildly on his vine from the impromptu Femme attack. "Oh, George's knickers, I think I'm going to be ill..."

Jack shrunk down lower in defense, panic creeping into his voice. "Crain, I'm out of my league here—help me!"

From Crain's perspective, the world was darkness punctuated with streaks of lamplight and shadowy trick-or-treaters as he swung around and around. His carved eyes were at a loss in his search for some distant point to focus on, recalling his months spent retching over the side of their warship as they sailed to recapture the New World and were thrown into titanic yaws by an indifferent Atlantic. He had just about given up on trying to keep his guts and seeds down when a slowing rotation allowed him a glimpse of some familiar figures. Could it be…?

"Sir!" he cried, choking back his sickness. "Sir, there they are! Dead ahead, Sir!"

Jack looked past his captors, scowling in confusion. All became clear in that instant, and he straightened to his full height as he caught the scent of his prey. Slamming the end of his staff into the sidewalk, a billow of fireball exploded from Crain's face, inciting howls of pain from the beleaguered lieutenant. The Firelight Femmes squealed and took a collective step back. Seizing the moment, Jack roared at the taciturn troop leader and yanked the scooter from her grip. Propping the staff and Crain over his shoulder, he clumsily tried to emulate his foe's use of the contraption, balancing precariously on the narrow plane as he pushed off towards his quarry, now within his grasp once more.

ELYSE WRAPPED HER cape around herself with a shiver as she watched Ms. Blithe, desperate for any kind of response to her brief explanation of a deranged tall tale chasing them across town because of some weirdo book. The street was busy as they waited outside the Grasshopper Café, but Ms. Blithe seemed removed, adrift on the waves of deep thought as she considered this condensed reasoning for Elyse's urgency. Elyse shifted uncomfortably from foot to foot as she looked back at Colin, who was busy silently mouthing the words from the menu hanging in the Grasshopper's window—no reassurances there, either.

The clanking of a well-worn engine drew her attention back to the street, where Mr. Burnett was making a misguided attempt at parallel parking in his beat-up sedan.

"Sorry to interrupt your, uh, date," Elyse said as she and Ms. Blithe watched the vehicle pull forward and backward seven times.

"Oh, that's okay, dear," Ms. Blithe said with a sigh. "Between you and me, I think the Chamber of Commerce rounded up on that three-star rating." Elyse nodded sympathetically as her teacher turned to her. "You have to understand, Elyse, it's not that I don't believe what you're telling me—I believe that *you* believe what you're telling me, but I can't—"

She was cut off by the curious sound of mass squealing coming down the block. They craned their necks in the direction of the disruption and were alarmed to see the towering form of Spicy Jack bursting from a pack of Firelight Femmes on a wobbly scooter, his skull leering as he bore down upon them, flaming pumpkin in tow.

"What the—" Ms. Blithe started, her eyes expanding to owlish proportions behind her glasses.

"He's here!" Elyse gasped. "Colin, we have to go," she called over her shoulder as she grabbed the sleeve of Ms. Blithe's jacket and began dragging her to Mr. Burnett's car. The brake lights flared red as Elyse slapped the side of the vehicle while struggling with Ms. Blithe, who could not tear her eyes from Jack as he approached, the pink tassels of his absurd chariot flapping in the wind.

The driver's side door flew open, and Mr. Burnett popped his head up. "Hey, did I hit someone? You know, I almost had it that last time, but—*whoa!*" He caught sight of the skeleton man and ducked back into the car as Elyse ushered Ms. Blithe into the front seat. Colin dived into the back, his face as expressionless as ever. Elyse slammed the front door and spun around to follow him, catching a final glimpse of Jack's twisted face as she did so before pulling the door shut behind her.

"Step on it, Mr. B!" she shouted over the front seatback, and step on it Mr. Burnett did, flinging the car away from the overrated restaurant like an errant pub dart, the illuminated storefronts whizzing by in a rush of relief, and then—*screeeeeeeech!*

Mr. Burnett slammed on the brakes with both feet as they hit one of several red traffic lights, all of which were ostensibly posted for the wellbeing of the citizenry. Elyse looked out the back window and saw that the man who was surely going to kill her was taking full advantage of this safety outpost, having successfully jumped the curb with the scooter he was now using to weave through the idling traffic.

"Um, he's still behind us," she informed the front seat as Colin turned to join her at the rear window.

"Fast," he agreed, observing Jack's progress.

"Can somebody tell me what that thing with the sword and the hat is?" Mr. Burnett said, watching Jack's maneuvers through the rearview mirror.

"Green, John, green!" Ms. Blithe said, pointing to the traffic light. Mr. Burnett floored it, the squealing tires indicating the sedan's displeasure with these new driving demands. "Oh, this is no good," she muttered, staring ahead at the numerous stoplights that dipped low over the street like half-hearted Chinese lanterns.

"Take a left at this street, Mr. B—my house is only a few blocks away," Elyse said, grabbing the teacher's shoulder.

Their screams filled the car's interior as Mr. Burnett flung the wheel left, momentarily launching them onto two wheels and sending a flurry of dead leaves into the air behind them as they entered the old neighborhood of Bootville Proper. They were silenced almost immediately as Mr. Burnett slammed on the brakes once more, pressing them hard against their seatbelts and knocking the wind from their lungs. They'd hit a stop sign, beyond which rippled the endless throng of trick-or-treaters.

"Whoops," Elyse said, offering a sheepish grin as Mr. Burnett slowly eased the sedan into the swarm of costumed pedestrians. "Maybe we lost him?"

"Spicy Jack," Colin said in response, pointing out the rear window as the undead colonel rounded the corner.

"Can't we go any faster, John?" Ms. Blithe said, coming slightly unhinged. "Come on—you're from the city! They have car chases in the city all the time, right?"

"I didn't grow up on the set of *Bullitt*, Doris—we had subways and an expansive system of bus lines!" Mr. Burnett cried, melting down. He yelped and slammed on the brakes as a mummy ran out in front of the bumper. "I only got my license when I moved here in August—hey!" He braked sharply again as more bag-swinging ghouls laughed and howled their way across the street without a care in the world. "Look at this—they're just going wherever they want!" he yelled. "Don't any of you have any respect for safety!?"

Elyse peered out the rear window once more as the car shuddered slowly down the street in violent fits of stops and starts. The trick-or-treating crowd had flooded into their wake, and it was difficult to make out anything beyond the three-foot pool of red irradiance cast by the taillights. It seemed that Jack wasn't immediately behind them, and that had to count for something.

She turned back to the front seat and pointed at the next corner. "We're almost there, Mr. B—when we hit Thorn Street, take a right."

She fell back in her seat and stared out the side window at the shrieking silhouettes passing by. Her chest felt heavy, and she was overwhelmed by a burning desire to breathe a sigh of relief. Instead, she clenched her jaw, knowing it was not to be; the way this night was going, she wasn't sure she'd find any relief again.

JACK WAS GETTING the hang of the scooter as he kicked his way after the shrinking taillights. The smooth rolling motion and rumble of rubber on pavement were strangely intoxicating, and the thought crossed his mind to perhaps outfit his troops with such a device— providing he *had* troops again.

"Crain, I've never felt so free," he growled back to his lieutenant, who bounced up and down with every bump in the road.

"That's brilliant, Sir—argh!" Crain shouted back as a particularly aggressive pothole launched him over the end of the staff, his vine briefly slackening like a snapped fishing line. "Maybe you could drop me off somewhere so I can vomit on solid ground, eh, Sir?"

"There is no time to lose—they gain ground. We mustn't let them escape again." Behind him, Crain moaned.

The costumed mob of Bootville was becoming denser, leaving the colonel to coast slowly, his large frame hunched low over the handlebars. Yes, this was truly a magnificent invention—perhaps the only useful thing this strange world had to offer. He even liked the tassels.

His heavy boot gave a push, and he wondered why the surrounding hooligans were pointing and laughing at him. Well, let them. Before the night was through, they would see who would be left laughing. With a sinister chuckle, he reached down to the handlebars and rang the mounted bell with his skeletal hand, parting the crowd before him.

CHAPTER 23
Fish Tank Nocturne

THE BOOMING SOUNDS of rhapsody filled the Korbin house as Elyse, Colin, Ms. Blithe, and Mr. Burnett entered. They were taken aback by the sound of the old baby grand as it merrily rolled through a flurry of notes.

"Did you leave your stereo on?" Mr. Burnett asked Elyse, moving his head in time to the music. "What is that—Liszt?"

"Bugs Bunny," said Colin.

Ms. Blithe looked down to see Elyse sniffling.

"Are you all right, dear?" she asked, placing an arm around her with concern.

Elyse nodded and wiped her face. "I'm fine, Ms. Blithe, it's just…" she paused as the song built to its finale. "It's just that it's been so long. And he always plays the second Hungarian when he's in a good mood."

Ms. Blithe frowned. "When *who* is in a good mood?"

Elyse gathered herself and led them past the staircase and into the great room.

Patrick was putting on a show for no one but himself. His fingers flew across the keys, slamming and banging the song with such force that his translucent form would hover in the air with each chord struck as though engaged in a bizarre musical moonwalk.

Ms. Blithe gasped at the sight of him, clapping a hand over her mouth. Mr. Burnett's jaw hung slack in stupefaction.

Across the room, Will lay draped upon the sofa, lazily tossing a small, fossilized trilobite to himself. He looked over to the small group standing in the entranceway and gave a bored wave before jabbing a thumb in Patrick's direction with a roll of his eyes and miming the checking of a watch.

Elyse couldn't help but smile at the scene; for that briefest of moments, despite all that had transpired that night, things seemed almost normal. Or, at least, normal in the way 'normal' used to mean.

As Patrick played the final chords, he sang the orchestral accompaniment and raised his hands as dramatically as possible before plinking out the last few notes. With that, he gave himself a round of applause and a pat on his own back.

"Cracking good job, Korbin, you magnificent bastard!" he said to himself as Elyse laughed and Will sat upright, stretching with exhaustion.

At that moment Ms. Blithe, looking incredibly ashen, found her voice.

"*Patrick!*" she yelled, shaking.

Patrick turned to them and gave her a devilish smile.

"Ah, Ms. Blithe," he said with rakish charm. "I know it's Halloween, but I'm afraid we don't have any candy for you this year."

With a moan, Ms. Blithe's knees buckled, and she collapsed onto Elyse's shoulder. Elyse struggled to keep her on her feet, looking to Mr. Burnett for help.

"Mr. Burnett?" she said, straining from her teacher's dead weight. He ignored her and continued to stare gobsmacked at her spectral brother, who was now laughing hysterically and taking an obscene amount of pleasure at Ms. Blithe's state of shock.

"Um, okay… Will? A little help?" Elyse said, losing her balance.

"Right," Will said, scrambling up from the couch to help Elyse lead her teacher to an overstuffed armchair beside the aquarium, where she would be able to hyperventilate in relative comfort.

Patrick ignored this ado and made his way over to the others. "Colin, m'boy, she sounds great," he said, pointing to the piano. "Hummed it out, did you? I thought so. Where'd you dig these up?" he said, gesturing to the adults.

"Grasshopper," said Colin.

"Really? Man, I just *hate* the Grasshopper!" Patrick said, waving a fist at the very idea of the café. Mr. Burnett continued to stare, utterly dumbfounded, as Patrick walked over to him and stuck out his hand. "Pat Korbin. Season's greetings."

Mr. Burnett slowly shook his hand and mumbled, "John Burnett."

"I'll take your word for it. Nice wrist candy," Patrick said, taking note of his cufflinks.

Mr. Burnett looked down at the ghostly hand he was holding. "Okay. This is really strange," he said to himself.

Patrick smiled, amused by his guest's increasing befuddlement. "Yeah? What's that feel like?"

"Solid. Cold," Mr. Burnett replied, never for a second taking his eyes off the up-and-down motion of the handshake.

"Hm, that's good to know. Well, we're down to single-syllables with you—perhaps you'd like a seat, yes?" said Patrick, extracting his hand as Colin nudged his teacher to the sofa.

"Yes… yep, I think that's the thing to do," Mr. Burnett said, his voice distant, as though he'd recently awoken from a three-hour nap.

Elyse fanned Ms. Blithe with a magazine as the stunned teacher heaved sharp, gasping breaths. Will looked on, unsure of what to do.

"Where's Ike?" Elyse asked him, her voice harried.

"He's back in the kitchen, crying behind the stove," Will said. "He's a real train wreck, you know? We had a hell of a time—"

"And the *Macabrium*?" Elyse asked, eyeing her bag and violin case, which Will had piled beside the couch.

"Oh, uh, Ike has it. I told him to guard it—figured it'd be something for him to do. You know, take his mind off things and all that. What's the matter?" he asked, alarmed by her urgency.

"Jack saw us in town," Elyse said, trying to prop Ms. Blithe's head up with a small pillow.

"What!?" Will exclaimed, the hair on his arms standing up.

"It was crowded, and he couldn't get to us, but he may have followed the car," she replied.

"Really?" Will said, aghast.

"He stole a Firelight Femme's scooter," Elyse added.

"Why, that creaky maniac," Patrick said, shaking his head in disgust. "Wow—and all those girls want to do is sell you some scones and learn how to tie a sheepshank. He truly is evil, isn't he."

"We can't stay here," his sister said, ignoring him. "He could be here at any time."

"Okay, so let's evacuate," Will said. "What do you want to do about *them?*" He nodded to the bewildered teachers.

"Um…" Elyse stood before them, gathering her thoughts. "Okay, here goes. Ms. Blithe? Mr. Burnett?"

The teachers looked at her as she snapped her fingers. They were both dangerously shocked, their eyes as big as hubcaps.

"Wow, okay," Elyse said, grimacing at their respective nervous breakdowns. "Hi. Uh, we don't have much time here, so I'll make this quick. As half of you know, this is my big brother, Patrick," she said, pointing to him.

Patrick pointed at the adults with a casual pistol motion. "John-John, Doris—the pleasure's mine."

"Now, Ms. Blithe, as you know, he is dead. Or *was* dead," Elyse continued.

Patrick raised a playful eyebrow at Ms. Blithe. "I always knew you'd breeze back into my life one day, Doris. I never stopped believing." Ms. Blithe gave a small hoot of fear but said nothing. Elyse continued.

"Like I was telling you before, that book I showed you turned out to be a coded way to somehow bring him back—well, the details are kind of fuzzy, but it happened, and now… here he is."

Patrick shrugged and threw an arm around Colin.

"Cold," Colin said.

"Now, that large skeleton man with the pumpkin and the sword— you remember him, right?" Ms. Blithe and Mr. Burnett only twitched in response. "Well, we brought him back by mistake, and now he wants the book to do… whatever. Probably something very, very bad. And he'll kill us to get to it, so we need to evacuate, like, big time." She turned to Mr. Burnett. "Now, Mr. Burnett, I have to ask you something, and it's very, very important: are you in a coma?"

He looked up at her with glassy eyes. "I really don't know."

"Okay, good enough. I need you and Colin to get Ike from the kitchen and start the car, so we can get somewhere safe. Can you do that for me?"

He nodded slowly and stood up on shaky legs. "What's an Ike?" he asked, his voice barely audible.

"He's a…" Elyse stopped and thought for a moment. "Well, don't worry about that—I don't think it would help you very much right now."

"Okay," he said without argument. He followed Colin into the rear of the house and through the kitchen service hallway, shaking his head and searching his pockets for his keys.

"Elyse," Ms. Blithe whispered, grabbing her by the wrist and taking her by surprise. "What have you done?"

Elyse stared back, grasping for an explanation.

"Don't worry, Ms. Blithe," Patrick piped in, breaking the uncomfortable silence. "I feel like two million Canadian dollars, and we're all together again—things could be worse, right?"

As if on cue, the front door flew open, rocking the entire house. There, in a sea of fog, stood Spicy Jack, his sword drawn and Crain fully ablaze.

"Trickety-treats!" Crain shouted, bursting into maniacal laughter as Jack stormed into the great room, a giant of tremendous speed and fluid aggression. Instincts kicking in, Ms. Blithe alit from her chair and grabbed Elyse and Will by the arm, pulling them out of harm's way. With a swing of his staff, Jack swung Crain into a blur of fire that erupted from his carved mouth and incinerated the chair they had just been gathered around.

Without pause, he swooped in a great billow of cloak to face them as they scrambled to their feet, choking on the smoke. The tendrils of flesh remaining on his jaw pulsed with fury beneath his cockade hat as he contorted his face into a twisted effigy of death itself. He pointed his saber at Elyse and addressed her directly.

"The book," he growled.

Patrick popped up from behind the piano, appalled. "Hey, one-track-mind, that's my sister you're roaring at!"

Crain turned to him with a sneer. "You must be mad—can't you see the colonel's speaking? We *do not talk* when the colonel's speaking—that is rule number one!" Inhaling deeply, Crain spat out another fountain of molten pumpkin guts, igniting the lid of the baby grand and chasing Patrick back into hiding.

Jack ignored them, fixated on Elyse, who stared back in defiance. Behind her stood Will, his hands balled into fists. Ms. Blithe clutched Elyse's shoulders with shaking hands.

"You have no right to do this!" she shouted at Jack. "You don't belong here, and you'll find nothing here to help you! Now, leave her alone!"

"You do not dictate to *me,* future peasant!" Jack shouted back, shooting Ms. Blithe the briefest of withering glances before taking a step toward Elyse. Will put his arm in front of her and was about to charge the undead monster when Elyse stepped forward.

"Look," she said, grabbing her bag from beside the couch and opening it. "The book isn't here for you to take."

Jack grunted and eyed the contents of the bag. Sheathing his sword, he reached out his boney hand to her. "Give it here, girl," he breathed.

She threw the canvas bag at him with disgust. Jack caught it and began hungrily digging through its contents in search of the volume. To his dismay, Will could see Elyse's notebook with the *Macabrium* translations rattling around inside, but Jack took no notice of it as he clawed the bottom of the bag to no avail.

"Blast!" he shouted with rage before balling the bag up in his massive hands and shoving it into Crain's mouth, where it immediately became ash and ember.

"No!" Elyse cried out as Will and Ms. Blithe pulled her back.

Jack turned on them again, pointing. "You will bring it to me, or I shall set this entire nightmare of a village to the torch once more!"

Crain chuckled evilly at this as he chewed Elyse's bag, his carved eyes narrowing into slits.

"You can't do that!" Elyse gasped in horror.

"You will bring it to me, and I shall return to my *true* form and paint the wreckage of this world into whatever designs I choose."

"Yeah!" sneered Crain. "And me too, right, Colonel? Sir? Me too?" he said, turning to his superior. Jack ignored him and waited for his prey to do his bidding. Behind him, a flash of movement caught Elyse's eye. Taking almost cartoonishly sneaky steps through the front entrance was Patrick, clutching the giraffe skull from the main hallway.

Elyse's breath caught in her throat as Patrick nodded to her with a grin before putting a translucent finger to his lips in a shushing gesture. He pointed to himself, then the back of the room, and made a looping motion followed by a thumbs-up. Elyse understood—he'd snuck around through the kitchen service hallway.

"Sir?" Crain continued, oblivious. "You did say you'll fix me too, correct?"

Elyse felt Will tense up beside her as he also noticed Patrick crossing the room behind their captors. A moment later, Ms. Blithe inhaled sharply at the same sight.

Jack took another step forward, his heavy riding boots dropping like thunder upon the rug.

"You cannot avoid it," he hissed at Elyse. "I shall follow you to the ends of the earth…"

"They're just children!" Ms. Blithe cried out in desperation, pulling Elyse back a step.

"…I shall haunt your every night's sleep…" He took another step as Crain's flame billowed brighter. "…I will leave nothing but carnage and ruination in my wake…"

Behind him, Patrick crept onto the arm of the sofa, where he momentarily balanced in a crouch. Elyse watched in amazement as he tucked the giraffe skull under his arm and spit into the palms of his hands, rubbing them together with pleasure.

"…The world will suffer in your name until I have what I desire. I shall be the curse that hunts you and everyone you love…"

"Elyse…" Will mumbled, his eyes riveted on her brother.

"…And when I've captured you…"

Jack was now mere feet away from them, the details of his horrible, translucent disfigurations within arm's reach.

"…You shall know what true *suffering* means."

The threat floated, electric in the air, the only sounds in the room crackling from the pools of fire Crain had so violently put forth.

"You've forgotten something," Elyse said, breaking the tense silence, her voice quiet and steady. Jack and Crain were taken off-guard and exchanged frowns. "If you want to catch me, you'll need something very important."

"And what is that?" Jack asked, his voice dripping with condescension.

"Bait."

With that, Patrick slammed the giraffe skull into the heavy plate glass of the wall aquarium. The tank broke immediately upon impact as the weight of thousands upon thousands of gallons of salt water flooded out in a deafening tsunami, carrying forth dozens of species of fish, krill, starfish, and lobster. Will grabbed Elyse's hand, and she, in turn, latched onto Ms. Blithe's with the other as they began running in a desperate chain toward the back of the house. The water caromed off the walls, extinguishing the fires and crashing into the undead Redcoats, sweeping them across the broad expanse of the room.

With a howl of triumph, Patrick rode the top of the wave, his hands in the air and his off-color body spinning amidst the various reef denizens, who could only look at their new circumstances with surprised fish eyes.

"Faster, faster!" Ms. Blithe yelled as the angry waters bore down upon them in a torrent, following them through the back service hall and into the kitchen. "But be careful!" she added for good measure as Will shoved a chair out of the way before leading them through the back door. As he passed through the jamb, the wave caught up with them, easily lifting them off the floor before heaving them outside with a final *splat!* on the blacktop.

Mr. Burnett's beat-up sedan sat idling in the driveway as Colin ushered Ike into the front passenger seat. Mr. Burnett stood by, his face sheet-white once more at the sight of the ambulatory skeleton boy. The splashing of the others down the flume of the back steps made him turn, but his open-mouthed expression remained cemented in place.

Will stood up with a groan and cracked his back before helping Elyse and Ms. Blithe up from their soggy heap.

"Oh, that looked like fun," Colin said, peering at them from behind Mr. Burnett.

"Yeah, that was a real riot," Will said, wringing out his shirt and squishing in his sneakers.

Elyse twisted her cape, squeezing out the excess water. "Oh, Dad's not going to be happy about *that* mess," she said with a pitying shake of her head as she pushed her black hair out of her eyes.

"Hey, not if we're dead before he finds out, right? There's always a silver lining," said Will before pointing at Mr. Burnett. "We need to go—like, *now*."

Mr. Burnett nodded blankly as Will and Elyse helped a rattled Ms. Blithe into the car before piling into the back seat. Mr. Burnett took a moment to collect himself and remember how a car works. As if on auto-pilot, he threw it into drive and floored it towards the street. They made it about fifteen feet before screaming and slamming on the brakes as Patrick appeared from the darkness and pressed his face against the glass of Ms. Blithe's window.

"Wait, don't leave me here—I just broke the fish tank for you guys!" he said, bursting into manic laughter and holding up Elyse's dripping violin case. "Dad's gonna be *pissed!*"

CHAPTER 24
The Clouded Caravan

AND SO THEY drove, the strangest caravan Bootville had seen in a great many years, unsure of where they were going but trying to get there as quickly as possible. The half who were soaked shivered in the cool night air, prompting a hacky comment from Patrick about them giving new meaning to the term 'carpool,' which was either groaned at or ignored.

"Tough room," he mumbled.

The hour was growing late, and the neighborhood streets of Bootville Proper were draining themselves of trick-or-treaters as Halloween wound down to a close for the year. The fog was rolling in now, thick and smothering off the fens. Mr. Burnett drove with as much concentration as he could focus between shooting wary, sideways glances at Ike, who sat between him and Ms. Blithe, quietly weeping into his boney hands.

"So, ah… where to next then?" he said to no one in particular, the whites of his knuckles rocking back and forth in a death grip on the steering wheel.

"Yeah, Sis, what's the master plan here?" Patrick said, leaning forward in the back seat to see her at the other end of the car. "Consider: we've already raised the dead, kidnapped our teachers, and flooded the house, so let's just call those things, like, done, right? We can just check them right off the list. Where do we go from here?"

Will and Colin also turned to her, and the increasing pressure of expectation finally began to break her down into pieces of despair.

"I don't know!" she said, trying to choke back a high-pitched tone of helplessness. "How are you supposed to get rid of the undead!? They're *already dead.* It just doesn't make any sense!"

"As an Undead, I have to tell you, I feel pretty great," Patrick threw in. "I'd imagine Spooky Jack is much the same, fish tank and all."

"See!?" Elyse said to Will.

Will could feel things spiraling out of control but was at a loss for what to say to ease her worries.

"Maybe he'll give up?" he offered lamely. "I mean, he hasn't caught us yet, and aside from scooter technology, he's sort of at a disadvantage in dealing with the modern world, isn't he? Maybe he'll just leave or something." It was a feeble attempt, and Will knew it, but the tension in the vehicle seemed to require the possibility of all options presented.

Ms. Blithe gave him a skeptical look through the rearview mirror that implied he was not helping things by speaking nonsense.

"I'm afraid Jack seemed a bit more hell-bent on having his way than that," she said, frowning in thought. With their recent escape, she had begun to show signs of regaining her steely teacher's resolve.

"He's going to destroy Bootville," Elyse said, shaking her head at the idea.

"Sorry—what?" Mr. Burnett said, alarmed.

"Yeah, yeah," Patrick said, as though this was yesterday's news. "There were all sorts of threats and taunts and swords—"

"And reveling," added Will, "don't forget the reveling."

"Oh yeah, he did revel, didn't he?" Patrick mused. "It was pretty dramatic, all told."

"Is this normally what happens out in the boonies?" Mr. Burnett asked.

"What is it about this book?" Ms. Blithe pondered, ignoring him. "Why is he so fixated on it that he thinks it can—what was it? Let him 'return to his true form?'"

"And paint the world into whatever design he chooses, blah-blah-blah..." Will sighed. "See, there's some preemptive reveling for you."

"Hideous," spat Patrick. "Are we sure he's not just a day player from the community theater?"

Ms. Blithe turned in her seat to face Elyse directly. "Elyse, dear? This is very important—please tell us everything you know about the book."

Momentarily lost in thought, Elyse pulled the book from under her seat and ran a hand over its cover as though searching for further clues in the texture of the worn leather.

"Well…" she began, "it's a song, we know that much. I played what we thought was the tune encrypted in these markings, and Pat and Jack appeared from… wherever." She paused, racking her brain. "But that's all useless now–Jack destroyed my bag, my notes. It'll take days to work it all out again," she said, shaking her head in frustration.

"But we still have the book," Ms. Blithe said. "That's what's important right now. As long as we have it, Jack needs it from us, putting us in a position of power."

"What about Ike?" said Patrick, nodding his head to the doubled-over skeleton boy. "He was there when it all happened."

Ms. Blithe looked down at Ike, who stared at her with sad, empty sockets. "Oh my," she said.

Elyse reached over the seat and placed a gentle hand on his sweatshirt-covered scapula. "Are you okay, Ike?" she asked him.

His posture sagged as he tried to master his sobbing, to no avail. "I wish I were dead," he said, heaving with melancholy.

"Um, I hate to break it to you, son, but—" Mr. Burnett started.

"But he's *not,* don't you see?" Elyse interrupted. "Something horrible happened to him at the time, and this is what's left."

"You poor thing," Ms. Blithe said, awkwardly placing a hand where Ike's cheek would have been.

"Yes, but *what* happened?" Mr. Burnett asked, baffled. "I don't recall zombies in my college history courses."

"Me either," said Patrick. "And I would have totally paid attention if there were."

"Another crack in the armor of standardized testing," Will scoffed.

"Brain food?" Colin offered, shrugging.

"Yes!" Patrick said, giving him a high-five.

"Cold," said Colin.

"Yeah, yeah, I've heard it before…"

"Ike, ignore the hyena brothers and listen to me," Elyse said, leaning in to get his attention through his veil of grief. "Tell them what you told us about that night."

They all listened as Ike repeated the horror of his tale to Ms. Blithe and Mr. Burnett before breaking down into inconsolable weeping once more at the murder of Moira Asten.

"There, there," Ms. Blithe said, putting an arm around his gruesome form.

"That's unbelievable," said Mr. Burnett, shaking his head. "Tragic."

"And they'll do it again," said Elyse. "They won't stop until they have it."

By this time, they had driven to the outskirts of town, where the fog was nearly impenetrable, allowing for only a few feet of visibility as the headlights cut through the swirling grey-white.

"John, we need to turn around," Ms. Blithe said, her voice suddenly urgent.

"What?" he replied, giving her an odd look.

"We have to go back."

Mr. Burnett slowed the sedan down slightly but did not fully stop. "Doris, that thing is still back there. We have to put as much distance—"

"I know what to do," she firmly interjected. "It's a long shot, but we have to try. We can't run forever."

"Not to be obnoxiously contrarian, but actually, I believe we can," he replied.

"John, this is technically still a date, isn't it? Usually, that means I get my way, correct?" she said, giving him a pointed look.

"Really, Dor'?" said Patrick, casting a skeptical eye on Mr. Burnett. "And here I was, thinking we had something special…"

"Shut it, Pat," said Elyse.

"Turn it around, John," Ms. Blithe repeated. "We have to go to the Heights."

ELSEWHERE IN THE fog, Jack and Crain walked, each step now filled with more determination than ever, despite their spirits having been literally and figuratively dampened by recent events. Having extricated themselves from the remains of Mr. Korbin's prized fish tank, they now headed to the outskirts of town to fulfill their promised threat of destruction. Though he was brimming with rage, Jack found comfort in this new task; the promise of laying waste to this accursed town was like an anchor keeping him from drifting into the tumult of complete despair. It was both familiar and friendly to him, and he fed on it like a beggar before a banquet.

Crain was still dealing with his flooded gourd. "Argh, I cannot tell you how much I hate the bloody sea, Colonel," he said, spitting out a stray crab. "I mean, you expect it when you're traveling across an ocean, but at least we had the promise of war and the chance to do some proper soldiering. Now, where are we? No war, no army, and suddenly we're up to our necks in squid and scallops in a bloody sitting room! And I ask you: is this *insufferable* place even worth it!?"

If Jack had had proper eyes, he would have rolled them at his underling's incessant complaining, yet he could not help but agree with some aspects of this tortuous monologue.

What sort of world *was* this? Certainly, it was no more violent than the world from which they had come—Spicy Jack had seen more than enough musket balls ruin a good man or woman in his day. But it was the *way* the violence was executed that concerned him. Like an unknown creature scratching at a closed door, the idea had been plaguing him since they'd found themselves thrown into the dank cellar of that unruly tavern, and it now entered the remains of his brains, fully formed and hideous: the people of Bootville were no longer afraid of him. In fact, if their observations could be interpreted correctly, fear seemed to be something to revel in.

Starting at a young age, these people had inured themselves to fright. The children wore the faces of fear and celebrated it as though it was merely some parlor game, a thing fully conquered and robbed of its visceral impact. The decomposing remains he now stalked within, caged, injured, and hideous, meant nothing to them. No threat would move them, and no sword could sway them. Still, having recently read of the past centuries he had somehow unknowingly traversed, Jack found that he could not blame them.

The history books were crammed with page after glossy page of astonishing occurrences. The defeat of the king's army. The separation of the colonies into their own nation. The rise of contraptions capable of powering themselves into every facet of modern life. Artificially produced light. The magic of capturing an image so realistically that Jack felt as though he could reach through the pages and pluck out the tiny figures within them. Carriages capable of moving without horse or ox. A global population of billions. The empire in shambles, and now, if you could believe the words, allied with the Americans. It was all unthinkable, yet, if the streets they had walked that night were any indication, this unseemly fiction had indeed transpired.

Of course, there had been war (it never seemed to go out of fashion), but it was war that Jack's battle-seasoned mind could hardly imagine. He was dumbfounded by the many adaptations and uses of these inventions for killing, held up to history with such pride. Armored carriages clashing, guns throwing bullets at incredible speeds, cannons capable of launching explosives for miles and miles, ships made of metal, and perhaps even some contraption that could go into the air, free from the limits of land *and* sea. Absurd!

No wonder the people of Bootville ran around, cloaked in fear—how could they not? It was everywhere, the threat of an ultimate end bleeding through the very fabric of their culture. Their wild imaginings roamed the streets, and the glowing boxes of varying shapes and sizes projected images of death and suffering from across the earth. Meanwhile, the wrath of mechanized death, already unleashed several times over, skulked in every corner, forever ready to pounce.

Jack had witnessed the scenes time and time again that night; they were acted out in the front yards of all the oddly decorated homes of Bootville like a pageant of suffering. Monstrous half-human figures wielding the very devices they had thought up, intent on torturing and maiming one another. It was a blatant garden of rebellion they had cultivated, as though the embracing of their fears would prove their defiance of them.

Jack could respect this, having grappled with fear on any number of blue-smoke battlefields, and added it to his calculations when assessing his enemies. He mulled these things over for some time as they continued to make their way out of town, and he eventually arrived at a satisfactory conclusion: the modern world did not fear him, having been so far removed from the threats of his time. They lived in a messy peace, but at the cost of worldwide destruction. They distracted themselves from the horrors they had concocted by laughing in the face of their fear. However, the very existence of this defense *did* prove that fear still existed and could be exploited if one had the capabilities to do so. And Spicy Jack Cavendish knew he had those capabilities.

"I think perhaps it is time to remind these vermin of the impermanence of their security," Jack rasped, emerging from the misty fathoms of deep thought.

"I'd say so, Sir," Crain replied, swiveling on his vine to better see his superior. "They've made us look a right load of rubbish so far if you ask me."

"They have forgotten what can transpire when the elements meet one with the will to exploit their powers," said Jack, twisting his face into a satisfied grin.

"You do mean the fire, correct, Sir?" Crain said, suddenly excited once more. "So we *will* be burning it down? That wasn't just an idle threat?"

"The fire is ours to do with as we please, my vegetative friend. And it pleases us to feed it with the vile carcass of *Bootville*," Jack chuckled.

"Oh, the flames are hungry, Colonel!" Crain said, the fires within his carved pumpkin head jumping at the promise of being unleashed.

"This… 'Halloween' they prize so highly, shall make them remember what fear really is. Let us see how willing they are to embrace the mask of death when it's melting into their faces."

CHAPTER 25
Asten Hall

LIKE A SUBMARINE emerging from the murky ocean depths, Mr. Burnett's sedan finally broke the surface of the fog as it ascended the highland switchback road, leaving behind the grasping tentacles of mist. Such were the charms of Bootville Heights, long a safe haven from the wrath of the fens for the wealthier townsfolk in search of a clear sky.

"Why did Mayor Asten rebuild his house here instead of the old farm estate?" Elyse asked, staring at the silhouettes of angular pines as they flew past the window, lining the little-used blacktop road.

Ms. Blithe adopted her best storytelling voice. "It's said that Mayor Asten, being so distraught over the... the loss of his daughter," she began, casting a sympathetic look at Ike, who gave a sharp sob, "moved the site to protect the remainder of his household better."

"That's so sad," Mr. Burnett said, his voice somber.

"Mmm," said Ms. Blithe, nodding. "After the inferno, the old manor was nothing but rubble, and with no boot trees, the sawmill was considered useless. So, Mayor Asten had his new home built in the style of his homeland, quarrying stone so that fire would not be able to breach the homestead walls."

"Spooky," said Patrick.

"Says the ghost-boy," Elyse replied.

"It can't be that bad if the family's stayed there all this time, can it?" asked Will.

"Well, doubting William, you can decide for yourself—there it is," said Ms. Blithe as Mr. Burnett slowed the car in front of a twelve-foot-high gate of black iron.

The passengers craned their necks to see out the right-hand windows and found themselves confronted with a long driveway leading up to one of the most imposing buildings any of them had ever seen. Asten Hall hovered over them, a shadowy mass of mortared grey stones, a veritable fortress nestled within an expansive copse of looming evergreens. A handful of kerosene lamps lit the massive doorway and accented the tall windows running along the façade on either side of the entrance with their soft, flickering light.

"Spooky," said Will, drawing a rolling of the eyes from Patrick.

"Doris, what exactly is the plan here?" asked Mr. Burnett as he threw the car into park and let it idle outside the gate. "I mean, this is not exactly the sort of house where you go ring the doorbell."

"This is the sort of place where the doorbell rings you," Patrick mumbled.

"Shh!" said Elyse, scolding her brother with a scowl.

"Well, it looks like there's an intercom next to the gate," said Will, squinting into the darkness.

"Right, that's it then," said Ms. Blithe, now all business. "We'll just have to be open and honest and give them the truth of things as we understand them and hope they can help us. John, pull up to the intercom, please."

"Really? You're sure you want to go with the truth of things?" Elyse asked, gesturing to Patrick and Ike. "They'll have us committed."

"Oh, balderdash, dear," said Ms. Blithe, waving her off. "We don't need to get into that. We just need to let them know we have a… uh, an old family heirloom of theirs and see if they have any information on it."

Heeding his date's request, Mr. Burnett pulled the car up to the intercom and grabbed Ms. Blithe's hand as she made to put her window down.

"Doris," he said, staring at her intently, "you're sure about this?"

"I'm afraid we don't have any other options," she said, looking back at Elyse. "Here, come switch with Ike and sit by me in case I need you to explain things should they ask."

The two changed places by awkwardly climbing over the back of the bench seat, kicking several other passengers in the face while doing so. Elyse straightened her cape as Ms. Blithe rolled her window down and pushed the intercom buzzer. There was a long silence, intruded upon only by the crickets hidden amongst the trees. With a gasp of static, the intercom went live.

"Yes?" said a tinny voice. "Who is it?"

Ms. Blithe opened her mouth but did not speak. She gathered her thoughts.

"Um… hello?" she began.

"Hello," the voice replied. "What do you want."

"Oh, ah… well, my name is Doris Blithe, and I'm a school teacher in town," she said, pausing once more. "Some of my students have been researching a very old item they've come across that may have belonged to your family at some point, and we were wondering if you could tell us anything about it." She paused again. "It's for school," she added, as though that would lend some legitimacy to their request.

There was another pause as the intercom considered this. The speaker crackled to life once more.

"Seriously?" the voice said.

"Well, yes… seriously," Ms. Blithe replied.

"You are serious?" the voice asked again.

"Yes, I am. Look, I know it's unusual, but I thought perhaps you could help."

"At ten-thirty on a Monday night. Halloween night," the voice said.

"Yes, yes, I know—everyone's having a hell of a time tonight. Believe me, this wasn't in my plans either," Ms. Blithe said with a sigh.

"What is the item in question?" asked the voice.

"Well, it's an old book, and—here, Elyse, you explain it to him," she said, leaning back so Elyse could speak through the window.

"A book?" the speaker rattled.

"It's called the *Macabrium*," Elyse said. "We think it belonged to the town founder, Mayor Asten."

"The *Macabrium*," the voice repeated quietly.

"Does the name 'Jack Cavendish' mean anything to you?" Elyse asked, staring down the intercom as though it had threatened to swipe her lunch money.

"Who is speaking?" the intercom asked, its tone even.

"Elyse Korbin," she replied, her name suddenly sounding odd as it tripped off her tongue.

The intercom went dead, and all was still for a moment. Without warning, the gates swung open quickly and quietly on well-oiled hinges. The passengers inhaled sharply as their way was cleared.

"Pull up to the front, please," the voice said. "We don't have much time." With that, the speaker clicked off, leaving them to the crickets, unsure of what had just happened. Patrick turned from the window and poked his head over the front seat, eyeing his sister suspiciously.

"You know, Sis, it occurs to me that you and your cape hold a lot of sway around here these days."

"Seriously," agreed Will with a trace of awe.

"No way," Elyse scoffed, staring out the windshield into the inky night beyond.

"'Lyse, you're cooking up ghosts with your violin, getting weirdo books sent to you from some phantom librarian, willing locked gates open with your mind or something—I mean, what the hell is this?" Patrick asked, his see-through hands gesticulating wildly.

"It's called coincidence," she replied, failing to convince even herself.

"Uh-huh. Coincidence, sure," Patrick said, leaning back in his seat and shaking his head. "Hey—you're not like… the Chosen One or something, are you?" he asked with an examining stare. The rest of the passengers couldn't help turning to her, awaiting her response.

Elyse suddenly felt intensely uncomfortable. "No, I'm not Chosen!" she protested. "There's definitely been no Choosing, okay? Can we go now?"

"Of course, dear," said Ms. Blithe, patting her arm.

They stared ahead as Mr. Burnett reluctantly eased the car up the drive. The house grew more and more castle-like as they swung around the turn in the roundabout and parked in front of the mammoth door. Mr. Burnett turned the car off, and they spent a moment gazing up at the formidable hall, awestruck.

"It's a cozy little place, isn't it," Mr. Burnett mumbled to no one in particular.

"I wonder what a room goes for," Will said, shivering as a gale lashed through the surrounding trees, rattling the branches in a swell, then fading back into nothing. "Not a lot of foot traffic, I'd imagine."

"Comes with turn-down service, complimentary Continental breakfast buffet, and poltergeist," Elyse added, taking note of the hulking figure silhouetted in the doorway at the other end of the stone steps beside their vehicle.

"Well," Ms. Blithe began in a bright voice, which sounded only mostly forced, "as my mother used to say, 'No time like the present, unless it's the past, without which we'd be elsewhere, and getting there fast.'"

She had just popped her door open and placed one sensible shoe on the pavement when Patrick clamped his hand on her shoulder. She froze, every muscle in her body tensing at his touch.

"Sorry, I know it's cold," Patrick said, quickly pulling his hand away as she turned to look at him. He appeared more sallow than usual with the sedan's dome-light streaming through his translucence. "Shouldn't me and Ike wait here? No sense in us stopping the old boy's ticker, right?"

"Nonsense, my dear," said Ms. Blithe, regaining her composure. "If anything, we'll need you there to convince him that we're not a pack of lunatics—which we might actually be, though not about this. Okay then?"

Patrick shrugged, acquiescent, and they soon found themselves nearing the shadowy figure at the door.

He was a tall man, towering over six feet, with plain features, and of indiscriminate middle age. He ushered them inside with a small gesture and closed the door in silence. His crisp black suit and tie begged to be taken seriously, and indeed, the group's already-shattered nerves began to fray even more beneath his examining stare.

"You are here—" the man paused, double-taking at Ike, who gave a small wave, "—to see Mr. Asten." It was more of an instruction than a question.

Feeling as though some response was required, Mr. Burnett cleared his throat. "Yes, we are. Um… and who might you be?"

"You can call me Bellwether," the tall man replied. "I… work for Mr. Asten," he added, his voice revealing only that he was revealing nothing.

"Not a bad space to butler in, eh, Bulwarker?" Patrick said, taking in the vaulted foyer lined with medieval tapestries and polished slate floors. Will knocked on the thick, hardwood railing lining the staircase, which swept over them into the floor above.

"Hm," he said, as though this test had yielded favorable results. "Solid."

Elyse adjusted the *Macabrium* beneath her arm. She could feel Bellwether's eyes lock onto it and began to have second thoughts about this excursion.

"It's *Bell*wether," the suited man replied, his eyes flicking back to Patrick, slightly annoyed. "And I never said I was the butler—I just happened to be by the door."

"Yes, well—Mr. Asten," Ms. Blithe said, again in her most business-like voice. "Is he available?"

"He has been expecting you," Bellwether said, finally tearing his eyes away from the book.

"He has?" Ms. Blithe asked, confused. Mr. Burnett cleared his throat pointedly. "I mean, of course. He has."

"Yes, ma'am," said Bellwether.

"But how could—"

"This way, please," the tall man interrupted, moving deeper into the foyer.

They followed him to a set of heavy, sliding panel doors, which he pushed open easily, and into a dimly lit, book-lined study. It was much larger than the ordinary private library, appointed with leather couches, wingback chairs, small reading lamps, and a sizeable, crackling fireplace. At the far end of the room, in front of another set of doors opposite the entrance, was an impressive desk, behind which sat an equally impressive older man of wizened features and Scottish tweeds.

He rose slowly and leaned on the old mahogany, a strange half-smile upon his hawk-like face as he examined his guests.

"Well, well," he muttered softly. "What have the fens gifted me with on this haunted night?"

Elyse could not help but find it odd that the old man did not so much as flinch at the curious sight of her brother and Ike. It was as though the undead were as familiar to him as the vast array of trophy antlers hanging on the wall behind him.

"Bellwether, you should see to the, ah—well, you know," the old man said to their guide, who nodded and wordlessly slipped from the study, closing the panels with a small *click*.

Patrick pointed back to the doors. "Are you sure he's not the butler?"

With a slight chuckle, the older man straightened and began making his way around the desk. "No, no, he's not the butler, I assure you—though it might be amusing to offer him the position one of these days. He is simply a business colleague of mine, lacking in social graces." The old man now stood before them, his hands clasped behind his back. "You will forgive the strangeness of your welcoming tonight—as you must well know by now, strange things seem to happen as the witching hour approaches."

"You *are* Mr. Asten, aren't you?" Elyse asked, suddenly impatient with the smothering sense of being out of the loop. The older man fixed his gaze upon her with a smile and the look of a person who had just been spoken to in Ancient Greek.

"That is correct," he said briskly. "I am Arthur Aurelius Asten, and I'm afraid you have the better of me, madam."

"Elyse Korbin," she replied, her posture suddenly that of an Amazonian warrior. "This is Colin Niemann…"

"Hello, old man," Colin said flatly.

"…Ms. Blithe and Mr. Burnett, our teachers…"

"Hello."

"Hi."

"…my brother, Patrick—he's, um, been sort of dead…"

"But I feel great."

"…and that's Ike. He's also sort of dead—well, obviously…"

"A pleasure and an honor, my lord."

"…and this is Will Castle, he's… something, I don't know what."

"Thanks, 'Lyse."

"Delightful. Welcome all, and please, be seated," Mr. Asten said with a warm smile, gesturing to the sofas. He settled into an opposing wingback, his fingers steepled in front of his mouth as he considered them for a moment. "Now, I understand this late-night confabulation has something to do with my family. Is that correct, Ms. Korbin?"

"Yeah, well… sort of," Elyse began, unsure where the actual beginning was. "We think this book may have belonged to your, um, ancestors."

"Indeed," said Mr. Asten, looking at the book she held with deep interest. It occurred to Elyse that his omniscient gaze had not locked eyes on the *Macabrium* until that moment, despite it being such a glaringly antique volume in the home of an avid book collector. It was as though he had been purposely avoiding it. This, too, cast doubts within her mind about the older man's motives. However, feeling the pressure of seconds ticking away like oxygen breathed from a scuba tank, she ignored them and proceeded with her tale, beginning with the book's unusual arrival into her hands.

Soon, they were all pitching in as they assembled the data they had compiled from the night's unusual goings-on. Mr. Asten listened with a hungry fascination to this patchwork telling of their saga, interrupting them only to clarify some of the story's more confusing points. Throughout, Elyse found herself surprised by how well the older man was taking these odd occurrences. It seemed to her quite unusual, but then again, Mr. Asten and his house were both unusual in themselves.

"Incredible…" Mr. Asten breathed as they finished their tale with Spicy Jack's deadly ultimatum and their narrow aquarium escape. He leaned forward in his chair to get a better look at Patrick and Ike, who looked down at themselves, equally unimpressed.

"Yeah, I suppose we are, but I'm no good for shadow puppets anymore," Patrick said, attempting to cast a decent wolf's head in the pulsing firelight to little avail. "See? That used to bring down the house."

"'Incredible' is one way to describe it, but there are other words—less flattering and more ghastly and morally ambiguous words—that could also be used," Ms. Blithe said.

Patrick's jaw dropped in mock offense. "Hey! I thought I was your favorite."

"Of course, you are, dear," Ms. Blithe said, patting him reassuringly on top of his undead hand, this time without so much as flinching from his coolness. "It's just that your… *reappearance*, shall we say, is quite… unexpected, that's all."

"Oh, sure," Patrick said. "I've seen better days, true enough."

For a moment, Elyse felt overwhelmed by everything that had happened concerning her brother. It was as though they were all involved in some manner of interactive eulogy, and she could only compare the idea of where it must ultimately lead to drowning in quicksand. There would be some kind of finality, though what it would be like and when it would happen was both uncertain and frightening. She closed her eyes in an attempt to steel herself and focus on the moment. She reopened them to find Mr. Asten observing her, his expression neutral.

"Better days indeed…" he mulled, seemingly lost in a reverie.

"Um, may I remind us that our time to act before the frightening cadaver-man brings ruin down upon us all grows short?" Mr. Burnett said, shifting in his seat.

With a weary smile, Mr. Asten snapped back from wherever he had momentarily drifted in his thoughts. "Quite right, old fellow. Allow me to give you what you've all been looking for."

"And what's that?" Elyse asked, her eyebrow raised.

Mr. Asten turned to her, his eyes alight. "Why, an explanation, Ms. Korbin. For the reason you're here."

CHAPTER 26
Shadows Of Enlightenment

THE OLD MAN stood and began pacing the length of the fireplace.

"I have always been fascinated by how legends and tall tales—ghost stories, if you will—can blur with the truth of things so that one can become virtually indistinguishable from the other. Like most of you, I was raised with the legend of Spicy Jack and his brief reign of terror during the occupation. And as you know, it was my great-grandfather of many degrees who was mayor at that time, just as it was our estate that was consumed by the flames of the inferno bearing the family name."

Here, Mr. Asten began making his way across the study as the rest of the group watched, transfixed.

"Few of the family's possessions survived this disaster, but what *did* remain was enough to—and you'll pardon the expression—stoke the fires of my ancestry's imagination to this day. It is the only clue to a great mystery."

Mr. Asten now stood before a large chest of drawers, which sat recessed between two bookshelves and a few paces away from an ancient grandfather clock, which ticked its seconds away like a time bomb of bad tidings. He drew from his vest a pocket watch, attached to the chain of which was a small key. He inserted it into the top drawer, unlocking it and pulling from within a large sheaf of papers, now yellowed with age.

"These are all that remain of the mayor's personal papers and diary, and while most of it is a typical, if not exceedingly dry, account of life in colonial Bootville, there is one intriguing entry towards the end that makes reference to his daughter, Moira."

Immediately upon hearing her name, Ike began softly weeping into his hoodie, his skull-head hanging low.

Mr. Asten looked at him, alarmed. "My goodness—is he all right?"

"I'm sorry," Elyse said, putting an arm around Ike's boney shoulders. "It's just… well, it's the last thing he remembers—what they did to her. He's been pretty inconsolable ever since he got here."

"Yes, of course," Mr. Asten said as Ike sobbed into Elyse's arm. "How awful."

"You can keep going," Will reassured him. "He'll be like this for a while."

"Yeah, seriously—it's like this all the time," Patrick added.

Mr. Asten placed the sheaf of old papers gently on top of the sideboard and continued, his voice now grave. "Yes, well, the mayor makes mention of some extraordinary power his daughter had divined from an odd book of unknown origin from the original family library, which was sadly lost to the flames on that terrible night."

"What does he say?" Ms. Blithe pressed, leaning forward with anticipation.

"Unfortunately, he is vague concerning the details of his daughter's discovery, saying only that it was both extraordinary and fearsome."

"To say the least," muttered Mr. Burnett.

Elyse scowled and shook her head. "But, why would he be vague? He *knew* what he was doing when he sent Ike to the Widow's Watch with the book, just like *she* knew what it was when he gave it to her. How would they know that it would, uh…" she started, her eyes darting to the sorrowful voids of Ike's skull, "…um, you know—do what it did?"

"An excellent point, Ms. Korbin, and one I've often pondered—until this young man shared his story, that is," Mr. Asten said, gesturing towards Ike.

"What do you mean?" asked Elyse.

"Well, if they knew the book in question possessed some powerful, destructive property, they must have seen the results themselves—they must have seen this terrible power in action—"

"The butler," said Elyse, her gaze distant as the centuries-old puzzle pieces began to match up along jigsawed lines.

"Um, you mean, Bellwether?" Will asked, confused.

"Of *course!*" Patrick said, waving his fist in triumph.

"No…" Elyse said, shooting an exhausted look their way.

"Yeah, Will, no *way,*" Patrick said, easily changing course.

"The butler—the *actual* butler of Asten Manor—the one Ike buried," Elyse said, turning to Ike. "Didn't you say that the coffin was closed, and there were rumors about it being a skeleton and all that?" Ike nodded his skull, retreating further into his sweatshirt as all eyes fell on him. "So, something happened—somehow Moira Asten decoded the *Macabrium* and played it, and maybe the butler overheard it or was actually in the same room at the time or something…"

"It would be seen as murder," Ms. Blithe said, finishing her thoughts.

"Whoa, hold up—*murder?*" Mr. Burnett said, shifting uncomfortably.

"The mayor was protecting his daughter…" murmured Elyse.

"Wait, you don't mean—" Patrick started before slapping a hand over his mouth. "I'm sorry, I know this is awful, but… you're saying it was *literally* a cover-up?"

"Patrick!" Elyse said, shooting him a furious look and tilting her head towards Ike.

"Sorry! I'm sorry…" Patrick said, cringing. He turned to Will and mimed the shoveling of dirt while mouthing the words, *"He covered him up…"* Will nodded, his eyes wide.

"It would make sense, would it not, Ms. Korbin?" Mr. Asten said with the tone of someone five steps ahead of everyone else in the room.

"I guess so," Elyse replied. "In a crazy kind of way."

"Quite," Mr. Asten said, absentmindedly flipping through the corners of the pages beside him. "Naturally, as generations of my family have passed, this mysterious entry was seen as an anomalous metaphor of sorts, the product of a superstitious age. However, my research into the man has found the opposite to be true. The mayor was very much a swimmer in the intellectual currents of the time, and while ignorance was bliss for many, his actions always reflected reason and rational thought. A true product of the Enlightenment."

"Thomas Edison, you've done it again," said Patrick.

"Ah, not quite," Mr. Asten replied, offering a perplexed look to Ms. Blithe and Mr. Burnett.

"He's special," Ms. Blithe offered in defense.

"Indeed," said Mr. Asten.

"'The greatest part of our knowledge depends upon deductions and intermediate ideas; and in those cases where we are fain to substitute assent instead of knowledge, and take propositions for true without being certain they are so, we have need to find out, examine, and compare the grounds of their probability,'" Colin intoned while playing with the chain dangling from the reading lamp beside him.

The others stared at him in surprise for a moment as he turned the lamp off and then on again.

"Very good, Mr. Niemann," Mr. Asten said with a smile of baffled admiration. "John Locke, isn't it?"

"An Essay Concerning Human Understanding, The Fifth Edition with large additions, Book IV: Of Knowledge and Opinion, Section XVIII – Of Reason. Printed for Awnsham and John Churchill at the Black Swan in Pater-Noster-Row and Samuel Manship at the Ship in Cornhill, near the Royal Exchange," Colin responded, slowly pushing the lamp five centimeters away from him, his eyes fixed on the now-swinging chain.

Mr. Burnett eyed him, aghast. "Where in the world did you—" He paused. "You know what, forget it," he said with a sigh.

"He's special too," Will said to Mr. Asten.

"And yet he can't remember to bring a pencil to class," grumbled Mr. Burnett.

"I know, dear, I know," Ms. Blithe said, patting him reassuringly on the leg.

"Regardless," Mr. Asten continued, "the mayor never did deduce or explain the incredible offerings of the book, as shortly thereafter, his entries stop, naturally coinciding with the colonel's occupation. No more mention is made of it in his writings."

Elyse brushed a loose strand of black hair out of her face. "So, we still don't know *how* Moira got the book to do its destroying-thing."

"I'm afraid not," he sighed.

"That doesn't sound like much of a help."

"Quite right, Ms. Korbin," Mr. Asten said, examining her carefully. "He does, however, describe the book in question. *That* book." He pointed to the volume she held, balanced on her lap. "Might I see it?" he asked, stirring a sudden possessiveness within her.

We need his help, she thought, momentarily smothering her reluctance.

Slowly she stood and handed it to him, watching as he turned and walked back to the old mayor's papers. There he stood, referring to the yellowed pages, muttering to himself occasionally as he turned through the vellum of the *Macabrium.*

Temporarily relieved of the book's burden, Elyse began to feel rather stir-crazy, the anxiety over what was to come causing her stomach to clench like an angry fist. Unable to sit or face the anticipatory looks of her companions, she walked to the enormous, marble-mantled fireplace and stared into the flames in search of some quieting of her mind. The bright tongues of fire licked relentlessly up towards the flue, and while the hearth should have comforted her, all she could see when she looked into the blaze was a photonegative impression of the *Macabrium*'s strange markings. They flashed through her memory, familiar yet exotic, as though her biography was being read aloud by a stranger in heavily accented English. The turning of the imagined panels beat a soft but steady rhythm of printed lungs at work.

The vision ended, and Elyse found herself staring into the brilliant fire once more, though the impression of breathing remained. She slowly turned her head to the panel doors behind Mr. Asten's desk, which she had initially taken as a passage to deeper rooms and corridors elsewhere within the Hall. The sturdy, varnished wood of the doors revealed nothing, but there... yes, the quiet sound of inhaling and exhaling could be faintly heard above the crackling of the burning wood. The longer she focused on the doors, the more convinced Elyse became that there was something on the other side of them, listening, waiting. It was the white noise of *presence*, as unmistakable as prey being stalked by an invisible predator. The breathing filled her ears as the unnoticed will do upon being noticed, drowning out all other thoughts or sensations…

The massive grandfather clock struck its somber tone, breaking the spell. Elyse turned, shaking her head as the tone rang out, again and again, eleven times in all, and she saw by the clock face that it was indeed an hour until midnight. She looked over to the rest of the group, who eyed her with quiet concern until the sound of a drawer being slid shut and locked on the opposite end of the room drew their attention back to the enigmatic Mr. Asten.

The old man gazed at the clock as the last bell echoed throughout the room, the *Macabrium* tucked beneath his arm. After a moment, he turned to them, his face now grave with intent.

"The hour grows late. You haven't much time left," he said, walking over to them.

"But… but we still don't know what to *do*," Elyse said, her frustration mounting again.

Mr. Asten fixed his hawk face on hers as he approached. "On the contrary, Ms. Korbin, you know exactly what to do—you just haven't accepted it as a reality yet. You do have your instrument with you, yes?"

Elyse knew where this was going, and her heart sank at the thought. "I can't play it again. My notes were destroyed, and—"

"Nevertheless," Mr. Asten stopped her, "you do know it. You, more than anyone else, are familiar with the workings of this piece. It is of a language only you know how to speak with any fluency."

"No, it's way too hard—just look at the thing," Elyse protested with a shake of her head.

"The book is real, Ms. Korbin; there can be no doubt about that. Just as your gift of interpreting it is real. The physical proof of the thing sits before you in the shape of your brother, this distraught ruin of a boy from hundreds of years ago, and the knowledge of a monster who threatens the lives of this town," Mr. Asten said, a vein of accusation running through his voice. "You have started this thing, and so must *you* be the one who ends it too."

Mr. Burnett cleared his throat. "Surely, there must be some alternative to facing an undead madman. Maybe it would be best if we summoned the police, or even—"

"Does Colonel Cavendish strike you as the sort of creature who bows to authority?" Mr. Asten said sharply. "Or even operates within the same realm of sanity as the rest of us?"

"Point taken," Mr. Burnett said, swallowing.

"Well, wait a tick," Patrick said, straightening on the sofa. "I can do it—I played it before. I can remember it, I've got a crazy photo memory with music! Here, listen: Dum-dum-dee-dum—"

"*No!*" everyone cried as he sang out the opening notes.

Patrick stopped, mildly offended. "All right, no need to be absolute pigs about it—man alive…" he said, shaking his head. "But seriously, let's get us a little pianer out to the orchard—I'm sure you've got some groovy piece of Steinway kicking around this dive—and I'll bust out some nocturnes, maybe ease into some Well-Tempered Clavier, then—"

"Mr. Korbin," the old man interrupted, raising his hand, "I'm afraid that is quite impossible."

Patrick paused, confused. "Well, okay… so we get a, uh… a synthesizer, and Colin hot-wires it to the car battery—"

"Mr. Korbin…"

"Okay, wait! This is really important—does anyone here have access to a key-tar?"

"*Mr. Korbin,*" Mr. Asten said with finality. "This is not an option."

Patrick was baffled. "Well… well, why not?"

Mr. Asten scowled at him. "Do you really think it wise to tamper with these unknowns in your current state of… disrepair? What would happen if you ended up falling prey to whatever passage is conjured to send Spicy Jack away from here, and you are vanished with him? Or any of you, for that matter? In fact, it is *essential* that only Ms. Korbin—the player of the piece—be present at the moment the song is completed. The risks are too great. The sooner we accept that we are at the mercy of the *Macabrium* and not the other way around, the sooner we can be free of the matter."

Elyse gave him a hard look and, sensing her window of opportunity for disclosure being firmly shut, decided to call the old man out. "You're not telling us everything," she said with a coolness that surprised even herself. "What *is* all of this?"

Mr. Asten did not flinch, and behind his unblinking gaze, Elyse could see that there was more to this hawk-faced man than good-natured smiles and grandfatherly platitudes. While one pocket of his tweeds might hold freely distributed toffees, the other surely kept a well-oiled switchblade. Here was a person of will and resolve, one who had been judged and was capable of judgment.

"Well, of course, you're right, Elyse," he replied, surprising her both with his candor and by the informal use of her first name. "I am *not* telling you everything. We haven't the time, and even if we did, this is hardly the *right* time. There is still much left to transpire and be decided. We mustn't let the strength of our curiosity get the better of us before then."

"So… you're not comfortable giving us the big picture, but you have no problem sending us to maybe get killed," Elyse jabbed, shaking her head. This old man was a real piece of work.

"I will tell you this," Mr. Asten said, addressing everyone. "There are times when we must invent a frame of reasons to work within when the larger picture has yet to reveal itself fully. It gives us purpose to accomplish what needs to be accomplished, even if we are not entirely sure why.

"That said, I warn you to take *nothing* about this for granted. None of this is what you think it is. *This*," he said, pointing directly at Patrick, "is not what you think it is. But for now, when the unknowns outweigh the knowns, it is reason enough."

The room sat quiet, stunned at the thought of so many mysterious variables in play. The situation was overwhelming, like being punched in the face by a kangaroo: half of you wants to cry while the other half is simply excited that somehow there's a kangaroo in the kitchen.

Mr. Asten turned to Elyse once more. "Ms. Korbin, I'm going to give you the opportunity to save us all." Elyse sighed and shook her head as the old man continued. "There are two conditions I must insist upon in doing so. First, I give this book to you with the understanding that it will be returned to me, as it is too dangerous to be in public circulation. As I'm sure you, of all people, can understand," he added, passing the old volume to her. She accepted it, the familiar weight and worn leather bringing a relief she had not anticipated.

"And the second?" she asked.

"I shall need to speak with your brother," the old man said, turning to Patrick. "Alone."

Everyone in the room turned to the ghost brother expectantly. He was still in mild shock at being silenced by Mr. Asten and being called a 'that' rather than a 'he.' He stood there, his hands raised at his sides, palms up, in a posture of incomprehension. Receiving no further explanation, he shrugged. "Uh, yeah… okay. Whatever you want, man."

"Very good," said Mr. Asten with a clap of his hands, turning to everyone. "Now, you must meet the colonel at Ash Orchard, where the old home once stood."

Will gave him a skeptical look. "Yeah? Is that, like, *legal?*"

Mr. Asten smiled at him. "Why, it's legal if I say it is, Mr. Castle—that property has never left the family."

"Oh, so a lot of this is old cider money, huh?" Patrick mused, gesturing to the book-lined wealth surrounding them. "Who knew?"

"So, wait—do you know old man Leo?" Will asked.

"You mean Mr. Aberfoyle?" Mr. Asten replied, a glint in his eye. "Of course I know him—he works for me. As such, I can say for certain he will not be at the orchard tonight. You shall have free reign over the place."

"Leo *Aberfoyle…* " Elyse said, examining the old man.

"The serendipitous inclinations of a small world, eh, Ms. Korbin? The Astens have always believed in keeping their allies close at hand."

Patrick turned to Ike. "Who *is* this Leo guy? He sounds totally fascinating." Ike shook his head, his lower jaw sliding sideways in bewilderment as Mr. Asten continued.

"Play the song, Ms. Korbin, and play it well. Only then will we be freed from this… unending nightmare." He sighed, his eyes losing focus. "We can run centuries away, and still, the past catches up with us in the end."

THEY STOOD IN the foyer with the heavy silence of defendants awaiting a judge's verdict. It had been several minutes since they'd left Patrick to his private audience with the eccentric old man. The despair they departed with had left them quiet with exhaustion as their minds grappled with the knowns and unknowns of the task ahead of them. Bellwether had been waiting in the stony, tapestried hall and now watched them from where he leaned against the wall beside the front door. His posture was casual, but his eyes spoke otherwise.

Elyse looked down at Will's hand clutched in hers, a physical echo of a simpler time, exactly one year earlier. She wondered if her life would ever feel as normal or as right as it had for those brief minutes before it had been upended.

The whoosh of the panels drew their attention as Patrick stepped out of the study. If a ghost could look like it had just seen a ghost, his face was what that would have looked like.

"Patrick?" Ms. Blithe said, her voice brimming with concern. "What… what did he say?"

Patrick turned to them with bleary eyes and looked briefly at Bellwether, who measured him with an unblinking stare.

"He said… uh, he said we have to go now," Patrick mumbled, his voice thick. With that, he led them to the front door. Elyse was the last to follow and stared back into the study as Bellwether began pushing the panel closed. Mr. Asten stood within, staring into the fireplace, just as she had only minutes before. He looked over to her, his eyes distant, and nodded as the door clicked shut.

CHAPTER 27

A Reaping In The Whirlwind

WITH THE HOUR late and the streets fully cleared of holiday revelers, they made the journey back across town in record time. Turning north onto Flareback at the lamppost crossroads, Will looked out the window at the brooding stone heap of the Widow's Watch and wondered if he would ever see his home again.

The others seemed to be entertaining similar thoughts, and the drive had been mostly silent as they cut their way back through the fog, except for Elyse's brief attempt to pry more information from her brother.

"What did Asten say to you? I mean, really."

Patrick laughed and shook his head. "Oh man, Sis, you wouldn't believe me if I told you. He's a real character, that old man is—I mean, *wow.*" He twirled his index finger next to his head in the 'he's-absolutely-bonkers' motion.

"You're really not going to tell me?"

"No-can-do, it's totally secret. It's like he said—there's more to all of this than we realize."

"Oh, that helps," she said, rolling her eyes.

Patrick shrugged and turned away to stare out his window, effectively ending the conversation. Only when they had parked the sedan in the Ash Orchard lot did they begin looking each other in the face again.

"Well then," Mr. Burnett said, trying his best to sound like this excursion was as normal as the field trip they had taken earlier, now 65 million years ago, to the same spot. "Here we are. We are here."

Despite being the same place, the difference in atmosphere was alarming; the dense mist filtered the old mill into a foreboding tower from the dark ages and revealed the first few rows of apple trees as mere shadowy outlines. Their branches spidered into the gloom like indistinct troll arms, beginning nowhere and ending nowhere. What in daylight had been cheerful and inviting was now alien and freaky.

"I want you four to wait in the car," Ms. Blithe said, turning back to the boys. "There's no need for you to be out there—"

"What!?" said Will.

"John and I will go with Elyse, and you will wait here," Ms. Blithe shot back with all her teacher authority.

"She's right, Will," Mr. Burnett said, looking at him through the rearview mirror. "We only need to make sure that she can play the song, and then it'll all be over, and we can go home."

Patrick propped himself up on the back of the front seat. "Now, Doris, if you really think I'm going to let my baby sister put herself in harm's way without my undead fists of fury for protection—"

Will opened the door and ran out to the orchard, followed closely by Elyse, book, and violin in hand.

"—then apparently, you're absolutely right," Patrick finished as the remaining passengers watched the two run into the fog. "Uh, okay… come on then, fellers, let's do this," he said, sliding himself out the open door and running after them. Colin and Ike exchanged looks before shrugging and following suit, leaving Ms. Blithe and Mr. Burnett to sit in the idling vehicle, frozen in shock.

"Well, I'm glad we've made these plans," Mr. Burnett sighed as the teachers watched the pack of kids swarm the grassy clearing.

Will ran up to the tree line and tried to make out anything through the dense fog. "Hey, Jack!" he screamed. "Yeah, you! The gross one! You want the book, you come and get it!"

Elyse watched from several paces back but saw no sign of response. Patrick ran up beside her, gasping for breath.

"Hey, Sis," he said, doubling over. "Oh man, if I'd known being a ghost meant so much running, I'd have said 'forget it.'" He spat on the ground and straightened, eying his best friend, who was now pacing in front of the orchard trees like a penned bull, his hands balled up into fists. "Wow, Bill's really flipped his lid, huh?"

"Yes, he has," Elyse replied with a smile of admiration.

"So... let me ask you this," Patrick said, watching as his friend stalked the clearing and hurled more insults into the trees.

"What's that," said Elyse.

"You and Willy-boy there..."

Elyse crossed her arms and turned to her brother, her face set. "Yeah?"

"Well, I mean, I feel kind of weird talking about it, but... are you two, uh—"

"Pat, don't you start too."

"Hey, I'm just asking!" he said, throwing his hands up. "So, what's the deal then?"

"What deal? There's no deal."

"Uh-huh. You know, I'm lacking a pulse, not my eyesight. The guy's had the hots for you for, like, *centuries* now."

Elyse looked away. "You don't know what you're talking about," she said, her voice distant.

"Oh, don't I? The dude's an eligible bachelor with a lucrative career in the dish-washing industry, yet it seems like he's been spending all of his time doing whatever you ask him to do."

"It's complicated, Patrick."

"Yeah, and how's that? You don't like him or something? Because it also seems like you haven't minded his company either."

She turned back to him. "Look... ever since you died, Pat, I haven't trusted myself to feel *anything.* Especially about him."

Patrick was quiet for a moment as he processed this. "Well... well, so I died—so what?"

"What do you mean, 'so what?'"

"I mean, what does it matter? Just because I died doesn't mean you did—or him, for that matter. Why would *you* stop living just because *I* did? It doesn't make any sense."

Elyse sighed. "You know, for a ghost, you're being really difficult right now."

"Well, look, Sis—all I'm saying is, *I* would want my two best friends to be happy. But it doesn't even matter what *I* want—I'm dead. I've been dead."

"But you're here now."

"Yeah, but what if I wasn't?" he said, waving her off.

Elyse frowned. "What? But you are—"

"Yeah, but if I *wasn't*. I'm not supposed to be, you know. If Mom and Dad were doing a field study of life and death tonight, they'd probably put all of this down as being 'anomalous,' right? I mean, unless you've got a *Macabrium* lying around. So, what if tomorrow comes and *poof!* I'm gone."

"You're not going anywhere," she said, her voice wavering. He was behaving weirdly—and with Patrick, this was really saying something—and she didn't like it.

"Look," he said, turning away, "I'm just saying that you'd have to keep living. And not for me—hell, I didn't even know I was gone until you told me—but for *you*. With or without him, I don't care, but if there's something there, you should probably check it out. Because life's too short. Obviously," he said, gesturing to himself.

Elyse was at a loss for words. It was strange to hear him speak so openly, without the layers of one-liners and eccentricities in which he usually disguised himself.

"I'm gonna go be a jerk with Will now before he uses up all the insults," Patrick said, taking a few steps toward the orchard. He turned back to her as he walked and flashed a grin. "You could do worse, you know—he'd do anything for you. Think about it."

With that, he turned and ran to join their friend, leaving Elyse to wonder what it was he knew that she did not. She turned at the sound of footfalls and saw Colin and Ike trotting up behind her, with the murky silhouette of Ms. Blithe trailing several yards behind.

"What on earth are they doing?" her teacher called as she approached, adjusting her glasses as she watched the two boys hurl insults into the grove.

"They're trying to lure him out," Elyse said, shaking her head.

"Oh dear," Ms. Blithe sighed.

Will had taken to throwing stones into the trees while Patrick reveled in this excellent excuse to speak loudly and often. "Come on, you disgusting coat rack! You putrid, scabrous museum piece! Your clothes are out of date, and your pumpkin stinks of rotting soft spots, you pathetic, substandard produce-shilling, voice-pushing, poor excuse for a boogie-man *creep!*"

Patrick looked over to find Will staring at him with a strange mixture of respectful awe and disgust. "Gee, Pat—why don't you tell him what you really think?" he said, grinning.

Patrick shrugged. "He set my piano on fire—the guy's a total scumbag."

They stood in silence, breath bated, waiting for any kind of response. They received only a gust of cold wind, which carried down the gutter between the center rows of apple trees, pushing the fog and cutting through them with an arctic bitterness. Elyse's cape billowed out behind her while Ike shivered and pulled the hood of his sweatshirt over his skull. Still, no sign of life, death, or anything in-between emerged.

"Oh, *come on,*" Patrick said, looking back to the group huddled together. "What's *with* this guy?"

"Maybe he called it quits for the night?" Will said.

"Yeah, he probably got a room at the Watch, figured he'd sleep on it and look at his haunting problems in the morning with fresh eye sockets," Patrick said, looking at Will in disbelief.

Will scratched his head. "Maybe he wants us to catch our death of cold—"

In the distance, a fireball bloomed skyward, cutting through the haze as the defenseless apple tree it engulfed became mere tinder within. They watched in wide-eyed terror as the flames began their threatening dance. Within moments a second tree erupted, then a third and a fourth, each driving them back a step at a time as the column of flame approached. The heat hit them like an open blast furnace, causing Ike to pull his hood back down with trembling skeletal fingers.

"I guess he's here after all!" Patrick yelled over the roaring fire as the trees nearest them exploded into a brilliant orange.

"Nice work, Bro—at least you've managed to severely piss him off," Elyse called back.

"Must've been that bit about how he's putrid," Patrick said.

Ms. Blithe latched onto Elyse's shoulders. "How are you going to do this?"

"I don't know!" Elyse said. "We need to distract him long enough to play the whole song."

"A distraction, right," Ms. Blithe said, thinking. "I have a plan—you stall." With that, she ran back in the direction of the car, vanishing into the dissipating fog.

From the depths of the fiery column of crackling trees emerged the now-familiar figure of Colonel Jack Cavendish, his cloak expanding behind him, his pumpkin lantern bursting with flames and malicious laughter. His heavy brow jutted from beneath the brim of his cockade hat like the drum of a steamroller, lending his hollow black eye sockets even more menace.

Stepping with one heavy boot beyond the hellish portal of the blazing tree line, he reached into the recesses of his long cloak and pulled something from within.

"I believe this belongs to you," he said, throwing a lobster from the aquarium at their feet, where it landed, now fully cooked and red, in a puff of dirt and smoke.

"Hey, Mr. Big Entrance—you're gonna have to pay for that!" Patrick shouted at him.

"Surf and turf," Colin mumbled.

"Damn right!" Patrick said, high-fiving him and spitting in Jack's direction.

"Now, now, children, that's not playing very nice," Crain taunted, rocking back and forth on his vine like a hypnotist's pocket watch. "Look here, we've all had a very long day, and I'm sure we'd all like to get back to our normal such-and-such. I know the Colonel's tired—just look at that face; the man needs a lie-in, who wouldn't agree with that? I know *I'm* absolutely *parched* after setting things on fire all night. I'll be honest with you, it wreaks havoc on my insides, and I could use a cold drink and the rest of the week off. The orchard back there was a pleasure to destroy, but I would have no problem skipping the rest of the town. So, why don't we pass by your exciting rescue attempts, and you just hand us what we need? Give us—"

"The book, right?" Will said. "You want the book, you *need* the book, you *have to have* the book—this is the nerdiest bargaining chip I've ever heard of!"

"Yeah, get a hobby," Patrick added. "Try in-line skating—it's supposed to be all the rage."

Jack and Crain exchanged a glance and began chuckling. "No, no, no," said Jack. "I'm afraid you misunderstand our intentions. The book, yes, but we also require… the *girl.*"

Elyse felt a fresh river of adrenaline course through her. Of course. Of course, they needed her—the *Macabrium* was a useless bunch of pages without her. Never mind that she would have no idea how to do what they wanted; to them, she was the one who could make things *happen.*

"Like hell," she said, rooting herself to the ground in defiance as Jack leered at her.

"Oh, it *will* be," he said as Crain burst into a fresh torrent of laughter.

As the impasse reached its zenith, the sounds of a rumbling mechanical beast erupted from one of the sprawling arms of the orchard. Everyone turned to the noise, and they were astonished to see the dashboard-lit, terror-stricken faces of Ms. Blithe and Mr. Burnett barreling towards them as the sedan bounced its way along the uneven ground at an awesome pace. There was no time to react, and before Jack could even finish saying "What?" the practical, secondhand vehicle was upon him, bathing him in the mesmeric white light of the high beams. The car collided with his hip and launched him into a cloak-wrapped tornado of bones that touched down several feet away, collapsing into a useless heap.

Elyse watched as the sedan swerved with the force of the impact, carving deep tire ruts into the grass as it abruptly turned back towards the orchard, where its motion was suddenly arrested by the sideswiping of a tree trunk.

"Ms. Blithe!" she yelled, immediately running toward the inert vehicle.

"Whoa—did that just happen?" Patrick asked, turning to Will.

"That was the most amazing thing I've ever seen," Will replied.

Elyse came upon the slightly crumpled sedan just as Ms. Blithe was climbing out of the passenger side, her hair skewed into a potential bird's nest. "Are you guys okay?" she asked.

"We're fine, dear," Ms. Blithe said, taking a step and nearly tumbling to the ground. "Mr. Burnett's taken a little bump to the head, I'm afraid."

Elyse looked into the car to find Mr. Burnett holding his palm to his forehead and looking completely spaced out. "Nice driving, Mr. B—I think you really maimed him!"

He turned to her in surprise and offered a wave. "Okay then, I'll have the ravioli on Friday!" With that, he slouched forward and passed out, his face pressed against the steering wheel.

"Oh dear," Ms. Blithe said.

"So, what's your plan?" Elyse asked as Will, Patrick, and Colin ran up behind her.

"That *was* the plan!" Ms. Blithe said, throwing her arms up.

"We should get out of open ground—we don't stand a chance like this," Will said.

"Will's right, dear," Ms. Blithe nodded. "You should go to the mill."

Behind her, Mr. Burnett woke with a start, his eyelids drooping and his index finger raised. "Mother, I told you the windows don't need washing—the *democracy* already did it!" He collapsed again and began to snore.

"I should really see to him," Ms. Blithe sighed. "You run to the mill now while you can."

"What if the door's locked?" Elyse said with a trace of panic.

"Elyse, you're with three *boys!*" Ms. Blithe said. "Don't worry!"

Patrick stood at attention and fired off a snappy salute. "Consider the door already broken and any food inside already eaten, my Captain!"

"See? Now go!" Ms. Blithe said, shooing them away as lightning flashed in the churning skies overhead. "And be *safe!*"

SPICY JACK UTTERED a groan from beneath his cloak and began to stir his wasted limbs. He'd landed on the hilt of his sword—it was amazing to him that despite his decrepit state, he could still feel pain. Lifting himself onto all fours, he swept the cloak over his head and grabbed his battered cockade hat. Crain lay several feet away in the damp grass, spitting seeds out of his carved mouth.

"Oh, Sir—this has really not gone well for us tonight. If we ever have to draw up a report for Parliament about all this, I'm especially leaving out the last five minutes."

Jack grunted as he fixed the hat to his head and watched the four dim figures run towards the distant mill. His jaw clenched as he straightened and felt several of his lower vertebra grind against each other as they rearranged themselves back into something vaguely spinal. "Come along, Lieutenant. She must not get away," he said with a decided lack of enthusiasm as he bent to retrieve his staff. Righting himself with his aide-de-camp swinging at his side once more, he turned toward the mill and froze in his tracks.

Blocking their way was a shorter, trembling skeleton wearing a bizarre hooded jacket. The interloper's boney kneecaps knocked together as the figure jittered with fear, looking from side to side as though assistance might materialize from thin air.

Jack sighed. "What now…"

"Y-y-you'll not h-h-hurt her," the skeleton stammered, worrying his hands against one another.

"I beg your pardon?" Jack said, rubbing his temple in sheer exhaustion.

"You'll not hurt the girl. I-I-I won't let you."

Crain's mouth fell open as he recognized the voice. "Oh, I can't believe it—Sir! Do you know who that is!?"

The peculiar sensation of reliving a moment from the past began to prickle its way down Jack's spine. The heat of burning trees behind him, the strange figure before him…

The dam of memory burst, and he was overcome with disbelief as the memories that had been so dirtied by time were washed clean in the flood.

CHAPTER 28
The Asten Woods Inferno

SPICY JACK CAVENDISH came to with the distinct impression that the ceiling had been calling his name. He found this odd in that he didn't recognize the ceiling, nor had he been aware of any ceiling's ability to speak. He frowned at the heavy timber beams, dimly lit and far away.

"Colonel?"

There it was again. But, no, that wasn't the ceiling speaking—the voice was coming from somewhere beside him. He turned his head with great effort and was surprised to find that he had been lying on the floor amidst a pile of cartographic clutter and a table flipped sideways.

How unusual, he thought.

"Colonel..."

Jack eyed an empty pewter tankard on its side a few feet away. His vision blurring as he gathered up the strength to do so, he rolled over, his head throbbing. Propping himself onto one elbow, he reached for the tankard and held it close to his face.

"Yes, mug? Did you call my name?" he asked, suddenly noticing how disgustingly boney his hand had become.

"No, Sir, this is not a mug talking to you," the disembodied voice continued with an impatient sigh. "Behind the table, Sir, if you would."

Dropping the tankard with a clatter, Jack reached for the table's edge and shoved it aside with a groan, revealing the empty expanse of the Widow's Watch dining room. The familiarity was enough to incite his memory into piecing together a coherent idea of what had just happened.

For a moment, he thought his eyes were deceiving him as he watched a pumpkin roll its way across the floor in a sloppy zig-zag, seemingly independent of any outside influence. With a heave, the gourd rolled itself upright, its long, mottled-green vine curling behind it as though it had just uprooted itself from its spot in a patch. Jack watched, his exposed jaw hanging open as eye and mouth carvings appeared on the smooth orange of the shell. The voice in which it spoke was clearly Crain's.

"Sir, I don't know what happened! I swear, I tried to stop her—"

"Aaargh!" Jack cried out, scrambling several feet back on his hands and knees before drawing his cloak around himself for protection. His pumpkin lieutenant eyed him, slightly appalled by this reaction.

"Sir, I hate to bring it up, but you're not looking like a prince right now, either. In fact, you look exactly like every representation of death I've ever seen—I half expect you to start passing out handfuls of black plague to the entire village."

Jack unfurled his cloak with a grunt and stared at his boney hand again. He reached up and touched the spot where his face used to be. He heard the clacking of bone skittering across bone as his fingertips traced the hollow remains of his features.

"What is this?" he rasped. "What has happened to me?"

Climbing to his feet, he took two long strides across the room and grabbed Crain by the vine before turning and racing out the front door. Clutching his lieutenant in the crook of his arm, he ran down the side of the building to the hitching post, along which ran a trough of filmy black water. He fell to his knees, tossing an annoyed Crain aside as he leaned over the trough. Gripping the wooden edges, he pressed his face close to the surface. His dull, torch-lit reflection stared up at him, a gruesome visage unfit for man or beast.

"No…" he whispered before dashing the water with his skeletal fist. "*No!* This cannot be!"

"I know, Sir, it's hideous, isn't it," Crain consoled, spitting out dirt beside the trough. "At least you've still got a body, right? Can you imagine if we were both round and legless, just rolling around all over the place—we'd look ridiculous."

Jack ignored him, fixing his attention on the village green before him, now covered with a thick blanket of fog. The torches of the officers' encampment were lit, but no movement could be seen or sound heard.

"Where is everyone?" Jack asked, suspicious of this placid atmosphere and knowing for a fact that dark works were unfolding everywhere.

"I reckon they've followed orders and gone on to Collartown, Sir," Crain replied with a sigh. "I suppose it's best we move out as well, eh, Sir? Wouldn't want to miss the battle now, would we."

"But what about our disgusting, rotting selves?" Jack cried out. "This place has made us into monsters, Crain. They must suffer the consequences."

Using the Watch's stone wall for support, he stood on boney legs as Crain watched from the ground. "Um, yes, Colonel? You're sure you want to deal with this now? We could always come back and do this—whoa!" Jack lurched forward and grabbed Crain by his new vine. He stalked his way to the front of the Watch, stopping only upon reaching the crossroads. There stood the lone, flickering lantern, signaling the outskirts of civilization for all weary travelers. Jack considered the dancing flame as its soft luminescence played shakily on the sockets of his skull.

Watching him from where he was being clutched by his superior, Crain recognized the madness of Jack's posture as he unhooked the lantern. "Um, Sir? Where are we going with this? I know it's unusual for us to operate this way, but can we momentarily agree to not act solely on impulse and try to—*argh!*" Jack smashed the lantern into Crain's carved face before his lieutenant knew what was happening.

The gobsmacked pumpkin spat out bits of glass and thin metal while his insides began to move with the light of the flame, now burning slowly within his abominable self.

"Why, Sir!? Why in the world would you do that!?" Crain hacked. "I'm on your side!"

Jack ignored him, now fully fixated on his revenge. He tossed the smoking wreckage of the lantern frame aside and ripped the knotty post from which it had hung from the ground. Jack wound the vine around the staff amidst a steady stream of protest from his lieutenant, suspending the pumpkin like a morbid vegetable hangman. Holding Crain's illuminated face before him, he made his way across the road and onto the village green, his rage so vibrant that even the fog seemed to scatter before him, running off to wait amongst the dense foliage of the forest undergrowth.

"Bootville!" Jack shouted, his ragged voice echoing off the façades of the shops lining the square. "People of Bootville! Behold the monster you have created!"

Along the boardwalk of storefronts, the townspeople could be seen peeking out of their windows while others dared to step outside to see what the commotion was about. All were horrified by the grim, skeletal figure of the wicked colonel possessed by this strange madness.

Casting his cloak away from his body, he drew his sword and extended his arms in a grand gesture, the master of ceremonies overseeing a theater of destruction. Crain's newly-lit fire radiated a sphere of golden light that arced across the lower canopy of the boot trees, illuminating the village green and throwing it back to the days of ancient pagan rites found the world over when humanity waded in more primal waters.

"These woods have sheltered you for too long," Jack continued, sweeping the saber's blade in a circle beneath the black, creaking boughs. "You hide behind them to shelter yourselves from the outside world, just like every other pathetic town across these colonies! Well, I have news for you, wretches: the world has come to call, and you shall conceal yourselves no more!"

Jack released his grip on the sword with a flick of his gnarled wrist, deftly spinning it 180 degrees against his palm before gripping it anew and driving it point-first into the grassy knoll. The saber stuck fast, buried halfway up the blade and quivering with the force of the motion. Using both hands, Jack gripped the staff and began swinging it over his head, Crain crying out as he began a deliberate, ever-quickening rotation over the colonel's crested hat like the head of a medieval chain mace. Faster and faster, he spun, the night air feeding the fire behind his carvings until he appeared as nothing more than a hoop of flame hanging above the death's-head face of Spicy Jack.

With a final roar of effort, Jack gave the hypnotically circling weapon a final, powerful snap of his arms. Crain's mouth spewed a fountain of white-hot fire into the air that spiraled outward into a vortex of flame and expanded in the atmosphere so that it seemed as though the sun itself had risen over the green. The gawking townsfolk were thrown backward at the deafening whoosh of the volcanic sky as the wheel of fire was caught by the enclosing network of autumn-grey branches. The inferno lit the trees up like torches, adding the crackling and snapping of wood being consumed to the rumble of the blaze as it jumped from treetop to treetop, a booming of thunder without end.

Those people of Bootville who could still walk screamed and shouted to one another as they gathered their weeping loved ones, their icy demeanors having melted in the face of the disaster. They ran panicked into the woods as the fire-eaten branches began to fall from overhead, lighting the undergrowth and chasing them away from what was once their home.

In the center of it all stood Spicy Jack, surveying the destruction he had wrought, the light of the fire playing on his cranial lacunas, animating his decomposed face into something demonic. Beside him, Crain swung from the end of his vine like a pendulum, his rough-hewn features discharging plumes of acrid smoke.

Without warning, a percussive blast echoed out over the din of the inferno, and Jack's head snapped down as some invisible force yanked his cloak taut against his frame before falling slack once more.

"What was that?" Jack growled in surprise. He grabbed the cloak with his free hand and held it up to his face, finding a ragged, singed hole.

"That sounded like a gunshot, Sir," Crain hacked through his cloud of foul deeds.

Jack turned in the opposite direction his cloak had moved, retracing the path of the musket ball to the stoic façade of the Widow's Watch. There in the doorway, clutching a musket emitting a wisp of blue smoke from the barrel, stood Isaac Morgan. His work clothes hung limp on his skeletal frame, the withered remains of his inner organs heaving with the effort of staying upright. He dropped the gun on the wooden planks of the Watch and collapsed against the jamb, pointing a boney finger at Jack and Crain in defiant accusation.

"Murderers!" he cried out across the square.

Jack tilted his head to the side in curiosity as he took in the ghastly appearance of the boy. "Crain, what in the world is *that?*"

Isaac tried to right himself, propping his form up with the bones of his forearm against the heavy timber doorframe. "You killed Moira! You've murdered my girl!" he screamed, his ragged voice breaking with a mournful sob.

Crain's watchful eye carvings narrowed with dawning comprehension. "Is that the… Colonel, it's the lad from the Asten house! The one who was playing hero!"

Jack leaned forward, fascinated. "Can it be?"

"I'd know that pathetic voice anywhere, Sir," Crain assured him. "But look at him! He's hideous—just like you!"

With a snarl, Jack began stalking determinedly across the green towards the inn with tremendous strides, the wall of flame swelling behind him.

"These people," he growled through gritted teeth. "They never know when to *quit.*"

As he approached the crossroads, he swung the staff behind him in a smooth motion before wheeling it overhand towards the figure in the doorway. A molten fireball launched from Crain's mouth and flew through the air, striking Isaac in the chest and enveloping his fragile remains. The force of the impact carried Isaac back into the dining room, where he writhed on the floor, his clothes reducing to cinders.

Jack burst into the room, his jaw twisting into a malicious grin at the sight of the tortured boy. Crain began laughing uproariously as Isaac contorted himself in agony, desperately trying to bat out the flames.

"Ha! Oh, look at him squirming, Sir!" he cried out as Jack slowly circled the human pyre.

"You dare defy me, boy?" Jack rumbled. "You think a wretched *peasant* will be my undoing?"

"I think he does, Sir…" Crain said in a taunting sing-song as he swung back and forth on his vine. As he arced towards the kitchen, the lieutenant caught a glimpse of Moira's motionless body slumped over the keys of the clavichord, now stained crimson with her throat's blood. There, still propped above her ashen face, sat the strange book she had been reading from while playing that cursed song—the song that had ruined them and spoiled their glory.

"Sir!" Crain cried out as Jack watched the howling Isaac try in vain to force himself up into a kneeling position. "Sir, the book! Grab the book—there, in the corner!"

Jack's head whipped around to the clavichord sitting before the mountain of pumpkins, his eye sockets alighting upon the mysterious black markings that had nearly finished him.

With a flourish of his cloak, he began crossing the room in front of the gaping maw of the fireplace to capture what may have been his only hope to fix himself. He had almost made it when he saw a brilliant light unexpectedly hurtling towards him in his periphery.

"Sir, look out!" yelled Crain as the enkindled skeleton of Isaac Morgan, making a final, valiant charge, struck Jack in his midsection. Together they sailed through the dining room and into the hearth, which exploded with a shower of sparks as they landed entwined, hero and villain, now nothing more than food for the flames.

CHAPTER 29
Breaking And Entering And Breaking

"I DON'T SUPPOSE Old Man Leo left this unlocked," Elyse said as they approached the heavy timber door of the mill. Grabbing the old iron handle and giving it a sharp tug followed by an equally aggressive push, her head sank. "Of course."

"Say what you will about the man's hygiene, Leo apparently runs a very tight ship," said Will.

"It's never easy," Elyse muttered as she stood aside and pointed to the door. "Well, go ahead. Do your breaking-thing."

"Um…" began Will as he considered the thick, banded lumber.

"Wait," said Patrick, his foot propped on the enormous cylindrical grinding stone beside the entrance, "I learned how to do this in an issue of *Danger League.* You've gotta give it a good kick right beneath the handle."

"Yeah?" Elyse said, her voice tinged with doubt.

"Oh yeah—works every time." Patrick took a step towards the door, then stepped aside, beckoning Will forward. "Come on, Will, you're a real tough guy, right? Kick the door in."

Glaring at Patrick, Will stepped up and reared back onto one leg. The impact of his shoe landing on the wood and the door not budging was enough to make the Korbins wince as pain rifled through Will's leg, sending him to the ground. As he lay there clutching his foot and forcing back tears, Patrick examined the door again.

"Well, I guess that was a long shot," he said, rapping his knuckles on the door. "Yeah, see, that's pure boot tree right there. Very durable. Very resilient."

As Elyse reached to help Will to his feet, Colin appeared from around the corner of the mill, clutching an ax. "For the chopping," he said, holding it out.

"Ah-*ha.* Give it here, Collywog," Patrick said, his eyes lighting up as Colin handed it to him. Resting the head in the grass and the handle against his leg, he pushed up the sleeves of his skeleton jumpsuit. "Just like Granddad would've done," he said in his toughest voice as his skinny arms hefted the brutish instrument.

"Yeah, Granddad was a chemist, moron," Elyse said, shaking her head. Seven labored swings later and the door swung free, the wood around the handle now completely annihilated.

"Now *that's* how you destroy everything you touch," Patrick said to Will, his face smug. He tossed the ax aside, where it bounced off the grinding stone, splitting the handle and sending the rusted blade into the dark with a metallic quiver. "And that too."

The inside of the building was a welcome shelter from the increasing wind, which howled through the mill walls but did not enter, leaving the air thick with the dormant smell of damp wood and the sharp tang of mutilated apple flesh. In the dark, the tall structure seemed even more cavernous, the walls reaching upwards without limit, the ceiling an elusive idea buried in the shadows and night. Across the cluttered expanse of flooring could be heard the droning rush of the Whirry River eddying around the stationary paddles of the waterwheel.

As the boys slowly rocked a barrel of apples into position to keep the newly destroyed door closed, Elyse surveyed the terrain of machinery, wishing she'd paid more attention earlier in the day. The floor was crowded with gears, arms, flywheels, belts, conveyor chutes, and all other manners of antique water-powered technology mixed with more modern adaptations as needed. The heavy white filter blankets used over the apples during a pressing hung along the back wall like death-shrouded sentries gathered in ceremony beside the cider vat. Overhead, the enormous pressing stone, the length and width of a bus, hung suspended in mid-air with all the anticipation of a sarcophagus lid about to be closed.

Elyse's eyes affixed on the steep wooden steps leading up to a maintenance balcony. "There," she said, pointing to the platform. "I'm going up there."

"Yeah?" Will said as the boys craned their necks to see the small overhang flash its shape as lightning pulsed through the slats of the walls.

"You know, Sister, going into the sky has rarely been the safer option for humans," Patrick said.

"I need time to play the whole song," she said, adjusting the shoulder strap on her violin case. "I just need you guys to distract him until I get up there, and then you have to get out. Maybe take his weapons if you can. Go for the pumpkin."

Will nodded. "Right. That way, he can't set fire to the place."

"No, he won't—if he burns it down, he loses the book," said Elyse. "I just don't want to listen to that thing talk anymore."

Outside, the wind whipped with a sudden fury, moaning in muted anguish as it assaulted the building. "Heh," Patrick said with a nervous grin. "That sounds like Ike, doesn't it? 'Boo-hoo-hoo…'"

"For real," said Will.

"Come on, you guys, be nice to him," Elyse said, frowning. "Where *is* Ike anyway?"

"YOU," SAID SPICY Jack.

"Bloody George Washington," Crain sneered. "Still rattling around these parts, eh? You know, lad, there's nothing more pathetic than being a townie."

"You're a murderer," Ike said through chattering teeth. "I won't let you do it again."

Jack's eyes darted to the mill, where his prey had vanished. He found himself amidst a violent hate triangle, pulled in two directions by pressing business and a need to carry out unfinished vengeance. Decisions, decisions.

"I don't have time to deal with you now, boy," he snarled, brushing past him with a sweep of his cloak. He fixed his eye sockets on the mill while Crain protested in his ear.

"Aw, Sir—he deserves a good boxing of the ear-holes!"

Jack was about to offer his scathing retort when he felt himself lunging forward as the weight of Ike landed on his back. The boy slid one arm around Jack's neck and began walloping him on the back with his free fist. Jack began to run towards the mill, his torso twisting abruptly in different directions as he clawed his free hand on his back in an attempt to rid himself of this troublesome burden.

A roll of thunder sounded, shaking the earth, while Jack roared in frustration. Ike's boney fist collided again and again on the colonel's shoulder while Crain screamed something about a door.

The warning came too late, and as Jack dropped his shoulder in one last attempt to cast Ike away, he met the timber head-on, smashing it to pieces. As he tumbled into the black belly of the mill, Jack felt momentarily comforted, glad to be swallowed up by the past for once rather than the future.

EVERYONE JUMPED AS the door and barrel exploded and Jack's towering frame burst inside with Ike and Crain in tow. The concussion sent them sliding and sprawling amongst the shards of wood into a motionless pile of bone and fruit. Elyse looked at the others as a nanosecond of silence controlled the room.

"Go," said Will, waving her to the stairs, and within seconds she was ascending. He pointed at Patrick. "Grab Ike!"

Patrick nodded and pulled the skeleton boy by the hood of his sweatshirt, peeling him off the felled colonel. "Ike, buddy! Nice work there, fella!" he said, righting the boney figure and dusting him off.

Will turned to Colin, who was watching the proceedings with blank-eyed interest. "A distraction?"

Colin nodded. "Yes, I am."

Will gave him a curious look. "Right, get to it." As Colin scampered off through the maze of machinery, Will hauled himself up onto one of the barrels of apples lining the walls, then onto a double-stack, next to which was a triple. Finding his balance on the wooden lid, he heaved himself at the triple-stacked barrel, every muscle straining as he tried to move the heavy load. It refused to budge.

Below, Patrick and Ike hid beneath the staircase and watched as Spicy Jack began to stir with encouragement from Crain. "Come on, Sir, this isn't anything we weren't dealing with five minutes ago— up you go!"

"Um, Will, you might want to, you know… do something," Patrick called across the floor as Jack stood and drew his sword.

Sweating with the effort, Will looked down to see the grim-faced colonel on his feet again. In desperation, he angled his body against the wall and used it to push off with his legs. Everything hurt, from his wrists to the foot he'd used to unsuccessfully boot the door in, but he pushed harder as he felt the barrel begin to tip onto one rounded edge. With a final clamor, he felt himself drop onto his side as the unwieldy container finally gave way and toppled off its stack.

Jack turned to the noise just in time to see the avalanche of reddish fruit break free of the lid and rain down upon him in a thunderous deluge. He collapsed again as Crain screamed, and they were partially engulfed by hundreds of pounds of apples, which rolled in all directions like dropped mercury. The barrel hit the floor beside them, shattering and adding its broken slats to their momentary burial.

"Yeah!" Patrick cried, pointing at Will in triumph. He turned to celebrate with Ike, but the skeleton only shivered with his usual anxiety. Patrick shrugged. "Well, okay, whatever, I guess. *I* thought it was cool."

Will looked up as the sleeping machinery overhead shuddered and groaned into motion. A string of dusty light bulbs spanning the space flickered to life, offering dim light. From his high vantage point, he could just make out the dim form of Colin standing beside a lever that apparently unlocked the sluice gates for the 16-foot-tall waterwheel outside. He watched the shadows of the massive paddles through the cracks of the far wall, slowly accelerating with the unleashed flow of the Whirry. Colin gave him an uncertain smile and waved. "A distraction!"

"Hey, Will!" Patrick called over the sounds of splashing and grinding gears. "Sword or gourd?"

Will frowned. "What!?"

"Sword or gourd?" Patrick pointed to Jack, on his hands and knees, trying to free himself from the debris.

Will grinned. *"Sword!"*

As he crouched low on his barrel like a heroic teenage gargoyle, he wondered if Elyse could see him and hoped he wouldn't make too much of an ass out of himself. Taking a deep breath, he aimed for Jack's sword arm as best he could, closed his eyes, and leaped into the fray below.

ELYSE WASN'T PAYING any attention to what was happening on the main floor. Having scaled three flights of steps, she finally set foot on the dusty maintenance platform, which creaked much louder than she would have liked. As she cleared a spot for herself on the filthy planks, she tried to ignore how high up she was. Her stomach lacked the same willpower and hung equally high in her guts, poised to drop like an elevator inside her. It reminded her of how she felt when Patrick had reappeared.

As she set the *Macabrium* down and opened her violin case, the back corner of her mind registered the strange collage of bangs and shouting emanating from below. Noise was good—it meant the boys were doing their job, which also meant they were still alive.

The familiar smell of lacquer and resin washed out of the case as she removed the violin and bow, incensing the musty space around her and momentarily comforting her shattered nerves. *Der Sturm.*

Her hands moved fluidly with practiced motions as she plucked the four strings and made slight adjustments to the tuning pegs. Tucking the bow under her arm, she reached for the book and flipped it open at its center, carefully unfolding the three panels on each side. Lightning flashed through the rafters overhead, briefly illuminating the angry teeth of the design into stark black-and-white contrast.

Blinking the flare out of her eyes, Elyse bent low, tracing her finger over the surging jags. She paused, her brow furrowed as she tried to make sense of what she was seeing. Something felt wrong.

She started at the beginning again, rifling through the file cabinets of her memory to match the arcane markings with the decoded notes she'd once written in her trusty workbook, now gone the way of the dodo. She stopped once more, consumed with the feeling of finding herself lost in the woods; the main trail had to be somewhere nearby, but the overwhelming unfamiliarity of the wilderness obscured all sense of direction.

Her breath caught in her throat; she refolded the pages of the left side and flipped them to reveal the first page. As her eyes scanned the shaky scrawl, she felt her internal elevator drop several floors. She flinched and snapped her head to the side as the mighty cogs beside the platform clanked to life and slowly began grinding against one another, starting a chain reaction across the mill as the rest of the machinery slithered into action.

"That's going to lead to trouble," she muttered as she turned back to the book and closed the cover to see the familiar black lettering of 'Macabrium' embossed in the leather. "What the hell?"

It was unfathomable. She felt any semblance of control in her loosely constructed plan slip from her grasp as she flipped to the front page again and reread the words in disbelief: *To Lose the Living.*

The book had changed.

CHAPTER 30
Melee Unlimited

WHILE ELYSE BEGAN to lose control of the situation on the balcony above, chaos ran the floor below. Ignoring the extreme cold that came with wrestling the ghostly undead, Will had latched onto Jack's arm and found himself being thrown in all directions by the colonel's brute strength. Patrick was an equal nuisance on the other side, yanking on the lantern staff. But Jack was powerful, and their efforts seemed only to slow him down as he began to drag them around the pressing vat towards the heavy machinery of the waterwheel in a snarl of limbs.

"Colonel, do something!" Crain cried, whipping around the end of the staff.

"Oh yes, 'Daddy, please help me!'" Patrick mocked as he forced the end of the knotty wood in the opposite direction Jack was moving.

"Oi! You watch your mouth, lad," Crain shouted at him. "When I get my body back, I'm going to tuck you back into the nursery you crawled out of and make you drink a cup of poisoned milk! Ha!"

"You really think *you're* the funny one around here?" Patrick sneered, locking his arms as he pulled back with all his weight, his feet sliding as Jack continued to haul them across the mill.

"That's right! As a matter of fact, I *am* the funny one here!" Crain shot back. "I was one of the great wits of the army, celebrated and beloved by drunken imbeciles across the empire! I have added levity to this disastrous excursion into your disgusting world, haven't I, Colonel!" Jack ignored him, leaning towards Will and snapping his jaws like an angry bear as they continued to grapple for control over the sword.

Patrick changed position, swinging the staff end over his shoulder and pulling in the other direction. "You don't understand comedy!" he said through gritted teeth as he leaned forward. "Your observations are broad and obvious…"

Crain watched as the staff began sliding through Jack's gnarled finger bones. "Sir! You've got to hold on, Sir!"

"…Your pop-culture references are dated…" Patrick continued, squeezing his eyes shut with the effort.

"Please, Sir! *Please* don't let me go!"

"…And you laugh at your own jokes!"

"Sir, save me!"

Finding himself torn in two directions, Jack looked back at Crain's predicament, saw his panicked pumpkin face, and offered him a baleful grin.

Crain's carved eyes went wide with realization. "No, Sir, *no!*"

Jack released his grip, sending both Patrick and Crain flying forward. The force of the broken tension sent Crain's end vaulting over Patrick's shoulder like a catapult arm, snapping the connective vine. Crain hurtled through the air and banked high off the far wall, the impact shooting him downward at a steep angle, where he landed in a pile of mashed apples with a *splat!* beneath the grinding hopper.

Relieved of his vociferous lieutenant, Jack took his newly-unencumbered hand and grabbed Will by the ankle, taking the last few steps towards the massive gears spinning off the vertical shaft leading to the waterwheel's axle. Pulling sharply, he broke Will's grip on his arm and held him above the cogs. Will struggled as Jack lowered him head-first into the grinding teeth of the gears, laughing sadistically.

"Will—no!" Patrick yelled as he watched this horror unfold. He'd only taken two steps towards them when he was cut off by a billow of white. Colin emerged from the shadows and leaped at Jack, wrapping an unfurled filter blanket over his head and pulling down on it as he fell to the floor. Jack's covered face jerked backward as he was about to release Will to the gnawing wheels, allowing Will's

hands to fly out in front of him. He felt his palms unexpectedly touch the rotating shaft and grabbed on without thinking.

The spinning machinery tore him from Jack's grip, swinging his body around parallel to the floor. Through his surge of panic and adrenaline, Will decided to take a gamble and let go as he swung around to where he'd started. The gear shaft launched him feet-first like a pitcher releasing a fastball, his legs folding beneath his torso as he hit Jack in the ribcage.

The blanket-covered colonel flew backward, sliding on the wooden planks, his sword clattering from his grasp. The boys watched in awe as his hulking frame smashed into the lowest layer of stacked apple barrels in an explosion of dust. As the debris settled, the sound of stressed wood cracking could barely be heard over the whir of machinery and the river churning. A moment later, the entire wall of barrels collapsed on Jack with a deafening rumble that threatened to shake the entire mill down to its foundation.

Patrick turned to Will. "Dude. That was *awesome.*"

"I totally didn't plan that at all!" Will said, grinning with the unabashed relief of having artlessly dodged death.

"Help! Colonel!? Sir, please help me!" The sound of Crain's voice wafted feebly from the pile of apple mash as he rolled back and forth through the gunk. "I can't believe you did that to me, Sir! You're so... you're so *evil!*"

Colin eyed the mechanism beside the vat and tugged on Patrick's sleeve. "Up," he said, pointing at a familiar lever, "and down."

"Right you are," Patrick nodded, scrambling up the side of the vat as Colin took his position beside it. With a grunt, Patrick leaped onto the massive pressing stone, sending it rocking back and forth as he landed, the taut ropes bound to each corner creaking with the added weight.

"Up..." said Colin, staring up at the howling pumpkin. He threw the lever. "...and down." As the apparatus engaged, the grinding flume opened, sending Crain screaming down in a slide of whitish apple flesh and onto the pressing platform.

Patrick straightened himself on the rocking slab and pointed to Will. "Sword?" Will ran to the abandoned ghost sword and tossed it up to Patrick, who flinched slightly as it arrived but still managed to grab it by the handle.

"No!" Crain sputtered with rage on the platform, spewing apple chunks into the air as he tried to regain any kind of control over his situation. "You bloody animals, don't you dare!"

Adjusting his grip, Patrick struck a heroic pose and slashed the sword in front of him with an unpracticed flourish. "Ha-*ha!* I am el Zorro, the fox, and I've come to sign your merchandising contracts!" He carved an imaginary 'Z' into the air, then bounded over to the back corner of the stone, cutting through the rope with a mighty swing of the blade.

"No! Nooo! You'll pay for this, you *peasants!*" Crain screamed as the freed corner crashed down behind him, the unsupported weight snapping the other ropes one by one. *"Nooo!"*

Patrick howled a frenzied battle cry as he crouched low on the slab, riding it crashing down onto the platform. The entire vat crumpled beneath the weight, finally silencing the undead lieutenant.

Will and Colin cheered as Patrick stood up on the stone and pointed the sword at them. "Ha-*ha!* Thank you, my friends," he said, pushing his voice into a manlier register. "And, please, always remember this: death is easy—*comedy* is hard." He whipped the blade of the sword up to his face in a dramatic gesture and then hopped down to join them.

"Elyse!" Will shouted up to the balcony. "We have successfully disarmed him!"

"Yeah, they didn't stand a chance!" Patrick added, shrugging as Will gave him a look.

Elyse stuck her head over the railing. "Nice work, guys! Now get out of here while you still can. I'm gonna start—"

She was cut off by a boom of thunder and lightning accompanying a movement from the barrel wreckage as one skeletal hand clawed its way free of the debris.

"No *way!*" Patrick gasped, suddenly drained of all bravado.

"Come on, we have to go," Will said, looking up to the balcony. "Elyse! Don't take any prisoners, all right?"

"Yeah—no mercy!" Patrick shouted, jabbing the blade of the ghost sword into the air.

"Get out of here, you boneheads!" she shouted, waving them away.

"Good luck, Sis," Patrick said as he and Colin ran for the gaping hole where the door used to be.

"Subsequent crocodilian!" Colin said, waving.

"Yeah, that's not how that goes…" Patrick said, rolling his eyes and pulling him outside.

Will started to follow them, then stopped and looked up at her again. Her dark eyes stared back at him as he hesitated in his search for the right words…

"Will," she said, nodding to the door.

"I'll see you outside," he said before vanishing into the darkness and wind.

CHAPTER 31
To Lose The Living

ELYSE STOOD FROZEN to the railing and watched as the boys departed. It was as though her brain had seized up and required professional maintenance. She was in trouble, this much she knew. She'd managed to work out that this was probably the same song Moira Asten had played all those years ago at the Widow's Watch, but how the book had changed itself was seriously blowing her mind. How was she going to play these strange new markings? How was she to execute a song she'd never heard before? She'd always been lousy at sight reading, but with a few practice run-throughs and a sneak listen to a recording, she'd always managed to fumble her way through. This, though… this was a chasm too wide to fake her way across.

She was taken out of this brief, paranoid reverie by the sight of Spicy Jack casting aside the mangled barrels, his movements sending more apples rolling down the planks of the mill floor. He'd lost his hat in the scrum, and his bare skull sitting atop his cloaked shoulders somehow made him look more nightmarish than ever. Lightning flashed, throwing her into silhouette and exposing her to his black eye sockets. They were fixed on her as he was driven with blind rage to extract himself from the debris.

Her own cape rippling behind her, she darted back to the *Macabrium,* laid out on the balcony floor. Her time had run out. Taking a deep breath, she shouldered her violin and rested her chin atop it. Her eyes moved to the first curved marking, which had momentarily deceived her in that it must have been the same starting point as the first song. Deciding that it was as good a start as any, she drew her bow to the strings and slowly began to play.

JACK COULDN'T DECIDE who he hated more—the children or himself. As he picked and stumbled his way through the ruins of what was once a charming cider mill, this debate swung back and forth through his mind on repeat like a broken neck in a noose. He, Spicy Jack Cavendish, scourge of the colonies, had been mastered by a pack of feral *children?* It was simply appalling.

Yet the fact remained, he had failed himself. He had been too lenient, too soft on these swindlers, too overwhelmed by this torturous modern world, too indecisive about taking what he wanted, and it had cost him. Well, no more.

The sight of the girl above him, literally looking down on him as he flailed through the mire of his humiliation, was enough to send his rage boiling over the sides of his black cauldron heart. *She* was to blame. She may not have started his decline, but she was the one who stood in his way time and time again, and *she* would be the one who would signify the end.

Having finally cleared his limbs of the destruction, he moved across the floor towards the balcony, scanning the shadows with an anxiety he had not felt since his first campaign. Back then, he'd been surrounded by the dense forests around the Monongahela River, where a French musket lurked behind every tree trunk, and a Potawatomi tomahawk was grasped beneath every thicket of underbrush. The shrill cries of the Indian war-whoops still rang clearly throughout his memory.

As he neared the steep staircase, he heard a sound floating from above and came to a halt. The girl was up to something, and as the tone shifted to another and then another and another in the cultivation of a melody, Jack realized that he had heard this song before. A wave of nausea washed over him, and he felt the unpleasant sensation of being unbalanced.

"No..." he said, shaking his head to rid it of this sudden vertigo. He looked across the expanse of the mill floor and saw the cavernous space begin to warp like a stirring of the sea. "No, not again!"

He collapsed onto one knee, catching himself before he fell completely. Sweeping his cloak aside, his bones shook as he brushed off the enveloping pain and willed himself to stand. The aching consumption seemed to expand as each second dripped away, and, through this agony, he knew he was running out of time.

AS ELYSE IMPROVISED her way through each reading of a new mark, the song she was playing entered that fraction of a percentage her consciousness had not dedicated to this task. These few neurons skulking in the corners of her mind began to fire with recognition. Her channeling of the *Macabrium*—this new, dirge-like *Macabrium*—had roots in her fingertips and seemed to grow outward from the rich wood of the violin in expanding sonic vines that threatened to strangle the air with their tenacity. They compelled her to continue playing, crying out for a resolution, and in this compulsion, she began to acknowledge familiarity. But this idea was ridiculous—she'd never heard or played this song before. She didn't even know what it was *supposed* to sound like. Still, as the melody reached out across the mill, curling its tendrils around all it came into contact with, she felt as though she had tapped into a wellspring of inherent music, something she somehow *knew* without even knowing she knew it.

Without thinking, she lifted her dark eyes from the aged panels of the *Macabrium* and closed them as she carried on playing, her fingers digging out the mournful notes one at a time. She could feel the familiar distortion of the air around her, that rearranging of the atmosphere caused by this experimentation with the known-unknown. She was surprised to find that it reminded her of Will and how he seemed to do the same thing when they were together. It was not an unpleasant feeling.

She opened her eyes. Lightning flashed from outside once more, only now the light curved as it spilled over the grief-washed shoals of the music. Elyse closed her eyes again, content to let the song play her.

As JACK CLUTCHED the railing of the narrow staircase and looked up at the flights of steps, his vision contorted them into an insurmountable obstacle of dizzying height. To his dismay, he realized there was no time for such an excruciating climb and pushed himself off the rail, lunging to the center of the floor with off-balanced steps in search of an alternative. He locked eye sockets on the massive gearing he'd tried to kill the boy with and raced over to it, pitching and weaving as the crawling sensation that had eroded his body centuries ago began to dance on his bones and remaining flesh.

He leaped over the grinding teeth of the interlocking wheels and grabbed hold of the spinning gear shaft, locking his leg around it. His cloak spiraled around him as he spun with the shaft, pulling himself upward with one skeletal hand over another, the music growing louder as he ascended. He gnashed his teeth as the waves of pain began to break over him with more intensity.

Not again. Not this time.

The underside of the balcony flew in and out of his vision as he rotated closer with each arduous climb.

No, not this time...

ELYSE GASPED AND took a step back from the railing at the sight of Jack's hideous brainpan as it spun in ascension, drawing level with the balcony on every revolution like a screw being turned. Her bow slid along the strings as though possessed, her fingers flying along the neck with a fluidity she'd rarely experienced for so long, wringing out the song one drop at a time. Jack was howling through a clenched jaw, his already ragged voice breaking from the pain, and yet he carried on as though indifferent to the crippling torment he must surely be experiencing.

She tried to return her attention to her playing, unable to even consider what she should do if Jack reached her. If he did, it would be all over anyway—she had nowhere to go.

Still, she was close, she could feel it. Despite never having heard the song before, she could tell it was building to a conclusion, the harsh strain twisting itself inside-out in a diabolical tension hook that bashed through the air like whale flukes on whitecaps. She just needed time to finish…

She could see Jack judging the distance, curling his angular form in preparation for the strike, and before she could even think about thinking about what would come next, he was airborne. His long carcass stretched itself out like a diver before the jackknife, his hazy, off-color phalanges snapping open, hungry to be around her neck, and at that moment, confronted with her impending untimely end, Elyse felt strangely liberated. A numbness overcame her, diffusing the adrenaline, and for the first time, she felt free from her anxieties and inhibitions. She looked on as Jack's jaw cut through the morphing atmosphere, soon to be over her and ready to put an end to all of this, and she was *ready.*

The end, however, was not ready for her.

She was startled by an anguished scream behind her, nearly dropping the note she'd been pouring. A bolt of bone and sweatshirt came from her left side as Ike leaped from his hiding spot among the shadows of the steep staircase. His cry was primal, a berserker caterwauling offering a distressing counterpoint to the song of the *Macabrium* as he smashed into the flying colonel, wrapping his arms around him in a tackle that threw them both off-course.

Jack flailed wildly, his hands clawing to find purchase, and barely managed to grasp the edge of the balcony. The rest of his frame swung in a pendulous arc, the motion loosening Ike's hold and sending him downward. His translucent hand shot out at the last moment, grabbing hold of Jack's cloak, which he then began to scamper up, one shaky pull at a time. Jack's head was thrown back by the additional weight, the chain and clasp digging into his vertebra. Both screamed the screams of the tortured.

Elyse lunged forward, pulled by the notes and her own need to know what was happening as her fingers dug ever-deeper into the song, each successful execution of phrase casting aside years and years of nonsense and clutter. Lifetimes of historic emotional debris were scraped out in great handfuls to be thrown into the air, while feelings of silver were polished and meticulously placed at the feast of fear upon the heart. They were immediately masticated into slag while the slurry was spat out by those undulating wisps of black markings, those agonizing notes which ran across the mirror of her mind.

Her dark eyes glimmered as she aimed them into the black sockets of the monster now beneath her feet, reaching for her with his free hand. Ike and the cloak were pulled taut, the tension of the weight bending Jack's body backward like a bow set for the nocking of an arrow. She looked on in disbelieving horror as the individual bones of the sinister hand began to dissolve before her eyes, victims of self-destructive desiccation.

It was time-lapse decomposition, as seen on a thousand nature documentaries, but followed through until the end when even the bones are broken down and returned to the earth for recycling, as everything eventually must. The screaming echoed in Elyse's ears, fueling her will to finish. She pressed on with aggressive slashes of her bow and found the final run of notes in the face of Jack's last lunge at her black cape as his body fell apart around him like the surface of a collapsing sinkhole.

This long-sought vision of decay was marred by the sight of Ike desperately clawing up Jack's cloak, most of his sweatshirt and half of his ribcage already worn away to nothing as though he was being consumed by invisible acid. A downpour of guilt and distress flooded Elyse as she watched the skeleton boy throw his arm up and grasp Jack across the forehead like falcon talons on prey, pulling the great monster back. The wailing skull crumpled into motes of nothing beneath the finger bones, which immediately followed suit in their own dusty vanishing.

The bow cut against the strings as the dirge signaled its last in a bursting cannonade of notes that rang out and faded along with the death throe screams of those would-be cadavers, now finally, actually dead.

Feeling spent, Elyse collapsed against the balcony railing and watched through the stilling atmosphere as the off-color dust of both hero and villain rode a draft over the mill floor. It hovered like an oddly beautiful aurora before dissolving into a state of the unseen, both now everywhere and nowhere at the same time. As her violin swung loose from her right hand like a metronome and her eyes glistened in the lightning strikes overhead, Elyse couldn't help but feel much the same.

THEY HUDDLED TOGETHER, a wind-lashed mass of bodies bathing in the glow of the sedan's headlights. Will alternated between furtive glances at the mill and lengthy examinations of the electric sky while the others watched the column of burning orchard whip in the storm.

"At least the rain will put the fire out," Ms. Blithe said over the noise.

"Is it supposed to rain?" Mr. Burnett asked. He was clutching a rag soaked in cool water from the Whirry, pressing it to the corner of his forehead and feeling the slightest bit better.

"I hope so," Ms. Blithe said, ducking as a broken whip-like branch blew past her face, the sprigs of dried and curled leaves whapping her glasses askew. "Or this will all have been for nothing." She gestured to the pulsing clouds above, but it could have meant something more.

Blue-white light blinded the world while the thunderclap deafened it, and as Will blinked away spots, he saw the small, cloaked figure approaching them.

"Elyse!"

They ran to her, and she let herself be swept up in Ms. Blithe's arms.

"Are you okay, dear?" the teacher asked, examining her face. From where he was standing, Will saw that she was exhausted—nothing more than a scorched filament in evacuated glass.

"Oh man, I'm so glad you're not dead, Sis!" Patrick said, throwing her in a bear hug.

"Cold," she uttered.

"Whatever!" he replied, taking her violin and bag and handing them off to Colin. "What the hell happened in there!? Where's Jack—do we have to run around some more, or what?"

"He's gone," she said, her voice tired. "For good."

"You're sure, Elyse?" Mr. Burnett asked, his eyes searching hers for the truth.

"I saw it happen, Mr. B," she said. "Ike saved me."

"He did?" Patrick asked, baffled.

"Jack almost had me—he was *right there...* and then Ike stopped him. And now they're both gone. Dust."

"Crikey..." Patrick breathed. "Who knew the little guy had it in him."

"It was all of us," Elyse said. "We all saved each other." She looked up at Will, who was relieved to see her in one piece. His inner monologue shouted that he was more in love with her than ever.

"It's over, 'Lyse," he said in his pining double-speak. "Let's get out of here, huh?"

"Yeah, let's go home, Sis," Patrick echoed.

They turned towards Mr. Burnett's slightly crumpled car, Will with his arm around the girl in the cape, practically holding her up in her fatigued state. They had almost reached the vehicle when two lights appeared, rounding the corner of the drive like mobile will o' the wisps. Everyone froze and watched as they approached, the beams blinding them into squints before the vehicle courteously turned its nose away, revealing a sleek, onyx-black Bel Air of mid-1950s-make.

Will felt Elyse's hand grip his arm as the door of the idling vehicle opened and a tall figure emerged.

"You've got to be kidding me," Elyse said, her face steeling itself into lines of disgust.

"Congratulations, Ms. Korbin," said Bellwether, striding towards them like a well-dressed black mass, the white V of his dress shirt mesmerizing them with its luminance. "You have just saved Bootville."

Will felt his body tense automatically as the tall man halted before them. "No thanks to you," he said.

"We are facilitators, Mr. Castle."

"You guys should get that embroidered on the back of some snap jackets," Patrick muttered.

"Mr.—Bellwether, is it? Why are you here? Now?" Ms. Blithe asked, stepping forward. "These children have gone through things that no one should have to experience. They should be at home with their families as soon as possible."

"Yeah—what's this all about?" Mr. Burnett added. "Just who the hell are you people anyway? And do you *see* my car? There was a risk of some serious danger here."

"It is understood that you have been tried this night," Bellwether replied. "You'll have to trust me on that."

"Trust-nothing!" Ms. Blithe said, her frustration bubbling over. "They could have *died* tonight! I think they have a right to know *why.*"

"All in good time," he said, unfazed by her anger. He turned to a scowling Elyse. "The transaction has not yet been completed."

"What transaction?" Mr. Burnett asked.

"It's the book," Elyse said, stalking over to Colin in a huff and pulling the *Macabrium* from her bag. "He wants the book, just like everyone else. That's what all of this has been about." She held the tome out to Bellwether, her cape drifting to the side in the wind. "Here, take it. Have your transaction. I don't even care anymore."

Bellwether eyed her for a moment, then looked at Patrick, who stood behind her, his arms crossed. Finally, he reached for and accepted the volume.

"You guys are unbelievable," Elyse said, shaking her head.

"Oh, we are certainly to be believed, Ms. Korbin," he said. "Make no mistake about that."

"It changed, you know," she said, stepping back beside Will. "I don't know how, but it did. But then, you probably knew that already."

"We had our suspicions."

"Whatever," Elyse said, turning to the others. "Let's go."

"Um, Mr. Bellwether, what about the damage? The fire?" Ms. Blithe asked.

"It will be raining soon. The rest will be seen to," Bellwether intoned. He turned back to Elyse. "Mr. Asten wished it to be known to you that you will be handsomely compensated for your cooperation in this matter."

"I don't care," Elyse said, grabbing her brother by the arm. "Come on, Pat. Let's go home."

As Will followed them to the sedan, he noticed Patrick looking back over his shoulder at Bellwether, who nodded his head once.

Elyse turned to him, impatient. "Hey, let's *go.*" Patrick swallowed, looking ill, and allowed himself to be pulled by the sleeve of his scorched jumpsuit as Bellwether watched them depart, the *Macabrium* now in hand.

CHAPTER 32
Candlepower

THE WIND BLEW without mercy as the beat-up sedan rolled down Flareback Road, slowing and parking on the shoulder of the cracked pavement several yards from its crossing with Nightjar. There, the streetlamp still glowed like an inland lighthouse, warning travelers of the perilous crags of the Widow's Watch.

The short trip to the inn had been frustrating. Everyone was tired, their brains worn out from being forced into expanding themselves into frightening new territory over and over again, their bodies equally drained from hours of chasing and escaping. It was now technically November, and they were shot. Patrick hadn't helped anything by insisting they stop at the Watch first without explaining what exactly they were doing. This severely aggravated his sister, who wanted nothing more than to get him back to their house.

"This is ridiculous, Pat!" she'd said, her sharp eyebrows furrowed in annoyance. "What more do those people want from us? They got their stupid book back—we don't owe them anything."

Patrick had looked at her with eyes of cool resignation and slowly shook his head. "It's just part of the deal." He'd been quiet since their encounter with Bellwether, and this uncharacteristically somber attitude had permeated the vehicle. His spirit of life—unstoppable even when he was dead—was sorely missed.

Now, he lagged behind the others as they ran through the forceful gales towards the entrance to the inn, where the wooden sign shuddered violently on its iron rungs. Elyse turned to him and watched as he looked around the lamplit street, oblivious to the flying leaves and thunder, as though desperately trying to remember where he had hidden something.

"Patrick?" she said, snapping him out of his daze.

He looked at the others, mere feet from the Watch's heavy door, looking over their shoulders at him. "No, wait," he said, bringing them to a halt. He pointed to the back of the building. "Cellar door."

The damp basement was how they had left it hours earlier, crates smashed and clavichord exposed. Will walked over to the door leading to the kitchen steps and opened it.

"Top door's destroyed," he said, closing the bottom one quietly and flipping on the overhead bulbs. "I guess I know what I'll be fixing tomorrow."

Everyone was shivering as they watched Patrick pace in a small circle with his strange air of detachment. Ms. Blithe huddled close to Mr. Burnett, who put his arm around her.

"So," he said, "we're at a countryside inn—does this count as a second date?"

Ms. Blithe laughed. "In your dreams—you still owe me dinner."

Will and Colin began absentmindedly shuffling debris towards the stone walls with the sides of their shoes while Elyse leaned against the workbench and ran her fingers over the gouge left by Spicy Jack's sword, which was now tucked through the belt of Patrick's skeleton jumpsuit. The trio eyed each other before turning their attention back to their undead friend, who now stood by the clavichord, gently plinking the same note repeatedly, seemingly lost in his thoughts.

After a long moment of nothing happening, Elyse broke the silence. "Patrick," she said. He turned to her with bleary eyes. "What are we doing here?"

"We're supposed to wait," he replied.

Elyse frowned. "Wait for *what?* Are we meeting someone here, are we supposed to *do* something? What is it?"

Patrick shook his head. "Just wait."

Elyse was too frayed to deal with this. The night of coursing adrenaline had left her wasted, and she did not have the patience he was asking of her. Why was he bothering with this after all they'd been through?

She sighed. "Pat, let's just go home, okay? Don't you want to go home? Whatever this is, we can do it later. Tomorrow, if you want."

Patrick ignored her and looked at the teachers. "Mr. B, you got the time?"

Mr. Burnett peered at the face of his watch. "It's almost 1:30."

Patrick nodded and stepped towards the center of the dirt floor, nervously tapping the hilt of the sword with one finger as though sending a telegram. He looked up at the beams overhead, mumbling something to himself, then down at the packed dirt beneath his translucent feet. He traced a short line with the toe of his shoe.

Will's eyes darted back to Elyse for a moment as he crossed his arms. "Hey man, I'm not helping you dig up the basement floor tonight if that's what you're thinking."

Patrick looked up at them, and Elyse felt her internal elevator snap its cable as she registered the fear in his eyes and watched as he slowly brought his arms up and clasped his hands behind his head.

"Okay," he said.

"Okay, what?" said Will, stepping towards him.

Patrick looked at him, frozen in his position of surrender. "Protect each other."

The space behind him tore open with the sickening pull of a vacuum sucking the sound from the cellar. The portal's mouth widened like a tornado on its side, funneling away from Patrick.

"No!" Elyse yelled, the air of the vortex whipping at her hair and cape, devouring the word.

Patrick gave her a sad, crooked grin. "I love you, Sis," he said. As the words left his mouth, two sets of hands reached through from the other side, monstrous in their disembodiment, and hooked themselves through Patrick's raised arms, pulling him back, off his feet, and through the opening. No sooner had his ghostly sneakers flown past the point of no return than the sideways funnel spiraled its last, snapping closed with an explosive halo of light and leaving no trace of it having ever been there. It had all happened so quickly that no one had moved from where they were standing; they were simply shocked into immobility. Only now, with the silence ringing in their ears, did they begin to rouse themselves.

Elyse ran to the spot where he had been standing only seconds before and fell to the dirt floor, screaming her brother's name as that night's true horror revealed itself to be a never-ending cycle of losing what she loved. She felt then as though it was a loss she would be doomed to repeat until her final day, and this time cut just as deeply into her heart as the first, muting the room and everyone in it. Everyone except for the grieving girl in the cape.

"PATRICK!" ELYSE SCREAMED, and in an instant, they were there, kneeling beside his lightning-shocked body in front of the cemetery's iron gate, terribly unsure of what to do. With shaking hands, Will threw the loose head of his dinosaur costume back over his shoulder and watched as the dying wind carried wisps of silver smoke from Patrick's smoldering costume into the distance. The body was on its side, unmoving.

"Pat!?" Will said, tentatively touching his shoulder before pulling him onto his back. No reply. "Patrick!?"

Elyse was in hysterics, one hand over her mouth, stifling her weeping, the other wrapped around her knees as she rocked back and forth.

Behind her, Colin dropped from the tree trunk and scampered over to them, his spacesuit singed brown like a marshmallow off a bonfire, his heavy gloves black and smoking. He looked down at Patrick through the dome of his helmet, now half-charred, and mumbled, "Patrick."

Patrick groaned.

"Pat!?" Will said again, leaning over him. His heart sank as he saw his friend's face, sooty and suddenly very aged. The black crescents under his eyes bore a message of extreme wear on his body as he peered through half-closed lids, seemingly focused on nothing.

Elyse flew forward onto her knees, placing a gentle hand on the side of his face as he blinked into awareness. "Hey, Sis," he mumbled, a pained smile contorting his lips as he gasped a deep lungful of electrified air.

"Pat, don't move," Elyse said, stabilizing him with a shaking hand on his shoulder. She spoke evenly, but her voice was thick with panic. "You're hurt—we'll do something… *something*. We'll get you help—"

"I'm sorry," he said, shaking his head slightly beneath her palm. "I'm so sorry."

Tears welled in Elyse's eyes as she frowned at him and her hands moved quickly to unclasp her cape. "No, we're going to fix this—we'll help you, and everything will be fine. It will all be fixed…"

Her taut hands trembling, she whipped the cape off her shoulders and covered Patrick's body as it misted smoke like dusk on the fens. She sniffed back tears as she spread the black shroud over his legs with Colin's help, as though keeping busy could somehow delay the inevitable.

Delirious, Patrick uttered a quiet cough and a laugh as he closed his eyes and turned his head away. He opened them to find Will staring back, his face drawn, clutching a handful of his matted hair, as lost and speechless as he'd ever been. Patrick tilted his head up at him and smiled.

"Will? Is that you?" His eyes were clear and unblinking, as though he was now seeing something elsewhere, beyond.

"It's me, buddy," Will replied, placing a hand on his shoulder.

"It's good to see you," Patrick muttered. His tone was unnerving in how genuine this sounded.

"Yeah, buddy," Will said, nodding grimly. "How you feeling?"

Patrick barked a laugh and shook his head slightly before resting it on the ground once more. "Oh, man…"

Will looked up at Elyse, who had buried the bottom half of her face into her arm while she watched her brother close his eyes, and was taken aback when Patrick's hand flew up and grabbed his wrist, his eyes wide and maniacal.

"I just wanted you to know…" Patrick wheezed. "…we didn't light the candle… the candle lit us."

He released his grip as he lay back, closed his eyes again, and laughed. His body shook as the laugh became a sob, his smile departed, and he became still.

And because the dead cannot weep, the sky parted and cried for him.

CHAPTER 33
The Heights

THE EVERGREENS LISTED in the soft breeze, their needle-heavy limbs scrubbing the air as Elyse and Will crunched their way through the gravel beside the blacktop river that wound its way through the foothills of Bootville Heights. Elyse had her face buried in her thick scarf and her arms wrapped around herself. The bottom of her long, black topcoat billowed at her knees like her cape, now conspicuously absent, had done for a year.

Will walked beside her, his hands in his jacket pockets, his eyes focused on the vaporous clouds he exhaled with each breath. Winter was unpacking its bags, and the change made the events of that busy night the week before seem even further away than they really were. Today was the first he'd seen of her since the teachers had swept her away to her house following Patrick's disappearance. She hadn't been to school, nor had she taken any calls. Mr. and Mrs. Korbin were still stranded in Polynesia, and only Ms. Blithe had been able to get through to her.

"She's having a very hard time right now," she would tell Will every day when he would ask about her. "Just give her some time to cope with everything."

Perpetually unable to give her any time, he and Colin had gone to the Korbin house but found no answer at the door. Until that moment, he hadn't been sure how or what she was doing. However, standing on the porch that day, the answer filtered through the drawn drapes, a familiar tune that started and stopped with no resolution. Now, finally with her in person, he could see the calluses on her right hand standing out shock-white against her already pale skin, betraying her frustrating days and nights of trying to hunt down and recapture the memory of that one incredible song.

Will understood—he'd also been trying to pin down the elusive. As the early days of November escaped him, so too did the solidity of his recollections, and it was already starting to feel as though Halloween had never happened. In a move practically oozing with conspiracy, the *Bootville Boilerplate* had reported nothing about a fire at Ash Orchard and had only buried a blurb about the property closing early for the season due to 'winterizing.' Will could only imagine the look of dismay on old man Leo's face upon walking into his thoroughly trashed mill the morning after their adventure. Winterizing, indeed.

And what of Mr. Korbin's aquarium? Unable to fathom what might have happened to its contents, which were now presumably strewn throughout the ground floor in a grand buffet of dehydrated Perciformes, he'd asked Ms. Blithe about it. Her eyes had immediately taken on the haunted, thousand-yard stare of one who has peered into the abyss of unspeakable things.

"I'll never be able to look at sushi the same way again," she'd mumbled in response, refusing to offer further details.

Still, it was the details he wanted, as though they would somehow cement what had happened to reality's memory. It was important to him, if only because it was important to Elyse.

He'd been in a terrible trough without her, the storm fronts of his various moods and feelings colliding in his head in an endlessly obsessive tumult. As a coping mechanism, he'd buried himself in his work, which meant being partially submerged in soap suds for hours on end. Still, it was distracting enough to refocus a fraction of his attention somewhere other than his depression. The table settings had never been so clean, and his mother had noticed and was worried.

That afternoon, he'd been plodding through another shift with his sink and black mood close at hand. He opened the back door to toss some garbage bags and was surprised to find Elyse waiting for him. It was strange to see her without her cape.

"You want to take a walk with me?" she asked, the circles under her eyes almost black in the awful November light.

Of course, he did, and so they had, marching from the outskirts through Bootville Proper and downtown, then up and up into the fir-lined estates of Bootville Heights, all without saying more than two words to each other. He hadn't needed to ask where they were going, and his intuition soon proved itself correct as they rounded the last turn of blacktop and found themselves before the gates of Asten Hall.

It looked deserted in the waning daylight, like the wing of a castle closed for repairs and set to reopen by next summer's tourist season. He watched as Elyse pressed the intercom buzzer several times in a row, waited, then tried again. After many minutes of this, she slapped the speaker box in frustration and stood back, staring at the distant, sleeping house.

"Damn," she said, wiping a stray tear from her eye. Will walked up beside her and put a hand on the small of her back, following her gaze through the heavy wrought iron and up the empty drive. "I should never have given it back," she said.

"You didn't know."

"I should've guessed. They were acting so weird, and I was distracted... I should have known better."

"You knew they weren't going to answer."

"Yes. But it felt like something I had to try, at least. I mean, you have to *try*, right?"

"Yeah."

"I would've settled for an explanation. I want an explanation."

"We'll keep looking for one."

"I miss him."

"I know you do. I do too."

"And I miss you."

Will stared down at her in surprise as she leaned her head against him. "You do?"

"Of course."

He bent down and kissed the top of her head as he'd always wanted, and her raven hair smelled amazing, as he'd always imagined it would. She took his hand in hers and led him back down the river of road.

"Take me to the Watch," she said. "It feels safe there."
"Even after everything?"
"At least it's not lonely. It feels like home."
"Tomorrow, I'll help you with the encyclopedias."
"You will?"
"Sure—it's something to try, isn't it?"
"Yes. It's something to try."